THE LINE BETWEEN HERE AND GONE

THE LINE BETWEEN HERE AND GONE

ANDREA KANE

MIRA®

MIRA®

Recycling programs
for this product may
not exist in your area.

ISBN-13: 978-0-7783-1337-3

THE LINE BETWEEN HERE AND GONE

For questions and comments about the quality of this book please contact us at Customer_eCare@Harlequin.ca.

www.Harlequin.com

Printed in U.S.A.

First printing: July 2012
10 9 8 7 6 5 4 3 2 1

To Myrna and Bob, who helped me bring the Hamptons to life,
who acted as consultants extraordinaire for the year it took me to
create this novel, and whose love and support mean the world to me.

CHAPTER ONE

December
Manhattan

Amanda Gleason gently rocked her infant son in her arms.

A new baby was truly the reaffirmation of life. If she didn't know that before this moment, she knew it now. He was her child, her miracle.

Her responsibility.

She hadn't planned on facing motherhood alone. In fact, when Paul had disappeared from the picture, she hadn't even known she was pregnant. Maybe if she had, maybe if she could have told him, things would have turned out differently.

But they hadn't.

And now the weight of the world was on her shoulders.

Decisions had to be made. Pressure she'd never even imagined. And a bittersweet pain that came every time she held Justin in her arms.

She touched his downy head with one finger, stroked the peach fuzz of his hair. As she whispered softly to him, his eyes opened wide and he stared at her intently, visibly fascinated by the sound of her voice. She gazed into those eyes—Paul's eyes—and her chest tightened. They were a lighter brown than Paul's, probably because they had yet to mature to their true color. But the shape, the lids, even the thick fringe of lashes—those were all Paul's. As was his nose, a tiny version of Paul's bold, straight nose with the slender nostrils. He even had the dimple in his cheek that was Paul's. Other than his golden-brown hair color and small, pursed mouth—both of which he'd inherited from her—he was very much Paul's son. And even at three weeks old, he was developing a personality—easygoing like Paul, inquisitive like her. He spent hours staring at his fingers, opening and closing them with a fascinated expression. And he was always looking around, seemingly transfixed by the world.

Thank God he didn't know how much of a battlefield his world really was.

"Ms. Gleason?" A young nurse touched her gently on the shoulder. "Why don't you get something to eat? Maybe take a walk? You haven't done either all day." She reached for the baby. "Justin will be in good hands. You've got to take care of yourself or you won't be able to take care of him."

Numbly, Amanda nodded. She held Justin for one more brief, desperate moment, then kissed his soft cheek and handed him over to the nurse.

How many times had she done that in the past few days? How many more times would she have to do it?

Tears dampening her lashes, she rose, retracing her steps through the reverse isolation unit and out of Sloane Kettering's Pediatric Bone Marrow Transplant Unit. She stripped off her mask, gloves and gown, and tossed them into the discard bin, knowing she'd have to repeat the same sterilization process when she returned. She stood there for a moment, head bent, taking deep, calming breaths to bring herself under control. The nurse was right. She'd be of no use to Justin if she fell to pieces. And she'd done enough of that already.

Walking down the corridor, stepping into the elevator, and descending to the main level, Amanda felt the physical pain tearing inside her that always accompanied a separation from Justin. She hated leaving him. She dreaded coming back.

Outside the hospital, the world looked surreally normal. It was dark. She hadn't checked her watch in hours, but it had to be after eight o'clock. Still, traffic sped up and down the New York City streets. Pedestrians strolled the sidewalks. Horns honked. Christmas lights blinked from green and red to a rainbow of colors, then back again.

How could everything seem so normal when her entire world was crumbling to pieces? When everything she cared about was upstairs struggling to survive?

Still operating on autopilot, Amanda reached for her BlackBerry and turned it on. She didn't really care if she had any messages. But she had to check—even if it was just to seek out some pie-in-the-sky miracle that would answer her prayers.

No miracle. Just the usual crap from the usual sources—

store sales, promotions, photojournalist magazine sites. Nothing personal. Everyone knew better than to bother her with anything short of a dire emergency.

Correction. There was one personal message. An email from a fellow photojournalist, a friend of hers who'd been traveling internationally for months and wouldn't be aware that Justin had already been born or that his condition had turned Amanda's life upside down.

She opened the email.

I'm in DC. I had to send this to you right away. Caught it on my cell phone yesterday. 2nd Street at C Street NE. Best quality I could get. But I swear it was Paul. Take a look. I know the baby's due this month, but thought you'd want to see this.

Amanda read the words, and, for an instant, she froze. Then she clicked on the attachment, staring at the cell phone screen and waiting for the picture to load.

The moment it did, she gasped aloud, her hand flying to her mouth. The image was a little grainy and was probably taken from twenty yards away. But clear enough if you were intimately familiar with the person photographed. And she was.

It looked just like Paul.

She zoomed in as close as she could, taking in every detail of the man who now filled her entire screen. Dear God, it was Paul.

A tsunami of conflicting emotions engulfed her. But she battled her way through them. Because one thought eclipsed all the rest.

What could this mean for Justin?

It was a mere ray of hope, a complex long shot. But, to Amanda, it was a lifeline.

She fumbled in her tote bag for the scrap of paper she'd been carrying around since last April. It was well past business hours but she didn't care. She knew they worked around the clock when necessary. She wouldn't call; she wouldn't give them a chance to turn her away.

As she unfolded the crumpled paper, she yanked out the file folder she carried with her at all times—just in case she ever followed through on her idea. Everything was in there. And it wasn't just an idea anymore.

She pressed a speed dial number on her phone—a call to her oldest and dearest friend, Melissa, who lived in Manhattan and who would never let her down.

"Lyssa," she said when she heard her friend's voice. "I need you to come over and relieve me. It's not Justin. He's okay. But can you come now?" She sagged with relief at the reply. "Thanks. It's an emergency."

CHAPTER TWO

Cold air. Bare trees. Christmas lights twinkling up and down the Tribeca street.

At 9:15 p.m. in this residential section of Manhattan, the four-story brownstone that housed the offices of Forensic Instincts was a secluded haven, isolated from the jungle of the city. Two sweeping willow trees marked either side of the brownstone, and a sense of peace made it seem more like a home than a workplace for Forensic Instincts.

Tonight was even quieter than usual. Casey Woods, the company president, was out holiday shopping with some friends. Most of the specialized team had taken the night off. They were all still recovering from the whirlwind of cases they'd tackled over the past month and a half—all of which had been dominated by an intense kidnapping investigation.

Marc Devereaux was the only FI team member who was

on-site. And he wasn't working. He was in one of the empty meeting rooms, doing a hundred push-ups, feeling the sweat soak through his workout clothes and hoping the intense exercise would help wipe away the mental ghosts that had come back, full force, these past few months.

They'd stayed quiet for a while. But since the kidnapping of that little girl…

He dropped to the floor, forehead pressed to the carpet, breathing heavily. Memories cut deep. Even for a former Navy SEAL. Especially for a former Navy SEAL. Everyone thought they were impervious to emotional scars. They weren't. What he'd seen during those years might have made him a better FBI agent, and now a valuable member of Forensic Instincts, but they'd taken away something that could never be restored.

And left something dark and destructive in its place.

Marc's head came up abruptly as he heard the front doorbell ring. It couldn't be one of the team. They all had keys and knew the alarm code for the Hirsch pad. Instinctively, Marc reached for the pistol he'd placed on the table beside him. Rising, he walked over and eyed the small window on the computer screen displaying a view of the front door from the video surveillance camera.

A woman stood on the doorstep.

Marc pressed the intercom button. "Yes?"

A brief silence.

"Is this the office of Forensic Instincts?" the woman's voice asked.

"Yes." Marc could have pointed out the ridiculous hour. But he'd worked for the FBI's Behavioral Analysis Unit for five years. He could read people and tones of voice. And this voice sounded dazed and shaken. Panicky. He wasn't about to ignore it.

"I...I didn't think anyone would be in. I just prayed you were." Her words confirmed Marc's assessment. "I was afraid if I called you wouldn't answer. Please...may I come in? It's urgent. More than urgent. It's life or death."

Marc had made his decision long before the end of her dire plea. He put away his pistol. "I'm on my way down."

He draped a towel around his neck and headed for the stairs. Professional dress decorum wasn't high on his list right now.

He reached the entranceway, punched in the alarm code and unlocked the door.

The woman standing there with a file folder under her arm was brunette and in her mid-thirties, although the strain on her face made her look older, as did the dark circles under her eyes. She was wearing a winter coat that enveloped her body, so it was hard to make out her build. Not to mention that she was clutching the coat around her as if it were a protective shield.

She stared at Marc, taking in his imposing build, the high cheekbones, dark coloring and aristocratic nose he'd inherited from his extensive French lineage, and the brooding, slightly slanted eyes that reflected his maternal grandparents' Asian background.

His formidable appearance made the woman nervous, and she wet her lips with the tip of her tongue. "You're not Casey Woods," she said, stating the obvious. She was not only uneasy, she was in a visible state of shock.

"I'm Marc Devereaux, Casey's associate," Marc replied in a voice that was intentionally calming. "And you are...?"

"Amanda Gleason." She summoned up her composure. "I'm sorry to come by so late. But I couldn't leave the hospital until now. I don't have much time. Please, can we talk? I want to hire you."

"Hospital? Are you ill?"

"No. Yes. Please…I need to explain."

Marc pulled the door open and gestured for her to come in. "Sorry for the casual attire. I wasn't expecting a client." As he spoke, a series of deep, warning barks sounded from above. The echo of padded paws announced the arrival of a sleek red bloodhound as he lumbered to the front door. He stood beside Marc and woofed at the stranger.

"It's okay, Hero," Marc said. "Quiet down."

Instantly, the dog obeyed.

"Hero is a human scent evidence dog and part of our team," Marc explained. "But if you're afraid of dogs, I can put him upstairs."

Amanda shook her head. "That's not necessary. I like dogs."

"Then we'll head to a meeting room." He indicated the second door to the left and escorted her inside.

"Hello, Marc," an invisible voice greeted him, along with a series of wall lights that blinked in conjunction with the voice tones. "You have a guest. The interview room temperature is sixty-five degrees. Shall I raise it?"

"Yeah, Yoda," Marc replied. "Raise it to seventy."

"Temperature will reach seventy degrees in approximately seven minutes."

"Great. Thanks." Marc gave a faint smile at the startled look on Amanda's face. She was peering around, trying to determine the source of the voice.

"That's Yoda," he informed her. "He's the inexplicable creation of Ryan McKay, the techno genius of Forensic Instincts. He's omniscient…and harmless." Marc pulled out a chair. "Have a seat. You'll probably want to keep your coat on until it gets a little warmer in here."

"Thank you. You're very kind." Amanda sank down into the chair, continuing to clutch her coat and her file folder. She looked like a terrified bird being chased by a predator.

"Now, tell me what Forensic Instincts can do for you."

Amanda drew an unsteady breath. "You can find someone for me. If he's alive."

Marc sank back in his chair, intentionally trying to put Amanda at ease, even though his brain was on high alert. "Who is it you want us to find and why aren't you sure he's alive?"

"My boyfriend. He was declared a no-body homicide. The police found his car, with blood splattered all over the driver's seat and windshield, out at Lake Montauk. There were signs that he was dragged to another car. The theory was that he was killed, and his body dumped in the ocean. The Coast Guard searched for days, using every form of sophisticated equipment they had. Nothing turned up. The case was closed."

"When did this happen?"

"In April."

"And you're first coming to us now, eight months later. Why? Do you have some new evidence that suggests he's alive?"

"New evidence and a new reason to find him immediately." Amanda rushed on to dispel the obvious. "I know you're thinking that, if he's alive, maybe he doesn't want to be found. Even if that's true, which I don't believe it is, he has no choice. Not now."

Marc leaned across the table and pulled over a legal-size pad. He preferred to take his notes in longhand, then transfer them into the computer. Typing into a laptop was very off-putting to clients who needed a personal connection.

"What's this man's name?"

"Paul Everett."

"And why is finding him so urgent?"

Amanda swallowed, her hands twisting in her lap. "We have a son. He was born three weeks ago. He was just diagnosed with SCID—Severe Combined Immunodeficiency. His body is incapable of fighting infection. He needs a stem cell transplant from a matched donor or he'll die."

Marc put down his pen. "I assume you're not a match?"

She shook her head. "The testing said I'm not even a candidate. I was in a car accident as a child. Thanks to the blood transfusions I received, I have hepatitis C. So I'm out of the picture. And so far, so is the National Marrow Donor Program Registry. They have no match for us. The best, maybe the only hope is Justin's father." Two tears slid down Amanda's cheeks. Fiercely, she wiped them away. "I could give you a full scientific explanation, Mr. Devereaux. It's consumed my life these past weeks, and I seem to know far more about how a human body can fail than I ever thought possible. But we don't have time. Thanks to me, Justin already has an infection and is showing symptoms of pneumonia."

"Thanks to you?"

"I was nursing him. Evidently, I'm carrying a dormant virus called CMV—Cytomegalovirus. I passed it along to Justin. He's started to cough and he has a fever—both of which are indicators that he's developing CMV pneumonia. Plus, he picked up parainfluenza during the two weeks he was home. His breathing's uneven, his nose is running.… I didn't know he had a compromised immune system, or I'd never have let him have visitors. It's too late to change that. He's on antibiotics and gamma globulin. But even those can only suppress the CMV virus, not cure it. They can also be toxic to a child. As for the parainfluenza, there's literally nothing they can give him. Justin is less than a month old. His tiny body can't sustain itself for long. This is a life-or-death situation."

"I'm very sorry."

"Then help me."

Amanda unbanded her file and opened it, pulling out a USB drive, a DVD and two newspaper clippings. She slid them across the table to Marc. "Here are the obituary and a small write-up of Paul's death from the *Southampton Press,* the local newspaper out there. Pretty sparse. Paul was a real-estate developer with no family. The only exciting aspect to report was the alleged homicide." She pointed at the disk. "A local cable TV station gave a brief broadcast when it happened. That was it for media coverage."

Marc glanced at both the write-up and the obit, making a mental note to contact both the newspaper and TV station. He slid his laptop over and popped in the USB drive. Two images appeared on his monitor, side by side. The first was of Amanda and a man—presumably Paul Everett—posing on a windswept beach in their ski jackets, arms wrapped around each other. The expressions on their faces, their intimate stance, said they were very much in love. The second image was of the two of them at some sort of formal gathering. They were smiling, looking directly into the camera as they posed for a photograph.

"Now look at this." Amanda pulled out her cell phone and placed it on the table for Marc to see.

There was a photo on the screen, and Marc shifted his attention to study it. Being a cell phone shot, it was a lot grainier than the other two photos. But it was obviously the image of a man standing on a busy street corner, impatiently waiting for a light to change. He was staring at the don't walk sign, which gave the photographer a chance to catch him face-first.

Marc could see that from the facial features, the expression and the stance, it was the same man as the one in the other two shots.

"When was this second photo taken?" he asked. "And where?"

"Yesterday. In Washington, D.C."

"By whom?"

"A friend of mine, a fellow photojournalist. In this case, my friend saw the resemblance to Paul. She didn't wait to get her camera ready. She just used the closest thing—her cell phone. She emailed me the photo a couple of hours ago. I had just walked out of the hospital to take a break."

"So she knew you and Paul as a couple."

"Yes. She also knew I'd never had a chance to tell Paul I was pregnant. She was hoping to give me that chance, along with the incredible news that Paul was alive."

Paul Everett had never known about the pregnancy, Marc thought. That eliminated one basic reason why he'd choose to vanish. Still, Marc would want to talk to Amanda's friend.

Amanda mistook his silence for skepticism. "I have no idea

why Paul would vanish without saying a word or why he'd start a new life elsewhere. Once I got this cell phone shot and realized he might be alive, I was relieved, but I was also furious. I felt—I feel—betrayed. When they told me Paul was dead, I was ready to raise my child alone. But now that there's a chance he could be alive, a chance that he could save Justin's life…my pride is a non-issue. I have to try to track Paul down."

Marc was still staring intently from the screen to the cell phone, looking for additional characteristics that would confirm the images as the same man. "Did you call the police about this new photo?" he asked.

"Yes, in the taxi on my way to your office. Two guesses whether or not they gave me any points for credibility." Amanda's lips trembled and tears began sliding down her cheeks. "That's why I'm here. I've been toying with the idea of calling you since last April when Paul disappeared, hoping you could uncover a miracle. But this photo clinched it. You have a reputation for solving cases that no one else can. Please. For the sake of my baby… Will you help me? I'll scrape together any amount of money to pay your fee. I'll give up my apartment, if need be. I don't care. I just want Justin to be all right." She broke down, dropping her face into her hands and openly sobbing.

"This isn't about money," Marc assured her, although she'd had him the minute she described her situation with her infant. "Our policy is to adjust our fees based upon our client's monetary circumstances." Thankfully, they could do that. Between the astronomical bonuses they received from their more affluent clients, and the trust fund Casey's grandfather had left her, Forensic Instincts was on solid financial footing.

"Then what is it?" Amanda asked as Marc fell silent.

Marc didn't answer immediately. The problem was, he was in the hot seat. Forensic Instincts had an unbroken rule: they never took on a case without first having a full-team discussion and a unanimous decision.

Well, these were dire circumstances. And given that no one else from the team was around and that it would take time to reach them all and get them over here—hell, there was a first time for everything.

"It's nothing I can't work out," he stated flatly. "We'll find Paul Everett, Ms. Gleason. If he's alive, we'll find him. And we'll do whatever's necessary to ensure his cooperation."

Amanda's head shot up, her tear-streaked face displaying a glimmer of hope. "Oh, thank you. Thank you. From the bottom of my heart, I thank you."

"Thank me when we've done the job." Marc's mind was on overdrive. "What hospital is your son in?"

"Sloane Kettering. He was referred there by the staff at Mount Sinai who made the original diagnosis."

"So you're staying there with him?"

"I haven't left until just now."

"Fine." Marc nodded. "I'll need you to email that cell phone picture to me. I'll also need some basic information from you—including the name and contact info of your photojournalist friend. Then go back to your baby. Give me a chance to assemble the team and lay all this out for them. We'll have a plan by morning."

Part of that plan, he knew, was going to include having his ass kicked.

CHAPTER THREE

"Marc, you're the one person I rely on to keep a consistent level head. You, of all people, know what it means to be a team member. What made you jump the gun like this?"

Casey Woods, the founder and president of Forensic Instincts, stood at the head of the sweeping oval table in the main conference room, her palms pressed flat on the surface, her spine ramrod straight. For a petite, strikingly attractive redhead in her early thirties, she had the commanding presence of an army general and the leadership skills to match. She was also a trained behavioral and investigative profiler with unerring gut instincts that enhanced her skills.

Right now, it didn't take a profiler to know she was pissed.

And not because it was close to midnight, and the entire FI team was gathered around the table, bleary-eyed, having been summoned for an emergency meeting. Business as usual at Forensic Instincts. But not for this reason.

Marc leaned back in his chair and met Casey's gaze head-on. "Amanda Gleason had to get back to the hospital to her gravely ill infant. An on-the-spot decision had to be made. I know you, Casey. I know the whole team. We would have agreed to take this case. So I bent the rules. Under the circumstances, I'm sure you can understand my rationale."

Glancing back down at Marc's notes, Casey blew out her breath. The fact was, she could see the merit behind Marc's argument. But it had still been a major breach of their team credo.

"I want to help this poor woman as much as you do," she said, calming down enough to lower herself into a chair and begin stroking Hero's glossy head. He was sitting up and looking around, visibly aware of the tension in the room. "But you know you could have gotten the whole team together, either in person or by conference call, in a matter of minutes. All you had to do was explain that to Ms. Gleason."

"You're right," Marc acknowledged. "I should have waited. But after the child kidnapping case we just wrapped up..." A brief pause. "Look. Stuff like this is my hot button. That's not news to any of you. Circumstances just made it easier to push it."

"I understand where Marc is coming from." Claire Hedgleigh spoke up. She was one of the team's newest members, and also its least hard-edged. Her abilities could be described as psychic; she preferred the term *intuitive.* Either way, her intangible connections to people and things were astonishing. They also made her more sensitive to Marc's plight.

"This is a newborn baby we're talking about," she continued. "Every moment counts."

"So do agreed-upon rules." Retired FBI Special Agent Patrick Lynch—also a new team member—spoke up. "If we don't have some kind of protocol here, we'll be tripping over each other, each taking on different, and maybe conflicting, cases." He arched a brow at Casey. "Actually, I think this is the first time we've ever agreed about rule breaking."

"We're coming from different places, Patrick," Casey replied. "So don't get too excited."

"Come on, Casey, take it down a couple of notches. Cut Marc some slack." Ryan McKay, Forensic Instincts' strategic whiz and techno-genius, made a disgusted sound. "He called us the minute Amanda Gleason walked out the door. I'm the one who should be complaining. I was in stage four sleep when Marc's phone call came. You know how I feel about my sleep."

Everyone knew how Ryan felt about his sleep. And no one wanted to be around him when he didn't get it.

On the other hand, with those drop-dead Black Irish looks, Ryan looked better with red eyes and bed head than most men did at a formal affair.

"I guess we were lucky you were alone," Claire commented drily. "Or you might have blown us off."

Ryan shot her a look. "Never happen." He angled his head toward Casey. "Well? What's the verdict?"

Casey stared at Marc's notes for another second, then raised her head and glanced at the team members, one by one. "I say we take it," she stated.

"Take it," Ryan echoed.

"Absolutely," Claire chimed in.

Patrick's nod was firm. "We could save a child's life. Take it."

"I'm still ticked off at you," Casey informed Marc. "But let's get on this case—now. Bring us up to speed."

John Morano's office was a dump, a ramshackle wooden building that smelled of damp wood, fish and salt water.

The location, however, was prime. His wharf and marina's dock service business for local fishermen was located right on the Shinnecock Bay in Long Island's affluent town of Southampton. He made good money because he was smart. But he was also a well-heeled real-estate developer with not only a big reputation, but equally big plans for the future. He was sitting on a gold mine and he knew it. He'd gotten in early. Now, as he'd expected, real-estate prices were skyrocketing, thanks to the construction of the nearby Shinnecock Indian Casino. It was the perfect time to act.

Morano could visualize the transformation that was about to occur. His dilapidated office would soon disappear; in its place a multimillion-dollar luxury hotel that would attract vacationers everywhere. The cash flow from his dock services would still be incoming. But there'd be a lot more than fishing boats making their way to his pier. Chartered yachts would soon conveniently travel between Manhattan and here, bringing affluent tourists to gamble in the casino and be pampered in his five-star hotel.

The pieces were falling into place. He just had to play his cards right.

The rickety office door swung open and a gruff workman walked in, carrying an empty toolbox.

It looked for all the world as if he was here to do carpentry or make repairs—and the place could sure use it.

But a short time later, the man left, his empty toolbox now filled with twenty thousand dollars in cash.

Just outside the office, he pulled out his burner phone and punched in the requisite number. "Today's repairs are done," he reported.

"Good," was the reply.

The workman headed to the gravel area where he'd parked. He walked past his truck and across the dock, stopping to hurl his phone into the bay. Then he reversed his steps, got into his vehicle and drove away.

Amanda hurried back to Sloane Kettering and the Pediatric Bone Marrow Transplant unit. She knew Melissa would never leave Justin's side during her absence. And she'd checked her cell phone twelve times since she'd called in an hour ago. But, despite Melissa's reassurances, her heart was still racing, her prayers still echoing inside her head as she rushed to see Justin, to make sure he was still alive and fighting.

She was startled to see the stocky man with the ruddy complexion and salt-and-pepper hair standing outside the BMT Unit, hands clasped behind his back as he stared inside.

"Uncle Lyle?" Amanda broke into a run. "What are you doing here at this hour? Has something happened?"

"No, nothing like that." Lyle Fenton patted his niece's shoulder. He wasn't an affectionate man. Never had been. He'd grown up poor, made himself rich, but had never included a family as part of the picture. But when his sister and her husband had been killed in a car accident, he'd felt some sense of responsibility for their only child. Amanda had been in photojournalism school at the time, and Lyle had already made a decent amount of money. So paying for her education and kick-starting her career had been his way of reaching out. It was easy enough, given she loved the Hamptons and had moved within ten miles of his estate.

Still, they rarely saw each other. Until now.

"I was in Manhattan on business," he told his niece now. "The meeting ran right through dinner and well past ten. So I stopped in to see how the baby—how Justin—was doing. I was surprised not to find you here."

Amanda released her breath. Thank God. Her uncle was just passing through on his way back to the Hamptons. Nothing had gone wrong with her precious baby.

"I only left for a few hours," she replied. "It was important. And, as you can see, I left my friend Melissa with Justin. She treats him like her own." With those words, Amanda glanced inside the unit, relieved to see Melissa sitting by Justin's side, talking softly to him in his crib.

"What was so important?" Lyle asked curiously.

"I hired an investigative firm to find Paul."

That came as a major surprise, and Lyle started. "Paul? He's dead."

"Maybe. Maybe not."

A heartbeat of silence. "I had no idea your thoughts were heading in this direction. Do you have something to go on?"

"Nothing solid. But tell me, Uncle Lyle, how else should my thoughts be headed?" Amanda spread her hands wide. "I'm desperate. *I'm* not a potential donor. *You're* not a potential donor. I have no other family. And so far the registry has come up empty. I don't know if Paul's alive. I don't know if he'd be a viable match. But I've got to try."

Lyle nodded, although the expression on his face was dubious. "I understand. Who did you hire? I could have given you some recommendations."

"I didn't need them. I hired Forensic Instincts. After the way they handled the kidnapping of that little girl, there was no doubt in my mind that they were the right company to track down Paul—*if* he's alive."

"They took the case?"

Amanda nodded. "They're meeting about it as we speak."

"Do you need money? An independent investigative team like Forensic Instincts doesn't come cheap."

"I'm fine for now. Plus, you're already paying for all of Justin's hospital expenses. I'm very grateful. But enough is enough."

"That's absurd, Amanda. I have the means. I'll offer a huge reward for the right stem cell donor, if that's what it takes. Don't hesitate to call on me."

"Thank you, Uncle Lyle. I'll do that. But right now I think Forensic Instincts is my ray of hope." Once again, she glanced into the unit. "I want to get back inside and relieve Melissa."

"The nurses said there'd been no change," Lyle informed her. "That's good, isn't it?"

"I don't know what good means anymore." Amanda was already rolling up her sleeves, getting ready to scrub up. "I thank God he isn't worse. But I keep praying he'll improve, that by some miracle he'll get better." She shut her eyes for a brief second. "That's a pipe dream, I know. But hope is all I can cling to. And I won't give up on my son."

"No, no, of course not." Lyle gestured for her to get back

inside. "Go and be with your child. I'll be in touch." He started to leave.

"Uncle Lyle?" Amanda stopped him with a gentle hand on his forearm. "Thank you. Not just for dropping by or for offering to help pay Forensic Instincts, but for having yourself tested. I know this isn't your thing. But it means the world to me that you'd try."

Briefly, he smiled. "It was hardly a sacrifice. I have more than enough blood—and money—to spare." Another awkward pat on her hand. "I'll be in touch."

Once her uncle had gone, Amanda went through the ritual of sterilizing her hands and donning the necessary gloves, hospital gown and mask. Then, she reentered the reverse isolation unit where her infant was fighting for his life.

"Go on home to your family," she said softly to Melissa. "And thanks so much."

Melissa rose and squeezed her friend's gloved hands with her own. "Call whenever you need me."

"I will."

Amanda approached the crib, relieved to be back, happy to be alone with her son.

She could never get over how small he was. Or maybe he just looked that way in his crib with a central line IV in his three-week-old chest and a blow-by of oxygen perched on his crib to enrich the oxygen content of the air around him. He'd been born full-term, a respectable seven pounds one ounce. Maybe that's what made it even harder. The preemies down in the neonatal ICU looked so much more fragile, so much more like they had the fight of their lives ahead of them. And yet, none of them was as sick as Justin, who faced a grim prognosis.

The middle-aged nurse who'd most recently checked Justin's vitals walked in behind Amanda.

"Ms. Gleason," she greeted her. "I'm glad you got out for a little while."

"Thank you." Amanda gestured at the medical apparatus, then at her baby, who had started waving a tiny fist and whining. "How is Justin? Is there any change?"

"No. The little guy is a fighter, though. And he obviously knows his mommy's voice. He was quiet until you walked in. Would you like to hold him for a while?"

It was a routine question—one that, in this case, the nurse already knew the answer to. Amanda held her baby every chance she could. It was one of the few things she could offer him at this point—the warmth of her body, the soft lullabies that soothed him, plus her constant prayers and love. Holding him was a bittersweet experience. The joy of cradling him close, having his tiny fingers curl around hers—the feeling was indescribable. But the guilt of knowing why she couldn't nurse him, why he couldn't even be bottle-fed, but instead had to get his nourishment from an IV catheter, why his breathing was raspy, and why he had an infection—an infection she'd given to him—ate at her like the vilest of poisons.

Now she gathered him close, being careful to avoid his IV, and rocked him as she began singing him the lullabies he seemed to love. He stopped fussing, his tiny body relaxing as he experienced the security of his mother's embrace and the melodic sounds of her voice. At that moment, all was right with his world—and Amanda's.

If Paul really were alive, he couldn't help but fall in love with this little miracle.

Tears welled up in Amanda's eyes, slid down her cheeks beneath the mask. Between the pain, the worry and the hormones, she cried at the drop of a hat. She'd even wept in front of Marc Devereaux, although he'd seemed to understand. He'd taken her case. He'd been confident. He'd reassured her. And she believed in him.

But would they find Paul? Was Paul alive to be found? Or was that just wishful thinking on her part?

She'd mourned him for so long. More so after she found out she was carrying his baby. They'd never talked about having children, nor about settling down together. It was too soon. They'd only been together for five months. But they were five intense months, filled with a love and a passion Amanda had never before experienced. Justin was the culmination of that. And Paul would never be able to share in the miracle that was his son.

Finding out that Paul might truly be alive had been a devastating blow to her gut. Disbelief, hope, confusion, betrayal, and most of all, anger had rushed through her, one sharp emotion at a time. But, with Justin's diagnosis, all that emotion channeled into desperation to find Paul. The fact that he might have been lying to her since day one and that he'd done a dump-and-run was insignificant. All that mattered was Justin. She had to save her baby. Even if it meant pleading at the feet of a man who'd made a fool of her.

Justin gave a little cough, then screwed up his face and kicked his legs. Amanda didn't like the sound of that cough. And she didn't like the way his nose was running. He looked paler than before. And he seemed fussier. Was that normal baby behavior or was it the pneumonia getting worse? She'd have to find Dr. Braeburn and ask him.

She stopped singing and kissed the top of Justin's silky head. *Please, God,* she prayed. *Please let Forensic Instincts find Paul. And please let him be a healthy match for Justin. Please.*

But Amanda was a realist. And she knew that prayers alone wouldn't be enough.

Ryan McKay's lair, as the team called it, took up the entire basement of Forensic Instincts. Usually, he was down there by his lonesome, with only his servers, his gadgets and his workout equipment to keep him company. But, at the moment, things were different. Even though it was after two in the morning, Marc was pacing around Ryan's space like a hungry lion.

Finally, Ryan swiveled around in his computer chair and faced Marc, hands folded behind his head.

"Nothing jumps out at me," he pronounced. "Our client is just who she says she is. A thirty-four-year-old photojournalist who lives in an apartment over a café in Westhampton Beach. Her only family is an uncle, Lyle Fenton, who's a rich business tycoon serving on the Southampton Board of Trustees. He put her through school after her parents died and used his influence to get her some high-profile jobs. Doesn't look like he's subsidizing her, though. She's on her own financially."

Marc nodded. No surprises there. Not about the information itself nor the scope of it. He didn't ask how Ryan had accessed Amanda's finances. Ryan could access anything.

"I also checked out Amanda's photojournalist friend," Ryan continued. "She's as legit as Amanda."

"Yeah, she's also cooperative," Marc added. "She didn't hang up on me when I woke her up in the middle of the night. She confirmed that she'd taken the photo, and when and where it was taken."

"Okay, so that takes care of those preliminaries."

"What about Paul Everett?" Marc demanded.

"Again, he seems clean enough on the surface. A real-estate developer, like Amanda said. Had some decent-size prospects, most of which are underwater, thanks to the economy. I can check around in the morning, see what I can find out from the people he worked with—assuming I can find them. Apparently, he owned a wharf and marina out in the Hamptons where local fisherman docked their boats. Looks like he had plans to grow it into something bigger. He was trying to get all kinds of building permits. Once again, I can't dig deeper until business hours start. No one's in the township office at 2:00 a.m. So we've got a seven-hour wait. What I can do until then is use my facial recognition software to compare the older photos of Paul Everett with the new one. It'll take time to enhance the cell phone shot. But I'll do it. And we'll have stronger confirmation that the two guys in the pictures are one and the same."

"At least we'll be using the time instead of wasting it," Marc concurred. "What about D.C.? Did Everett have any ties there?" Marc asked. "Any reason he'd be in Washington?"

"None that I can see. That doesn't mean he didn't start a new life after he took off—*if* he took off. Remember, we still have to consider the possibility that Paul Everett is dead and decomposing at the bottom of the ocean, or that he was dinner for a bunch of hungry sharks."

"Uplifting thoughts." Marc blew out his breath. "So no

signs of dirty dealings? No business contacts who would want him out of the way, or who he'd run from?"

"Not yet. This was a cursory search, Marc. It was meant to give us some starting points. I only scratched the surface. I'll go deeper. I'll dig up Everett's friends, business associates, partners, history—anything sketchy from his past. Whether he ran or was killed, he was into something over his head. It's up to me to give the team something to run with. I'll figure out if Everett was a victim or a slimeball. He can't hide from me." A smug grin. "No one can."

CHAPTER FOUR

Casey faced Amanda across a table in Sloane Kettering's institutional cafeteria.

Amanda shifted in her chair, staring into her coffee cup and stirring furiously. She was waiting for a reaction from the head of Forensic Instincts. Just because Marc was fully invested didn't mean the rest of the team would follow suit. And having Casey Woods fully on board was essential to the urgency with which they approached the case.

Casey alleviated her worries with just a few words.

"Marc made a compelling case," she stated simply. "The whole team feels as strongly about your situation as he does. We started working on the investigation just after midnight."

Amanda's head shot up. "Then you'll find Paul." It was a statement, not a question, one that was rife with faith that Forensic Instincts would succeed.

"We're going to determine if he's alive," Casey amended. "And if he is, my team will find him."

"Thank you," Amanda said gratefully.

She was an attractive woman, Casey noted. But she looked much older than her mid-thirties. She also looked dazed and battered, as if she'd been struck with a sledgehammer. The hell she was going through was unimaginable. Casey didn't have children of her own, but that didn't mean she was immune to Amanda's pain. Having your newborn son's life on the line, being helpless to keep him alive—Casey couldn't fathom anything more excruciating for a new mother.

"I have to ask you a few questions," she told Amanda gently. "I know your heart and mind are with your son. But the more help you can give us, the faster and more effectively we can do our job."

Amanda nodded. "Ask me anything you want."

"Tell me about you and Paul. Where and when you met. How the relationship progressed. Where things stood between you when he vanished. Anything the police said when they wrapped up the investigation into his possible death. How much you knew about his work, his friends, his business acquaintances. Any enemies he might have had. Any personal details that could explain his disappearing off the grid. Any reason you can think of that he'd be in Washington, D.C. Where he lived in the Hamptons and anything you can remember about his place—mementos, photos, anything that might reveal something more about him."

"Wow." Amanda blew out her breath, blinking at the deluge of questions Casey had just fired at her. "I assume Marc filled you in on what I told him and showed him?"

"He did. And some of what you tell me will be redundant. I realize that. But I want to hear it from you."

"Okay. Paul and I met at a political fundraiser. There was chemistry from the start. We got involved pretty quickly, and we were together for five months. He was a real-estate developer. I never met any of his colleagues. I met a few of his friends, mostly neighbors near the house he rented and a couple of his poker buddies. Paul and I were pretty wrapped up in each other. Most of the time we spent together was alone."

"So things were good right up until he vanished?"

A nod. "We hadn't talked in a few days, which was unusual. I assumed it was because he was busy. We were supposed to have dinner that night. He never showed. I called his cell phone all night. Then I went to his house."

"Which was where?"

"In Hampton Bays. It's a small cottage, close to Tiana Bay. He rented it year-round. It was about twenty minutes from Westhampton Beach, where I live. He was working on some big real-estate development project in Southampton. We didn't get into the details. But enemies? I can't imagine anyone hating Paul. He was easygoing and charismatic. And I also can't imagine why he'd disappear. Things were so good between us. And I never even got a chance to tell him about Justin." Amanda's voice quavered. "When I think that way, I'm sure he must be dead. Nothing else makes sense. But, on the other hand, where is his body? Why didn't the Coast Guard ever turn up anything? It makes no sense."

"The police dismissed the case," Casey continued. "Did they leave any doors open?"

"They said they had nothing to go on. No suspects, no

motives and no body." Amanda took a quick gulp of her coffee. "As for D.C., your guess is as good as mine. Paul never mentioned any friends or relatives there. Could he have gotten a project there? Of course. But I have no way of knowing."

"Okay, let's get to Paul's cottage. Do you know if it's been rented out?"

"I don't know," Amanda replied, looking puzzled. "But what difference does that make? All his things are gone. I donated everything to charity except items that had sentimental value to me."

"I'll need to see those items. Also, I'll need the name of Paul's landlord." Casey gave the simpler explanation first. "As for the house, I'd like to get permission to go inside. I don't know whether or not you're a believer, but Claire Hedgleigh, one of my team members, is a brilliant intuitive. She might pick up on something just from being in Paul's surroundings—especially if no one's lived there for the past eight months. And she'll definitely have a shot at sensing something from the personal items you're talking about."

"You're talking about a psychic."

Casey's lips curved. "Claire hates that term, but yes. A psychic. She was crucial to solving our last big case, and before she joined Forensic Instincts, she was tremendously successful working with law enforcement."

"If she can help tell us if Paul's alive and where he is, I'm all for it."

"Good. Then you won't balk at my next request. Last night when you spoke to Marc at the office, you met Hero. He's another unconventional member of our team—a human scent evidence dog. Between sniffing out Paul's place and sniffing the scent pads we'll make from Paul's personal things, he'll be able to zero in on Paul's presence within miles—if and when we get to that point. So, can you give me the information on Paul's landlord? I'll make a few phone calls and check the status of the cottage. Also, would you make a mental note of whatever mementos you have? We'll drive out to the Hamptons together either later today or tomorrow, depending on when you can make arrangements to leave your son."

Amanda shut her eyes for an instant. "Thank you for understanding," she said simply. "My friend Melissa has offered to stay with him whenever I need to leave. And it's not as if the hospital staff isn't in constant contact with me. I just feel better when I'm close by. It's not logical. It's just being Justin's mother."

"I don't blame you." Casey pushed back her chair and rose. "You go to your son. I'll call you as soon as we're good to go."

Ryan was leaning over his computer, deep in concentration, when Claire walked in.

"Where is everybody?" she asked.

"Ever hear of knocking?" Ryan's gaze never left his monitor.

"Why? Is this a private sanctuary?"

"Actually, yeah, it is."

Claire rolled her eyes. "Then put a lock on the door. Or at least keep it shut." She walked over to Hero, who'd jumped up from his nap the minute she walked in. He gazed at her hopefully, and with good reason. Claire was definitely the soft touch of the team, not only in her handling of the cases, but in her handling of Hero. Her sensitivity went right along with her pale blond hair, light gray eyes and willowy figure—not to mention the ethereal quality that emanated from her.

She didn't have many buttons that set her off. But Ryan McKay was one of them.

Now Claire's lips curved as she scratched Hero's ears. The bloodhound's gaze was locked on her.

"In my pocket," she told him, reaching in and pulling out a piece of cheese. She offered it to him. He slurped it up and swallowed it in one bite.

"You're a doormat," Ryan noted. "And you're going to put five pounds on him in less than a year."

"It's low-fat cheese. No harm, no foul." Claire scanned the room, taking in the workout equipment, the vast array of computers, servers and network wires, and the centerpiece of the room: a long line of semicompleted robots—all surrounded by a pile of metal and plastic parts that were just waiting to be used.

"I wouldn't worry about my touching anything in your precious basement," she retorted. "I'd trip and kill myself if I tried. Plus, I don't know what half this stuff is anyway. Especially your toy section. Robots were never my thing."

"No, you're more of a tarot card girl."

Despite her vow to remain impervious to Ryan's barbs, Claire grimaced. "You're so narrow-minded, it's sickening. And FYI, I don't do tarot cards. Or Ouija boards."

"Séances?"

"Nope."

"You're a boring psychic."

"And you're a pain in the ass."

Ryan spun his chair around, leaned back and folded his arms behind his head. He looked disgustingly amused. "Nice comeback. Cold, too. I'm getting to you."

Claire shot him a look. "Not a chance in hell."

"Then why'd you drop by? No one uses the basement but me. The conference room is two flights up." He pointed at the ceiling.

"I know where it is." Claire folded her arms across her chest. "Don't flatter yourself. I'm here because I got a call from Casey. She said we're having a full team meeting. I went straight to the conference room. When no one was up there, I chose the obvious—you. You live in this cave. So, I came down to check and see if you knew anything."

"Yup. A full team meeting it is. Casey called me, too." Ryan glanced at his watch. "She's on her way. So's Patrick. And Marc's in the kitchen, brewing a pot of coffee and probably eating my trail mix."

"Fine. Then I'll go up and wait." Claire hesitated. "Did you find anything?"

Ignoring Claire's question, Ryan leaned forward and pressed the print button on his computer. A handful of pages glided out. He strolled over and picked them up, perusing them as he did. "You'll know when everyone else does," he said at last.

Claire didn't answer. Trying to reason with a preschooler was pointless. She just left the room and shut the door behind her with a firm click.

Ryan glanced up at the closed door, his lips curving into a lazy smile.

★ ★ ★

All humor was off ten minutes later as the team gathered around the conference room table.

"I met with Amanda Gleason," Casey began, hands folded in front of her. "Marc was dead-on in his assessment. The woman is desperate. The situation is heartbreaking. Time is of the essence. And we're going to save this baby at all costs." She turned to Ryan. "What do you have for us?"

"Let's start with my facial recognition software. I did a comparison of the guy in Amanda's photos with the enhanced image of the guy in the cell phone picture. Using elastic bunch graph matching techniques and a cutting-edge sparse representation algorithm, I was able to determine..." Ryan glanced around at the table of blank faces. "Never mind the details. I'm ninety percent sure it's the same guy."

"Nice odds," Marc commented.

"Yup. I'm willing to bet that Paul Everett is alive."

"A fact that we're not going to pass on to Amanda Gleason," Casey informed them. "Not until we've ruled out the other ten percent."

"Agreed." Ryan nodded. "Moving on, I got in touch with a couple of Paul Everett's former business associates. Lots of praise. No red flags."

"So a dead end."

"Nope. Now comes the interesting part. Marc got me some personal info from Amanda—Everett's birthday, where he banked, a few key dates like when they first met—that kind of stuff. I did a little bit of strategic guesswork and a lot of poking around. It took me some time, but I managed to hack into the guy's banking records."

"And?" Casey perked up. She knew that tone of voice. It meant Ryan was leading up to something big.

"And Paul Everett had some hefty bank balances and some equally hefty withdrawals. The withdrawals followed a pattern. Same amount each time—twenty grand, and same time increments between withdrawals—six weeks. Interesting that this came at the same time that he was fighting for construction permits to upscale his dock operations into a waterfront luxury hotel. With all the amenities he planned and the close proximity to the new Shinnecock gambling casino, this would have been a gold mine."

"Sounds like our guy was paying someone off to get what he wanted." Marc stated the obvious.

"Sure does."

"So he wasn't so squeaky clean after all," Patrick stated. After thirty-plus years as an FBI Special Agent, he was a no-bullshit guy who played by the rules—mostly—and called it like it was.

The playing-by-the-rules part was a huge rub at Forensic Instincts. But Patrick was good—very good. And, as he put it, he kept the team as close to "legal" as possible.

Now he pulled over his pad and started scribbling. "We've got two main possibilities here. Either Paul Everett was paying someone off like Marc said, or he was being blackmailed by someone who had dirt on him. Either one could get him killed or convince him to disappear."

"So much for true love conquering all," Claire murmured.

"Self-preservation trumps true love plus a whole lot more," Ryan replied tersely. "And murder trumps everything. If I'm wrong—and I'm not—and Paul Everett's at the bottom of the ocean, he didn't exactly have a lot of choice about whether or not he hung around for Amanda."

"I get that." Claire looked thoughtful. "I wasn't suggesting that Paul should have—or could have—stuck around. I was just wondering if the relationship between him and Amanda was even real, or if he was just using her as a cover for whatever he was involved in."

"Good point." Casey's eyes narrowed as she scrutinized Claire. "Is that a random question or a feeling?"

"A random question. It's way too soon for me to have a connection with any of this. I haven't even met Amanda, much less gotten into her personal space or feelings."

"That's about to change." Before she elaborated, Casey turned back to Ryan. "Anything else?"

"Yup. Much as I hate to admit it, Claire's theory might have merit." Ryan sounded as if he might choke on his words. "Amanda's uncle is Lyle Fenton. He's a business tycoon who also happens to serve on the Southampton Board of Trustees. If Everett wanted to score points with him in order to get his building permits, it could be why he hooked up with Amanda. The fundraiser they met at was for Congressman Clifford Mercer. Amanda was freelancing for the guy. Her uncle got her the job. Everett could have easily found that out and made a donation to the campaign. That would have gotten him an invite."

"A congressman serves in Washington, D.C.," Casey noted thoughtfully. "Marc, you called Amanda's photographer friend, didn't you?"

"Sure did."

"Where exactly was that recent D.C. photo taken?"

"Second Street at C Street NE."

"Which is just a little over half a mile from the Capitol Building."

"And about a million other places," Ryan reminded her. "Casey, that's the business hub of D.C. It's a leap to assume Paul Everett was going to see Mercer."

"You're right." Marc's brows drew together. "But it's not out of the realm of possibility. Just because Everett vanished, doesn't mean he's given up on building that hotel. Like Ryan said, it's a gold mine. With Everett's ties to Amanda and her uncle severed, Mercer's a shrewd and logical person to win over to his side. He represents District One. That includes the Hamptons. Maybe Everett is looking for a more influential—and long distance—way to get what he wants without tipping off the wrong people to the fact that he's alive."

"We're all speculating." Casey gulped the last of her coffee and set down the mug, mulling over a list of assignments she'd drawn up. "It's time to act and find some answers. Here's what I propose—Patrick, you go down to D.C. and see what you can dig up. If you're down there for more than a day and have something solid to go on, one of us will join you. In the meantime, Claire, Marc and I are going on a field trip to the Hamptons with Amanda. We're taking Hero with us."

At the sound of his name, Hero's head came up and he watched Casey attentively.

"We've got to search Paul's place and make scent pads for Hero to sniff. We've also got to drive out to Montauk and visit the crime scene. On the way back, we'll stop by Amanda's apartment and get some personal items of Paul's for Claire to work with, plus hit some of the spots that Paul and Amanda used to go together."

"Wouldn't it be better if I went with Patrick to D.C.?" Marc asked. "Two former Bureau agents have twice the contacts and twice the resources."

"Probably," Casey conceded. "But I need you here for several reasons. Number one, you'll make things happen."

"In other words, he can break into houses and businesses, or question people under false pretenses," Patrick put in wryly.

A grin tugged at Casey's lips. "Actually, I have permission from the owner to search the house Paul rented. As for the rest—who knows what might come up? Another reason I need Marc here is because Amanda trusts him. For whatever reason, she is comfortable with him and turns to him for support. We need to use that to our advantage. This whole excursion to the Hamptons is going to have to be quick and productive. Amanda doesn't want to be away from her baby for long, and I don't blame her. So we leave in an hour. Ryan, you keep digging, and text me anything you find. Patrick, catch the first flight to D.C. Is everyone okay with that plan?"

"Yup." Marc answered for all of them.

"Good. Then let's make this thing happen."

CHAPTER FIVE

The Hamptons were quiet.

If this had been July, Montauk Highway would have been a parking lot, and getting through the bumper-to-bumper traffic would have been a nightmare of untold proportions. All the rich, beautiful people with summer "cottages"—a euphemism for multimillion-dollar estates—would have been heading out here to enjoy the Hamptons's elite shopping, popular clubs and private beaches. They were the Citidiots, as the locals called Manhattanites—the semiannual residents who helped define the Hamptons as a finely manicured alternate world, a playground for the mega-rich.

But, thankfully, it wasn't July. It was December, way offseason, and only the sparse population of full-time residents were out here. All the better for the Forensic Instincts team. No crowds, the ability to move faster and more productively, and fewer false leads. Besides, Amanda and Paul's relationship had happened off-season. So this was the best way to recreate the scenario, witnesses and all.

Their first stop was Hampton Bays and the cottage Paul had rented.

Farther out on Long Island than Amanda's Westhampton Beach apartment, Hampton Bays was a combination of modest and expensive homes, nestled between Westhampton and Southampton. Right now it was sleepy, strung with Christmas lights that would be beautiful after sunset, but one couldn't help but imagine how hopping the place would be during the summer season. The beaches along the bay were beautiful, and it was a hop, skip and a jump to dining, shopping and nightlife.

The FI team had made a joint decision with Amanda to drive out to Paul's cottage first, then forty-five minutes away, out to Lake Montauk and the spot where Paul's car had been found. After these two site visits, they'd backtrack and stop at Amanda's apartment on the way home. The reasoning was simple: Amanda and Paul had spent more time at his place than at hers. And since Lake Montauk was the crime scene, Casey and Marc could search the area from there to Gosman's Dock, checking for anything the police had overlooked—assuming they'd really been looking. At the same time, Hero could learn Paul's scent, and Claire could immerse herself in Paul's surroundings and see if she picked up on his energy. Whatever personal items of his that Amanda had kept, particularly those with sentimental value, were at her place, and would be sifted through on the return trip.

Casey turned the van into the driveway leading to the cozy little cottage Paul had rented. She'd been watching the road most of the way with an occasional direction from Marc, who was eyeing the GPS. But Claire, who was sitting in the backseat, was finely attuned to the change in Amanda as they neared their destination. She got quieter and quieter, her fingers clasped so tightly together that her knuckles were white. And there was a pained, faraway look in her eyes. She was remembering. She clearly hadn't been out here since Paul's disappearance. And the waves of memory were overwhelming.

Gently, Claire put her hand on Amanda's shoulder. "Are you all right?" she asked.

Amanda gave a slight shake of her head. "Not really. I didn't expect this to be so hard. And Montauk—I'm not even sure I can do it."

"Yes, you can—you can do it for your son. Whatever time you need to compose yourself, to work through what you need to—just take it. We have plenty to keep us busy inside the cottage."

"Thank you," Amanda replied softly.

Marc glanced over his shoulder at Claire and scowled. She knew what he was thinking—that the clock was ticking and that Claire's advice to Amanda to take her time was absurd. Claire gazed steadily back at him, conveying her certainty that this was the right way to go. If they pushed Amanda, they'd get less out of her. She needed to deal with her emotions. It was the only way this day trip was going to yield any results.

Reaching the top of the drive, Casey turned off the ignition and sat back, studying the small wood-shingled house with the rocking chair porch. It was a cottage in the truest sense, not the massive estates some of the wealthy locals referred to as their "summer cottages." It couldn't have more than two bedrooms and a bath, but it was perfect for a single guy whose career was based out here.

Even with the van's windows only slightly cracked for Hero's sake, you could smell the salty air, a sure indication that the bay was close by. A charming cottage, a good location—clearly, Paul Everett had been faring well.

"I can see why you and Paul spent most of your time here," Casey said tactfully.

Amanda nodded. "The inside is lovely, too. And the place is well maintained, even though it's fifty years old. Paul got lucky. The owner is a wealthy East Hampton guy who bought the cottage as an investment. He liked Paul. He rented it to him at a great price, especially because Paul wanted it year-round and not just as a summer vacation house. I think Paul would have eventually bought it if…" Amanda's voice trailed off.

"Let's go inside," Marc suggested.

Amanda hesitated.

Casey glanced at her in the rearview mirror. "Do you have cell reception?" she asked in a casual tone, as if she didn't already know the answer.

Amanda glanced down at the phone that was perpetually on her lap or in her hand. "Yes."

"Then why don't you stay out here for a minute and check in with the hospital? The owner of the cottage told me he'd leave the door unlocked. Claire, Marc, Hero and I will get started while you get an update on Justin. Then, when you're ready, you can join us."

"I appreciate your compassion." Amanda wasn't just referring to Casey's concern for Justin. She wasn't stupid. She understood that the team was trying to give her the space she needed to prep herself for a painful walk down memory lane.

"No problem." Casey's gaze slid to Claire in the rearview mirror and she gave a quick nod.

All three team members climbed out. Marc went around back of the van and opened the double doors so that Hero could jump down and join them.

With a quick lap of his water, Hero scrambled to the gravel drive, waiting obediently while Marc leashed him up.

"All set?" Casey asked.

"Ready and raring to go."

"Then let's do it."

Amanda watched the FI team head into the house—Paul's house—and her throat tightened. How many times had she and Paul stepped through that door, sometimes toting grocery bags, sometimes laughing and talking, sometimes pulling off each other's parkas in their haste to make love?

Being back here was surreal, like being plunged into a vivid, bittersweet memory and being forced, by one's own mind, to relive it.

This was hitting her much harder than she'd expected. After all, she and Paul had been together less than half a year, no matter how intense their relationship had been. Amanda was far from a weak and clingy woman. She'd been on her own since college, and had loved the freedom of her own independence. Meeting Paul had been the last thing she'd expected. Yet it had happened, and, from the moment it did, she'd sensed that her life was about to be changed in a major way.

Losing him had been unbearable, especially after she realized she was carrying his child.

But she'd gotten through it and survived. Her life had gone on.

Except now there was Justin, a precious gift—but one who'd come with a reality she'd never imagined in her worst nightmares. And the unfathomable possibilities were staring her in the face.

So maybe it was the combination of Justin's precarious health and her postpartum hormones that were making this walk down memory lane so painful.

Or maybe it was because she'd so successfully blocked out the happy times and allowed them to be replaced by grief, anger, hurt and resentment.

Today was going to be one long confrontation with the past. More unnerving than that was the question of what their investigations would uncover. If Paul was alive, what kind of man had he really been? What had he been involved in that he'd kept so well hidden?

Squeezing her eyes shut for one long, aching minute, Amanda picked up her cell phone and snapped back into the real world—the one she'd been battling for almost a month now.

Justin.

She pressed the speed dial number for Sloane Kettering.

Please, God, she prayed, as she did every time she picked up the phone or walked back into the Pediatric BMT unit. *Please let him hold on. Please let us find a miracle.*

And, for good or for ill, that miracle had to be Paul.

★ ★ ★

Casey headed up the stone path that led to the cottage. She turned the knob, and, as promised, the door was unlocked.

The place was cozy and charming—one large and one small bedroom, a full bath, a galley kitchen, a little eating area and a family room with a brick fireplace. The back door opened to a wooden deck and a dense cluster of trees. Not exactly woods, but certainly the foliage offered privacy from probing eyes.

Hero immediately went to work, snout to the floor, dragging Marc every which way as he took in all the new and interesting scents. He zigzagged through the house, investigating every inch of his surroundings. Marc let him take the lead. The more comprehensive Hero's olfactory experience was, the better it would be when Marc made scent pads of anything they found that belonged to Paul. Paul's scent would be that much more recognizable to Hero, which could be a key factor down the road.

It wouldn't be the first time Hero had lived up to his name.

"It's a pretty secluded half acre," Marc commented a short time later, standing on the deck beside Casey and gazing around. "No houses in back. Set back far enough from the road. And with lines of trees on either side that block the neighbors' view. Interesting."

"Very," Casey agreed. "If someone wanted to stay as inconspicuous as possible, this is a good place to do it."

Marc nodded, glancing down at Hero, who was sniffing the length of the deck. "It also tilts the scales slightly in favor of Paul Everett being alive. If someone killed him, why do it out in the open, on a road in his car where a passerby could witness it? Why not kill him here, where it's private, then clean up the mess, toss the body in the trunk of your car and drive it to the ocean to dump it? There'd be no evidence of a murder at all."

"Unless the murder wasn't premeditated," Casey pointed out. "If Paul met someone for an illegal dealing of some kind, it would explain the seclusion of his car's location. And if that meeting ended violently, the rest of the police's suggested scenario plays out."

"True." Marc frowned. "It just doesn't feel right. I'm not sure why."

Casey's lips curved slightly. "Maybe because it sounds like a low-budget B movie. Besides, I don't think Paul Everett was an idiot. And only idiots drive out to deserted, sinister places in the middle of the night to meet someone, even for illegal purposes. Paul wasn't some random drug dealer who hid in alleys to make a drop."

"That would be the low-budget B movie part," Marc said, chuckling. "I agree. From all the info Ryan's given us, Paul Everett was a smart, white-collar businessman."

"Whose murder is starting to feel more staged by the minute."

"Casey?" Claire's voice echoed from inside the empty house.

"Coming." Casey glanced at Marc. "Keep looking around. Let Hero keep sniffing out all the smells. If you find anything, make a couple of scent pads. I'll see what's up with Claire."

Marc nodded.

Casey went back inside, going straight to where she knew Claire would be—in the master bedroom.

"What are you picking up on?" she asked.

Claire had been standing by the window, staring into the room, her brows knit in puzzlement, her expression shaken. She looked uncharacteristically off balance.

"Contradictions," she replied. "There are conflicting energies in this room—and throughout this house. Dark and fervent, light and joyous. It's exhausting to be here. I'd guess Paul Everett felt the same way—like he was being torn in two. The pull is especially strong in this bedroom. He went through some powerful emotional struggles in here."

"Probably because he and Amanda spent some powerful emotional hours in here." Casey eyed Claire's face. "But that's not what's got you so weirded out. What is it?"

"Paul. His energy," Claire said. "I've never experienced anything like it. His energy keeps clicking in and out, like a light switch being flipped—on, off, on, off. It's not just weird. It's creepy. I don't understand what it means."

One of Casey's brows rose. "You're not talking about an identical twin scenario, are you?"

"No." Claire gave a hard shake of her head. "Nothing like that. This is all Paul—here and then gone. Like some binary energy I can't wrap my mind around."

Casey pursed her lips. "What can I do to help you get a clearer picture?"

"I'm not sure. As you well know, this isn't an on-command ability. I either sense it, feel it, or I don't. And it doesn't come with an instruction manual." Claire dragged a frustrated hand through her long blond hair. "The only thing I can suggest is that we bring Amanda in here. She might trigger something stronger, clarify this strange intangible energy. Also, I know that Paul's personal items are at her apartment, but maybe she has something of his that she carries around, something meaningful to the two of them. This isn't about just Paul. It's about him and Amanda as a couple."

"I'll get her." Casey left the house and walked back to the van. Amanda was sitting in the backseat, just as they'd left her. Only her head was bowed and she was openly weeping.

Casey's gut knotted.

"Amanda?" she said quietly through the slit in the window.

Amanda's head came up. Her cheeks were wet with tears and her expression was haunted. "I just spoke to Dr. Braeburn. He's head of the pediatric bone marrow transplant team at Sloane Kettering. Justin's fever spiked. Not a lot. But enough. Dr. Braeburn isn't sure whether it's because the antibiotic isn't doing its job or because it's the parainfluenza that's getting worse. There's no antibiotic treatment for parainfluenza like there is for CMV. Most people just fight it off. But with Justin's lack of an immune system, he can't…"

"Do you need to get back?" Casey asked at once.

Amanda swallowed and shook her head. "No. Dr. Braeburn said that, right now, they're not making any change in Justin's antibiotics and there's no imminent danger. My little guy is still holding his own. He's a fighter. And Melissa is right by his side. Frankly, the doctor thought it was far more crucial that I continue trying to track down Paul. And, much as my instincts are to rush right back, the truth is I'm not doing Justin any good hovering over him and getting hysterical. I've got to help him. I've got to find Paul."

Seeing the determination on Amanda's face, hearing the firm tone to her voice, Casey got her first real glimpse of the strong woman beneath the grieving mother. Amanda Gleason was nobody's doormat. She'd do what she had to. And she was ready to face whatever she had to about Paul.

"Can you come inside, please?" Casey opened the door. "Claire thinks it might help her."

"Of course. That's what I'm here for." Wiping the tears off her face, Amanda slid out of the car and preceded Casey to the front door.

Claire was standing in the middle of the master bedroom when they walked in. She glanced up, clearing her expression of anything negative or alarming, and acknowledging Amanda with a compassionate look. "How are you holding up?" she asked.

"Not great. But I'm not the concern here. Justin is. Did you sense anything from your tour of the cottage?"

Claire explained the same thing to Amanda that she had to Casey—omitting the unnerving part and sticking to the conflicting energies she was picking up.

Amanda gave a sad nod. "That doesn't surprise me. If Paul was wrestling with something ugly or illegal and keeping it from me, it probably was gnawing away at him—that is, if he actually cared about me at all."

"He did." That Claire said without hesitation. "One of the positive energies I can pick up on is love. There was genuine emotion here, especially in this bedroom. I can sense intimacy, passion and tenderness. But it's all tangled up with guilt and a dark, underlying purposefulness. I can't promise you there was no manipulation involved in Paul's relationship with you. I can only tell you that he was torn—and that he did care for you." Claire pointed at the area on the long wall. "What was there?"

"Paul's bed."

A nod. "That explains why the emotions I'm picking up on are the strongest there. There's a raw vulnerability and a clarity there that make it easier for me to connect. There's no divisiveness—only pained confusion. Paul was definitely battling feelings for you versus other commitments."

"What commitments?" Amanda asked. "What was he involved in?"

Claire frowned. "I don't know." She turned, pointing at the opposite wall. "What used to be there?"

"Paul's desk. His small file cabinet. His laptop."

"And intensity. Not emotional. Mental. This is where plans were reviewed, strategies were devised…" A pause. "And phone calls were made. Not on his regular cell. On a separate one. One he kept locked in his desk drawer and used only when he was alone. He was a different man during those calls. He wasn't the person you knew." A pause. "He was running. To something, and away from something. Again, that same binary energy. No clear images of the to or the from—or the why. Just flashes of Paul in motion."

"Paul did run—in the literal sense," Amanda supplied. "Five miles every morning, no matter what the weather. Here. At my place. No matter where we stayed. Could that be the running you're envisioning?"

"Sometimes." Claire was concentrating, hard. "I can see him in his sweats. Panting as he makes his way rhythmically along the beach. Stopping to make a phone call—on that private phone again. He enjoyed his run, but he used it for more than exercise. And the running isn't just literal. It's more complex than that." Claire squeezed her eyes shut, and then gave a frustrated shake of her head. "That's it. I just can't pick up on any details."

Casey was studying the anguished look on Amanda's face.

"Let's walk the rest of the house," she suggested. "We'll

see if Paul inadvertently left something behind—something you didn't notice when you had his things removed. If we find anything, I'll make some scent pads for Hero. By now, he'll have memorized every smell in the cottage. Then we'll head out to Montauk." A quizzical glance at Amanda. "If you're up for it."

"I've got to be up for it." There was no hesitation in Amanda's voice. "Any pain I feel over Paul pales in comparison to my pain over Justin. I hired you to find Paul. I don't plan on being an obstacle in your search. Let's drive out to the crime scene—now. If Justin can fight, so can I."

CHAPTER SIX

Patrick Lynch was very good at everything he did—whether it was as a private investigator, a security consultant or as an FBI agent, something he'd done for most of his life.

He'd worked for the Bureau for more than thirty-two years, starting in the days before the New York Field Office had moved to Federal Plaza and, instead, had occupied just several floors in a building on East Sixty-ninth Street and Third Avenue. He'd handled everything from white-collar crime to violent crime. Things had been so different back then—no computers, only shared telephones among the agents, and fewer, less-easily accessible resources.

But one thing hadn't changed: Patrick worked within the letter of the law—always.

Consequently, he'd never expected to find himself part of a team like Forensic Instincts, whose methods were as different from his own as could be imagined. But events in life, especially the recent kidnapping case that had introduced Patrick to FI, had taught him that sometimes, sometimes, the end really did justify the means.

That didn't mean he was ready to abandon his principles—only that he was willing to bend them a bit when it became absolutely necessary.

The team considered him to be the seasoned and steadying voice of reason at Forensic Instincts, the guy who played by the book and acted as the anchoring fist on the kite strings of the other team members. Patrick considered himself to be the guy who kept his colleagues out of jail.

But, hell, he respected their talents. And on the flip side, they respected his.

In this new case, Patrick felt totally comfortable with the first assignment Casey had given him. He knew D.C. like the back of his hand and his task was solid. He might not have Hero's nose, but he was damned good at tracking down people.

He landed at Reagan National around noon and took a cab into D.C.'s Capitol District. Ryan had enlarged the mystery man's photo on the computer, fine-tuning it as sharply as possible so the man's image was clear, the background less blurry. The pictures of Amanda and Paul were close-ups and needed only minor tweaks to make their images crisp.

Patrick stood on the corner of Second Street and C Street NE, and glanced around. Just as he recalled. Government buildings, St. Joseph's Church and throngs of people moving rapidly along. And that was just what was within line of sight. A short walk away there were a couple of coffee shops, a bagel place, a café and a supermarket. Farther on was Stanton Park, and north was Union Square Station.

He had lots of territory to cover. And nothing but a few photos and his gut instincts to go on.

One thing about the Hamptons. It literally shut down in the wintertime. The same applied to Montauk, which was at the far eastern tip of Long Island. Even the avid fishermen, who braved the cool autumn days to cast their lines, were long gone by December.

Although cars drove by it year-round, Lake Montauk was deserted when the team arrived. A stiff breeze had kicked up, reminding them all that it was nearly Christmas-time. And the chill in the air was accentuated by the proximity of the water.

"Here. Stop here," Amanda told Casey as they rounded a bend on West Lake Drive.

Casey braked, bringing the van to a halt. "You're sure?" she asked quietly.

Amanda scanned the lake before her gaze shifted back to the road. "Yes, I'm sure. I'll never forget this spot." She swallowed hard, her face sheet-white. "Let's get this over with." She turned the door handle and stepped out of the van.

Casey and Marc exchanged quick glances.

"It's the right spot." Claire answered their unspoken question from the backseat. "There's a dark aura of violence here. Something ugly happened within yards of where we are." She opened her own door, brows drawn together as she stepped out. "The feeling is strong. And equally as complex as what I was feeling in Paul Everett's house. So many conflicting emotions coming at me all at once." She stayed where she was, squeezing her eyes shut and trying to zero in on something concrete.

"Do what you need to do. Marc, you and Hero do your thing, as well. I don't want to leave Amanda alone." Casey had already turned off the car and was out and moving. "This has got to be the most torturous part of her day. We've got to tread carefully in our questions and the depth of our interrogation."

"Yes. We do," Claire agreed.

Marc nodded, getting out and going around back to leash up Hero.

Amanda had walked a short distance away, then stopped, wrapping her arms around herself in an instinctive act of self-protection. She bowed her head, staring at the road. But Casey could tell that she wasn't really seeing it. She was seeing Paul's car, the driver's seat covered in blood, and the nightmarish hour that had followed.

"Hey." Casey came up behind Amanda, putting a gentle hand on her shoulder. "I can't even imagine what you're feeling right now. I'm sorry you have to go through this."

"So am I. But it has to be done." Amanda's chin came up as she steeled herself. "It's an odd combination of emotions. Some of it's cutting pain. Some of it's anger and resentment. Obviously, that's justified if Paul's still alive. But even if he's dead—the feelings are the same. If someone drove all the way out here just to kill him, there had to be reasons for it. And Paul clearly agreed to the meeting. So how could he have not played some part in getting himself killed? He had to be involved in something illegal. I loved him, but I guess I never knew him. And Justin…" She drew a slow, shaky breath. "I realize Paul had no idea I was pregnant. Still, I blame him for not being here when Justin needs him. I guess that's irrational."

"No, it's human." Casey's reply was filled with conviction. "Paul's death was a life crisis. Justin's illness is a bigger one. Your emotions might be all over the place, but every one of them is justified. Don't beat yourself up."

"Thanks." Amanda glanced behind her as the sound of approaching footsteps announced Claire's arrival.

"Do you need more time alone?" Claire asked, scanning the area. She gazed past the tree-lined street, down to the water. The lake was rough, the waves keeping pace with the wind, slapping the sand with the impact that announced winter's impending arrival.

Amanda shook her head. "I need resolution."

"Then let's get it." Casey gestured around. "Describe everything you remember in the order it happened."

"I got a call from the police reporting that they had found Paul's car and where. They asked me to meet them. I raced out here like a lunatic." Amanda's tone was flat, as if she were replaying a scene she'd long since memorized. "I knew the car was Paul's. I saw the license plate as I drove up. And I saw a few personal things—his sunglasses case, the peppermint candies he kept in his cup holder and the suction-cup heart I'd given him was stuck on his dashboard."

"So you identified the car to the police."

"Yes."

"A Mercedes SL63 AMG convertible," Casey stated. "That's quite a car."

"Paul was a successful real-estate developer. That much, at least, he told me. Then again, I guess he couldn't lie when he was driving a hundred-thousand-dollar car."

"True." Casey refrained from making a judgmental comment. "Real-estate development can be very lucrative, if the developer is smart and lucky. So let's skip that part. Go on."

"The door to the driver's side was wide-open. There was blood all over the seat and on the windshield."

"How much blood?"

"Enough to convince the cops that Paul was dead. It was written all over their faces."

"According to the police report, they found tracks leading from the car. Is that why they wrote off the lake as a potential place for the body to have been dumped?"

A nod. "They did drag the lake. But the bloody tracks were pretty convincing. They headed north, up the west side of the lake toward Gosman's Dock. The theory was that Paul had been dragged to another car and driven up to Gosman's Dock, where he was dumped into the water."

"That's quite a supposition. I get the other car part. But what convinced them he was dumped into the water?"

"The proximity of Gosman's Dock. The fact that there's an open inlet between the jetties there that leads from Block Island Sound out to the ocean. The fact that high tide last April occurred in the middle of the night, which would make it possible for the body to be carried away by the tide…to the ocean—" Amanda's voice quavered "—and the sharks. The fact that the killer chose Lake Montauk for the meeting. And, most of all, the fact that there was no body."

"All compelling evidence. Still, a lot of supposition. They didn't investigate further?"

Amanda sighed. "They did. But most of the work fell to the Coast Guard. No body turned up. Not in the ocean or anywhere else. Meanwhile, there was no tangible proof that

Paul was alive *or* that he was dead. The amount of blood on the car seat spoke volumes, but there were no suspects, no motive and no body. After a few weeks, maybe a month, there was no way the cops could justify pouring any more resources into the search. So that was it."

"What about you?" Claire asked, tucking a strand of pale blowing hair behind her ear. "What did your gut instincts tell you?"

A shrug. "My instincts? They were clouded by my emotions. I'm not even sure I knew Paul at all. So how could I trust myself?"

At that moment, Marc and Hero made their way over. Hero circled the section of road right around the women, then sat down and gazed directly at them. He emphasized his point with a bark.

"You're right about the spot where this happened," Marc noted. "I found an old T-shirt and a bath towel back at the cottage. I made some scent pads and let Hero sniff them. He's picking up the same smells here. I'm sure dozens of people have been by this spot since, but Paul was definitely here at some point." Marc stroked Hero's head and gave him a treat. "Unfortunately, that gives us nothing we didn't already have—except confirmation that Hero is finely tuned to Paul's scent. Which is a huge plus. It could be significant when we need it."

Casey nodded her agreement. Then she turned to gaze quizzically at Claire. "Anything?"

Claire was still looking around. A subtle but odd expression—different from the one she'd displayed earlier—flickered across her face. This expression was so fleeting that no one but Casey would notice. But Casey did notice. She also noticed that whatever it signified was, evidently, not something Claire wanted to explain.

Instead, Claire spread her hands in a helpless gesture. "There's way too much energy coming at me to pinpoint something exact. So many people have been here, which means an onslaught of sensitizers. Even violence, which is a powerful force, isn't enough to crystallize into something tangible. I got nothing off Paul's towel and T-shirt. Maybe if I could hold one of the personal items Amanda described it would make a difference. But as things stand..."

"I have the suction-cup heart at my place," Amanda interrupted. "It's one of the things I kept. Foolish sentimental value, I guess."

"Maybe *important* sentimental value," Casey amended. "I've seen Claire get something off a personal object more readily when she's actually been in a place where that object mattered."

"That's sometimes true," Claire acknowledged. "It's far from a guarantee. But now that I've stood at the crime scene, I need to hold that memento. If it's something Paul had a strong attachment to, I might sense something. *Might,*" she stressed. She glanced down toward the lake, and that recent odd expression reappeared, then vanished. Something new was clearly bugging her.

"Can we leave now?" Amanda asked. Her voice and body language were tense, and she looked away from the crime scene, pained by the memories, compelled by something stronger. She looked at her watch. "It's getting late. I don't want to leave Justin any longer than is absolutely necessary. And we still have to drive back to Westhampton Beach and go through my apartment."

"Okay." Casey had a lot more to ask, wanting to urge Amanda to recall while she stood on the spot where she'd learned of Paul's alleged death. But the woman had had enough. And the visit to her apartment was imperative. So they had to go—for now.

The ring tone on Casey's BlackBerry sounded. She pulled it out and glanced at the caller ID.

Ryan.

"You go on ahead," Casey told the group. "I'll catch up in a minute."

She waited, watching as they walked away. Instinctively, Amanda positioned herself beside Marc. There was no doubt that she found comfort in his presence. It could be because he was the first team member she'd connected with, and the one who'd listened to her heartbreaking situation and agreed to take on her case. Then again, Marc had that same reassuring effect on everyone—except the offenders he went after. They shook in their boots when he approached with that killer look in his eyes and that lethal Navy SEAL presence.

Casey's BlackBerry continued to ring. She was about to answer it when she saw Claire pause, her chin up as her troubled stare scanned the periphery of the lake. A moment later, she reluctantly turned away and followed Marc, Amanda and Hero back to the van.

Making a mental note to question her when they were alone, Casey put her BlackBerry to her ear. "Hey," she greeted Ryan. "Do you have something for me?"

"Don't I always?"

A hint of a smile tugged at Casey's lips. There was nothing like Ryan's cockiness to add some levity to a tense situation. "Yes, wise-ass. What's up?"

"A lot. Let's start with the project Paul Everett was involved in when he vanished—building that mega luxury hotel. Apparently someone bought the land and took over the project a month or so after Paul's disappearance."

"A colleague of his?"

"Nope. A developer who paid an arm and a leg for the land and the construction plans. I can't find a single connection between the two men—except for their insight into how awesome a concept this is. And, believe me, I dug. Deep."

"I don't doubt it," Casey replied. "Too bad. It would be a huge lead if there was some link between the developers."

"Tell me about it. But that's a dead end. Anyway, the Shinnecock Indians had just finished building the casino on land adjacent to their Hamptons reservation. It was being advertised big-time, and business was booming. Long before that, the local inns had waiting lists a mile long. Now there's not enough room to accommodate all the additional patrons who want to shop and gamble at the casino."

"So a luxury hotel on Shinnecock Bay would be a major windfall for the developer." Casey stated the obvious. "We already knew that."

"We also knew what a perfect spot for the hotel Paul had picked. He bought that run-of-the-mill wharf and marina for a steal. The fishing industry is hurting. The old-timer who owned the property was thrilled to unload the place—along with the fifty acres of undeveloped land that came with it. It was a gold mine, right down to the ready-made port. No one was being cut out. Any fishermen who still wanted to dock there were welcome. But they were no longer the priority. The plan was to expand the wharf and the docks, bulldoze the wooded land and tear down the shack of an office Paul was using to make way for the hotel. A dredging company would then do their thing—dig a deeper trench on the ocean floor and widen the channel so that large passenger ferries and private yachts could pass through. The ferry service would travel from Manhattan to Shinnecock Bay, along with hundreds of tourists."

"They could reach their hotel in a fraction of the time it would take to battle the highways by car." Casey considered the ramifications of that. "We're talking about a massive undertaking. Paul would have needed all kinds of permits, cooperation from the town of Southampton, and the right construction companies."

"Yup, although we already knew that. Here's something we didn't know. Paul was still working on the permits and the town's cooperation. But as for the construction companies, he was already lining them up at the time when he either took off or died. All of them are legitimate. Most of them jumped at the chance to be part of this moneymaker. Except for one holdback—the dredging company. Because of the company's strong rep, Paul was still working on them for a commitment. Still, it was an interesting choice of companies, as it turns out. Way too coincidental."

There was that *ta-da* note in Ryan's voice again. Whatever he was going to say next was going to be a biggie.

Casey waited expectantly.

"Fenton Dredging. Name ring a bell?"

"Fenton. *Lyle* Fenton?" Casey asked in surprise.

"None other. Major business tycoon who owns a pretty substantial empire. The dredging company's just one arm of it. Plus, as I mentioned before, he's also on the Southampton Board of Trustees. And, most significant of all, he's Amanda

Gleason's uncle. His spot on the Board of Trustees didn't seem relevant before. It sure as hell does now."

Casey pursed her lips. "No way that's a coincidence. When did Fenton and Paul start doing business together?"

"They didn't. Not until Paul started pressing Fenton to take the dredging job. Fenton was holding back. I don't know why. It sure as hell wasn't due to a low margin. He had to know he'd make a killing from this deal."

"You think that's who Paul was paying off?"

"Could be. On the other hand, Fenton's a pretty prominent guy. And a rich one. Would he risk exposure just for some drop-in-the-bucket payoffs? Sounds like a dumb idea to me."

"I agree. So let's take another approach. If Paul needed Fenton's cooperation, maybe that's why he made it his business to meet and get close to Amanda. Maybe he was hoping that a relationship with her would tip the scales in his favor."

"Now *that* makes sense."

Casey dragged a hand through her hair, which was whipping around from the wind. "Let's get back to the guy who took over Paul's project. Who is he and what's his deal?"

"His name's John Morano. He's a well-established real-estate developer with even more resources than Paul. He got wind of the opportunity Paul's death had opened up and he jumped on it, purchasing the property with a preemptive offer to Everett's estate."

"And is he moving ahead with the same contractors as Paul?"

"Seems like it. The important thing is, Fenton's still a holdout. I don't know what the deal is with this guy, but he has some kind of agenda. Cash, power, who knows? But he wants something to agree to do the job."

"Damn." Casey glanced at the van, where Amanda was seated in the rear, her posture stiff at she anxiously studied her watch. "We need more time out here. We have to talk to Morano, interview Fenton and talk to the other contractors Paul was dealing with. Not to mention we haven't visited any of the places where Amanda and Paul hung out together, nor have we questioned Paul's neighbors and poker buddies. But right now we don't have time for any of it. Amanda's jumping out of her skin. She called the hospital, and the baby's temperature is up. We're lucky she agreed to stop at her apartment before heading back to the city."

"Poor kid. So what do you want to do?"

"Leave Marc behind to work his magic. I'll bring Hero home with us. He'll have completed his job out here. So will Claire."

"Hero? Yes. Claire? Iffy. Paul might have left some boxers there for her to commune with."

"Ryan." There was a cut-it-out note in Casey's voice.

"Okay, okay." The clicking sound meant that Ryan was back on his keyboard. "I'll get all the names and addresses I can. I'll text them to Marc. If anyone can get maximum info in minimum time, it's him. I'll check into Fenton's schedule. He shoots back and forth from the Hamptons to Manhattan." A pause. "Interesting. He's meeting with Congressman Mercer in D.C. tomorrow morning."

Casey didn't even question how Ryan had tapped into Fenton's schedule so quickly. "Perfect. That's who we originally thought was Paul's target to get the support he needed.

Now we have both men in the same place at the same time. Find out where Mercer likes to eat lunch."

"*Likes* to eat lunch? I'll find out *where* they're eating lunch and what time."

"Of course you will." Casey smiled. "After that, text Patrick. Maybe we can kill two birds with one stone and give Marc more breathing room to talk to the rest of the people on the list. I don't want him gone for more than another day. I need him home, and so does Amanda. Of the whole team, she leans on him the most."

"I know. And he'll get to see every one of the names I send any way he has to."

No elaboration was necessary. They both knew what that meant.

"Let me get back to the van," Casey said. "Text me whatever I need to know. Send the rest directly to Patrick and Marc. The fact that the baby's fever is up means we have less time and more pressure."

"On it, boss."

CHAPTER SEVEN

It took Patrick all afternoon questioning people to get a bite, and even that bite was only a nibble.

It was during his third trip to the coffee shop, purposely planned to coincide with the arrival of the pre-dinner shift. That's when the strategic move paid off. One of the waitresses—a buxom, middle-aged woman named Evelyn—thought she recognized Paul from the photo of him and Amanda. She wasn't sure. But if it was him, he came in mornings at around 7:30 a.m. for a roll and coffee—possibly every day, but definitely on the mornings she worked the early shift.

If Patrick wanted to follow up on that lead, he'd have to spend the night in D.C.

Then again, there wasn't any choice—not unless he was desperately needed at home base.

He was just about to call Casey when his cell rang. It was Ryan.

"Hi, Ryan," he greeted him. "I was just speed dialing Casey. I might have a lead at a local coffee shop, but it would mean waiting till morning to check it out. Do you need me back in the office?"

"Actually, we need you right where you are." Ryan explained the situation, which was too long and complicated to text. "Fenton's lunch with the congressman is set for twelve-thirty at the Monocle Restaurant on Capitol Hill," he concluded. "I made you a reservation under the name of Jake Collins. Some poor lobbyist just had his lunch reservation canceled. No loss. I didn't like the douche bag's politics anyway."

"Looks like I'm booked for both breakfast and lunch," Patrick replied drily.

"So get hungry."

The FI team made record time from Montauk to Westhampton Beach. It was imperative that they got as much quality time with Amanda as possible before she insisted on getting back to the city and to Justin. They quickly parked, mobilized and took the flight of stairs from the street level up to Amanda's apartment.

The apartment was an airy one-and-a-half bedroom place with lots of light. It was located directly over one of the stores that lined Main Street in Westhampton Beach. That meant tons of street noise, especially over the summer. On the other hand, that's what made the rent affordable. And Amanda was one of those lucky people who could block out the world when she was working. So her photojournalism career didn't suffer. Her sleep, on the other hand, did, particularly if she wanted to press the snooze button and catch some extra shut-eye. But Amanda was a night owl and new motherhood didn't exactly lend itself to sleeping in.

All in all, it was an ideal arrangement for her, keeping her close to her work projects and to the water, where she did her best thinking. And the small den, which counted as the half bedroom, had been converted to an adorable little nursery—a nursery that, sadly, had been occupied for just a few short weeks. Now it seemed oddly hollow, despite the animal-babies wallpaper and linen, the matching mobile over the crib and the flowing primary-colored accents that decorated the room.

Amanda turned away from the nursery as quickly as possible, barely even crossing the threshold. Her pain was a palpable entity that all four of them—including Hero—picked up on. He made a small whining noise, ceasing only on Marc's quiet command.

"This is home," Amanda concluded with a wave of her arm. She paused, following the others as Claire wandered back into the master bedroom.

"Paul's presence is strong here," Claire commented. "Even though he spent less time here than in his cottage. My guess is that this is where he felt most comfortable, most able to be himself."

"Which self?" Amanda asked in a bitter tone.

"The self that loved you." Claire placed a gentle hand on Amanda's arm. "May I see those personal items we talked about?"

"Of course. I'll get them." Amanda hurried down the hall

to the coat closet in the foyer. She stood on tiptoe, rummaging around in the back of the top shelf.

Casey wasn't surprised by the location of Paul's things. Amanda had obviously distanced herself and her intimate, personal space with the impersonal, across-the-apartment placement of the coat closet. It was another way to push away Paul's memory and to sever her emotional ties to him as best she could.

Meanwhile, Casey used these few minutes wisely, since they were the first ones she'd had alone with her team since Ryan's call. "Marc, I need you to stay out here another day. I'll brief you while Amanda's with Claire. Hero will come home with us."

Marc nodded, accepting Casey's request without questions. He'd reserve those for later, when time permitted.

Casey then turned to Claire. "What was gnawing at you when we were at Lake Montauk?" she asked bluntly. "You stopped in your tracks and looked around, not once, but a couple of times. What were you sensing?"

Claire frowned. "Danger. And not past danger, imminent danger. It was very disturbing. But it was distinct. It was out there somewhere—somewhere close by." She paused, her brow furrowed. "I think we were being watched."

"Watched," Casey repeated. "By whom?"

"I don't know. But whoever it was— As I said, there's danger."

"Then I'm glad I brought my gun," Marc said calmly. "No one's getting near Amanda. Or us," he added. He looked at Casey. "You sure you want me to stay behind? It might be better if I went with you."

Casey gave a hint of a smile. "Thanks, Mr. Bodyguard,

but we'll be fine. We're not going to say a word about this to Amanda. No need to alarm her. And I have my Glock with me, too."

Marc arched a brow. "You're a ball-breaker, Casey, but you're also five foot four and petite, not to mention untrained in hand-to-hand combat. If someone *is* following us, I'm a lot more qualified to do significant bodily harm and to scare the shit out of them."

"I'll have to take that chance. I need your skills out here."

At that moment, Amanda returned from the hall, the handles of a small, somewhat crumpled shopping bag in her hand.

"Here they are." She extended the bag to Claire.

Claire took it and sank down on the edge of the bed as she removed the items one by one. First, the sunglasses case, then the unwrapped peppermint candies, and finally the suction-cup heart. She lingered over each item, starting with the eyeglasses case.

"Blood," she murmured. "The image of a car seat saturated with blood is strong. This eyeglasses case must have been near the driver's seat."

"It was," Amanda confirmed.

Claire's expression intensified. "I keep getting the same conflicting vibes. Darkness and light. Resolve and hesitation. And pain. Not just physical pain, emotional pain. Regret—and yet, purpose. It's like Paul was perpetually torn in two about who he was and who he wanted to be. His energy… It turns on, it turns off. In surges." Claire pressed her fingers to her temples. "The impact is powerful enough to make my head ache."

"Do you know how he was killed or hurt?" Amanda asked, visibly unsure if she wanted to hear the answer.

Claire shook her head. "There was a struggle. Many struggles. I'm not getting any clear images. Just flashes and sensations. I can't get a grasp on any of them. They just keep slipping through my fingers." She picked up two of the peppermint candies and rubbed the cellophane between her fingers. "Nothing. Paul didn't touch these that day."

"Not exactly a shocker," Marc commented drily. "People fighting for their lives—or faking their own deaths—don't generally stop to freshen their breath."

Claire didn't laugh. She was too busy holding the suction-cup heart, moving her hands over it. "You're right about the sentimental value in this, Amanda. I'm feeling deep emotional attachment." A pause. "This was the last thing Paul looked at. Then he was gone."

"Gone, dead? Or gone, gone? Did he die? Was he dragged to another car? Did he just walk away and never look back?"

Claire shut her eyes tightly, concentrating as hard as she could as she clutched the plastic heart.

"A black car," she murmured. "Not Paul's. But he was in it. I don't know if he was dragged. He's crumpled on the floor in the backseat. I'm not picking up life—or death. Just urgency from whoever's driving the car." Claire gave a sigh of frustration. "It's like there's a filter separating me from the events, from the feelings. A plan is in motion. I don't know what, why or how. And I can't zero in on any vibes from Paul. They just keep disappearing. The harder I try, the more nonexistent they become."

"Does that mean he's dead?"

"No." Claire was determined to protect Amanda from

the worst-case scenario, since she herself was swimming in unchartered waters. "It means that, for whatever reason, I'm not connecting. That doesn't always imply death. It could imply secrecy, or just an unlucky coincidence. I can't control what I sense. And that doesn't always work in our favor."

"I see." Amanda's shoulders sagged. "What else can I do to help you get that connection?"

"Right now, nothing." Claire released the heart. A troubled look flickered in her eyes. "You should get back to the hospital," she said.

Amanda's expression was one of sheer panic. "Why? Is Justin…?"

"He's the same. Nothing drastic has happened," Claire reassured her quickly. "I just feel as if it's time for you to be with him. He's fussier since the fever spiked. He'll be soothed when you're holding him. Most of all, so will you. We've reached a place where your anxiety is escalating. It's to the point where it's the strongest aura I feel. Soon it will block out all the other energies."

Claire rose, placing all the objects back in the shopping bag. "Let me take these three mementos back to the city with us. Let me handle them when I'm alone."

"I thought this process works better if you're in an environment where Paul spent his time."

"That's usually true. But sometimes it's the other way around. Sometimes when I'm in the quiet of my own space without interfering energies, I can focus only on the object I'm holding." *And I can try to make sense of this binary energy,* she added silently.

"Okay." Amanda dragged both hands through her hair. She was visibly coming apart at the seams. Claire's assessment of her was accurate. "I'm sorry," she murmured. "We have so many places I didn't have the chance to take you. Places where Paul and I used to go."

"We can come back," Claire replied. "But this is enough for one day."

"Amanda, I'll be staying out here for another day." Marc spoke up in that deep, calming voice of his. "I've got some old-fashioned detective work to do. Give me a list of the places where you and Paul hung out. I'll show his picture around. I know the cops already did that, but I might have more luck."

That panicky expression was back on Amanda's face. "What kind of detective work? Is there something you're not telling me?"

"Nope. I just want to talk to some of Paul's poker buddies, maybe his neighbors." Marc purposely omitted whatever bigger purpose Casey was about to share with him. "The passage of time is a funny thing. Sometimes people forget. Other times, they remember. You'd be surprised at how often clarity occurs later rather than sooner."

A slow nod. "All right."

"Would it be a problem if I crashed at your place?" Marc asked. "The team and I will need a home base for tonight and for any return trips we might have to make to the Hamptons."

"Of course. Stay here whenever you need to. I'll give you my extra key. I won't be living here until Justin's with me—healthy and well." She glanced at her watch for the hundredth time. "It is getting late. And Claire's right. I'm getting too antsy to concentrate. I want to call Dr. Braeburn and check in. And I want to get back to Justin." She paused. "If you do need to come back, maybe you can do it without me. It's just too long a day. I can't be away from my baby." Tears glistened on her lashes. "Unless…*until* we find a donor, I don't know how much time I have with him. I can't waste a moment of it."

"Agreed." Casey met Claire's gaze. "Could you go out to the van with Amanda?" she asked. "She can get settled and you can give Hero a quick walk before we head back to the city."

A hint of a smile touched Amanda's lips. "In other words, she can babysit me. I'm really okay."

"I know you are. But someone has to unlock the van for you. As for Hero, I'm sure nature calls. He's been on duty all day. He needs a walk, some food and some water. Claire can do that while you call the doctor. Marc and I will lock up. I just want to get his and my schedules in sync before we leave."

The drive back to the city was quiet but tense. Amanda insisted on sitting alone in the backseat where she stared out the window, lost in her own thoughts. Casey just drove, alternately glancing in the rearview mirror to see how Amanda was doing and slanting a sideways look at Claire, who was still showing distinct signs of uneasiness.

The silence in the van was deafening.

Trying to appear casual, Claire shifted in her seat, turning to peer past Amanda and—ostensibly—into the hatch area of the van. "Hero's exhausted," she noted. "He's out for the count."

She turned back, feeling Casey's stare, knowing she was

well aware that Claire hadn't just been checking on Hero. She was checking to see if they were being followed.

Casey herself had kept a watchful eye the whole time they'd been driving on the Long Island Expressway. She'd seen nothing and no one suspicious. Obviously, neither had Claire, or she'd be conveying that to Casey right now.

But that didn't mean Claire was happy. True, she hadn't spotted any car that stood out as being on their tail. But that didn't ease the knot in her gut. The LIE was jammed with traffic, as always. And someone was out there. Whether they were near or far, she couldn't say. Nor could she determine if they were following the FI team or Amanda, and what their intentions were. But, whatever they were, they weren't good.

The van reached Manhattan, and Casey dropped Amanda off right in front of Sloane Kettering.

"I hope all is well," she said as Amanda got out of the car. "Keep us posted."

"I will. We'll talk later." Amanda shut the door as she spoke. Her mind was already in the Pediatric Bone Marrow Transplant Unit with Justin.

Casey eased the van away from the curb and back into traffic. "They're still following us?" she asked Claire as she headed up East Sixty-seventh Street toward Park Avenue, en route to Tribeca and the FI brownstone.

"I don't know." Claire spread her hands wide, palms up, in a gesture of sheer uncertainty. "Maybe. Their presence isn't as strong as it was on the expressway. But they're out there. I just don't know where. Or why. Or *who.* I'm not getting any flashes. Only vibes. Which makes this all the creepier."

★ ★ ★

One block behind Casey and Claire, a black sedan cruised slowly by Sloane Kettering. The driver paused, watching intently as Amanda disappeared into the hospital. From the passenger seat, his colleague peered through his binoculars, focusing on the FI van until it disappeared from view.

"They're gone," he announced.

The driver nodded. Then he punched a number into his cell phone to make his report.

CHAPTER EIGHT

Despite the brisk weather, Marc took a five-mile, predawn run through Westhampton Beach—down Main Street to Dune Road and around the beautiful beaches of Moneyboque Bay. He couldn't help but wonder if he was overlapping any part of the loop Paul Everett had taken during his own morning runs—the ones that had followed those nights he'd stayed over at Amanda's place. Had anyone seen him? Talked to him? Or had he made sure to limit himself to private areas where he could ensure himself the solitude he needed for his private phone calls?

There was no way to know. Not unless Marc had the time to locate and interview every Westhampton Beach resident. Which, clearly, he didn't.

He'd spent the night at Amanda's vacant Main Street apartment, rather than a motel, out of sheer convenience. At least that was the part of his decision he'd conveyed to Amanda. The truth was, he also wanted to take a private look around their client's residence. He didn't plan on violating Amanda's privacy. He just planned on focusing on the areas of her apartment that he hadn't had the opportunity to scrutinize in her presence. He wouldn't open drawers, closets or cabinets—not unless something he saw compelled him to do so.

He didn't get very far in his endeavors. He'd barely had time to shower, pull on the standard pair of jeans and a T-shirt he brought along as his emergency change of clothes, and guzzle down two bottles of water while sifting through Amanda's unopened mail in the kitchen, when the doorbell rang. He stayed very still, not moving as he heard the thump at the front door, the retreating footsteps and the roar of a truck as it pulled away from the curb.

A delivery. He didn't need to look to know that. Nor did he need to guess who the package was from.

With a hint of a grin, Marc crossed over and opened the front door. Bending down, he retrieved the large box from the stoop. He couldn't wait to see what Ryan had come up with this time.

Taking another belt of water, he carried the box inside and opened it.

A suit, tie and shirt were folded neatly inside. In an envelope was a driver's license issued to Robert Curtis but bearing Marc's photo, along with falsified press credentials from Crain's business magazine in the name of Robert Curtis. Last, there was a note telling Marc to check his email ASAP.

Quickly, Marc laid his business clothes out on the sofa. Then he sat down beside them and opened his laptop, checking his email box as instructed, and seeing the email from

Ryan that had arrived seconds ago. The damned genius even knew the exact time when the FedEx truck would show up.

The email was strictly an audio attachment. Marc clicked on it, and Ryan's voice filled the room.

"Good morning, Mr. Curtis," he said soberly, in true *Mission Impossible* style. "Your assignment today, should you choose to accept it, is to interview John Morano and learn all you can about him, his real-estate development project and anything he knows about Paul Everett. If there are any leads to be gotten, you're the guy to get 'em. You have an appointment scheduled with Morano at eleven o'clock this morning—right after his 9:00 a.m. breakfast with Lyle Fenton. Oh, as an aside, sorry I let myself into your apartment, but I had to get you proper business attire for a stick-up-the-ass journalist. And while I'm still on the aside, your wardrobe's boring. Remind me to give you some pointers. Back to business. I've included all you need to be a real live news correspondent. This email will erase in ten seconds. Good luck, Robert."

Marc couldn't resist watching and counting backward from ten—although he had no doubt that the inevitable would happen. Sure enough, the instant he muttered "zero," the email vanished from his screen and his in-box.

Another Ryan-ism. The guy might be full of himself, but he had good reason to be.

Putting down his bottle of water, Marc rose. He had his work cut out for him. He glanced at his watch—7:45 a.m. Enough time to do some comprehensive indoor sleuthing, drive over to Paul's neck of the woods and chat up a few neighbors and maybe a poker buddy or two, and then head out for Morano's dock.

It was going to be a productive morning. Marc could feel it in his bones.

John Morano walked into the Living Room, the Maidstone Inn's rustic but upscale restaurant in East Hampton. He peered around, shifting from one foot to the other as he searched the room.

Lyle Fenton was relaxing at a quiet corner table, sipping a cup of coffee and glancing over the menu with the casual ease of someone who'd memorized the whole damned thing.

Morano waved to catch the hostess's attention, pointing at Fenton to indicate he'd be joining him. When the hostess nodded her understanding, he went straight over to join Fenton.

"Good morning, Lyle." Morano pulled out his chair and sat down on the bright, primary-colored upholstery.

"Morano." Lyle acknowledged him with a gesture at the silver urn in the center of the table. "Coffee?"

"Sure." John poured himself a cup, then accepted the menu the hostess handed him. "I'm glad you could meet me."

"Your message sounded as if it were important. So I made some time. But not a lot of it. I'm flying to D.C. for lunch." Lyle turned to the waitress. "I'll have the smoked salmon and onion omelet," he instructed, passing back the menu. "And a glass of fresh-squeezed orange juice."

"Yes, sir." She jotted down his order.

John glanced down quickly, scanning the options. "Two eggs over easy, please, with bacon, crisp." He nodded his thanks at the waitress as he, too, returned the menu to her.

"What's on your mind?" Lyle asked.

John folded his hands on the table and leaned forward. "I

need those permits. I need you to get them for me. I can't start construction without them. And I need you on board once I get them."

Anger flashed in Lyle's eyes. "You called me here for that? We've had this conversation, Morano. You know my terms."

"Yeah. I also know my pressure. I've been paying these guys off for months now. I've only got so much cash to go around. You know who I'm dealing with. They don't play games. And they sure as hell don't take MasterCard. I don't want to wind up like Paul Everett."

"I'm afraid that's in your hands. Being on Southampton's Board of Trustees, I have my own pressures. It'll take a lot of calling in favors on my part to get those permits approved, and a lot of feather-smoothing to get the necessary people to accept my company's involvement in this venture. Turning Southampton into a mini-Manhattan is not a popular idea with the locals. I've got to resort to all kinds of incentives. And I never do something for nothing. You know that. You also know what I need from you. This project of yours has the potential to bring in big money. I want a major chunk of that."

"I promised to give you ten percent of the profits over and above the generous amount I'll be shelling out to your company. I'll have documents drawn up to that effect."

"That's not enough."

John blinked. "How much do you want?"

"I want an ownership stake. I believe I mentioned that."

"No, you definitely did *not* mention that."

"Then I'm mentioning it now. I'm also mentioning that I want the ability to bring in my own people as investors."

John's coffee cup paused halfway to his mouth. "You're joking."

Lyle's gaze was steely. "I never joke about business."

"What investors? Who are these people?"

"That's not your problem."

"Not my problem? How do I know these investors of yours aren't more dangerous than the thugs I'm dealing with now?"

"You don't. Life's a gamble. The way I see it, you could start demolition, ground-breaking and dredging before winter, or you could go broke and probably wind up dead." A shrug. "Your decision."

"Great choice."

"One other reminder while you make your decision. My company only uses union labor. You'll have to get the business agents on board with this project."

John frowned. "It's one thing to be union on your end. I'm not sure I can afford an entire project using union labor."

"Again, that's your issue, not mine."

"I'll have to straighten that out with the business agents."

"Indeed you will." Lyle paused, nodding at the waitress as she placed their breakfasts in front of them.

"Now I'm going to sit back and enjoy my breakfast," he informed John as soon as they were alone. "I suggest you do the same. No more on this subject. You know where I stand. My demands are not up for negotiation."

John's jaw was working. "Fine. You win. Get me my permits."

"I'll have my lawyer draw up the papers." Lyle calmly chewed and swallowed a bite of his omelet. "Once they're signed and locked away in my safe, I'll get you what you need."

"How long will that take?"

"Not long." A tight smile. "My lawyer gets paid by the hour."

Claire had tossed and turned all night.

Her dreams were plagued by shadowy figures looming close by, threatening...someone. Or *someones*. Was it the team? Amanda? All of the above? She didn't know. All she knew was that the vision incited a new dark energy inside her—one that was in addition to the eerie vibe she was already trying to make sense of.

Around dawn she sat up in bed, arranging herself in lotus position—her automatic pose for keeping her mind and her body open to whatever energy surrounded her. She loved the serenity of her East Village studio—her little oasis away from the Manhattan madness outside her window. Everything in her home was the antithesis of the congestion, wild pace and loud noise of the streets below. Her apartment was perfect—one spacious living room/bedroom, a galley kitchen and a bathroom. The large room was done in muted pastels, and consisted mostly of uncluttered space. Claire was a minimalist. It gave her room to breathe and to be. Even her furniture itself was open and airy, all natural wicker with pale aqua and sand-colored cushions. Ditto for her bedding. The walls were that same soft sand color, and they were adorned only by a few of her favorite landscape paintings.

She shut her eyes, letting the morning energy flow through her, hoping it would ease the tight knot in her stomach.

It didn't. Too much wasn't right. Something had definitely

happened to Paul Everett. But it wasn't death. It was something that conveyed mixed energies—positive and negative—to no energy at all. Maybe he'd barely escaped death? Maybe he'd briefly experienced it? No. Neither of those things felt right. Nor did they explain the perpetual binary energy surges she was experiencing. If Ryan hadn't all but stated beyond the shadow of a doubt that the man standing on that street corner was Paul Everett, she'd wonder if perhaps he was in a coma, drifting in and out of consciousness.

But she wasn't visualizing a hospital setting. Then again, she wasn't visualizing anything at all. Damn, it was frustrating.

The shadowy figures unnerved her equally as much as the eerie flashes of Paul. Danger factored into this equation. She had to zero in on the how, the why, and, most importantly, the who.

Abruptly, another, more painful energy shot through her—and this energy was as clear as glass.

The baby. Oh, no, the baby.

Amanda was dozing beside Justin's crib when his whining and restless shifting awakened her. She was on her feet in an instant, and she knew something was wrong the minute she touched him. He was hot. Very hot. And his breathing was raspier than it had been. His tiny chest made a rattling sound each time it rose and fell with a breath.

She raced for the door, nearly running down a nurse who was on her way in.

"Get Dr. Braeburn," Amanda said frantically. "Justin's worse. He's burning up with fever. And his breathing is bad. Please. Get the doctor."

Not two minutes later, Dr. Braeburn strode into the reverse isolation unit and straight over to Justin's crib.

He examined him quickly, took his vitals and listened carefully to his chest. "It looks like we're dealing with a new infection in addition to the others," he told Amanda, gesturing for the nurse to come in.

"What kind of infection?" Amanda asked in a high, thin voice.

"That's what we're going to find out. It could be anything from bacterial sepsis or pneumonia to a fungal infection." He turned to the nurse, issuing instructions. "I'll need blood cultures drawn, as well as chest X-rays..." A pause. "Make that a chest CT. We'll start broad spectrum antibiotics. If I don't like what I see on the CT, I'll want a bronchoscopy." Seeing the terrified look in Amanda's eyes, he explained. "A bronchoscopy sounds far worse than it is. It's only a test to check Justin's lungs. We'll insert a flexible tube through his nose into his lungs and take some tissue and fluid samples. He won't feel a thing. He'll be asleep. We'll do the procedure in the ICU. Once we know what we're dealing with, we'll know how to treat it."

"You're already adding more antibiotics. How else would you treat it? What is it you're looking for?"

"I suspect that Justin has bacterial pneumonia on top of the parainfluenza pneumonia," Dr. Braeburn replied as gently as he could. "In which case I'm going to put him on a pediatric ventilator to ease his breathing."

"A ventilator?" All the color drained from Amanda's face.

"Yes. But it's likely to be temporary," Dr. Braeburn hastened to add. "Once we get the infection under control, we might be able to remove the ventilator support."

"Might."

"Let's take this one step at a time, Amanda. First, let's run the tests, find out what we're dealing with. Then we can proceed."

"Another hurdle." Amanda was trembling. "He's so tiny, Doctor. How many more complications and procedures can he take before…" She broke off, clenching her teeth to fight back the tears.

Dr. Braeburn cleared his throat. "No other donors have turned up yet. Have you had any luck locating Justin's father?"

"No." Amanda met his gaze. "But, as you know, I've hired an excellent investigative team. They're working round the clock."

"Good. Round the clock is what we need."

He didn't have to elaborate. Amanda saw it in his eyes. And she knew exactly what he was telling her.

Marc arrived at the marina at ten-fifty. He climbed out of his rental car and stretched, simultaneously taking in the dock, the boat masts and the run-down shack that was John Morano's office—for now.

But what a location.

Shinnecock Bay was beautiful, even in December. There wasn't much activity going on, other than some fishing boats. But there was something incredibly invigorating about the cold air mixed with the smell of salt water. Extreme sports addict that he was, Marc had the sudden urge to go windsurfing.

Not going to happen now, he reminded himself, turning away from the temptation and restoring the ironclad discipline that had been ingrained in him since his days as a Navy SEAL. Today was about getting information from John Morano. It had to be done with finesse, not threats or violence. He was supposed to be a news writer. That meant words, not muscle. But, dammit, it would be a challenge to keep himself in check if he suspected Morano knew more about Everett than he was willing to say. An infant's life was on the line. An innocent baby. The clock was ticking. And accepting failure wasn't in Marc's DNA—especially where it came to kids.

His early-morning interviews hadn't yielded much. Paul's neighbors described him as friendly but private, not the type to attend block parties. And his poker buddies—at least those Marc could track down on such short notice—knew only that he was a real-estate developer with great ideas and a great sense of humor, and that he'd become a less familiar face around the poker table once he got involved with Amanda. They'd ribbed him about it mercilessly, but they were pretty easygoing guys. Besides, Paul was a relative newcomer to the game, so he wasn't a regular, meaning that his absence didn't break up the game. And Amanda, who dropped by once or twice during a game, was a sweetheart. So the guys went with the flow. They were pretty shaken up by Paul's murder, but not one of them could think of a reason why he'd been killed.

All that added up to was a whole lotta nothing.

This meeting had to be different.

Marc straightened his tie, picked up his writing tablet and stuck his hand in his pocket to ensure that his ID was there. Check, check and check.

He pulled out the ID, clipped it to his lapel, then walked across the wooden deck and knocked.

"Come in," a male voice called.

Marc swung open the rickety office door and stepped inside. He was immediately struck by the smell of damp wood and fish—both of which he'd expected. And John Morano looked pretty much like he'd expected, too. Maybe a little taller and broader-shouldered than he'd imagined. But a well-put-together guy who, beneath the surface, Marc could sense was a little rough around the edges, the kind of businessman who could handle himself in down-and-dirty dealings. Again, no surprise, since, according to Ryan, Morano had made his way from the bottom up. He wore an open-collared business shirt and a Hugo Boss jacket—okay, so he was definitely not hurting financially, but not rolling in money. either. Not yet.

Morano rose from behind the desk, buttoning his sport jacket and giving Marc a cordial smile. "Mr. Curtis?" A swift confirming glance at Marc's credentials.

"Mr. Morano." Marc extended his hand. "I really appreciate your seeing me on such short notice."

"No problem. And it's John."

"Rob," Marc replied.

"Rob it is." Morano shot a quick glance around the room. "Sorry for the less-than-comfortable quarters."

"I have a feeling they won't stay like this for much longer."

"You're right. They won't. In fact, my office will be disappearing altogether." He gestured for Marc to sit down, although he himself remained standing. Marc followed suit. It leveled the playing field when one party didn't loom over the other, something Marc avoided—unless he was the one doing the looming.

"Would you like a cup of coffee?" Morano indicated a

drip coffeemaker on the shelf behind him—one that looked older than the hills. "It's hardly high-tech, but it makes exceptional coffee."

"That would be great. Never enough caffeine for me."

"I hear you." Morano grabbed a couple of mugs. "How do you take it?"

"Black. Thanks." Marc waited until Morano had handed him one of two steaming mugs and reseated himself behind his desk. Only then did Marc lower himself to the wooden chair across from him.

"I'm flattered that Crain's is interested in talking to me," Morano said, setting down his coffee mug.

"How could we not be? Real-estate prices in the vicinity are already skyrocketing in anticipation of your project. That, combined with the Shinnecock Indian Casino—it's a windfall waiting to happen." Marc took an appreciative gulp of coffee and then placed his cup on the desk.

He pulled out his writing tablet, simultaneously shifting the chair around on the rickety wooden floor until it was on somewhat stable ground. Taking notes while balancing on a wobbly chair was less than optimal. "What you're striving to accomplish here could result in a local economic boom—a rarity in today's strained business environment."

"That's exactly what my goal is." Morano leaned forward, propping his elbows on his desk and steepling his fingers. "I can't claim to have thought up the concept myself. But when the opportunity presented itself for me to take it over, I jumped on it."

"I don't blame you." Marc began jotting down notes. "You have an impressive real-estate development background. But nothing of this magnitude."

"True." Morano nodded. He was clearly on sure footing—for now. "I'm lucky that my timing and resources made it possible for me to go forward with this project."

Damn, that would be the perfect segue to bring up Morano's predecessor. But it was way too soon. Any mention of Paul Everett at this point would raise major red flags. This article was supposed to center around John Morano and his ambitious project, not the guy who'd originated the concept and laid the groundwork. Patience was essential in this all-important interview. And Marc was trained to have plenty of that.

"Describe your ultimate vision to me," he began instead. "How do you see the hotel in its finished state? Its layout, what kind of new luxury amenities you have in mind, that sort of thing. If you have a sketch or architectural drawings, that would be great. Next, how will your guests travel from Manhattan to here and back? And, finally, how does the new Shinnecock casino factor into the equation?"

Morano chuckled. "In other words, tell you everything, soup to nuts."

"Something like that, yes."

"I'm not ready to release the drawings. Let's just say that the hotel will be opulent and spectacular, even for the Hamptons. I'm having a comprehensive brochure printed up, which will describe the key architectural and design elements, as well as all the planned amenities. Simultaneously, I'll be launching a website dedicated just to the hotel, which will include details about the entire experience, both to and from Manhattan, and to and from the casino. But it's way too soon to be releasing all that."

"Right." Marc nodded his comprehension. "If you start

the buzz too soon, your prospective guests will either get impatient and pissed off or lose interest. You want maximum impact at just the right time."

"I couldn't have said it better. But off the record?"

He waited for Marc's nod of professional courtesy before continuing. "I'm going to offer both a chartered luxury yacht service and scheduled ferry service. The former will be more picturesque and exclusive, the latter will be quicker and more frequent. That way, everyone's needs will be provided for—those who want to savor the overall experience, and those who want to get to their destination ASAP. As for the casino, the hotel will provide private car service there and back." A hint of a smile. "No shuttle buses, not for this crowd. Just town cars and, for those who prefer it, limos."

"With fully stocked bars, of course."

"Of course."

"How does the casino feel about getting barraged with this overwhelming influx of patrons?"

"They're thrilled. The casino is large enough to accommodate my hotel guests, and to provide them with an exclusive gaming experience. It was the choice of the Shinnecock Indians not to use up a major portion of the acreage they'd allocated for the casino on a hotel resort—at least not initially."

"And perhaps not at all," Marc commented.

"Exactly. They opted for the concept of a casino on the bay, which was a brilliant business move. They created the ultimate gaming facility and an islandlike beach experience. They're about to add to that by building an entertainment arena, two stories of exclusive stores and restaurants, and a theater for their guests' shopping, dining and entertainment pleasures. But, for now, they know what I have in mind.

And it's far more lucrative for them to leave the luxury hotel aspect of things to me. We'll complement each other, and have a mutually beneficial business relationship."

"It sounds like a win-win relationship," Marc noted. "And a genius of an idea. Can we go back on the record now?"

"Sure," Morano agreed magnanimously.

"Let's talk about the local fishermen. Will you be phasing out your wharf and marina's dock service business?"

"Not at all. I don't plan on abandoning the locals. Shinnecock Bay is an ideal spot to supply local restaurants with the freshest catches. The fishing boats will still be coming and going from here—just a little farther down the way." Morano pointed out the window, over and to the right. "A newer, larger pier will be constructed to accommodate more fishing boat traffic and to provide the fishermen with ample warehouse space. Meanwhile, the current pier will be redesigned and become a private pier for the hotel guests."

"For their yachts and ferries," Marc supplied. "I like it. An upscale environment. A local flavor. Very smart."

And he meant it. John Morano was a shrewd businessman. By continuing to offer services to the fishermen, he'd win a whole lot of goodwill while giving the tourists a flavor for the area. Not to mention the cash flow from his dock services would still be incoming. Fishermen would have more customers—thanks to Morano's hotel restaurants. It was good news all around.

On to a stickier subject.

"What about the town of Southampton?" Marc asked. "They're typically very strict about minimizing the influx of tourist traffic. The locals like things the way they are—

fairly quiet, except during the season. This will change all that. Was it difficult to obtain your building permits?"

A heartbeat of silence. Just a heartbeat. But Marc didn't miss it.

He glanced up from his notes just in time to see the look of discomfort that crossed John Morano's face.

It vanished as quickly as it had come.

"It's a challenge. But nothing I can't handle. The town is being very cooperative. I'm in the process of getting all the necessary permits," he replied, his tone so smooth that it almost dispelled any doubt or anxiety.

Almost.

"That's great," Marc said, casually watching John's reactions. "What about your contractors? Do you have all those lined up?"

John paused for a sip of coffee. But this time he kept his game face intact. "Sure do, other than a few estimates that are still coming in. Everything should gel within the next week or two. Luckily, it's supposed to be a mild winter. That'll make it possible to break ground right away."

"So you're moving forward aggressively on this project?"

Morano's lips curved slightly. "I move forward aggressively on everything, Rob. Otherwise, I never would have snagged this opportunity before the slew of other developers who are now kicking themselves."

That was Marc's cue.

His brows arched—just a fraction. Not enough to be imposing. Just enough to be inquisitive. "The original developer…" He skimmed through his notes, as if trying to recall the name. "Paul Everett. Did you know him?"

An easy shake of the head. "Never met the guy."

"My notes say he was killed about a month before you bought in, even though no body was ever found. I guess I sound like a bad spy novel, but do you think it's possible his murder had something to do with this project?"

John's teeth gleamed. "You do sound like a bad spy novel. The truth is, I have no idea why Paul Everett was killed. Like I said, we never even met. Most of the contractors I'm dealing with are the same ones he hired, since they're the best in the area. They all have spotless records. And none of them has spoken badly of Everett, or implied that he was shady in any way, if that's what you mean." A shrug. "But who really knows the private life of another person? He could have been killed over anything. I feel bad for the guy, but I'm not worried about my contractors. They're all insured, well respected and highly recommended." It was Morano's turn to look quizzical. "Why do you ask?"

Marc shrugged. "Just an overactive imagination, I guess. It's certainly not on my list of questions. Part of me was just wondering if you ever worried that the project was jinxed."

That elicited a rumble of laughter. "Jinxed? Hardly. This project is a grand slam. The casino will boom, the hotel will be sold out year-round, tons of vacationers will reap the benefits and I'll be a very rich man."

"Sounds good to me." Marc scribbled down a few final notes. "In fact, I wish I'd come up with this idea. My job doesn't even pay enough for me to stay in your hotel overnight."

"I tell you what," John said, rising from his chair. "I'll arrange for you to enjoy a complimentary weekend as soon as we open. In return, you can write a follow-up article describing your experience, which I have no doubt will be incredible." He stuck out his hand.

"I can't wait." Marc grinned, shaking Morano's hand. "Interviewing you has been a pleasure, John."

"Thanks. When will the article appear in the magazine?"

"Either next week or the following week's issue would be my guess," Marc replied. "Do you have a business card with your contact information on it? I'll email you the specifics once I know them."

"Certainly." Morano fished in his pocket and pulled out a card. "There you go."

"Excellent." Marc gathered up his writing materials. "Enjoy the rest of your day."

"You do the same."

Morano's smile faded the minute the door shut behind Marc's retreating figure. He waited until he heard the car drive away. Then he picked up his cell phone and punched in a number.

"We've got a problem," he informed the person at the other end. "And it could mean trouble."

CHAPTER NINE

Casey spent the morning leaning over Ryan's shoulder, then following up on anything he produced. Intermittently, she called Amanda to check on the baby's condition. What she heard didn't sound good. Neither did Amanda. She sounded as if she were coming apart at the seams. And who could blame her?

The clock inside Casey's head ticked loudly.

They needed more time. They didn't have any.

Her lips tight with frustration, Casey paced back over to Ryan, folding her arms across her chest and tapping her toe on the floor.

That did it.

"You know, I don't work well with people breathing down my neck, boss," Ryan flat-out stated. If he didn't speak up, he'd lose his mind. "Not only does it drive me nuts, it also slows me down."

Exhaling sharply, Casey walked away and began fiddling with one of Ryan's gadgets. "Sorry. I just hear the sheer panic in Amanda's voice and I feel helpless. I don't do helplessness."

"I hear you. But I'm on the verge of hacking into John Morano's bank accounts. I want to see if he's got the same kind of pattern going as Paul Everett did—whopping bank balances, equally whopping withdrawals. I also want to see if he's paying the same twenty grand at the same six-week time intervals as Paul Everett was. If he is, then it's a safe bet that the payoffs have to do with the hotel construction. If not, then Everett was in over his head about something else. Either way, we need to know."

Casey nodded. "We also need to know if his payment methods are the same—cash, rather than bank transfers. To me, that screams organized crime. This isn't a kidnapping, so it's not ransom money. And big wheels who extort money do it through anonymous wire transfers to overseas accounts, to places like the Cayman Islands."

"Yeah, all the data seems to be pointing in that direction." Ryan's brows knit in concentration. "Interesting. As hard as it was to break into Everett's account, it's harder to break into Morano's. Anyone less talented than me would never get through."

Despite her somber mood, Casey's lips twitched. "You really should work on your self-esteem, Ryan. It sucks that you think so little of yourself."

A shrug. "Just being honest. You hired me because I'm the best. And I *am* the best. I'm just wondering if, after Paul Everett had to be dealt with, whoever dealt with him decided to tighten the reins so it would be near impossible to get into John Morano's… There!" Ryan exclaimed, leaning back and pumping his arms in a "yes-s-s-s" motion. "I'm in."

"Okay, you win." Casey was appended to his side again. "You're a techno-god. I bow to your genius. Now let's see what you found."

They both peered at the screen as Ryan scanned through a list of bank entries and withdrawals. "Look." He pointed at a series of lines. "Same pattern. Same dollar amount. Same time frame. But still ongoing." Ryan angled his head toward Casey. "Maybe that explains why he's still with us and Paul Everett is—in whatever capacity—gone. Maybe Amanda's boyfriend refused to play nice anymore. And that made him a liability rather than an asset—especially if he threatened to report the blackmail to the cops."

"What would make him do a one-eighty like that?" Casey asked. "First he's playing ball with the bad guys and then he suddenly stops—why? You can't tell me that love for Amanda transformed him into another man—not when it meant risking jail time. No real-life relationship is that strong."

Ryan snorted. "This is *me* you're talking to. I don't deal in romantic crap."

"Well, something made him stop. Something or some*one.*" Casey was thoughtful for a moment. "Let's talk about Lyle Fenton. You said that he was the one holdout in terms of lining up contractors."

"Yup. That's true with Everett and it's still true with Morano. He didn't sign on with either of them. I don't know what he wants, but I'd love to ask him. He's clearly holding out for something."

"Patrick is playing fly-on-the-wall during Fenton's lunch

with Congressman Mercer today. He'll see if there's any tie between them, beyond financial support for his political career. That's step one toward getting inside Lyle Fenton's head." Casey shot Ryan a quizzical look. "You checked Fenton's itinerary?"

A nod. "His private jet is scheduled to land at Long Island MacArthur Airport in Islip at 5:30 p.m."

"Islip. So he's going straight back to the Hamptons, not stopping in Manhattan."

"Right, or he'd be flying into JFK."

"Good. Then he'll be home in the evening. Let's hear what Patrick has to say. Then I'm giving Amanda a call and asking her to set up a meeting for Marc and me with her uncle—for tonight. She already told him she hired us. Given the urgency of Justin's condition, there'll be no question about our timing. Marc's already out there. I'll jump in the car and join him."

Ryan's brows raised. "So you're making this all about the baby. I get that. But Fenton was already tested to see if he was a donor match. He wasn't. So what else is there to ostensibly talk to him about that's so urgent—unless you plan on telling Amanda the truth about our suspicions and asking for her help in fabricating a reason?"

"No way. I don't want Amanda knowing a thing about that until and unless it becomes necessary."

"I didn't think so. But Fenton's not stupid."

"No, he's not. Neither is Amanda. But you're coming at this from the wrong angle, Mr. Strategist. Remember, we're hunting down Justin's father. And he and Fenton were business associates."

Abruptly, comprehension lit Ryan's eyes. "I'm with you

now. Smart move. If you come at it from that angle, Fenton will think we're interviewing him strictly to learn what we can about Paul—not the blackmailed Paul, but the colleague Paul. He'll think we're hoping to gain any insights that might lead us in the right direction. Naturally, he'll think he's controlling the conversation. The truth is, he won't even be controlling the reason behind it—that we're actually checking into *him*."

"Bingo. Our real goal will be to figure out why Fenton's continually holding out on the dredging contract for the new hotel—and if he has any connection to the payoffs that Paul made, and John Morano is still making."

"That should be fun to accomplish."

A hint of a smile curved Casey's lips. "Have faith. I can read anyone, and Marc can get information out of people they didn't even realize they had, much less spilled. You've got a double-dose of the best. How can we possibly fail?"

"You really should work on your self-esteem, Casey," Ryan parroted her words. "It sucks that you think so little of yourself. Marc, too, for that matter."

"Yeah." Casey grinned. "It's a team problem. Maybe it's contagious."

"Well, you know where the buck stops," Ryan clarified cheerfully.

"With the person who puts those bucks in your pocket." Casey arched a brow.

"Ouch." Ryan pretended to wince. "Okay, you win. You're the boss. And the boss is always right."

Casey considered that. "Well, not always. Just most of the time."

★ ★ ★

Patrick was *not* in a good mood.

After all his years with the Bureau, working cases that took aeons before—and if—they were solved, he still hated investing his time and coming up empty. And that's exactly what had happened this morning.

He'd gone to that damned diner at 6:30 a.m., just in case the guy the waitress had tentatively identified as Paul Everett came in earlier than his customary seven-thirty.

Not only didn't he come in early, he didn't come in at all.

Great. With Patrick's luck, the guy had scheduled his annual physical checkup for this morning.

Dragging breakfast out as long as possible, Patrick had ordered poached eggs—which took a while to make—and toast, along with three cups of coffee, lingering over each bite and each damned sip, until he was flying on caffeine. Still nothing. Finally, he'd given the waitress his name and cell phone number, plus a fifty-dollar tip, and asked her to call him ASAP if the guy in question dropped in—and not to mention to the guy that Patrick was looking for him. The unspoken message was that, should she be successful, there was more where that came from. She'd quickly agreed, dollar signs gleaming in her eyes.

From there, Patrick had shown Paul Everett's picture around to the morning commuters. Zilch. At that point, he'd had enough time only to work off his breakfast at the hotel gym, shower and get ready for lunch. Most people would relish this kind of workday. Lots of eating. Not lots of demanding tasks. Patrick didn't. If something didn't materialize at lunch, he was going to punch someone.

★★★

He strode under the green-canopied entrance of the Monocle Restaurant on Capitol Hill at twelve-twenty. The restaurant was pure class, but it wasn't huge. So he could easily scan the dining room from the waiting area. No sign of the congressman or Fenton. Which meant he'd beaten them there. Good. He wanted to be settled and inconspicuous by the time his quarry arrived.

He didn't have long to wait.

He'd just opened his iPad in front of him and was presumably hard at work on something when Mercer walked in, closely followed by Fenton. The two men shook hands vigorously in greeting.

Patrick recognized them from the photos Ryan had given him, although he would have recognized them anyway. Mercer had been interviewed on several news shows, and Fenton's picture had appeared in the business section of a couple of New York newspapers.

Neither man was imposing in stature, yet each of them had his individual type of commanding presence. Mercer was much younger, probably in his mid-forties, and he was an avid sportsman. So he was muscular and fit. Although Fenton looked pretty damned good for a man in his sixties. Hours of golf would do that for you. He was just stockier than Mercer, with a little more flesh on him. Still, he had a full head of salt-and-pepper hair, and a tan that looked year-round. Yup. Money and power definitely agreed with him. And Mercer probably couldn't allow himself the luxury of a December tan. His constituents might think he was slacking off, spending time at the tanning salon.

Patrick cut his evaluation short as the waiter handed him

his menu and filled up his water glass. Simultaneously, the maître d' was showing Mercer and Fenton to their table. Patrick kept his head down, his eyes on the screen of his iPad. He murmured a "thanks" to the waiter and shifted his attention to the menu, scanning it and waiting until the two men had passed by. He almost had to laugh aloud when he saw where they were being seated—at the table diagonally to the right of his. Ryan was a friggin' magician.

Well, it was time for Patrick to call on an enviable skill of his own. He had a rare ability to totally shut out all surrounding noise and activity, and focus just on the one thing that interested him—whether it was a conversation, an interesting article on the internet or a football game. When he was singularly—and intentionally—focused like that, there could be an earthquake around him and he wouldn't notice.

He called this ability a gift. His wife called it something else—especially when she'd asked him the same question five times and he still hadn't answered her.

Before he could start his tune-in process, the waiter reappeared at his side. "What can I get you, sir?"

"An Angus burger, extra peppers." Quick and easy.

"How would you like that cooked?"

"Medium."

"And to drink?"

Patrick indicated his glass. "Water's fine for now. Maybe coffee later." He handed over his menu. "Thanks."

"Very good, sir." The waiter was well trained. He sensed when a patron wanted his or her space. So he didn't dawdle. He simply took the menu and left to place the order.

From his ideal seating location, Patrick had no trouble following Fenton and Mercer's conversation. And, clearly, he hadn't missed very much, because the two men were still exchanging niceties.

"You look great, Cliff," Fenton said, settling himself in his chair. "A little tired maybe. But that'll be remedied soon enough. Congress is almost out of session and you'll be free to come home and enjoy the holidays with your family. How is Mary Jane?"

"She's great." Mercer's smile was practiced, whether from force of habit or because Fenton made him uncomfortable, Patrick wasn't sure. "Looking forward to having me home." A chuckle. "Looking more forward to having the kids home. Finals are over next week, and the twins will be flying in right afterward."

Fenton's brows drew together as he searched his memory. "Tom's at Caltech, right?"

A nod. "And Lisa's at Northwestern. I can't believe they're finished with the first semester of their freshman year. To me, it flew by. To Mary Jane, it lasted an eternity. I actually think she's looking forward to doing laundry—mass quantities of it. Lord only knows what those two are bringing home with them."

"Straight As, I'd imagine," Fenton commented.

"They're doing well." Mercer sounded like a proud father. "Most of all, they're enjoying what they'll later learn is the happiest stage of life."

"They're successful. They take after their father. Good genes clearly go a long way. You're doing a fine job. I'm very impressed."

"I appreciate that." Mercer cleared his throat. "Your support during the campaign made all the difference. But I think you know that."

"I do." Fenton paused as the waiter approached their table, holding up his palm. "I don't need a menu. I'll have the crab cakes and a glass of sauvignon blanc." He glanced at Mercer. "Do you know what you want?"

"I do indeed." Mercer gave the waiter a pleasant smile. "I'll have a chicken club and some sparkling water. I've got meetings all afternoon," he explained to Fenton. "So no wine for me."

"Understood."

There was a moment of awkward silence at their table after the waiter left, which seemed to be on Mercer's part. Clearly, there was an elephant in the room. Patrick just didn't know what it was, or if Mercer was going to address it.

Leaning forward, Patrick propped his iPad in the upright position. He fired up the FaceTime app and switched to the back camera to record Fenton and Mercer in action. Simultaneously, he listened intently, watching their expressions over the top of the iPad.

Unfortunately, the waiter chose that exact minute to deliver his lunch. It wasn't the poor guy's fault that Patrick was on a mission that had nothing to do with food. Nevertheless, the interruption was a pain in the ass.

"Your lunch, sir," the waiter announced.

"Thanks." Patrick accepted his Angus burger with a courteous nod at the waiter, hoping the guy wasn't going to hang around. Once again picking up on his customer's vibes, the waiter took his cue. He paused only long enough to tell Patrick to let him know if he needed anything else, then turned and left.

"Any news about those maritime contracts?" Fenton was asking in a low tone.

Ah. Business. Finally.

Patrick picked up his burger one-handed and took a bite, watching Mercer's reaction.

To his surprise, the congressman appeared almost relieved at Fenton's choice of subjects. Whatever it was that Mercer was reluctant to address, this clearly wasn't it.

"No worries on that score," he assured Fenton. "I already spoke to the Army Corp of Engineers. Your company will get its government maritime contracts."

"Excellent." Fenton looked pleased, but not surprised. Obviously, he was accustomed to Mercer coming through for him. "I'm glad to hear it. When will it be official?"

"Soon. But, trust me, you can relax. Fenton Dredging's got a strong reputation and a wide regional presence. It didn't take any arm-twisting to get my recommendation unanimously approved."

Okay, so Fenton was seeking U.S. government maritime contracts. Made sense. His company was a maritime construction company, and landing government contracts would mean big money—money that Mercer was helping him achieve. One hand washing the other. More evidence that Fenton had used his leverage to get Mercer elected.

The arrangement might be sketchy, but it was an everyday occurrence in politics. Unless there was more to it. How deep in Fenton's pocket was Mercer?

As if to answer Patrick's question, Mercer continued.

"Where do things stand on the Southampton hotel? I'm getting pressure from both sides—the ayes and the nays."

"Which side is exerting more of that pressure?" Fenton inquired. He didn't sound too concerned.

"It's pretty damned close to fifty-fifty. And both sides have solid reasons to back them up. The financial gain versus the intrusion to their way of life. Hey, I'd love to see the profits and the job opportunities for my constituency. But I'm a local myself. I get it. No matter how I position myself, this is going to cause a major outcry—one it'll be up to me to keep a lid on. I need to know which side you want me to come out in favor of. Are you signing onto this project or not?"

"You know the answer to that. I'm a businessman. To me, profit trumps resistance to change."

"Then why the hesitation, first with Everett, now with Morano?"

"I had my reasons." Fenton sidestepped the question, blatantly stating that he planned to keep those reasons to himself. "But all that's about to be resolved. My plans are to sign the contracts and take on the dredging project. That hotel is going to rake in millions. And if I let another dredging company do what mine can do better, I'll lose out big-time."

Mercer blew out a resigned breath, although he showed no sign of surprise. "So Morano's ferries and chartered yachts will have a direct route to a newly constructed hotel dock."

"Yes, they will. And a professionally dug channel to get them there." Fenton shot Mercer a purposeful look as their food arrived. "So, if I were you, I'd start preparing my district for an influx of capital—and people."

"Don't worry. Strategies are already in place for whichever way you go. I wasn't about to put myself behind the eight ball and have to improvise at the last minute. Although I guessed which way you'd turn."

"Good. Then we're on the same page."

"Yeah." Mercer paused again, toying with his silverware as

the waiter arranged their plates, then placed Fenton's glass of wine in front of him and opened a bottle of sparkling water.

Patrick studied the congressman as the waiter filled his glass. He could be waiting for privacy. But Patrick didn't think so. That elephant was back in the room. Was that elephant more about the hotel contracts, or was Mercer pulling other strings for Fenton, as well?

Taking another bite of his Angus burger, Patrick enjoyed a bit of his lunch as the waiter finished his work at Mercer's table, asking the usual hospitable questions, and then disappeared with his empty tray.

A few silent moments passed, during which Patrick waited with curious anticipation. Fenton was sipping his wine. Mercer was staring into his glass of sparkling water.

At last, he looked up, swallowing as if he'd steeled himself to broach a very difficult topic.

What came next was the last thing Patrick had expected.

"Your niece—Amanda—how is her baby doing?"

Fenton set down his wineglass. For the first time in this conversation, he showed a strong emotional reaction. "Not well." A muscle twitched at his jaw. "Amanda's son is losing this battle a little more every day. I'm not sure he can hang on much longer."

There was steel in his tone. Clearly, he was furious—whether at the situation, the doctors, or his own inability to fix things, Patrick wasn't sure.

"I'm very sorry to hear that," Mercer replied—carefully, as if he were walking a very fine tightrope.

"Sorry doesn't cut it, Cliff. I need more."

The almost-military command made the congressman

do a double take. "More? What more can I offer you? You don't need my money..."

"No, I don't." Fenton stopped him in his tracks. "I need a donor match. And I need one now." He leaned forward, interlacing his fingers tightly in front of him. "Amanda's hired some investigative firm to find out if Paul Everett is alive and to hunt him down. We both know I can't wait for that to happen. I need you to be tested. Immediately."

Mercer did another double take. "Why? To sidetrack Amanda from searching for Everett?"

"You know damned well why—and why you could quite possibly be a match. Besides, my reasons aren't in question. The bottom line is, my great-nephew is my last shot to hand my business empire over to blood. I'm not going to lose it. So just do what I say."

"And how will I justify my sudden involvement—not only to the world, but to Mary Jane?"

"Easily. It's not as if I'm a stranger. I've had dinner in your house, been a strong supporter of your career since the beginning. Your wife is very fond of me. She knows the crisis my niece is going through. Tell her how desperate Amanda is. Tell the same thing to your constituents. Hell, make a public announcement. Remember, Amanda is a local herself. The fact that her congressman would care enough to extend himself in such a personal and meaningful way would earn you a shitload of votes for the next election. And, for God's sake, we're only talking about a blood test. I'm not asking you to donate an organ."

A long pause as Mercer considered Fenton's words.

"I'm not asking you, Cliff. I'm telling you. Consider the scenario I've just conjured up for you to be a bonus gift. But the testing itself is a given. You'll have it done at Southampton Hospital, where you can get maximum exposure for your act of compassion. You'll be flying back with me tonight and tested tomorrow in plenty of time for the evening news cycle. That'll give your Chief of Staff all of today and tonight to get the word out. I also want the twins to be tested. They can do that at their respective schools. There'll be goodwill stretching from Long Island to California."

"The twins?" Mercer sounded ill. "How do I explain that?"

"There's nothing to explain. You've got an altruistic family. Mary Jane included. Let her go with you and be tested herself. She's a loving mother. She's devoted eighteen years to raising your kids. She'll probably race you to the hospital tomorrow. Think how compelling the front page of the Southampton newspapers will look with your photos front and center."

"God." Mercer pressed his fingers to his temples. "How am I going to pull this off? No matter how you spin it, there are going to be questions."

"Field them. That's what you have a staff for. Say you became aware of the urgency of the situation when we had our business meeting today." A quick glance around. "We're having lunch on Capitol Hill, Cliff. Half of Washington probably already knows we're together, and wondering what we're discussing. Now they'll know. We discussed your support for Fenton Dredging Company's commitment to the Hamptons communities. After that, you asked about Justin. I told you. You immediately contacted your family and took action." Fenton gave an impatient wave of his hand. "I might as well be your campaign manager at this point. I've just written the whole script for you. Now do it."

Mercer's mind was visibly racing. "I've got meetings tomorrow morning."

"Move them to late afternoon. You'll be back in plenty of time. My jet will get you here." Fenton took a bite of his crab cake. "Now eat your lunch. Make your phone calls. We can talk business on the plane."

"Sir?"

Patrick's concentration was broken as he realized the waiter was talking to him, and apparently had been for the past minute or two. "Is everything all right?"

With a swift glance at his barely eaten burger, Patrick nodded. "Excellent. I was just absorbed in my work. But now I have all the important aspects of it under control. So I can sit back and enjoy my lunch."

He did just that, texting Casey as he ate. The phone call would come later, when he was back at his hotel and had some privacy.

But, damn, it felt good to finally make some headway.

And major headway at that.

CHAPTER TEN

Casey was perched at the edge of Ryan's desk, scratching Hero's ears and gripping her phone as she prepared to hear Marc's update, when Patrick beeped in.

"Hang on a sec," she told Marc. "Let me see what's going on in D.C."

She switched calls. "Patrick. I got your cryptic text message. Now tell me, what did you find?"

"Nothing at breakfast. A windfall at lunch."

"Well, now I'm screwed," Casey replied. "I've got both you and Marc on the phone simultaneously, and each of you has a significant update. Who goes first?"

"Talk to Marc," Patrick answered quickly. "I'm done here. I'm at the airport, about to jump on a plane. I'll be home in a few hours."

"Can the information wait till then?"

"Yeah. Besides, it has to. I need Ryan there when I review it with you. Is he in the office?"

"Yes." Casey glanced at Ryan, who was still staring at his monitor, this time delving into John Morano's employment history to see where he'd worked previously so as to determine how he'd managed to amass such large sums of money. "He's here. I'm sitting in his lair right now. But I won't be for long."

"Why not? I need your insights and Ryan's eye."

"Can you get my insights by phone?"

"I suppose so. Why?"

"Because I'm about to leave for the Hamptons. Long story. I'll fill you in later. Let me get back to Marc so we can make plans. Fly safe." Casey switched lines again. "Hey, Marc. Patrick's on his way home with information he sounds very hyped up about."

"I'll be back at the office by then," Marc replied. "I'm grabbing something to eat at Simon's Beach Bakery Café. You remember it. It's that place with the yellow awning right down the street from Amanda's place."

"I remember. I also remember that it's a spot Amanda mentioned where she and Paul ate pretty often."

"I can see why," Marc informed her drily. "The pastries look amazing. I'll do a hundred extra push-ups tonight. But it'll be worth it."

"Eat as many pastries as you want. You'll have the time. You're not leaving Westhampton just yet. I'm meeting you out there. We have a date with Lyle Fenton tonight."

"We do?"

"We will as soon as I talk to Amanda. I'm heading for the hospital now. Then I'll try to beat rush hour traffic out to

Long Island." Casey glanced at the clock as she spoke. "It's three-thirty, so I should be okay. Are you speaking to anyone in particular at Simon's?"

"Anyone and everyone, from Simon the owner to the employees to the patrons. This place is a real hangout, not just during the season but all year round. There are quite a few locals here. I'm hoping someone will have a meaningful observation or two about Paul."

"So you struck out with his neighbors and friends?"

"Essentially, yes. They were all willing to talk to me, but I didn't learn anything of consequence. If the guy had an alternate life, he kept it very well hidden."

"So would I if I were involved in something criminal."

"Right. In any case, I've got more to accomplish. I was going to bag it and come home so I could make decent time on the expressway before rush hour screwed me up. But now that I've got a few hours, I'll cover more territory. I want to talk to some of the contractors Paul Everett hired."

"Good idea." Casey's wheels were turning. "By the way, if it wasn't Paul's neighbors or poker buddies who piqued your interest, I'm guessing it was the meeting with Morano. Is that what you want to discuss? Did Morano say something that related to Paul Everett?"

"Nothing as straightforward as that. But, Casey, that guy is way too smooth. He answered my questions like a practiced politician. And I don't mean because he's used to handling the press. I doubt he's done anything except local interviews at this point. He prepped himself, or was prepped, far more than necessary, not just about what to say but about how to say it. I can buy that he'd be comfortable talking about his business. But when I brought up Paul Everett, he was overly laid-back about it."

"In what way?"

"You'd think that Paul had just reneged on a business opportunity, rather than being killed. Having your predecessor murdered would throw anyone. Not Morano. He laughed it off as if I'd made a joke that fell flat. At the same time, he was definitely curious as to why I wanted to know about Everett. And, smooth or not, I know his antennae went up. The whole interview felt wrong. No concrete reasons. Just gut instinct."

"That works for me."

And it always did. It wasn't just because Marc had worked as a profiler with the FBI's Behavioral Analysis Unit. It was because he was Marc. Every single member of the Forensic Instincts team had that same knack—each in a different way—of just knowing. Together, it made Forensic Instincts exceptional.

"Okay," she said. "Then here's what I suggest. Go do your thing at Simon's. Then take care of your other stops and drop off your rental car. I'll give Claire a call. She, Patrick, and Ryan can convene at the brownstone as soon as Patrick lands. I'll drive out to the Hamptons. You and I can have a conference call with the rest of the team when I get there." Casey paused. "Oh, speaking of Claire, there's something you should know. She had some upsetting insights earlier today."

"About?"

"The baby. So I called Amanda. Justin had a setback today. And not a minor one. His fever spiked, he's getting a chest CT and some other more invasive tests. The doctor thinks he has an escalating lung infection of some kind. He's concerned about the baby's breathing. He'll probably put him on a ventilator. The scenario isn't good. Neither is Amanda. She was bordering on hysteria."

Marc blew out a breath. "That poor woman. And that poor, innocent baby."

"That's the other reason I'm dropping by the hospital before I drive out to you. I'm hoping I can calm her down by giving her some hope. I'll mention that you're at Simon's, asking around. And I'll tell her Patrick's on his way home from D.C. with some information. I've got to walk a careful line here, since I'm guessing the information Patrick's bringing back involves Lyle Fenton. I'm not ready to clue Amanda into our suspicions about him yet. But they've escalated. Ryan's been making some progress. And the one common denominator in all this is Fenton. When we connect all the dots, I have a feeling the details surrounding Paul Everett's disappearance might include Amanda's uncle Lyle."

"No shocker there."

"As I said, you and I are paying him a visit tonight. Ryan says he's landing from D.C. around dinnertime. You and I will show up during dessert. We'll keep our questions focused on Paul—what he was like, why Fenton would or wouldn't choose to work with him, did he ever mention where he might go if he left the Hamptons—that sort of thing. We'll key it up to look like we're all about needing Fenton's help in finding the father of Amanda's baby. Which we are. But while we're at it, we're getting a read on this man. He seems to be there at every turn we take."

Casey pursed her lips thoughtfully as she disconnected her call to Marc.

"Are you leaving now..." Ryan cut himself off as he

pivoted around to face Casey. "Uh-oh. I know that look. Whatever you just came up with means more work for me."

A grin. "You've been hanging around Claire too much, Ryan. You're becoming psychic. You're also full of it. You love this. The more I throw at you, the happier you are."

"Yeah, well, don't spread that around." Ryan sobered. "What's up?"

Casey rose and shrugged into her coat. "I want you to do another background check on Paul Everett," she said. "I need the results by the time I get out to Westhampton."

Ryan's brows drew together. "You need me to go back further? Or dig deeper? I already did a thorough check into his professional background. You want educational details? His college grades? Major?"

"No. I want you to cross-check him with John Morano. You did a cursory search of Morano's background. Now do an intensive one. Get details. Then see if he and Everett were in any of the same places at the same time—anywhere they might have crossed paths. If you need to go back to their school days, do it. I want to make sure these two didn't know each other."

"And that Morano wasn't part of Everett's disappearing act."

"Exactly."

"Consider it done." Ryan's fingers were already flying across the keyboard. "I'll have answers for you in time for our conference call."

The man was parked a few buildings down from the brownstone, his car concealed by a pile of garbage. Dusk had already settled over the city, since the December days were so short. He was dressed in black and between that and the fading light, he was nearly invisible. Still, he wasn't taking any chances. He ducked down behind the wheel of his car when Casey exited the building. She crossed the street and walked into a garage. A few minutes later, the FI van flew up the ramp, turned left and drove off.

He waited a moment. Then, two.

Quietly shifting into Drive, he pulled away from the curb and followed behind her.

Claire was sitting cross-legged on her futon, holding the suction-cup heart that Amanda had let her take home. Of all Paul's personal possessions, this one triggered the strongest reaction. She could feel that binary energy flowing through her like a river. She could visualize Paul and sense his conflicting emotions. Suddenly, she couldn't visualize him at all, and the emotions she was picking up from the plastic heart dissolved into dust.

The reasons behind it were driving her crazy. She had to clear the cobwebs from her mind and get to the core of her response. In her gut, she knew that when she did she'd have something concrete to draw from.

Claire started as her cell phone rang. She didn't want to be interrupted in her attempts to figure out Paul Everett's energy. Whoever it was could call back.

Meanwhile, the ring tone was invading her cerebral space. She leaned over and picked up the phone, fully intending to press Ignore and send the call to voice mail. Then she glanced at the caller ID. Casey. She couldn't blow off a call from her, not now.

Setting aside her frustration, she punched a button on the phone and put it to her ear. "Hi, Casey."

"Hi. Sorry to intrude. I know you're working with the personal items Amanda gave you. But I wanted to keep you posted and ask you to go to the office in a few hours. We're arranging a full-team conference call so that..."

"Stop." Claire's interjection was sharp. "I'm sorry to cut you off. But something's wrong."

"Wrong? You mean with the baby?"

"No. I mean with you. That feeling I had. It's back. Casey, someone's watching you." A pause. "Where are you?"

"In the car."

"Then he's following you. He's wearing black. I can't see his face, just a shadowy form. But his energy is dark. Lock your doors. And don't drive anywhere remote. Stay in traffic."

"No worries there," Casey said drily, searching her rearview mirror for a suspicious-looking vehicle. "I'm in Manhattan. I'm stopping at Sloane Kettering and then driving out to the Hamptons. That's about as remote as Times Square on New Year's Eve." She shifted in her seat. Despite her flippant attitude, she wasn't happy. "Is he armed?"

"I don't know." Claire sounded terribly unnerved. "But he's only going to follow us and Amanda for so long before he does something. And whatever that something is—it's ominous. *He's* ominous."

"I hear you." Casey wished she could figure out which car in the converging traffic was the one. "I'll make sure I'm not alone. I won't park in the hospital garage...I'd have to walk through that connecting tunnel to get to the building. I'll drive to one of the lots on Sixty-ninth between First and

Second. That way, I can drop the car off up front and walk, blending in with the crowd. It's the end of the workday. Everyone will be rushing out of their offices to head for home. I'll just be another rat in the rat race."

"Do that. I don't have a good feeling about that tunnel. You wouldn't be safe. The hospital's being watched, too." Claire pressed her fingers to her temples. "My head is pounding. There's too much happening at once. And none of it's good."

"The baby, too?" Casey asked quickly.

A heartbeat of a pause. "Get to Amanda," Claire replied, her voice low and tense. "She needs you."

CHAPTER ELEVEN

Casey nearly ran from the parking garage to the hospital building. She reached the Pediatric Blood Marrow Transplant Unit in minutes. It was quiet…too quiet. Not just the kind of quiet that went along with the gravity of the unit. The kind that made Casey know that something was wrong.

She stopped the first nurse who passed by.

"Is Amanda Gleason here? I believe she's with her son, Justin."

"And you are?" the nurse inquired.

"A friend. My name is Casey Woods. You're welcome to clear me with Amanda."

"She's not here, Ms. Woods. She's with Justin in the Pediatric ICU. That's all I can tell you."

Oh, God, Casey thought silently. "Where is that located?"

The nurse gave her directions. "But you won't be allowed in."

"I know that. I'll just get a message to Amanda that I'm here."

Casey took off again, arriving at the Pediatric ICU tense and out of breath. She spoke to the first hospital attendant she saw, who obviously got a message to Amanda, because she came out and met Casey in the waiting area a few minutes later. She moved robotically, her posture stiff, her face sheet-white and lined with worry.

"What happened?" Casey asked without preamble.

"The bronchoscopy results came back," Amanda replied in a wooden tone. "They showed that Justin has bacterial pneumonia. That's in addition to the parainfluenza pneumonia. Dr. Braeburn put him on a ventilator. His breathing is so labored, Casey." Amanda's voice broke, tears sliding down her cheeks. "We're at a crossroads I can't face. Because if the antibiotics don't work... If the ventilator isn't enough..."

"Don't talk that way," Casey interrupted. "Don't even think that way."

"How can I not?" Amanda turned her palms up in a helpless gesture. "The doctor all but told me we'd better find a donor. Urgently."

"We're going to find Paul." Casey didn't miss a beat. "I told you we would and we will. Marc is questioning people at Simon's Beach Bakery, and Patrick's on his way back from D.C. with information that sounded significant. In the interim, Justin's a fighter—you said so yourself. He'll hang on." *He has to,* she thought silently.

Amanda's nod was dubious. "I have to get back inside. The nurse said you needed to see me."

"I do." Casey began her diplomatic mission. "We've been talking to everyone who dealt with Paul, even casually. We need to talk to your uncle."

"My uncle?" Amanda blinked. "Why? He barely knew Paul. And if he had any information on him, he would have told me the instant Justin was diagnosed."

"I'm sure he would have. But it's our experience that people sometimes have information they don't realize they have. It's possible your uncle picked up something from Paul in a conversation or a business meeting that seemed so insignificant he forgot all about it."

"And you think you might be able to jostle his memory." Amanda sounded more thoughtful than she did suspicious. Then again, she'd have no reason to believe Casey was being anything other than straightforward. "I doubt it will work. Uncle Lyle has a steel-trap memory. On the other hand, he believed Paul was dead—which would eliminate him from my uncle's thought process altogether. So I guess it's worth a try."

Casey jumped right on that. "Given Justin's health, we shouldn't waste a minute. I want to drive out to the Hamptons, pick Marc up and head over to your uncle's East Hampton estate so we can talk to him tonight. Do you think he'd agree to that?"

"Of course—if he's home." Amanda frowned. "I don't know his schedule. He might be anywhere, even Manhattan." She took out her cell phone and turned it on. "Let me find out before you waste a long drive."

Casey waited while Amanda made the call. It took a few minutes with several pauses before she got an answer and turned off her phone.

"I spoke to Frances, his housekeeper," she explained to Casey. "Apparently, my uncle was in Washington, D.C., today. But he'll be back tonight. Frances contacted him and he said you and Marc should come by around eight o'clock. Does that work for you?"

"We'll make it work." Casey squeezed Amanda's hand. "Go back in to Justin. But don't lose faith."

"I'm trying. It gets harder with every hour and every setback." Amanda pressed her lips together. "Go. If my uncle can help you, he will."

Oh, he will all right, Casey thought. *More than he realizes.*

Amanda watched Casey walk away, battling the white panic that was building up inside her, eclipsing all else. Forensic Instincts was talking to her uncle. To them, that was a step in the right direction. To her, it was grasping at straws. Even if Uncle Lyle remembered something crucial about Paul—which she doubted he would—how long would it take to get concrete results and find Paul? Weeks? Longer?

Justin might only have days.

It was time for her to grasp at her own straws.

She'd nixed the idea when Melissa had first suggested it, when she'd urged Amanda not to put all her eggs in one basket. But now Justin was worse. Amanda was beyond desperate. And the idea was promising. She had the contacts. Melissa would make all the arrangements.

There was no need to mention it to the Forensic Instincts team—not until it was a fait accompli. It would sidetrack them from their current path and it would piss them off, neither of which would work to her advantage. All she wanted to do was to expand the number of people looking for Paul.

And maybe, just maybe, the right someone—the someone who'd seen Paul—was out there and would respond.

She had to try.

FBI
New York Field Office
26 Federal Plaza, Manhattan
Office of the Assistant Director in Charge

Supervisory Special Agent Neil Camden, head of the Vizzini Criminal Enterprise Task Force, didn't enjoy being reamed out. Least of all by the head of the entire New York Field Office

But that was precisely what was going on at the moment.

His superior at Headquarters, James Kirkpatrick, Section Chief of Criminal Enterprises for the Americas, had been advised in advance of this meeting. He wasn't happy. Still, given how many resources had been poured into this operation, it didn't come as a surprise. What it did do was make Camden feel more ineffective.

"What have you and your team been doing?" Assistant Director in Charge Gary Linden demanded. "I went out on a limb with this. I expected results. This is a priority investigation. We have limited time and even more limited funds."

"I understand that, sir." SSA Camden could feel a fine sheen of perspiration form on his brow. "We have made progress. We know for a fact that Lyle Fenton is involved."

A brief nod. "No surprises there."

"Also, the video feed we planted in John Morano's office caught his payoffs to the mob. We ran the pictures. They're definitely from the Vizzini family. And, since the Vizzinis own the union leaders, there won't be any construction until the Vizzinis are happy with the terms."

"Great," Linden said sarcastically. "None of this is news. The reason I let your task force pick this up isn't to catch some punks collecting bribes or some mob bosses controlling union workers. What we really need to know is who's behind this whole operation. *All* of it, not just some extortion scheme. Is it Fenton? Someone else? And how deep does it run? Are other families involved? Who's running things for the Vizzinis? I want it all—and I want the evidence to go with it. Otherwise, we're going to look like idiots kicking a dead horse."

Camden nodded. "I realize that, sir. And we're right on the brink. We just need a little more time."

"We're running out of time. And money. So you need to figure out who's behind all this and find the evidence we need to convict him. And not soon, Camden. Yesterday."

Closeted in Amanda's apartment, Casey and Marc situated themselves on the living-room sofa and dialed into their conference line at the agreed-upon time.

"Everyone here?" Casey began.

"Yup," Ryan replied, speaking for the group. "All present and accounted for. Right down to Hero, who's eating my trail mix and slobbering on my shoes."

"Good. Patrick, let's start with you, since I've already caught up with Marc, who'll fill you in later. What did you find in D.C.?"

Succinctly, Patrick relayed his day's findings, starting with the less-promising lead at the coffee shop, and moving on to the more significant revelations he'd gained from the lunch between Fenton and Mercer. "I'm hoping to hear back from that waitress, Evelyn, soon," he concluded. "I was concerned that if I hung around much longer I'd scare Paul Everett off—assuming it's him who's frequenting that coffee shop. So that lead's a maybe—although Evelyn did seem pretty certain it was Everett. That having been said, my lunch was a real eye-opener."

"That's an understatement," Casey agreed. "Least of all because Mercer's clearly in Fenton's pocket, which doesn't come as a huge surprise. But let's concentrate on the real issue at hand—Fenton's slamming Mercer against a wall by dragging him back home to get tested as a potential donor for Justin. That's not fueled by political manipulation. It's very personal, and very pointed. Not to mention the fact that Fenton is also demanding that Mercer's kids get tested. From what you just said, Patrick, Mercer's wife was an afterthought, just to keep up appearances."

"You got it." Patrick's tone was intense. "I caught the whole thing on my iPad so you can check it out yourself. In addition, I've followed up since then. An hour after their lunch, Mercer's PR department issued a press release stating that whole BS story Fenton spouted at lunch. Sounds like a heroic gesture on the part of a congressman and his family to save a dying infant whose mother is part of Mercer's local constituency. The Hamptons press will be swarming around that hospital tomorrow morning, snapping photos of the compassionate, heroic congressman, and writing articles filled with accolades."

"No doubt. But we all know that Mercer's motives aren't based on altruism." Casey paused. "Ryan..."

"Already on it," Ryan came back. "My facial recognition software and I are hard at work. I'm comparing Fenton's features, bone structure, etc. to Mercer's. If there are any physical traits that suggest a genetic tie, I'll find them. I've also pulled up whatever photos I can of the twins. Their Facebook pics are good, but not good enough for me. I'm going after better ones. I want to be as precise as possible, so I can catch even the slightest resemblance between Fenton and the Mercer crew. Not to worry. I'll hack into whatever network's necessary. I'll have what I need within the hour."

"I never doubted it." Casey chewed her lip thoughtfully. "This changes Marc's and my priorities when we see Fenton tonight."

"It sure as hell adds to the long list of them," Marc commented.

His voice made Claire chime in on a different matter. "Marc, you picked up on something in the Hamptons. Something in your meeting with John Morano. What was it?"

"She's not being Claire-voyant," Ryan clarified in that "gotcha" tone he reserved only for Claire. "I told her what Marc said when he called in. She also got a glimpse of the research I was doing into Morano's and Everett's backgrounds. So her question is based on facts, not psychic inspiration."

Claire gave an exasperated sigh. "I was asking a question, Ryan. Not issuing a proclamation."

"Just making sure that was clear."

"It was," Marc reassured him with a wry grin. "As for Morano, the guy is way too scripted. And way too blasé about Paul Everett and any connection his murder might have had to the development of that five-star hotel. Something's up. I'm just not sure what."

"I'm still running those background checks on Morano

and Everett, digging up every detail I can." Ryan scanned the results of his work. "I've checked the trade groups each of them was affiliated with, any certifications they may have, and the companies they've worked with and for. I did a detailed analysis of their finances, right down to where they do their banking. Next, I'm moving on to their families, including any estranged relatives who might know each other. From there, I'll dig into their full educational backgrounds. I'll include all the activities that accompanied their academics, from summer camp to sports teams. I'll go back to friggin' kindergarten, if I have to. But, as of now, I don't see Everett's and Morano's paths crossing, or even being mentioned in the same paragraph."

"Not until the hotel project and the controversy around it," Marc guessed.

"You got it. Once that came into play, the newspapers jumped on the story of the infiltration of the Citidiots and the divided opinions of the locals. But even in those articles, Morano and Everett are discussed as separate entities. Everett was killed. Morano picked up the reins. Period."

"Do the newspapers get into Everett's murder at all?" Casey broke in to ask. "Any speculation as to who killed him?"

"A paragraph on the unsolved homicide—but the tone was more dramatic than it was speculative. You know, like was Paul Everett an innocent victim or was he a high roller who got in with the wrong crowd and paid the ultimate price? Clearly that was old news, so it wasn't the focus of the articles. The building of the hotel was."

"Remember, no one paid much attention to Paul's murder," Marc reminded them. "That's why Amanda brought me next to nothing mediawise when she first met with me. Paul wasn't a celebrity. He was just a shrewd real-estate developer who happened to buy into a good thing. There was no construction under way, so most of the public didn't even know about his plans for the hotel. Only the locals. And they'd have no reason to connect his murder with a project that hadn't even gotten off the ground."

"Clearly," Patrick concurred. "Or the police would have pursued that angle more thoroughly. They didn't." A pause. "Of course, there are people who can pull off that kind of murder without leaving any leading evidence behind."

"Paul Everett is *not* dead," Claire stated. "I can't explain how I can be so sure, especially since my connections to his energy are so weird and binary, but I am. I just wish I could make a deeper connection. I spent hours on end today holding that suction-cup heart and trying to analyze its energy. It's like I'm right on the verge of opening a window and peering inside, and then it's gone. Not just the opening. The whole window. It's driving me crazy."

"That tells me what my gut already knows," Casey replied. "That either Paul Everett or whoever dragged Paul Everett off wants it this way. Which makes Paul either a criminal or a victim. All the more reason to find him. Most importantly, for Justin. Secondarily, for justice—or rescue. Right now, the 'whys' don't matter. All that matters is that we find what right now looks like Justin's only chance of survival."

"Then I think we all have our tasks cut out for us," Ryan said.

"I want to visit Amanda in the hospital," Claire stated. "I have the perfect opportunity tonight, since both Casey and Marc are away. After them, I've spent the most time with her. I want to check on her and the baby. I want to touch something of the baby's—maybe a sheet or blanket he came in contact with that's no longer in the ICU with him. And I want to see if I pick up on anything weird on the way to the hospital."

"What do you mean by weird?" Ryan asked.

"She means that she's been sensing we're being followed," Casey supplied. "Us and Amanda."

"Why?"

"I don't know," Claire said. "But it's getting pretty sinister."

"You're sure?" For once, Ryan didn't taunt Claire for her gift.

"Positive."

"You shouldn't go alone," Patrick jumped in. "I'll go with you. I'm a trained investigator. Maybe I'll spot something you missed. Besides, I'm in a holding pattern, anyway. I can't just sit on my hands and wait for the waitress to call me. I need to do something."

"Good." Casey liked that idea. Patrick had a sharp eye, Claire had a psychic gift and there was also safety in numbers. "So we're all in sync for this evening's activities. We'll report in if there's something to say. If not, Marc and I will be home by midnight. We can resume our discussion then."

CHAPTER TWELVE

Lyle Fenton's East Hampton estate was the size of a suburban cul-de-sac.

Marc was doing the driving tonight, giving Casey a break after her monster trip out. He turned in to the paving stone driveway and waited for his entranceway summons to be answered. After the video cameras surveyed their van and the intercom exchange confirmed who they were, the iron gates swung open and the van was allowed to pass through.

Using Ryan's night-vision-enabled camera, Casey shot a few photos of the grounds and the mansion as the van wound its way up the serpentine driveway, past the guesthouse to the megamanor.

"Impressive," Marc commented drily. "A bit extreme for my tastes."

A smile curved Casey's lips. Marc hated extravagance.

And pretentiousness. "Yeah, I'd say so. Too much for me, as well. I'd get lost just going downstairs for a bottle of water." She glanced down at her camera. "You never know when these shots might come in handy. Not that I think Fenton has any incriminating evidence on his front lawn. I'm sure I'll get a lot more off Patrick's iPad video. Still, you never know when we'll need a frame of reference."

"Agreed." Marc was a big believer in visuals, not to mention being superthorough. The more data they collected, the better. "Fenton's probably going to be rough around the edges. But he'll also be smart. No one builds the kind of empire he has by stepping in shit. Clean or dirty—and we both know which of those applies to Fenton—he's got brains. We're going to have to tread very carefully to get what we want."

A nod. "I know. I'm glad we ran through our planned script. But we both know we'll be deviating. Fenton will have his own agenda—not just what he wants to know, but what he has no intentions of saying."

"Then we'll wing it. But we'll get the job done."

Casey shot him a sideways look. "Nothing threatening, Marc. I don't want to clue Fenton in to what we're digging for."

"I promise not to rough the guy up." It was Marc's turn to smile—a tight, restrained smile. "That doesn't mean I won't want to. Especially if he's responsible for keeping Paul Everett away from his critically ill son."

"That's what we're here to find out." Casey looked out the window as the van pulled up to the front of the house. The front door was already opening. "It's showtime," she muttered.

* * *

Lyle Fenton looked like a combination of a filthy rich businessman and a retired prizefighter. He was stocky—dense and muscular rather than pudgy. His powerful shoulders strained at the jacket of his two-thousand-dollar suit, and his physical presence totally reminded Casey of a bulldog. His complexion was ruddy, accentuating the tough-guy veneer, and he had thick salt-and-pepper hair. Expensive clothing or not, he lacked the polish and presence he was trying to convey. He'd clearly grown up in the school of hard knocks and had elevated himself to his current position of wealth and authority. If he'd made the transformation honestly, he'd be admirable. But if he was the sleazy guy Casey suspected he was, admiration was the last thing she'd feel.

He showed them into the study himself and shut the door. "Ms. Woods. Mr. Devereaux." He shook both their hands, studying Marc for one hard moment before looking away. Marc had an intimidating presence when he chose to. And now he clearly chose to. "Amanda's told me all about your company and your efforts on her behalf. You have my thanks."

Okay, the guy was putting on a show. Casey sized that up in about a minute. He'd been home for a couple of hours now and hadn't even loosened his tie, much less changed into some comfortable clothes. He was dressed and ready for them—the business tycoon and the concerned uncle. Too bad his facade was fake, his manners forced. He was the walking epitome of a street rat turned rich, and trying to act as if he'd been born that way. The discomfort was all there, from his überstiff handshake to his tight lips and jaw, to the fact that he wouldn't look them in the eye. And that last bit of body language, well, that smacked of a lot more than just superficial deception.

Lyle Fenton was playing a role—and not very well.

"That's our job, Mr. Fenton," Casey replied, intentionally clasping his hand in a firm handshake and staring directly at him as she spoke. "We were hired to help Amanda. We appreciate you seeing us on such short notice."

As Casey had hoped, Fenton's gaze darted quickly to hers, and there was a glint of surprise reflected there. No shocker. Fenton was used to dealing in a man's world. To meet a strong, assertive woman was a rarity, if not a first. This would definitely work in Casey's favor. With a modicum of luck, she could keep Fenton slightly off balance, tipping the scales in hers and Marc's direction.

"Please have a seat." Fenton gestured at the tufted leather chairs that sat across from his desk. The desk was formidable—large, mahogany, expensive and situated in front of a wall filled with power photos. Photos of Fenton in his company headquarters. Photos of Fenton at a ribbon-cutting ceremony, in front of a Welcome to Bayonne, New Jersey, banner. In that photo, he was holding a bottle of champagne and christening yet another vessel, all with the backdrop of towering cranes and Fenton's extensive—and expensive—fleet.

And, in the center of all the other wall photos, a marble-framed photo of a sleek and stunning ship, its elegant bow boasting the name *Big Money*.

The whole package—the desk and the wall—made a perfect boundary between Fenton and his guests.

Sure enough, he walked around to the buttery-soft brown leather executive chair behind the desk. "Can I offer you anything?" he asked before he sat. "A glass of wine? A soft drink?"

"Nothing, thanks." Marc answered for them both in that tone of his. Hard. Tough. He, too, was setting the stage, showing Fenton the entirety of what he was up against. All kinds of strength, both mental and physical. Neither the successful businessman or the tough street fighter would scare them. So he could forget it. "Nice ship." Marc pointed at the center photo.

A proud smile curved Fenton's lips. "My first. All these years and still going strong. Are you a seafaring man, Mr. Devereaux?"

"You could say that. I was in the navy."

"He was a Navy SEAL," Casey amended.

"Oh, I see." Once again, Fenton looked taken aback—and out of his league. He'd been comfortable with the conversation for exactly thirty seconds. Marc had made quick work of that.

Casey almost started to laugh.

"We'd really just like to get started." Marc forged on while Fenton was still at a disadvantage. "As you well know, we're racing the clock."

"Yes, I know." The grim expression that crossed Fenton's face was genuine. He settled himself in his chair and folded his hands stiffly in front of him. "How can I help? I've offered Amanda a blank check—anything she needs to launch a wide-scale search for a donor. She's fixated on the idea that the baby's father is her only answer. I even offered to pay your fee. She's proud. She won't accept any more of my financial help."

"Speaking of the baby's father, that's the reason we're

here," Casey replied, pulling out a writing tablet and pen. "Tell us about Paul Everett. What was your take on him? How well did you know him? What was your reaction to his supposed murder?"

"Supposed?" Fenton's brows rose. "Are you saying you agree with Amanda in thinking that Everett is alive? Or just that you're following every possible lead to make sure that he's not?"

"You mean, pursuing an avenue that involves taking Amanda's money—or your money—in the process." Casey spoke Fenton's thought aloud, and continued without waiting for confirmation. "No, Mr. Fenton, we're not just humoring your niece. Forensic Instincts is known for our direct approach to our cases and our clients. If we didn't believe Paul Everett was alive, we'd be laying out that fact for Amanda. And we'd be encouraging her to discontinue our services. Rest assured, our company is on solid financial footing. We don't need to squeeze money out of our clients. Nor would we. Our company's growth relies on our reputation. I'm sure you can relate to that."

"Of course." Lyle Fenton was definitely off balance. Whatever he'd expected, it hadn't been this. "I didn't mean to insult you. I'm just surprised that you sound so certain about Paul. Do you have proof he's alive?"

"Nothing concrete," Marc replied. "But our leads are strong enough to convince us to pursue this aggressively. That's really all we can say. Client confidentiality. I'm sure you can understand. I'm equally sure that Amanda will answer any questions you have directly." He leaned forward, gripped his knees. "Paul Everett?" he prompted.

"Yes… Paul." Fenton relaxed as he mentally recalled whatever speech he'd prepared. "I didn't know him well. He had a great reputation in his field when he moved into the area. And his idea about converting the marina into a luxury hotel was intriguing. It had the potential to bring in big money, jobs..."

"And tourists," Casey finished for him.

"Exactly. Which is why I was so ambivalent about signing on with his project. My dredging business would have profited greatly. But I'm not just a businessman, Ms. Woods. I'm also a local, and a member of the Southampton Board of Trustees. I had an obligation to do what was best for my community."

"Which explains why you never committed to Paul."

"Not only why I never committed my company resources. Also why I never threw my full support behind him. I had a lot of due diligence facing me. Permits had to be obtained—environmental, engineering, building—and I had no idea if the town would cooperate. It was my job to figure out what my town wanted before I moved forward."

A regular Boy Scout, Casey thought in disgust.

"We know that your niece was in a committed relationship with Everett," she said. "Did that ever sway you in the direction of helping him out?"

"No." Fenton's answer was quick and adamant. "I never mix business and personal matters. I couldn't have built the kind of empire I have if I did."

"Did Everett pressure you?" Marc asked.

A shrug. "He was a businessman. He saw the opportunity to make a killing. Did he keep after me to sign on? Sure. Did he harass me? No. I'm not sure what else you want to know."

"We want to know if Paul Everett was as upstanding as

Amanda thought he was," Casey supplied. "Did he ever threaten you? Do you have reason to suspect he used illegal means to get what he wanted—blackmail, bribery, hooking up with the wrong crowd?"

"Right," Marc added. "The kind of crowd who could make things happen—for a price."

Fenton's brows rose slightly. "Are you talking about organized crime?"

"I don't know. Are we?"

Marc's tone seemed to throw Fenton a bit. Or was it his subtle implication that Fenton could have that kind of knowledge?

"If Everett was working with the mob, I certainly didn't know about it," he denied quickly, keeping his tone even. But his gaze was still darting around, never settling directly on them. "I suppose it's possible. No one dies—or is attacked and disappears—under violent circumstances without a reason. But, as I said, he and I weren't friends. I have no clue who he associated with or where his cash sources came from."

"What kind of a man would you say Everett was—personally?" Casey opted to veer in a slightly different, less confrontational, direction.

Fenton pursed his lips as if contemplating the question. "He was a personable enough guy. Our dealings were fine. But I know he had a temper. I heard him on the phone several times reaming out contractors. Then again, that's not unusual for a real-estate developer. Paul was a perfectionist. His contractors weren't. That causes friction."

"So you'd say he was volatile?"

"I suppose so, yes."

Convenient, Casey thought. *Interesting that that was* not *a trait Amanda had even slightly alluded to in her description of Paul.*

Curious about where Fenton wanted this to go, Casey played out the point. "Would you say Paul's temper was enough to win him enemies?"

Another shrug. "Probably. Then again, most of the people in my business have tempers and enemies. That doesn't mean they resort to violence. Or illegal dealings."

But you'd love for us to think it did with Paul. And to distance yourself from him as much as possible. Well, aren't you the ultimate Good Samaritan?

Time to catch Fenton off guard.

"What about John Morano?" Casey asked.

A startled expression. "What about him?"

"Are your dealings with him different? We know he's picked up the reins where Everett left off. Will you be working with him?"

Fenton clearly felt he was in the hot seat. "Until now, I wasn't sure. I had the same misgivings I had with Paul. But, as of today, Morano and I made a verbal agreement. My company will be doing the dredging work for the hotel marina."

"Really?" Marc arched a brow. "Why is that? Did you figure out what the Southampton locals want? Or is it just that you'd rather do business with Morano than with Everett?"

"I had nothing against Paul Everett, Mr. Devereaux. I already told you that. Do you think I'd encourage a relationship between him and my niece if I felt otherwise?"

"Of course not." Picking up on Fenton's growing agitation, Casey took it down a notch. "We're just trying to get at anything that might give us a clue as to the way Paul Everett's mind worked. You're a shrewd businessman with shrewd instincts. We value anything you can tell us—even if it's something you hadn't considered before, when you assumed that Paul Everett was dead."

That did the trick. Fenton calmed down. "I understand. No, to answer your question, my change of heart had nothing to do with Paul. I've just had more time to talk to my peers and to my fellow community members. The general consensus is that the influx of jobs and capital outweighs the inconvenience of the additional traffic. So I'd like to hope I made the right decision for the town."

"I assume the Board agrees with you?"

A nod. "I think Morano will get the necessary permits to get his hotel off the ground."

"That's great." Casey was careful to keep her tone noncommittal. "Speaking of which, I understand you're a strong supporter of Congressman Mercer."

As Casey had intended, that came at Fenton out of left field. And it didn't take a behaviorist to see his reaction. Surprise. Discomfort. His eyes widened and the pulse at his neck beat faster.

"As a matter of fact, I am." The street fighter in Fenton was there in full force. "Why? What does the congressman have to do with this?"

"Just that I was curious where the congressman stood on this issue. He's been fairly ambiguous up to this point."

"Ambiguous? I'd say he was weighing the pros and cons, just as I was. He's determined to do what's best for his constituency."

"So you've discussed this with him?"

"As a matter of fact, I have. He seems to be of the same opinion as I am. That's part of what swayed my decision."

"Did the congressman know Paul Everett?"

"Only casually. I introduced them at a political party—the same party where Paul and Amanda met."

"If they didn't know each other, why was Everett there?" Casey asked, feigning puzzlement.

"Paul was a big fan of the congressman's. He believed he was the real deal. He'd contributed to his campaign. So he got an invitation." Fenton had had enough. "Why are we talking about the congressman? You can't possibly think he's connected with Paul's disappearance?"

"Of course not," Casey assured him. "We just thought that if he and Paul knew each other, we could interview the congressman in the hopes of learning something. But you're saying they were barely acquainted."

"I doubt they said a dozen words to each other. There's nothing the congressman could tell you, believe me."

"I do. It's obvious that you and Congressman Mercer are close personal friends. I think that's wonderful."

Fenton was not happy with the turn this conversation was taking. "As it happens, our families have known each other for years. But what made you jump to the conclusion that we're close personal friends?"

"We were listening to the news on our way over here," Marc supplied. "We heard that Congressman Mercer had flown in from D.C. to have himself tested as a potential donor for Justin."

"Oh, I see." Fenton calmed down. "Yes, that's true. But it's not because we're friends—although we are. It's just the kind of a person Cliff is. Caring is in his nature, whether it's for one or for many. I told him how critical the situation with Justin is. He offered to see if he, or anyone in his family, were donor matches."

"It's refreshing to hear a political figure described that way. Most of them do things like that to impress the public."

"Not Cliff. He's a genuinely fine man. And a genuinely fine public servant."

"That explains why you were so instrumental in his campaign," Casey noted.

That didn't sit well with Fenton. "He's the best thing that's happened to Southampton in a long time. So if you're implying that this is a case of one hand washing the other, it's not. If you knew the congressman, you'd know he isn't for sale."

"I'm sure that's the case. The fact that you think so highly of him speaks volumes."

If Fenton picked up on the ambiguity of Casey's statement, he didn't react. "I'm far from the only one. Cliff won his seat by a landslide. And he certainly didn't need my help to do it."

Casey nodded. Time to bring this interview to a close—for now. "Marc and I won't keep you any longer, Mr. Fenton." She rose, with Marc smoothly following suit. "We appreciate your time."

Fenton came to his feet, visibly unsettled by the abrupt closure to a conversation that had steered way off course. "I'm not sure I helped."

"You gave us some insight into Paul Everett. That's all we expected. The rest of it—the heavy lifting—is our job." Casey handed him a business card. "If you think of anything else, please give us a call, any time of the day or night. We're working 24/7 to find Justin's father."

"With very little time to do it in," Fenton amended, that genuine distress crossing his face again.

"We're narrowing things down." Marc sounded more threatening than he did reassuring. Some of it was the role he was playing, and some of it was pure Marc. "I told Amanda we'd find Everett, and we will—through whatever means necessary."

Fenton met Marc's hard stare, then wet his lips and glanced away. "I hope so. Amanda swears by you. And I'm aware of your reputation. This is one time I hope you earn it."

Five minutes later, Casey and Marc were back in the van, heading up the serpentine drive toward the gates.

"What a scumbag," Marc stated flatly. "He's dirty in more ways than we can count."

"No argument." Casey waited for the gates to open, then steered onto the main road. "The only thing about him that's genuine is his feeling for Justin. He's worried. Enough so that if he were directly involved in Paul Everett's disappearance, he wouldn't leave it that way."

"Don't be too sure," Marc muttered. "Fenton's drive for self-preservation trumps everything. Even the baby's life."

"That's exactly *why* he'd save the baby's life," Casey refuted. "Justin represents his legacy, which is the only thing he gives a damn about."

"So you think he *wants* us to find Everett?"

"I didn't say that. I think *he* wants to find Everett. I think he believed he was dead. I wouldn't be surprised if he played a part in whatever happened. And if he is guilty of something, he's probably frantic to find Paul before we do. That way, he can clean up whatever Paul has on him, and then make him disappear again, this time for good. Whether that means killing him or paying him off, I don't know. There's a menacing quality about that guy that tells me he's capable of both."

"Yeah. I think you should have let me beat the crap out of him. It would have made me feel a whole lot better."

Casey understood Marc's frustration. He rarely made comments like those—comments he would never act on. He was way too disciplined to opt for physical violence unless it made sense. In this case, it would only have resulted in FI getting fired and Marc getting arrested—all of which would have brought them no closer to finding Paul Everett.

"He flipped out when we got onto the topic of Mercer," she commented.

"Ya think?" Marc frowned. "There's definitely a connection there, and not just a political one. Although I'm sure having Fenton's money in his coffers sweetened the deal for Mercer. But I'm glad Ryan's running that facial recognition software. It should be interesting to see if we're barking up the right tree."

"You know we are, and so do I. There's a blood connection here. How close a blood connection, and why it's being kept a secret, are the questions we need answers to."

"Okay, so we know Fenton's freaked out about Mercer." Marc's eyebrows knit. "He's also freaked out about Morano. Why him more than Everett—especially if he's involved in Everett's disappearance?"

"Maybe because he had rehearsed his entire speech about Everett and he wasn't expecting us to get into Morano." Casey continued driving toward Westhampton Beach, where they'd collect Marc's stuff and head back to the city. "Fenton was like an actor on the stage, and not a particularly good one. First, he tried to intimidate us with his wealth and his demeanor—right down to the custom-tailored suit he opted not to change out of before our visit."

"Yeah, I noticed that. Pretty transparent. Nobody stays in a monkey suit a minute longer than necessary. You'd think that a couple of hours after getting home, he'd be in casual clothes."

"You would indeed. Now let's get to Paul. Fenton ran through his litany about Paul like a memorized script. He didn't lose footing until we touched on the mob. That struck a nerve. So did our curiosity over what Morano did to tip the scales in his favor. Fenton was definitely thrown by that. Why? Are he and Morano proverbially in bed together?"

"Wouldn't surprise me," Marc replied. "On the other hand, who's Morano paying off? Who was Paul paying off? Fenton would be my first guess."

"In which case, they're both in this, but on opposite sides."

"Yup. I told you how staged Morano was during our interview today. Maybe afterward he clued Fenton in on the interview—and the fact that 'Robert Curtis' had asked about Everett. Maybe he was nervous that Crain's business magazine might decide to take the article a step further and talk to others involved in the project."

"Which would explain why Fenton was so scripted about Paul Everett."

Marc chuckled. "It would also explain Fenton's reaction when he first saw me. If Morano described me to him, then Fenton must have recognized me—and not as Robert Curtis." An exaggerated grimace. "And here I thought my mere presence had scared the shit out of him."

"It probably did. Doubly so, if he put the pieces together." Casey sighed. "If you're right, it means they're onto us. I knew that would eventually be unavoidable. I just wish we could have avoided tipping our hand a little longer. Now, both Morano and Fenton will be on their guard. So will Mercer, if he's in on this. And Fenton will make sure to mention something to Amanda that'll either upset her or make her wary of us." A quick sideways glance. "She trusts you, Marc. I think you should do some damage control ASAP."

"How much do you want me to say?"

"That we were thorough and direct with her uncle. That he seemed uncomfortable with some of our questions. That we had no intentions of offending him, but that it was our job to cover every base—including some that dealt with Paul's possible criminal involvement. And that we're sure he understands, since he's as eager to find Justin's father as we are."

"Got it. The truth, only sprayed with perfume."

"Right. Then, no matter what Fenton says to her, Amanda's reaction will be tempered. After all, there were no accusations made. If Fenton has a guilty conscience, that's his problem." Casey shrugged. "I have a feeling that the deeper we dig, the more we're going to find on Fenton. Eventually, Amanda's going to have to be told. For now, she has enough on her plate. Her focus is on Justin, as it should be. Her uncle's peace of mind is low on her priority list. And if it turns out that Fenton had something to do with her losing Paul... Let's just say that I doubt she'll be too concerned about hurting his feelings."

Marc glanced at his watch. "Let's get my stuff and get back to the office. I want to hear what Ryan's figured out so far."

"And what Claire and Patrick got from visiting Amanda at the hospital. No one's called or texted. Which means everything's still in the works. We'll have more to discuss when we're all together."

As if on cue, Casey's cell phone rang. *Caller Unknown* registered on the dashboard screen. It could be anyone, threatening or otherwise. That never stopped Casey; it only made her cautious.

She pressed the button on her steering wheel and picked up the call. "Casey Woods."

"Kyle Hutchinson," a deep, masculine voice replied.

"Hutch." Relief surged through her. Hutch's voice was the last one Casey expected to hear. She was mentally wrapped up in the investigation, and this call was unexpected. The sound of Hutch's voice was a welcome balm, and brought with it the usual surge of pleasure. More so than usual, since they hadn't spoken in weeks, which was a rarity. "Are you back in Quantico?"

"Just finished up my assignment. I'm at a stopover in London. I'll be flying back to the States tomorrow."

Hutch didn't elaborate and Casey didn't ask. Despite how involved they were, she knew better than to pry. Hutch worked for the FBI's Behavioral Analysis Unit, and most of his assignments were on a "need to know" basis. He'd just transferred from the BAU-3—crimes against children—to the BAU-2—crimes against adults. He was much happier. The former had started to get to him. Kids being hurt, killed or worse. He'd had enough.

He and Casey had been committed to their long-distance relationship for months now, and they'd managed to make it work. Their professional lives had crossed just once—on the kidnapping case Forensic Instincts had worked in October. The two of them had butted heads—it hadn't been pretty.

"Hey, Hutch," Marc chimed in. "I'm here, too, before you say anything that'll make me blush."

A chuckle. "Thanks for the warning." Hutch knew Marc from his BAU days. They were friends. In fact, Marc had been the one to introduce him to Casey.

"Are you working?" Hutch asked.

"Round the clock." Casey blew out a breath. "It's a rough case."

"You'll tell me about it tomorrow. I'll be landing at JFK a little before six o'clock—early enough to take you to dinner."

Casey blinked. "You're coming to New York?"

"Yup. I've been working nonstop for weeks. I've got a few days of R & R. I chose to spend them in the Big Apple."

"That's great." Casey hated feeling torn. "But Hutch, the case I'm working on..."

"Not to worry. I'll claim whatever snatches of time you have. Otherwise, I'll be eating three squares and sleeping in. I'm hungry and I'm beat."

"Okay." Casey felt another surge of relief. There was something very steadying about Hutch. He was intense, but he knew where to draw the line. He had to. He'd been a cop, now he was FBI. He had nerves of steel. She had the nerves, but she had problems drawing the line. Despite her best efforts, her cases got inside her. Hutch helped her find balance.

"See you tomorrow," he said. "And tell Hero he'll be sharing the bed."

Casey smiled as she disconnected the call.

"You know," Marc mused aloud. "Maybe we could clear it with Amanda, and ask Hutch for his help. We'll tell her he's an FBI consultant. He might give us a fresh take on Paul Everett."

Casey's brows rose. "Hutch and me working together? The death toll could be high."

CHAPTER THIRTEEN

It had taken a half hour of pleading and persuasion on Amanda's part to get the ICU staff to agree to her request. But when she explained what she was desperate to accomplish, they'd finally agreed.

A professional videographer and his assistant showed up just before 7:00 p.m. Amanda thanked her friends profusely for the huge favor. Her instructions were brief—record a five-minute video right outside the PICU window where Justin was sleeping in his crib. They'd have to work overnight to have everything ready and posted on YouTube by morning.

It wouldn't be easy. But it could be done. And they'd do it.

The video went smoothly. The entire event—from arrival to departure—took seventeen minutes.

Its repercussions would last far longer.

★ ★ ★

Bleary-eyed and weary, the Forensic Instincts team trudged into the main conference room and reconvened around the expansive mahogany table just after midnight.

As they entered, the wall of floor-to-ceiling video screens began to glow. A long green line slid across each panel, pulsating from left to right as it appeared.

"Hello, team," Yoda welcomed them. The green line bent into the contour of his voice pattern. "Room temperature is currently at sixty-eight point three degrees. Due to the body heat generated by five humans and one canine, the room temperature will rise to exactly seventy degrees in eight minutes and thirteen seconds. Shall I maintain seventy degrees?" Yoda paused, awaiting further instructions.

"That's fine, Yoda," Casey replied. "We're just fine."

"Fine?" Ryan muttered reflexively. "How much sleep have you had in the past few days?"

"If you're addressing me, I don't sleep, Ryan," Yoda responded. "You programmed me not to require it. Lumen, Equitas and Intueri were designed to ensure my uninterrupted service."

Yoda was referring to the three servers that made up the server farm in FI's secure data center, located downstairs in Ryan's lair. Ryan himself had named his custom-built servers, giving them the Latin names for light, justice, and intuition.

"I am available twenty-four hours a day, three hundred sixty-five days a year," Yoda continued. "And three hundred sixty-six days every four years, plus or minus an occasional leap second as needed—except, of course, for the century year twenty-one hundred, per the leap year algorithm."

"Gee, Ryan, and here you claimed you were Superman."

Claire's tone was dry, but her lips were twitching. "Yoda is clearly superior, needs no sleep and is a lot easier to get along with."

"Thank you, Claire," Yoda said politely.

"Oh, shut up, both of you." Ryan looked as if he'd like to short-circuit his creation. "Yoda, chill. We'll let you know if we need you."

"Very well, Ryan." Yoda fell silent, and the glowing line receded.

"Now that you've finished having it out with Yoda, can we discuss our respective evenings?" Casey inquired. "And that doesn't include your lack of sleep, Ryan. Suck it up."

Ryan knew that tone of voice. Casey wasn't in the mood for bullshit.

He nodded. "Sorry. Although I want to go on record as saying that everything Yoda knows, I taught him." Being Ryan, he couldn't resist adding that, along with darting Claire a sideways look. "In any case, do you want me to report my findings first?"

"Actually, I think Marc and I should go first. That'll provide a good baseline for Lyle Fenton. Then, yes, I want to hear what your facial recognition software showed."

Casey and Marc went on to detail the meeting with Lyle Fenton and their take on it.

"Got it," Ryan said, summing it up for the team. "A dirtbag and a scumbag."

"Is there a difference?" Claire asked, amused.

"Yeah. A scumbag's a slimier dirtbag."

"Ah. Thanks for enlightening me."

"No problem." Ryan pursed his lips. "As far as Fenton getting all weird when you brought Mercer into the conversation, I can explain that one—although I think we already know the answer."

"Go on," Casey urged him.

"I'll spare you the mathematical details and just get to the bottom line. I ran a whole bunch of different facial recognition algorithms, just to see if the results came out the same. They did. There's more than an eighty-percent chance that Lyle Fenton and Congressman Mercer are related. The percentages drop down somewhat when you compare Fenton with the twins, and even more when you compare Mercer with Amanda. But that's to be expected, since the relationships are once or twice removed. They're still high, though. High enough for me to conclude that there are blood ties across the board. Most important, in my opinion, Clifford Mercer is Lyle Fenton's son."

"No shocker. But it adds a whole new dimension to this investigation." Casey tapped her fingernails on the table—a gesture that meant she was digesting and analyzing the situation. "Mercer's being illegitimate wouldn't mean the end of his career, not these days. But the fact that his biological father has as much to gain from this relationship—now that's a whole different story. It's bad enough to be in someone's pocket. But being in the pocket of the man who's secretly your father? A pocket deep enough to make or break your career? That's a scandal-waiting-to-happen." She gave Ryan a quizzical look. "Who's Mercer's mother?"

"She *was* Catherine Mercer, born Catherine Wilmot. She died of cancer four years ago." Ryan glanced at his notes. "No eye-openers about her background. Middle-class. Born and bred in a less affluent section of Bridgehampton. Got married at twenty-one to Warren Mercer, a rich, significantly older attorney she met as a secretary in his law firm."

"Let me guess. One child, Clifford, who was the light of his father's life."

"You got it." Ryan shot Casey an admiring look. "Nice assessment."

"It doesn't take a rocket scientist," Casey replied. "If there were other children, keeping the secret wouldn't have been as crucial. Catherine would still be tied to her husband through the other kids. But an only child? And a son, to boot? Catherine wouldn't risk her marriage by letting the cat out of the bag."

"Are we sure Clifford Mercer isn't adopted?" Claire asked. "We can't assume Catherine had an affair with Lyle Fenton."

"Sorry to burst your naive little bubble, Claire-voyant, but they were hot and heavy for a couple of years," Ryan informed her. "I checked with a few of Catherine's old friends. At first, they were guarded. But I managed to charm them into talking to me."

"And how did you manage that?" Claire asked. "I doubt they'd be interested in a trade—their cooperation for one of your Superman comic books."

"Nope. No need to trade." Rather than pissed, Ryan looked amused. "Just some finesse on my part. I told them I worked for Congressman Mercer, and that I'd been assigned the job of protecting his political future by preserving his mother's good name. I asked them to tell me what they knew about her extramarital affair so I could squelch it. Loyal friends that they were, they were happy to supply me with the information."

"What about Warren Mercer?" Claire demanded. "Did

they say whether or not he knew? Or is he still in the dark after all these years? Actually, is he even alive?"

"Oh, he's alive," Ryan assured her. "He was Lyle Fenton's lawyer. And the two of them were golfing buddies."

"Were?" Casey jumped on the past tense.

"Yup—were. Right around the time of Catherine's death, all that went to hell. Warren Mercer dropped Fenton as a client right after Catherine died. And from everything I could dig up, he and Fenton had no further dealings after that, business or personal."

"I smell a deathbed confession," Marc surmised aloud. "Catherine probably had to clear her conscience. Her son was a grown man, so she wasn't worried about his reaction anymore. And she probably knew her husband wouldn't cut off ties with Cliff, not after forty-plus years of being his father."

"I agree." Casey's brows were still knit. "The question is, when did Fenton find out? Did she also tell him when she was dying? Or did he know beforehand? Clifford Mercer certainly didn't tell him. By the time his mother died, the man was a political figure. The last thing he'd want is to give Fenton that kind of power over him. No, my guess is that Fenton already knew. But for how long?"

"My gut feeling?" Marc replied. "For a long time. Maybe even before Cliff was born. We're talking about a man with tons of street smarts. He sure as hell knew how to count. And, given the timing of the affair, he had to suspect that he was potentially Clifford's father. On the flip side, when he went to Catherine and she assured him the child was her husband's, Fenton was probably überrelieved. He's a lot of things, but a family man is not one of them."

"I agree with that," Patrick said. "I watched the two men

together at lunch. There's no father-son bond there. If anything, they're distant when it comes to personal matters. Fenton asked about the twins as if he were discussing the neighbor's kids. He got more intense about business than he did about family. Except where it came to Justin. Then, he was single-minded. He practically forced Mercer to get tested."

"Justin represents his future," Casey replied. "A new life, like a blank slate waiting to be written on. A last-chance hope for being the future of Fenton's business empire. When the congressman was born, Fenton wasn't thinking along those lines. He was young, unconcerned about the future."

"Let's not forget that DNA testing for paternity didn't come into play until the 1980s," Ryan supplied. "So even if Fenton had a paternity test, it wouldn't have been conclusive. I doubt he pushed for it, though. I agree with Marc. I'm sure he backed off with great relief."

"The truth is, he didn't even want to know he had a child." Claire's gray eyes were filled with disgust. "But eventually he found out. So how could he walk away? Better question—what prompted him to come back? Was it because he wanted something out of Clifford Mercer?"

Casey turned toward her. "Are you getting some kind of sense?"

"Nothing." Claire shook her head. "I'm as stymied as you are. Remember, I've never met either Fenton or Mercer."

"Maybe it's time you did. Maybe it's time we all did."

"You want to show up at the hospital tomorrow." Marc's statement was a conclusion, not a guess.

"I sure as hell do. Not just me. You and Claire, too. And Hero. I want him to pick up some initial scents from the congressman. Who knows how corrupt he is? Not just by being in Fenton's pocket, but worse. What if he's connected to Paul Everett's disappearance? For all we know, Everett found out the truth about Mercer and Fenton and blackmailed them. Maybe that factored into his disappearance. And, if it did, we can add Mercer to the list of people who might know where Paul is." Casey's gaze shifted to Patrick. "I'd love to get your firsthand take on this, but we can't risk it. Not when you were sitting next to the congressman and Fenton at lunch. If Mercer were to recognize you, it would blow everything."

"That's okay." Patrick waved away Casey's explanation. "You're right. Besides, I want to do some old-fashioned digging of my own. I'll see what I can learn about Fenton and Mercer, and any mutual ties they had to Paul Everett. That might give us a path to follow."

"Good." Casey glanced from Patrick to Claire and back. "Your turn. What happened when you saw Amanda at the hospital tonight?"

"Ladies first." Patrick gestured for Claire to talk.

Claire blew out her breath. "Justin is the same. Hanging on. Fighting for his life." A hard swallow. "I saw him through the ICU window. He's hooked up to so many machines. The ventilator is helping him breathe, and the antibiotics are battling the infection. But he's so tiny. I don't know how much longer he can keep up this fight." She swallowed again, this time to bring herself under control. "On a separate note, something's up with Amanda. I felt it the minute she walked out to greet us. She was uncomfortable, like she wished we'd go away. She spoke quickly, assuring us that there was no need to stick around, that she was fine and just needed to be with her son. But it was a smokescreen. I could feel her anxiety and her impatience. It wasn't related only to Justin's health. There was something else."

Casey frowned. "It couldn't have been a reaction to our meeting with her uncle. We didn't even arrive at his estate until eight o'clock."

"And we were long gone from the hospital by then." Claire shook her head. "No, it had nothing to do with her uncle. I think Amanda was expecting someone. Whoever he was, we've never met him."

"Him?" Ryan was all over that one.

Claire rolled her eyes. "It wasn't some secret lover, Ryan. It was business. Personal business, which I think had something to do with Justin."

"Then why wouldn't she talk to you about it?" Casey asked. "What is there that she'd prefer we not know?"

"I can't answer that." Claire turned her palms up in a gesture of noncomprehension. "I asked her a few questions, but she only got more anxious and more distant, which clouded the energy between us even more. So I backed off. I decided it would be more productive to try talking to her again in the morning, when she was less on edge and I could get a clearer read."

"Okay," Casey agreed. "We'll find out what time the congressman is being tested, and we'll work a visit with Amanda around that."

"He's due at the hospital at 11:00 a.m.," Ryan supplied. "Perfect timing for the evening news cycle. He and his wife will give blood, answer the media's questions and then leave. He'll be back in Washington before dinner."

"Okay, then we'll head out to Southampton first, and be

at Sloane Kettering in the late afternoon. I want Marc to do some damage control with Amanda anyway, just in case Fenton spins our conversation in a way that throws her for a loop." Casey shifted her gaze to Patrick. "What about you? You obviously have something for me, too."

"Yeah." He nodded. "Claire's right. We were definitely being followed. Both ways. And whoever did it is a pro. He stayed far enough behind us so I couldn't catch his license plate. And when we pulled into the parking lot, he drove right by, tinted windows raised, so I couldn't get a good look at him. But he was right behind us on the trip there, and two cars behind us on the way back. I could try to get security footage from the hospital, but I guarantee it won't show anything."

"We're making people very nervous," Claire murmured. "And those people aren't just pros. They're dangerous."

"Then I say, let's keep pushing their buttons." Marc had that hard, steely edge to his voice. "Eventually, they'll slip up and let us know who they are."

CHAPTER FOURTEEN

It was after 5:00 a.m. when Ryan finally crawled into bed. He wasn't going to get a hell of a lot of sleep. But he'd be getting more than the rest of the team. They'd be on the road by nine o'clock, right after rush-hour traffic. He didn't envy them. At least he could catch a good five hours before he was needed.

That idea was blown to hell at 8:30 a.m. when the *Star Wars* theme music began blaring through his room in triplicate—from his BlackBerry, his iPhone and his Droid.

He bolted up in bed, simultaneously groping for the closest phone, his BlackBerry, which was sitting on his nightstand. The screen was furiously flashing Yoda. That meant he'd find the same name on all three screens. Clearly, it was an emergency.

"Yeah, Yoda, it's me," he said, waiting a split second for the voice recognition to register.

"Ryan," Yoda replied. "We have a comm server overload. I repeat, a comm server overload."

Ryan blinked away the final cobwebs of sleep, although he was totally confused. Why the hell would they have a comm server overload?

He got out of bed and crossed over to his laptop, quickly logging onto the Forensic Instincts server. "What the fuck…?" He stared at the huge volume of phone calls that were pouring in. "I'm coming in, Yoda."

Twenty minutes and one subway ride later, Ryan was in his lair, punching computer keys and monitoring what he soon realized was a big-time screwup on their client's part and a major communications crisis at FI.

He watched the video on YouTube, redirected to voice mail the incoming calls responding to Amanda's plea, and then called Casey on speed dial.

"What's up?" she asked, briskly towel-drying her hair.

"I'll tell you what's up. Amanda went public—and I mean public—last night. Our server can't handle all the calls coming in as a result. You'd better get a bank of receptionists in here, now, or we're in trouble. Screw that, we're already in trouble."

"Ryan, slow down." Casey tossed the towel aside. "Where are you? And what did Amanda do?"

"I'm downstairs. Come on down and take a look. And then call a temp agency, or whoever you call in situations like this, and get some people in here to answer the damned phones."

"I'll be right there."

Casey was already dressed. She grabbed her BlackBerry and raced down the four flights of stairs to the basement. Ryan was standing up at his desk, visibly freaking out at the number of red lights that were flashing throughout his lair.

"Yoda called me," he explained briefly. "The phones are blowing off the hook. Wanna see why?" He gestured for Casey to come over.

She complied, staring at his computer screen as he got on the YouTube site and called up what he was looking for.

The video was very clear. It was Amanda, standing in the corridor of Sloane Kettering's Pediatric ICU. She was just outside the window where Justin's crib was situated, and the curtains were pulled open. The viewer could see inside and clearly make out the infant, along with his medical apparatus, through the glass. In a voice that was shaky and filled with tears, Amanda explained Justin's condition and why it was imperative that they find a donor match immediately. She held up a photo of Paul, announcing that he was the baby's father and the prime option, but that he'd been away and had no knowledge of Justin's health crisis. She begged everyone to call immediately if they knew anything about Paul Everett or his whereabouts. She concluded by saying it was literally a matter of life or death, pleading with the world to save her child.

Throughout the three-minute video, Forensic Instincts' name and phone number were posted prominently at the bottom of the screen, to be contacted on any and all potential leads.

"Dammit." Casey dragged a hand through her tousled hair. "I can't believe she did this."

"Me, either. Now what are *we* going to do?"

Casey was already going through the contact list on her BlackBerry. "I'm going to call the first person on my NYU phone chain."

Comprehension flashed in Ryan's eyes. The whole team knew that Casey taught a biweekly human behavior seminar to a class of psychology students at NYU. "Phone chains are for class cancelations," he reminded her.

"True." Casey found the number she was looking for and pressed *dial home.* "But the kids have out-of-class hours they need to put in before Christmas—a fact I'm sure they've procrastinated away. Here's their chance to fulfill those hours and get a great experience in human behavior." A grin. "Even if they did finish partying and/or cramming for exams at dawn." A brief pause. "Hi, Marcy. It's Casey Woods. I need a favor."

A minute later, she hung up. "Marcy's calling the next person on the list. There are ten people in that class. We'll get at least three-quarters of them, trust me. Our server won't explode. I, on the other hand, might." Casey's features tightened. "I understand that Amanda is desperate. But she should have come to us first. Not just because it's our phone number she's listing. But because any hope we had of keeping this under the radar is now shot to hell."

Ryan scowled. "Even if we got her to pull the video, it's had thousands of hits already. The damage is done."

"It sure is." Casey sighed. "Well, now we know what vibes Claire was picking up on last night."

A grudging nod. "Yeah, even I've got to admit that Claire-voyant knew what she was talking about. And if you repeat that, I'll deny having said it."

"Your rivalry with Claire is low on my priority list right now." Casey's mind was racing again. "I'm not the right one to handle Amanda. Not now. I'm too pissed. And I want to get my interns settled at the phones before I take off for Southampton. I need to quickly throw together an interview script. Train them to use it. Something simple, easy to follow, but designed to flag any useful leads." She pressed Marc's number on speed dial. "I'll get Marc to go over to Sloane Kettering. He's the best man for the job. He'll stay cool. And he has a soothing effect on Amanda."

"He has a soothing effect on everyone—except those he beats the shit out of," Ryan muttered.

"True." Casey turned her attention to the phone, which Marc picked up on the second ring, sounding alert and ready to hit the road. Bless the man. Once a Navy SEAL, always a Navy SEAL. He'd probably done a hundred push-ups before dawn. The man never slept. "Hey," she began. "We've got a situation."

Just after the morning rush hour, Investigative Detective Rick Jones of the New York State Police Department's Bureau of Criminal Investigation was settling himself behind his desk when the phone rang.

"Jones," he answered, simultaneously juggling the receiver and his foam cup of coffee so it didn't spill over the mounds of paper on his desk.

"The girlfriend released a video on YouTube," the voice at the other end of the phone informed him. "It spells out everything, including a photo of Everett and a plea for any news on him. The video was released at 6:30 a.m. It's already had over a hundred thousand hits. There's no getting away from it. Everett's homicide is going to be in the headlines and the goddamn media will be up your ass."

"What do you want me to do?" Jones asked.

"Pull the whole case file and work it."

"What whole case file? It's a couple of sheets of paper."

"Beef up the file. Make the investigation you conducted look thorough. Backdate it. Get rid of anything that points to your passing off the case to the Coast Guard. The media's going to be all over this. And that sucks for all of us. Is all that clear?"

"As glass."

"Good. Now go do it—fast."

Marc sat in the Pediatric Intensive Care Unit waiting area, downing a cup of coffee and waiting for Amanda to come out.

When she did arrive, it was stiffly, with slow, weary steps. She pulled off her hospital mask, and she had the same weary expression on her face. "Hi," she greeted Marc.

"Hi." Marc took another slow, calm drink before setting down his cup on the end table. "How's Justin?"

"The same." Amanda sank down on the institutional sofa, her yellow paper hospital gown making a rustling sound as she did. "Oh." She seemed to notice the gown and the mask for the first time. "I should have tossed these. I'll need sterile ones when I go back in." She dropped her face into her hands. "Why doesn't the antibiotic work? Why won't his fever come down?"

"It's only been a day," Marc soothed. "I know it feels like a lifetime. But it's not. Give the medicine and your son some time to combat the infection."

"And then what? There'll be a new one?" Amanda looked up, the agony on her face too acute to miss. "He's struggling so hard. And there's not a damned thing I can do."

"You certainly gave it your best shot last night." Marc's comment was pointed but gentle. The woman was unraveling. She'd reached out in desperation, clawing at a chance to find Paul. Sure, it had complicated their investigation. And it had almost melted Ryan's precious server. But it's not like their search was classified. And, as for the server, its load had been lifted. There were a bank of people at the office now, taking calls.

How furious could he be? It was her baby's life at stake.

Amanda stared blankly at him, looking completely out of it. It was almost as if she had no clue what Marc was talking about. Then, comprehension dawned in her eyes. "You're talking about the video."

"Yup. Very impactful. Succinct, heart-wrenching, and great videography. You've got talented friends. Plus, you accomplished your goal. You captured the world's attention. Hell, the number of YouTube hits are off the chart. And our server practically self-destructed from all the phone calls pouring in."

"Are any of the calls worthwhile?" she asked, a plea in her voice. "Has anyone given you information on Paul?"

"No. So far, it's been a lot of crank calls and reporters." Marc leaned forward, held Amanda's gaze. "Not your best idea. Grandstanding like that tends to bring out all the crazies. It wastes precious time and resources. Getting a worthwhile lead is like looking for a needle in a haystack."

"I wasn't grandstanding. I was using my contacts to reach

as many people as possible." She studied his face. "You're angry. I'll pay for any damage to your server."

Marc almost laughed, just visualizing Ryan's reaction to that statement. "Don't worry about the server. It can take it. We also had to scramble to get a bunch of college kids into our office to field the phone calls." A pause. "We're not big on broadcasting our phone number round the globe. But then, you already knew that. You also knew we'd cut you off at the knees if we'd known your plan. That's why you didn't mention a word about your plan to Claire and Patrick."

"You're right." Amanda licked her lips. "It was a calculated risk, but one I had to take. I knew it could backfire. I told Melissa so when she first suggested it. But then Justin got worse. And I had to try. I knew you might write me off as a client. But the idea of reaching so many people in one fell swoop—any one of whom might have seen Paul... I had to do it. I'm ready to ask my uncle to offer a reward for any information on Paul's whereabouts." She gave a resigned shrug. "In any case, if you're the one assigned to ream me out or kick me to the curb, go for it."

She looked like a small, broken bird, and Marc felt another huge wave of compassion. Emotion wasn't normally his thing, and it felt weird to be reacting this way. But a child... no, not just a child, a newborn—talk about his Achilles' heel.

Images of what he'd seen in years past—children being torn from their parents, sold like livestock, used as human shields, shot and killed before they'd even had a chance to live—those images flashed through his mind like some heinous movie. They'd never go away. They'd haunt him forever.

And here was a mother who'd lain down her life for her

child. How could he berate her for that? If Justin survived, it would be his mother's love and tenacity that made it happen.

Marc had taken Amanda's case before talking to his team. It had been personal to him from the start. It still was.

"I'm not going to kick you to the curb," he said. "I'm going to tell you not to act without talking to us first, because impulsive acts rarely pay off, and because you hired us to do the job and do it right. I'm going to tell you that we need you to help us, not impede us. And then I'm going to buy you a large orange juice and an egg sandwich. You need protein and electrolytes. You're about to collapse."

Amanda nodded. "You're right—about everything. Clearly, my first instinct was the right one. I never should have jumped the gun without talking to you first. I'm sorry."

"You might have been surprised by our reaction. We're not big rule-followers. We could have found a better way to pull off that video—a more controversial one, actually. One that could have pushed all the necessary buttons—while probably pissing off some people in the process—but that didn't put us in the limelight. We could have set up a special toll-free number for the incoming phone calls. So don't sell us short. You hired us because we're the best. So let us be the best."

A weak smile. "Point taken. And, speaking of being the best, I never had a chance to thank you. I just found out that your whole team had yourselves tested as potential matches for Justin. That was incredibly kind."

"It was something we chose to do," Marc replied.

"Nonetheless, I'm grateful." Amanda drew a slow, exhausted breath, then rose. "I'll take you up on that OJ and those eggs. I'm feeling really shaky. And Justin needs me to be strong."

"Agreed." Marc glanced at his watch. "Let's head down to the cafeteria. I can only stay a few minutes."

"Ah. You drew the short straw and had to deal with me first, then head straight back to the office to do telephone damage control."

"Nope." As always, Marc went for the no-bullshit approach. "Like I said, the phones are under control now. Yeah, some of us are pissed. Especially Ryan, who got woken from his beauty sleep by Yoda reporting an overheating server. He'll get over it. We all will. But Casey thought I'd be the easiest one for you to talk to. And I'm not heading back to the office. I'm heading out to Southampton."

"Southampton? Why?" Amanda looked startled, and then thoughtful. "Does this have something to do with your meeting last night with my uncle? Because I forgot all about it. How did things go? Did he ask you to come back and meet with the Town Board?"

Marc gestured toward the elevators. "Let's get you fed. I'll fill you in along the way."

CHAPTER FIFTEEN

John Morano sat in his decrepit, run-down office and shoved aside the legal documents that Lyle Fenton's attorney had drawn up. Frustrated, he rubbed his eyes, feeling the pressure deep in his gut. He popped two antacid tablets, washing them down with a bottle of water. He wished it were bourbon. But at 9:30 a.m. with an ugly confrontation about to occur, the last thing he needed was to have his faculties compromised.

He was taking a huge risk, and he knew it. Cutting off kickbacks to the Vizzinis could backfire big-time. They controlled the unions. Teamsters. Ironworkers. Even the service workers that would staff his hotel. As a result, they'd been controlling him. He couldn't jeopardize this project, much less his life. But he couldn't keep paying twenty grand every six weeks for nothing. There was only so far a dwindling cash balance could be stretched. And only so much manipulation he could successfully juggle.

He'd managed to get Fenton on board, which meant he'd get his permits—at a much steeper price than he expected. Talk about manipulation. Fenton's rules. Fenton's profits. Fenton's investors.

And Fenton's pressure.

Things were about to come to a head. And Morano had to keep his eye on the prize.

The door to his office swung open and Sal, the gruff workman aka slimy mob soldier who paid Morano collection visits, walked in. He was wearing jeans and a work vest, and he had his usual toolbox, although he wasn't expecting to leave with it filled. It was weeks too soon for that. No, today was a different kind of scheduled visit, one that had been requested by Morano.

Sal shut the door behind him, grabbed himself a chair and sat down. He plunked the toolbox on the wooden floor and folded his arms across his chest. The fingers of his right hand brushed the top of his vest pocket, in close proximity to the gun that, no doubt, was concealed inside.

Morano intentionally avoided staring at the vest, instead fixing his gaze on Sal's pockmarked face.

"What do you want?" Sal demanded.

"To renegotiate." Morano got straight to the point, keeping his tone and his expression hard, his jaw set. "This time by my rules. We're done. I'm finished paying. Tell your boss enough is enough. No more bullshit. I'm cutting ties. I've got other mouths to feed on this project. I've coughed up a fucking fortune to keep him happy. Time to move on."

Sal's dark eyes narrowed. "You're making a huge mistake,

Morano. You need us. And I don't need to remind you what happened to Everett, do I?"

Morano went very still. "Is that a threat?"

"A threat?" Sal shrugged. "Call it a helpful suggestion from a concerned associate. What happened to Everett was an unfortunate coincidence. You're not into unfortunate coincidences, are you?"

"No. But I'm also not into being bled dry. You got your pound of flesh—and then some. We're more than even. I'm done with these visits. And I want the decks cleared for my project."

"Not happening. And not smart," Sal replied.

"Maybe not. But necessary." Morano rose slowly, hands in front of him. "So that's that. Now what? Do you plan on gunning me down?"

A crooked smile twisted Sal's lips, as he, too, came to his feet. "Nope. I plan on delivering your message. I'm guessing you'll be getting one in return."

The parking lot outside Southampton Hospital's brick building was crawling with press when the FI team drove in.

"Wow," Casey commented drily. "Mercer's whole PR department deserves a raise. The media here isn't only from New York's First Congressional District. It's from all of Long Island, Queens and Manhattan. Which means the networks and cable will also pick it up."

"Damn straight. And not just thanks to Mercer's press office. All these reporters have probably seen Amanda's video by now," Marc reminded her, studying the crowd as Casey cruised along, looking for a parking space. "Mercer couldn't ask for better publicity. The whole crowd is tweeting as they wait for his appearance. This altruistic act of his will be in everyone's face in minutes."

"How are we going to get close enough to him to accomplish anything?" Claire asked from the backseat of the van. "He's going to have security around him when he arrives and when he leaves the hospital."

"That's not what our problem's going to be," Marc said with a frown. "FI is already on everyone's computer screen as the go-to place for anybody with information on Paul Everett. We're smack in the middle of this saga. The problem is going to be getting to Mercer without being bombarded by the media. Once they hear who we are, it's all over. Not to mention Lyle Fenton, who's sure to be showing up with Mercer. He'll recognize us instantly and stand between us and the congressman."

"Maybe we can pull this off without identifying ourselves." Claire was thoughtful as she stroked Hero's glossy neck. "At least not until we're close enough to Mercer to keep our conversation private."

Casey glanced at her in the rearview mirror. "I'm listening."

"You two are the only members of the team that Lyle Fenton has met. No one knows Hero or me. And we've both learned how to be very good actors. Right, Hero?"

Hero turned his soulful eyes on her and made a sound deep in his throat. Then he licked Claire's hand, slobbering on her ski jacket. Clearly, he knew he was being discussed.

"I hate being stereotyped as the vapid, helpless blonde," Claire continued. "But it can sometimes work to our advantage. When the congressman shows up and heads for the door, I'll take Hero for a walk. I'll issue the necessary command for him to lurch into high gear. We'll practically crash into Mercer. I'll act pathetic enough for his security to shift into at-ease position. Then I'll quietly tell Mercer who I am and that we need to speak to him about that video after he and his wife donate their blood. If Fenton is with them, he won't be happy, but he won't freak out, because the video wasn't on YouTube when you had your meeting last night. He'll probably want to sit in on our chat with Mercer, but we can't help that. At least it'll gain us access without causing a riot."

"Nice," Marc praised. "And you're right. Fenton won't make a scene—and that's true even if he is thrown by our talking to Mercer. He'll be as eager as we are to keep the lid on who we are. The last thing he wants is a public spectacle—especially if that public spectacle shifts the limelight off Mercer." Marc was nodding as he spoke. "It could work."

"Okay, then let's go for it." Casey pulled into a parking space a good distance away and turned off the ignition. She glanced at her watch. "Mercer should be here any minute."

As she spoke, Fenton's private limo turned into the hospital parking lot.

"Go," Casey urged Claire.

Claire leashed up Hero and was out of the car in a minute. They quickly crossed the parking lot, cutting through the rows of cars and reaching the hospital entrance at the same time as the limo did.

The limo stopped, and Fenton emerged, followed by Mercer and his wife, and two assigned security guards whose job it was to ward off the press and leave a clear path for the congressman to do what he'd come here to do.

Claire glanced down at Hero and issued a quiet command.

Instantly, Hero bounded forward, nearly colliding with the congressman's legs before Claire regained control of him.

"I'm so sorry, sir," she said to Mercer, breathless and embarrassed. "My dog got startled by all the excitement. Heel, boy," she instructed the bloodhound.

He sat down—but not before giving the congressman's shoes a thorough sniff.

Mercer chuckled, patting Hero's head. "No harm done. And you've got a pretty impressive dog. I wish my kids listened to me half as well."

By this time, security had backed off and the press was moving in like vultures. So was Fenton, who was a half dozen steps away.

Claire turned her back to them all, Fenton included, so that the only people who could hear her were Mercer and his wife. "My name is Claire Hedgleigh and I'm part of Forensic Instincts," she said in a low tone. "The team and I need to talk with you about the video Amanda Gleason just released. It's important. We wanted to avoid a media frenzy. So we opted to approach you this way."

Mercer looked momentarily surprised, but he recovered like a true politician. "I appreciate your discretion. I'll arrange to have you and your team admitted through the back entrance of the hospital lobby. I'll come find you right after I get my blood test."

Claire nodded. "Thank you." With that, she raised her voice to a normal level. "Again, I apologize, Congressman." she said. "My overexuberant dog and I will get out of your way now."

By this time, Fenton had walked around to join them, and she could feel his stare boring right through her. Talk about negative energy. It permeated the entirety of Fenton's persona. She was not getting the same vibe from the congressman but, then again, this was all a first impression. Claire would have to spend more time around them.

She reversed her steps, half watching the congressman as he waved at the crowd and called out that he'd answer questions after he and his wife had finished up in the hospital lab.

Reminded, yet again, why she hated politics, Claire tightened her grip on Hero's leash and jogged the remaining distance to the van.

"We're all set," she told Casey and Marc as she and Hero scrambled into the car. "Drive around back. Then let's give it fifteen minutes. Mercer's arranging for us to meet him in the back lobby."

"Nice work," Casey praised. "What did you tell him?"

"Only that we want to talk to him about the video. He got my point loud and clear. We're in the hot seat and we want to know where he factors into that. He was relieved at the discreet way I approached it. That was all I said. The rest was all Hero. Who knew he was such a great actor?" Claire scratched Hero's ears with a smile. "He not only played his part to perfection, he got a good, long sniff of the congressman. Good job, boy." She reached into her pocket and offered him a treat, which he gobbled right up.

"Let's talk about what we hope to accomplish in the five or ten minutes Mercer gives us." Casey shifted the van into Reverse and backed out of the parking space. "We're supposedly very upset about the video. We're really looking to get a read on Congressman Mercer. But we're not going on the attack. We're looking to make Mercer an ally. That'll put him at ease and keep Fenton from erupting."

"Got it, boss," Marc acknowledged drily. "This interview is about subtly figuring out if we think Mercer's relationship with Fenton includes the disappearance of Paul Everett."

"Right. And the way we do that is by sticking to questions about the video. We'll confirm that Mercer has seen it. Then we'll express our concern about the video not only putting us in the limelight, but putting Paul there, as well. We'll explain that, if Paul is in hiding and doesn't want to be found, this will only make him go further underground. We might even ask Mercer for his help in deflecting the attention off Paul and onto the baby. He can make a few public statements urging people to get tested, the way he did, to see if they're a match. I'm sure he'll agree to that."

"And in the meantime, we can read between a lot of lines. Good agenda." Marc gave a brief nod. "It all makes sense."

"I want to hear the most from you, Claire," Casey added. "Not necessarily during the meeting, but after. I want your take on both Mercer and Fenton. I want anything you pick up from them, insights or energy. And I want all our takes on the interaction between Mercer and Fenton. Patrick said they were stiff around each other. Let's see if we share that perception. Are we all on the same page?"

"Sure are," Marc replied.

"Absolutely," Claire echoed.

Hero stayed in the van with the window cracked open while the rest of the team went inside the hospital. A middle-aged man whom Casey recognized as one of Mercer's security guards walked right over to them.

"Please come with me," he said. "The congressman is waiting to speak with you."

He led them into a private office that clearly belonged to one of the hospital administrators, but which was now empty, save the congressman and Lyle Fenton.

"Congressman." Casey shook his hand with a respectful smile, setting the relaxed tone of the meeting. "Thank you so much for seeing us." A quick glance at Lyle. "Hello, Mr. Fenton. Nice to see you again."

"Ms. Woods." He gave a curt nod. "Cliff, this is Casey Woods, Marc Devereaux and..." His brows drew together quizzically.

"Claire Hedgleigh," Mercer supplied with a smile of his own. "Yes, she and I met, along with her bloodhound. Not an easy duo to forget."

Claire leaned forward and shook his hand, making the most of the personal contact. "Again, I apologize for the near collision. I just wanted to get to you without alerting the media."

"No problem. I appreciate your discretion—and your creativity." He shook Marc's hand, as well. "Mr. Devereaux."

"Congressman," Marc replied. "Good to meet you. I hope we didn't scare your wife off."

"Not at all." Mercer didn't miss a beat. "I had her escorted back to the car. The last thing she needs is to sit through another one of my meetings."

"Understood," Marc said with a nod.

"Why don't we all have a seat?" Mercer suggested. "And let's skip the formalities. It takes way too long to say Congressman Mercer every time you address me. It's Cliff."

Casey sank into a chair. "And we're Casey, Marc and Claire. You also met Hero. We're all part of Forensic Instincts."

"Yes, the name I've seen on every TV crew monitor I've walked past today."

That took care of ensuring Mercer had seen the YouTube video.

"Exactly," Casey confirmed, the smile vanishing from her face. "I'm sure you can understand how unhappy that video made us. We're trying very hard to fly under the radar." Another quick glance at Fenton. "I don't know how much you've filled Cliff in on."

Fenton looked as stiff as he had last night, and even more aloof after the tension generated by their conversation. "About your hunt for Paul Everett? Little to nothing. Cliff and I have been discussing Amanda and her baby. We both saw the video. Frankly, I was surprised you'd given Amanda permission to use your company as a contact point."

"Actually, we didn't. We didn't even know about the video until this morning. We were as surprised as you were." Casey carefully watched Fenton's expression. His gaze was still averted from hers, but he didn't fidget or exhibit any increased signs of uneasiness. Fine. He hadn't known Amanda was making that video. No shocker there. It wasn't part of his agenda. Very little Amanda did was—except saving her son. On the other hand, if, thanks to the video, Paul should crawl out of the woodwork, Fenton would be all over it like white on rice. So, if anything, Amanda had aided her uncle without realizing it.

Which meant he'd be sticking close to his niece—and keeping closer tabs on Forensic Instincts.

"This whole situation with Amanda and her baby is tragic," Cliff Mercer said. "She's a wonderful young woman, and a very talented photojournalist. She covered my campaign when I ran for reelection. My heart goes out to her."

Mercer was setting the stage, beginning by letting them know he had a good relationship with Amanda Gleason—a *working* relationship.

"What you did for her today was a kind and generous thing," Casey continued. "Not many public servants show that much compassion for one of their constituents."

A shrug. "As I said, I know Amanda. I consider her a valued colleague. Plus, I had very little to do. Giving blood is something I do regularly anyway. In this case, it was even more essential. It's a long shot that I'll be a match. Lyle and I both know that. But maybe it will set a precedent for others to do the same."

"That's what we're hoping," Fenton added. "I was about to offer a reward to the person who wound up being a donor match. But Amanda is convinced that person will be Paul. Besides, Cliff's gesture is much warmer and more personal than writing a check. I think it will touch people and make them take action."

Casey wondered if they'd run lines together. This certainly seemed like a scripted performance.

"What can I do to help counter the impact of that video?" Mercer asked. "I could have the calls routed to my office, to take some of the burden off you."

Right. And to make sure any leads went first to Fenton.

"That won't be necessary, although we appreciate the offer," Marc put in. "We've already put a bank of receptionists into place and routed the overflow to a call center we've hired. This way, we won't miss any leads, but we'll take the burden off our office."

"Then how can I help?"

"We were hoping you could continue to draw attention to the importance of being tested to see if there's a match for Justin," Claire said in that gentle, sensitive tone of hers. "Maybe make a statement about that to the press. Shift the emphasis off finding Paul Everett to saving an infant's life. That will ease the pressure off our investigation and onto Justin, where it belongs."

Mercer looked puzzled. "I have no problem doing that. But why would you want to downplay the search for Justin's father? Isn't he the best hope for a donor match?"

"Yes," Casey replied. "But he's also a controversial figure right now. The circumstances of his disappearance—or what was presumed to be his death—means that something criminal went on. We need to find out if that criminal activity happened *to* Everett or was made to happen *by* Everett. Either way, the last thing we need to do is to alert the wrong people to the fact that he's being hunted down by a professional investigative team."

"I see your point." Mercer nodded. "But hasn't that ship sailed already?"

"To a point, yes, thanks to the first three or four hours during which time the video went viral. But we've already done damage control on that front. We've worked with Amanda and substituted the toll-free number for ours and eliminated our contact information from the video. So if you check out YouTube now, you'll see a different message at the bottom. The phone calls and the connection to FI should start petering out."

"I see." Mercer's gaze flickered ever so briefly to Fenton's. "Then of course I'll help you. I'll issue statements to everyone out there, and send written statements to the rest of the press. I'll also be on live TV in—" he checked his watch "—seventeen minutes. I'll stress Justin's predicament and I'll have the stations air the toll-free number, if you give it to me."

"Thank you so much, Cliff." Claire was studying him as she spoke. "This could make all the difference in saving Justin's life."

"I hope so." Mercer rose. "So unless there's anything else?"

"Just one quick question," Casey said swiftly. "Mr. Fenton told us you barely knew Paul Everett. So I realize there's not much you can tell us. But it's clear to me that you're a good judge of character. When you met Everett, did you sense anything about him that made you uncomfortable or suspicious?"

Okay, it didn't take a psychic to sense the tension in the room. Mercer cleared his throat and blinked a few times. And Lyle Fenton looked pissed as hell.

Mercer recovered first.

"As you said, I met Paul Everett once, maybe twice. He was an enthusiastic supporter, which explains why he was at the campaign party where he met Amanda. We were introduced, he spoke highly of me and my political platform, and that was it. He seemed friendly, personable and intelligent. That's about all I can tell you. I didn't sense anything off-putting about him. Then again, I doubt he'd show that side of himself to me if it existed. He wanted my support in the construction of his hotel."

"That's true." Casey backed off as fast as she had started. She'd gotten what she needed. Now it was time to part friends. She never knew when they'd need to speak to Mercer again—as an ally or an adversary.

"I appreciate your time, Cliff," she said. "We'll leave the way we came. And thank you so much for helping us out."

"My pleasure," the congressman replied.

Hardly, Casey thought. *I wish I could be a fly on the wall when we leave you and Fenton alone.*

CHAPTER SIXTEEN

The Forensic Instincts team had just driven out of the hospital parking lot when Casey's cell phone rang.

The caller ID flashed *Unknown*.

Glancing at the other occupants of the van, Casey pressed the button on her steering wheel.

"Casey Woods."

"Ms. Woods, this is Detective Jones of the New York State Police's Bureau of Criminal Investigation. I need to speak with you about the case you're currently working on—the one that involves Paul Everett's homicide."

Casey slowed down the van and pulled over to the curb. "May I ask why, Detective?"

"I'd rather not get into details on the phone. When can I meet with you at your office? Time is of the essence."

Casey could have told him that she was driving by his

neck of the woods right there in Long Island. But she didn't. "I'm out of the office right now," she said instead. "I won't be back for several hours."

"I see." Jones cleared his throat. He was dying to ask her where she was and why. Casey could sense it as clearly as if he had spoken. Just as she had a strong hunch that he knew exactly what she was working on.

"Would it be easier to meet outside the office?" she asked, intentionally letting him know it would be closer to his troop. "I assume you're located in Suffolk County."

"Yes, in Farmingdale."

"Republic Airport?" Casey asked, specifying the headquarters of Troop L, which handled all of Nassau and Suffolk Counties.

"That's right."

"There's a Starbucks nearby. Why don't we meet there at..." She glanced at the digital clock on the dashboard. It was almost noon. "One-fifteen?"

"That would be fine."

"See you then."

The doorbell at the FI brownstone rang.

It struck Ryan that it had probably rung a bunch of times before it registered with him. He'd been staring at the computer screen, lost in his own world. But the insistence of the rings told him someone had been standing on the doorstep for quite a while.

He glanced up at the monitor above his desk and focused on the center window, which displayed the live feed from the video surveillance camera that protected the front door. A tall guy, whose powerful build and authoritative presence dominated the camera lens, stood outside. Ryan's brows arched in surprise, and he rose, heading upstairs to the main level.

"Hang on," he called out. "I'm coming."

He punched the code on the Hirsch pad and opened the door. "Hey," he greeted Hutch, gripping his hand in a guy-to-guy handshake. "What's this—a surprise visit?"

"Nope." Hutch walked in and dropped his bag on the floor. "Just a surprise arrival time. My flight got in early."

"Good afternoon, Hutch," Yoda chimed in. "Your body temperature is low. A coat is required in winter weather. You must not be wearing one. A cup of tea will restore your body temperature to a normal 98.6."

"Thanks, Yoda," Hutch responded. "I'll take a hot shower instead."

"A satisfactory cure."

"What do you mean this isn't a surprise visit?" Ryan interrupted. "Casey knew you were coming?"

"Yup. Since yesterday."

Ryan rolled his eyes. "Nobody tells me anything."

"I wouldn't take it personally." Hutch gave him a sympathetic pat on the shoulder. "Considering how wound up Casey sounded when I talked to her on the phone, I'm guessing she's obsessing over the case you're working on. It sounds like a real house of cards."

Again, Ryan's brows rose. Casey was a stickler for not discussing ongoing cases, not even with Hutch. "She told you about it?"

"Not a chance. I just heard that intense note in her voice. So I looked up FI on Google just before I jumped on the plane to see if there was any new media buzzing around your company. And I found that YouTube video. Doesn't sound like the kind of advertising you normally do. I'm guessing it was your client's idea?"

"Oh, yeah. It came at us out of left field. Just ask Yoda. He woke me up right after I'd pulled an all-nighter. Our client almost fried my communications server."

"That's correct," Yoda supplied.

"Anyway, it's under control now. If you check out the video, you'll see a change in contact info. Casey saw to that in a New York minute."

"I'm sure she did." Hutch's lips twisted into a crooked grin—the only thing that ever softened his hard features. He looked every bit like the D.C. cop he'd been before joining the Bureau, right down to the jagged scar across his left temple. Despite his dry sense of humor, he was self-contained in a way that made most people squirm. He had a way of staring people down and waiting them out, staying silent until they felt compelled to speak. It was an asset in his professional life, and it spilled over into his personal life.

Hutch was very much an enigma. He kept his emotions in check and revealed very little of himself to others.

Casey was the exception to that rule.

"After Casey twisted your client's arm to get FI's name and number off that video, did she also ream her out?" Hutch asked.

Ryan shook his head. "She and I were too ripping pissed to deal with Amanda. Casey sent Marc over to the hospital to handle things. He has some magical, soothing effect on our client. She holds on to him like a life preserver."

"That shouldn't surprise you. Between that solid, calming way of Marc's and his feelings about little ones with their lives on the line—he'd be your go-to guy with this client."

"Yeah, I know." Ryan stretched, getting the kinks out of his body. "I wish I could get into more detail with you. This case is really gut-wrenching."

"Aren't they all?"

"Some more than others."

"I hear you." Hutch's sharp blue eyes swept the area. "I take it Casey's not here."

"Nope. Just me and my to-do list. Casey's out working the case with Marc, Claire and Hero, and Patrick's pounding the pavement. What time is she expecting you?"

"We have a dinner date. Till then, I'm on my own. Which is fine with me, because I'm beat. I slept a little on the plane, but not enough to make a difference. I think I'm going to crash in Casey's room, and then take that shower so I can be human when she gets home."

"Good plan. I'm taking a break myself. I'll be heading over to the gym. I need a two-hour workout to get my brain in gear—but I'll settle for one. The fallout from Yoda's phone call robbed me of that second hour."

"An unfortunate necessity, Ryan," Yoda said. "I apologize."

"No apology necessary, Yoda. You did the right thing. Then again, I programmed you."

"Again, that's correct."

"In any case," Ryan told Hutch. "My brain is on overload. Time to pump some iron."

Hutch nodded. Everyone knew what a gym rat Ryan was. Hutch just found it amazing that his full-scale workouts plus his eight hours of sleep a night left him time to be as productive as he was. But the guy managed to do it all, and do it better than any technology pro Hutch had ever seen in action.

"You need my key?" Ryan asked. "You'll either have to go out for food or get something delivered. I doubt Casey has much in her fridge."

"Nah. I'd rather sleep. I'll make up for the lack of food at dinner." Hutch picked up his overnight bag, yawning as he did. "Oh, and Yoda? I promise to use warm blankets. My body temp will rise in no time."

"Very good, Hutch."

Hutch headed for the stairs. "Enjoy your workout," he called over his shoulder to Ryan. "I'll see you in a couple of hours."

The two men met in a private office. Neither of them was happy.

"Have you seen the video?" The stockier of the two wasted no time on small talk.

"Yeah, I've seen it" was the equally terse reply.

"We've got a problem."

"I know. A big one."

"We need to have that video blocked. We can't risk him seeing it."

"That's no problem. He won't. But the rest of the world already has. Someone's going to say something to him. It's just a matter of time—and probably not a lot of it."

"Have him isolated," was the order. "And fast. It's the only way."

The second man nodded. "I'll figure something out and make it happen."

"Make it happen today."

★ ★ ★

The Starbucks near Republic Airport was crowded just like every other Starbucks Casey had ever been in. She sometimes wondered if the regulars actually lived there with their laptops, having their first cup of Pike Place at 6:00 a.m. and their final decaf latte at closing time, all the while clinging to the brownies and the Wi-Fi until they were forcibly removed from the store. It was even worse now, since it was lunchtime, which meant that there was a line for paninis that spilled out into the street.

Casey scanned the packed café, wondering how she was ever going to find the man they were here to see.

She needn't have worried. He found them.

Even in the lunchtime crush, Detective Jones had spotted the FI team and was now gesturing them over to the table he'd obviously claimed a long time ago. His venti coffee cup was sitting on the table, half-empty, along with a partially eaten blueberry scone and an official-looking manila folder. Customers were glaring at him and the three extra chairs at his table as they passed by, but he ignored them. And the few patrons who went up to the counter to complain were spoken quietly to, after which they shut their mouths and went away.

Okay, so the staff knew who and what Jones was. And no one wanted to mess with the State Police.

Jones was a middle-aged guy with a lean build and a balding head. He was wearing a white shirt and a staid red tie with dark blue stripes. The BCI were plainclothes detectives, and Jones epitomized the word *average.*

"Thank you for coming on such short notice," he began after the introductions had been made and everyone was sitting down. He cast a dubious eye at the long line of patrons. "Did you want some coffee?"

Casey followed his gaze to the line of people snaking from the door to the counter, and she gave a wry grin. "Not unless we want to postpone this meeting for a week. Let's get down to business. Why did you want to see us?"

Jones interlaced his fingers in front of him. "You're conducting an investigation into Paul Everett. More specifically, *finding* Paul Everett. I personally closed that file. So I'd like to know what makes you believe he's alive. Did you find something we may have missed?"

"I assume this conversation was prompted by the YouTube video?"

"Yes. It's pretty hard to miss."

"We didn't make it or give our consent to have it made," Casey clarified. "It was all done by our client on her own initiative. We didn't even know the video existed until after the fact."

"Why was your contact information withdrawn and replaced by a toll-free number?"

"For privacy and proper handling of phone calls." It was Marc who answered. "Trust me, Detective, if there were any content issues, we would have demanded the video be pulled—or dropped our client. We've done neither. Now that the cat's out of the bag, we're just hoping the video brings in more donors to check for possible matches—a long shot, but one that we agreed could at least make Amanda feel like she's doing something."

"So my question remains," Jones said. "Do you believe that Paul Everett is alive?"

"Yes," Casey stated flatly.

"What proof do you have?"

"We have a photo of a man that our facial recognition software tells us is Everett—a photo that was taken within the past few weeks. We have at least one person who believes she's seen Everett regularly and recently. And we have strong professional gut instincts that convince us he's alive."

"Gut instincts?" Jones's brows went up. "That hardly constitutes evidence. What are you basing these instincts on?"

"Experience—and me." Claire spoke up for the first time. "I don't know how much research you've done into the FI team, Detective Jones. But I suspect it was thorough. In which case, you know that I'm an intuitive. And there's not a doubt in my mind that Paul Everett is alive."

There was that typical look of skepticism that Claire had learned to expect—and to ignore.

"We're a private investigative firm, Detective Jones," Casey reminded him. "You require hard evidence. We don't. We're not going to court. We're trying to find a dying infant's father." She leaned forward, propping her elbows on the table and folding her hands under her chin in an aggressive stance. "But let me turn the tables. What solid evidence do you have that Paul Everett is dead?"

Jones's eyes narrowed. "I believe you called and made some police inquiries already. So you have your answers."

"I do. And everything I heard was speculative, suggesting, but not proving, a no-body homicide. Without a corpse, all you can do is draw a logical conclusion. But not a concrete one."

That one made Jones visibly uncomfortable. "Is your theory that the man's been walking around with amnesia for the past eight months? Or that he's in hiding?"

"Amnesia isn't really on the table," Marc replied with the same note of sarcasm in his tone as Jones had. "Other than that, anything is possible. I'm sure you checked out Everett's background, his business dealings, his potential enemies and his friends and colleagues. There could be dozens of reasons for his disappearance. But, frankly, that's your problem. Ours is just finding him."

Jones's eyes narrowed slightly. "Withholding evidence is a crime, Mr. Devereaux."

"And discussing our case is unethical, Detective Jones. Casey just told you the only solid evidence we have. If we had more, we'd be sharing it with you. I was an FBI agent. I know the law."

Casey had to bite back a smile on that one. Marc knew the law, all right. He also knew how to break it.

"We're the least of your concerns, Detective," Casey said aloud. "We have no plans of hiding any evidence from you that we stumble upon. But we will keep hunting down Paul Everett. And I believe we'll find him. In the meantime, you have more pressing problems to contend with. A few hours ago, Congressman Mercer met with the media and made a personal appeal to find blood donors for our client's infant son—an appeal that will make the evening news cycle. Once that happens, and once people start putting together the YouTube video and the congressman's plea, your phone will be ringing off the hook. So I hope you have all your ducks in a row—and a good media person. You're going to need it."

Jones's lips tightened. "Thank you for the advice, Ms. Woods."

"Anytime." Casey rose, placing her business card on the table. "Call us if you have any further questions. And we'll do the same with you."

Jones watched Casey, Marc and Claire leave. He waited until they'd walked their bloodhound, then climbed into their van and driven away.

He entered a number on his cell phone and pressed Send.

"It's Jones," he said when the call was answered. "Consider this a heads-up. This Forensic Instincts team has skills and smarts. They're not giving up. And they're putting the pieces together. I'm doing my part. I'll beef up my file and run as much interference as you want me to. But I'm telling you now, you don't have much time." He paused. "And neither do I."

"We're making a lot of people nervous," Casey stated as she accelerated onto the highway and headed for home. "Fenton. Mercer. The cops."

"Do you think Jones's division is just worrying about covering their asses, or do you think there's more here?" Marc asked. "Jones could be dirty."

"Everybody's beginning to feel dirty," Claire said in exasperation. "I haven't had a positive feeling all day—except when the Mercers gave blood."

"You think Cliff Mercer is a match?"

Claire shugged. "I have no idea. That's not what I meant. I just meant I had a sense that he was glad to help, even if he wasn't too happy about the reasons why."

"What else did you pick up on?"

"A slew of conflicting emotions. When I shook his hand,

my palm was actually burning. He was nervous, worried, resigned, caring in an ambiguous way and trapped in a tangled web, partially of his making." Claire chewed her lip thoughtfully. "There's no doubt that he's in Fenton's pocket, or that he has a personal tie to Fenton. A strong personal tie, which would go along with Ryan's determination that he's Fenton's son. But the real ugliness I picked up on was from Fenton. He's one cold, single-minded man."

"Capable of murder?" Marc asked.

Claire blew out a breath. "I can't answer that. Everyone's capable of murder. But has he committed one? I don't know. All I can sense is how guilty he feels, which is not at all. If he committed a crime but feels no regret, there's less explicit energy for me to pick up on. But negative energy? That's there in abundance. And, for the record, Hero didn't like him much, either. He barely glanced at Fenton when he walked over to Mercer in the parking lot. On the other hand, he sniffed Mercer out thoroughly. No negative reaction there. Just a good memorization."

"I'd have to agree with Claire's assessment," Marc said. "Mercer's smooth. But I don't see an evil guy. I'm sure he's way deep into Daddy's pocket. But that's not our problem. Paul Everett is our problem. And I just don't see Mercer having anything to do with his disappearance—at least not directly."

"Nor do I." Casey frowned. "But we're missing something here. I just don't know what. And without figuring out what that something is, we're not going to find Paul Everett."

CHAPTER SEVENTEEN

Ryan came upstairs the minute he heard the team's voices in the front hallway.

"Anything?" he asked, squatting down to roughhouse with Hero.

"Yes and no." Casey filled him in on what happened at the hospital and on the surprise phone call and meeting with Detective Jones.

"We're worrying the cops." Ryan rose, a speculative expression on his face. "That's interesting. Especially since I can't find a damned thing on Everett that doesn't make him sound like a Boy Scout—other than those periodic bank withdrawals. Same thing with Morano. But, clearly something exists. So I say we use the little critter to check out Morano's office. It's time to figure out what's going on—who he meets with, what his relationships are with his contractors, and who might be extorting twenty grand from him every six weeks."

"Ah, Gecko." Casey grinned. "I was wondering when you might use him."

"The little critter" as Ryan affectionately dubbed him—or "Gecko" to the rest of the team—was one of Ryan's most prized robotic creations. It looked a little odd, but what it lacked in appearance, it made up for in versatility and talent.

Gecko had suction-cup-like attachments on his feet and was small enough—not quite the size of a paperback book—and technologically sophisticated enough to walk up walls and inside ductwork. It sported miniature video cameras and microphones, and Ryan could manipulate it in any one of a dozen ways, including around corners.

All he had to do was get access to Morano's office and plant Gecko in an air duct or drop ceiling, then watch and listen from his laptop.

Breaking into an old, one-story wooden dump would be a piece of cake for Marc. He and Ryan would drive to Morano's place at night, Ryan would park the van a safe distance away, and Marc would do his thing. After that, they'd have front row seats to Morano, any visitors he might entertain and any phone calls he decided to make.

It was the perfect idea.

"We'll go late tonight," Marc said as if reading Ryan's mind. "Another road trip. I feel like I'm on autopilot to the Hamptons."

"I'll drive," Ryan said. "And we'll stay over at Amanda's. That way, we can make one more trip to Morano's office in the morning. We'll slap a GPS tracking device under his car. Then we'll know where he is at all times. The guy's entire life will be an open book." Ryan glanced at Casey. "That okay, boss? You're going to be busy anyway."

Casey shot him a look. "And you know this how?"

Ryan jerked his thumb upward. "You've got a guest crashing on your bed. He got in early and tired. But he promised to be refreshed by dinner. So my guess is you'll be occupied all night. It's been how long since the two of you saw each other?"

"Careful, Ryan." Casey's tone was firm, but her lips twitched. "Keep heading in this direction and I'll start spewing what I know about your love life. And it's a lot more interesting than mine. Not to mention the secret crush you have..."

"Okay, okay," Ryan interrupted. "My mouth is shut."

"Now that's a first," Claire commented, looking and sounding a bit thrown by Casey's comment. It had clearly never occurred to her that the team was aware of the whatever-it-was that hovered beneath the sharp banter between her and Ryan. She wasn't even ready to analyze it herself. "I've never seen you at a loss for words."

"I never am." Ryan shot her a lazy grin. "I just know when it's time to talk and when it's not."

Claire flushed, quickly changing the subject. "What's happening at Patrick's end?"

"He called in a while ago," Ryan replied, visibly enjoying watching Claire squirm. "He's seeing what he can do about figuring out who's following us. Then he's going home to spend some time with his wife. He's barely seen her since we took on this case."

"I think we can all use a few hours off," Claire said with a meaningful look at Ryan and Marc. "Let's grab something to eat. Then you two can catch some rest before you head back to the Hamptons, and I can go home and do some yoga. Some of my best insights come to me during that time."

"We could order in, if you want," Ryan suggested. "Hero can't go into restaurants."

"No. We can't order in." Claire's tone and look were so pointed this time that Ryan would have had to be dead not to notice them. "Hero's exhausted from his day. See? He's already sleeping on his favorite blanket. I doubt he'll even venture upstairs."

"Oh. Gotcha." A quick glance at Casey. "We'll catch you later."

Casey was trying hard not to laugh. "For a team of very discreet investigators, you were about as subtle as the Keystone Cops. But thanks. I appreciate the privacy."

Hutch had a towel wrapped around his waist and was briskly drying his hair with another when Casey walked into her bedroom.

"Wow," she said, leaning against the wall. "Is this an early Christmas present?"

He looked up, tossing the towel he was holding aside and giving her that lazy, crooked smile that got to her every time. "It's just the gift wrap. Wanna see what's inside?"

"Sure." She crossed over to him, unknotting the towel from around his waist and letting it drop to the floor. "Very nice," she murmured, gliding her hands up his chest to wrap her arms around his neck. "You have excellent taste in gifts. How did you know what I wanted?"

"I guessed." Hutch stopped talking. He lifted Casey up and pressed her flush against him. His mouth crushed down on hers and she wrapped her legs around his waist, kissing him back with the same heated intensity.

They toppled onto the bed, and he had her naked and under him in record time.

It was always the same. The first time was frantic, filled with the built-up sexual tension of being apart for weeks, sometimes months. Long, drawn-out lovemaking would come later, but right now, it was a wild rush for completion.

Casey tried to delay her climax, but she couldn't. It boiled up inside her the minute Hutch penetrated her body, and by his second thrust, she was crying out, arching to take him deep inside her as her spasms pulsed around him. Hutch didn't even try to fight the inevitable. He just let go, his fists making deep impressions on the pillow as he poured himself into her, throwing back his head and giving a guttural shout.

The silence in the room was punctuated by their shallow, ragged breaths as Hutch blanketed Casey's body with his. A semblance of sanity returned—slowly, in increments—not that either of them cared.

"I hope I'm not crushing you, because I don't think I can move," Hutch murmured into her hair.

"You're not." Casey wrapped her arms around his back, her legs too shaky to follow suit. She turned her face into his neck and kissed him. "By the way, I missed you."

"Yeah, I could tell. As for me, I've been taking cold showers for the past two weeks. A month and a half is just too damned long."

"I agree." Casey gave a sated sigh. "Fair warning. I doubt I'm going to let you rest for any length of time."

"I doubt I'll need to." Hutch propped himself on his elbows, scrutinizing her face. "You look gorgeous all flushed and naked."

Casey smiled. "You're pretty hot yourself." She reached up, brushing his damp hair off his forehead. "I think I undid the positive effects of your shower."

"Not a problem. I'll take another one, this time with company." Hutch kissed her, and what began as a slow, tender kiss soon turned into something more. He rolled onto his back, taking Casey with him, still buried inside her.

Casey pushed herself into a kneeling position, leaning back and deepening their joining, already feeling the familiar tingling of pleasure.

"Did you really want to go out for dinner?" she managed.

"No." Hutch had clutched her hips and was moving her up and down in a motion that took their breath away. "Dinner is highly overrated."

Casey was dead asleep when her cell phone rang.

She reached across Hutch and groped at her nightstand, until her hand made contact with her BlackBerry.

"Casey Woods," she mumbled into the phone.

"Casey?" It was Amanda's voice. And it sounded high and shaky.

Casey was instantly awake. Her first and only thought was Justin. "Amanda? What's wrong?"

"I got a phone call," Amanda said, on the verge of hysteria. "It was a man. His voice was…weird."

"Weird like he was using a voice scrambler? Like he wanted to disguise his identity?"

"I guess. It was as if he were in an echo chamber. But he knew me, Casey. He said my name. He told me what time

I'd come outside the hospital for some air. He told me what I was wearing. And he told me to stop looking for Paul—to tell you to stop looking for Paul."

"Did he threaten you?"

"Not in so many words. But he made it clear that he would be watching us to make sure. He didn't say 'or else.' But his tone of voice did. And, Casey..." Amanda's voice broke. "Right before he hung up, he said that he certainly hopes my son, Justin, gets well. Then he broke the connection. What does that mean? Does he plan on doing something to my baby?"

"It means he was going for your emotional Achilles' heel." Casey's mind was racing. "The more personal he makes this, the more terrified you'll be, and the more apt to listen to his demands. He's trying to scare you, Amanda, but he's the one who's scared. We're getting close. If anything, that's good news, not bad." She paused. "How long ago did he call?"

"Two minutes ago. I called you the instant he hung up. And there was no caller ID. It said *Unavailable.*"

"Check your phone again—but not for a caller ID. Do you have any missed calls? Messages?"

"I checked as soon as I got to the general waiting area where I was allowed to turn on my cell phone." Amanda was holding herself together by a hair. "There were no missed calls. A few messages from friends and a couple of pushy ones from the press. No hang-ups. Why?"

"Did this man call you right then—as soon as you turned on your phone?"

"As I was checking my last message."

"Then I'm guessing that either he or someone who's working with him is inside the hospital. It's the only way he'd know exactly when you were reachable."

"Oh, my God." Amanda lost it again. "That means he's close to Justin."

"Sloane Kettering is a big hospital." Casey battled Amanda's understandable panic. "He could be in any one of dozens of places and still keep you in his sight." Casey dragged a hand through her tangled mane of hair. "But we won't take any chances. I'll call Patrick and have him stand guard outside the PICU."

"Why Patrick? Why not Marc?"

"Because Patrick is the right person for this job. Before he joined Forensic Instincts, he was a security consultant for law enforcement and private companies—big ones. He's consulted for the NYPD, the FBI and a long list of other entities. And, before that, he was an FBI agent for over thirty years. No one will get by him."

"I'm sorry..." Amanda inhaled sharply. "It's just that..."

"I know you trust Marc. But trust all of us. Trust me. When I say Patrick's the one you want, he is."

"You're right. And I do trust you. I'm just a wreck." Another attempt at a calming breath. "When can Patrick get here?"

"I'll call him right now." Casey remembered Claire saying that Patrick had gone home to spend time with his wife. And home for Patrick was in Hoboken, New Jersey, a short ride through the Holland Tunnel and into Manhattan. "He'll be there within the hour. And I'm going to see what Ryan can get off your cell records. My guess is nothing, if this guy is a pro. But it can't hurt to try. And, Amanda, remember, no one's interested in hurting you or Justin. They just want to protect whatever secret it is they have—and that secret involves Paul. So keep a low profile. No more videos. No public statements. Let us take the lead and the risk."

"I will."

Casey disconnected the call and pressed Patrick's speed dial number. By the time they hung up, he was halfway out the door, on his way to Sloane Kettering.

Casey flopped back against the pillows with a heavy sigh.

"You okay?" Hutch asked, rolling onto his side and propping himself on one elbow.

"Frustrated."

"Then I didn't do as good a job as I thought."

Casey smiled. "Yes, you did. That's the only way I'm not frustrated. But this damned case..."

"Do you want to talk about it?" Hutch asked, playing with a strand of Casey's red hair. He was as respectful as she about not overstepping his bounds with her cases—at least until he sensed she was in danger. Then all bets were off. Casey often muttered that he was a caveman, although they both knew that wasn't true. Hutch was the furthest thing from sexist. His longtime BAU partner, Grace, was female, and they worked together seamlessly and respectfully. But Grace was a trained law enforcement agent. Casey wasn't. And Hutch had just seen way too much, first as a D.C. cop, then as a BU agent, to be okay with Casey throwing herself smack in the middle of big-time danger.

Unfortunately, that's what she always seemed to do.

"You know a lot of it already, thanks to YouTube," Casey said now, still staring at the ceiling with a troubled expression on her face. "Amanda Gleason's baby has a life-threatening autoimmune disease. He needs a stem cell transplant. No donor match has been found. His best chance of survival is his father. FI's job is to find that father—Paul Everett."

Hutch arched a brow. "Now why don't I think it's that simple?"

"Because you just heard me on the phone. And because your instincts are almost as good as mine."

"Thanks for the compliment," Hutch said drily. "How much can you tell me without violating client confidentiality?"

"I can tell you that Paul Everett is supposedly dead, the victim of a no-body homicide. That's the official police report. I can tell you the cops found his abandoned car, complete with a fair amount of his blood on the driver's seat, just east of the Hamptons on Long Island. And I can tell you that no one on my team believes that he's dead."

Hutch didn't need time to digest that speech. "That last part is the only thing we need to discuss—or not discuss. The rest is all fact, not investigative work."

Casey nodded, chewing her lip thoughtfully. Then, she angled her head toward Hutch. "I need to speak to my client. But, hypothetically, if I asked you to check someone out and see if they were on the FBI's radar for some criminal act, or because of some criminal act, could you?"

"You're not sure if this someone is an offender or a victim—hypothetically."

"Right."

"I could check our system, sure. If there's a federal crime involved, the BU would be as eager to solve it as you are."

"Then let me get Amanda's permission. I'm sure she'll jump at the offer. This isn't the kind of case she wants to keep under wraps. The sooner we find Paul, the better chance that Justin, her baby, will make it—assuming Paul's a healthy donor match. But from what I understand, the odds are good."

"I take it Amanda's not a match?"

"She's not eligible to be tested for health reasons," Casey replied carefully.

"Got it." Hutch studied Casey's face, a knowing glint in his eyes. "Go ahead and call your client. You won't get any sleep until you do. And, for what I have in mind, you need your sleep to recoup your strength."

CHAPTER EIGHTEEN

Ryan turned off the headlights as he slowed the van to a crawl, then pulled onto a deserted stretch of the Shinnecock Bay shoreline, just around the bend from the marina.

Marc was peering through his night-vision binoculars. "No one's around," he announced.

"What a surprise." Ryan grinned. "It's after 1:00 a.m. on a December night. Who wouldn't be basking on the beach?"

"I wasn't looking for sunbathers, smart-ass. I was looking for pot-smoking kids and anyone else who might want a dark, deserted spot to do their thing."

"The idea of kids smoking up or drug dealers doing business here—that I get. But you'd have to be really desperate to choose this spot to hop in the backseat and get laid. On the other hand, hormones do trump atmosphere when you're a teenager."

"Yup." Marc put down the binoculars. "You take Gecko. We'll go the rest of the way on foot. Although, like I said in the van, I doubt I'll need you. This is a one-story shack, not an office complex. You won't have to get access to the roof and feed Gecko down. I'll just jimmy my way in, unscrew a return and put the little critter in."

"Uh..."

"I know. No one touches Gecko but you."

"True. But it's not just that. I need to find a good location to plant my black box. It will pick up Gecko's video and audio feeds, encrypt them and route them over the internet using a secure tunnel between the black box and the Forensic Instincts firewall."

"Fine, whatever. Let's just get moving."

They climbed out of the van, both dressed in black, Marc with a fanny pack of tools, Ryan with Gecko. Staying low, they made their way toward Morano's cabin.

Abruptly, Marc came to a dead halt.

"Wait," he whispered, stretching his arm across Ryan to block him from proceeding.

Ryan obeyed, his head snapping around in surprise. "What is it?"

"Someone's coming." A pause. "A truck."

Ryan didn't question Marc's keen sense of hearing. No one on the team did. These were the moments when Marc was pure Navy SEAL.

"Is it headed in this direction?" Ryan asked in a low tone.

"Yeah. Listen. You'll hear the diesel engine in a minute."

A few moments later, Ryan heard precisely what Marc had described—the low roar of a diesel engine. The two of them crouched low to the ground as the headlights of a pickup truck drew closer to where they hid.

It stopped diagonally across the street from Morano's office, and the driver cut the motor.

"What the hell…?" Ryan muttered. "Why is someone here? We know Morano's not in the office. He's home. We checked, and saw him walking around his apartment. Those high-tech binoculars of yours don't lie. So who's here and why?"

"It's two 'who's,'" Marc identified. "I can see by the movement in the truck. As for why, we're about to find out."

Two shadowy figures emerged from the pickup truck and walked rapidly but stiltedly toward Morano's shack. "They're both carrying something," Marc added in a low voice. "Something heavy enough to be weighing them down. Maybe this is a drop-off of some kind?"

"I wish Gecko and the black box were already in place," Ryan said in frustration. "Then we'd know what they're up to."

"We'll figure it out. If they leave Morano's office without whatever their cargo is, we'll find it when we get inside and see what it is."

They fell silent and waited.

One of the men put down whatever he was carrying and hunched over the front door, concentrating. The other made his way around the back of the cabin.

"We can assume that Morano wasn't expecting them," Marc noted. "Since the guy out front is picking the lock. This wasn't prearranged." Marc gave a knowing grunt as the door opened and the man went inside. "Like I said, a piece of cake. A friggin' baby could get into that dump." A puzzled pause. "What's the other guy doing? There's no back door."

"Maybe he's climbing in a window?" Ryan suggested. "There must be at least one of those, or Morano would suffocate."

"Yeah, there are. Two windows. But it doesn't make sense. Even if he planned on jimmying one of them open, why bother now, especially lugging a heavy load? His partner could just whistle, letting him know he was in. Then the other guy could come around front, get inside ASAP and drop off whatever it is they came here to leave."

As Marc spoke, the second man reappeared, walking slowly around the perimeter of the shack. He was leaning forward, taking a few steps at a time, and sprinkling something from whatever it was he'd carried over.

"Gasoline," Marc diagnosed instantly. "He's pouring it all around the shack."

"I smell it." Ryan stifled a cough. "Shit, they're going to torch the place. What are we supposed to do?"

As he spoke, the first guy came running out of the cabin. Simultaneously, a light began flickering inside.

"He already lit something inside—probably a stack of paper or a pile of rags. That dump is a walking fire hazard." Marc grabbed Ryan's arm. "It's too late to do anything. That shack is gonna go up like a forest fire. Let's get the hell out of here." He tightened his grip, as he felt Ryan make an instinctive move to stand up and run. "No. Stay down. They're taking off at the same time as we are. They'll see us. Time to show me what you've got. Run like a duck."

As he spoke, the shack ignited. Just the way Marc said,

it erupted like a volcano, flames shooting skyward, wood burning like paper.

Ryan saw the two offenders race for their pickup truck.

He pivoted and followed Marc's lead, pausing only long enough to get a glimpse of what was involved. Marc remained squatting, and used his thigh muscles to take long strides away from the impending explosion.

Ryan followed suit, staying low to the ground and directly behind Marc.

They reached the van just as the pickup truck sped by. The diesel blocked out any other sound, and the two men didn't even glance out the window, much less see Marc or Ryan.

Ryan crept around to the driver's side, and Marc half rose, staring at the back of the truck, trying to make out the grime-covered license plate. He could barely catch one number and one letter, it was so dark. Ironically, the thing that helped him see was the eerie light burning from behind them as the cabin burned to the ground.

"They're gone. Get in," Marc commanded. He and Ryan jumped into the van. Ryan backed it up and swerved out of their hiding spot and onto the road, speeding away from the fire as far and as fast as he could.

Marc was on his secure cell phone, calling 9-1-1. "I'm on the Hampton Bays side of Shinnecock Bay, off Lynn Avenue. There's a fire at the marina. It looks bad. Send someone over ASAP." He disconnected the call. "That takes care of that."

"Shit." Ryan dragged a sleeve across his forehead, sounding off balance and exhilarated at the same time. "That was like something out of a movie."

A corner of Marc's mouth lifted. "If you say so."

Ryan gave him a sideways glance. "I guess that sounded pretty lame to you. I can BASE jump with the best of them. I'm just used to doing extreme sports for fun. I'm not used to doing military exercises to escape midnight arsonists."

"You performed well under pressure." Marc's official-sounding praise was genuine. "You're in great physical shape. And don't kid yourself. You might get good at things like this, but you never get used to them. Violence is still violence."

"Shit," Ryan reiterated. "Either that hotel project is jinxed, or there's something attached to it that makes the developer a target for killers."

Marc nodded. "Which seems to support the theory that Paul Everett was a victim, not a participant. Someone wanted him out of the way."

"Out of the way, but not dead. And now they're following suit with Morano." Ryan exhaled sharply. "This gets weirder and sketchier by the minute."

"Yeah." Marc looked thoughtful. "I think we'd better head over to Morano's now and plant that tracker on his car. Once the firefighters rush over here to douse the pile of rubble that Morano's office will soon be, and the cops show up to investigate, they'll call the owner. And Morano will be down here like Greased Lightning."

"Agreed. Not a good idea to plant a GPS tracking device with a swarm of cops and the owner of the car in your face. Let's head straight over to Morano's place before we drive to Westhampton Beach and crash at Amanda's. We can be at Morano's apartment in ten minutes and done and out of there in twenty."

★★★

Ryan and Marc had just finished their task and hiked up the flight of stairs to Amanda's apartment when Ryan's cell phone rang.

He glanced down at the caller ID.

"It's Claire," he told Marc. Punching on the phone, he answered Claire in a short, clipped tone. "Hang on a sec."

He waited until both he and Marc were inside the apartment, before resuming the conversation.

"What's up?" he asked.

"Are you okay?" Her voice was tight and anxious.

"Yeah, why?"

"I just got a quick flash that freaked me out. It was a fire, a big one, engulfing a shack on the water. I was afraid it might have something to do with you and Marc and your visit to Morano's. I'm glad I was wrong."

"You weren't wrong." Ryan dropped his gym bag and sank down on the sofa. "Morano's office just went up in flames. And it wasn't caused by a cigarette butt. Marc and I saw two men douse the place with gasoline and light the match."

A sharp intake of breath. "Who were they trying to kill? Morano or you two?"

"None of the above. Morano was at home—we knew that and I'm sure they did, too. And they never saw Marc or me. We hid out until they were gone. Then we got the hell out of there."

"So you weren't near the cabin when it happened?"

"We were near enough. We got front row seats. But we didn't get roasted."

"That's not funny."

Ryan leaned back on the couch, finding himself smiling.

"You were worried about me, Claire-voyant. I'm touched. I never knew you cared so much."

"I don't," Claire retorted, back to herself now that she knew things were okay. "It was Gecko I was concerned about. He's irreplaceable. I knew Marc could take care of you."

Ryan threw back his head and laughed. "I'm so flattered. But don't worry. We never made it inside the building. And Gecko was safely stashed inside my jacket. He's in A-plus shape—just like me."

"He's not nearly as arrogant."

"True. But he's not as hot, either."

"Debatable," Claire quipped. Then she grew sober. "They were giving Morano a message."

"Yup. A pretty direct one."

"The same one they gave Paul Everett, no doubt. The question is, who are 'they' and do they plan on making a similar disappearing act happen to Morano?"

"Any signs from the universe?" Ryan teased.

"None," Claire answered seriously. "I wish I had one. Maybe it would lead us to Paul Everett faster."

"You're still convinced he's alive?"

"Definitely."

"So am I." Ryan shrugged out of his parka as he spoke. "This kind of thing smacks of the mob. But where does Lyle Fenton fit in?"

"I don't know. But he plays a major part in this convoluted puzzle. The negative energy surrounding him is so strong, I could barely pick up on anything else with him in the room." A pause. "Are you sure that you and Marc are okay?"

"Never better. Marc's a pro when it comes to this stuff. He got us out of there like a black ops mission."

Another pause. "I know Marc's used to seeing arson and every other kind of violence there is. But you're not. You're shaken. That's to be expected, Ryan—even for someone as cocky and egotistical as you."

Ryan started to laugh. "Is that your way of saying you care, Claire-voyant?"

"Yes, you obnoxious pain in the ass, it is."

A split second of silence. Ryan wasn't laughing anymore.

"Thanks," he finally said, with no trace of banter. "I appreciate your worrying about me. But I'm fine. Honest. A little weirded out, but fine. Nothing a hot shower and a good night's sleep won't fix."

"Then I'll let you get both. Tell Marc to do the same. I'll see you tomorrow."

"Claire?" Ryan interrupted.

"Yes?"

This pause was a long one. "See you tomorrow."

He disconnected the call, staring at his BlackBerry for a moment, eyebrows knit.

"Oh, for God's sake, when are you going to stop being an asshole and do something about it?" Marc's question sliced the silence.

"What?" Ryan's head snapped up. He'd almost forgotten Marc was in the room, he'd been so preoccupied.

"You heard me. But if you need it spelled out, fine. You want Claire. You've wanted her since the day you met her. So stop doing this moronic dance and go for it. If it works out, great. If it doesn't, you can go back to killing each other."

Ryan shot Marc a look. “I don’t need lessons in hooking up with women from you.”

“Clearly, you do.” Marc stripped off his jacket and sweater and grabbed the gym bag that had his change of clothes. “I’m going in the shower. I’ll use up the hot water. That way, you can get the cold shower you so desperately need.”

CHAPTER NINETEEN

As he stepped out of the shower, Ryan could hear Marc talking. From the tone of his voice, it was obvious that it was Casey at the other end of the phone. Marc was, no doubt, filling her in.

Ryan pulled on some sweats and headed out to the living room.

Marc glanced up. "Ryan's here. I'll put him on." He handed Ryan the phone. "It's Casey," he informed him.

"I figured." Ryan put the phone to his ear. "Hey, boss. I assume Marc woke you up to report in about our boring night."

"He did—in detail," she replied. "Sounds like you became an instant action figure."

"Hey, you gotta do what you gotta do."

Casey laughed. "It's good to hear you're still yourself. Arrogant and cocky. Thanks for making me laugh. I needed it."

"Really?" Ryan perched on the edge of an armchair. "If I'm your best source of entertainment tonight, I'd say Hutch isn't doing his job."

"His job isn't to make me laugh," Casey returned drily. "So much for that subject. The reason I asked Marc to put you on the phone is to tell you that Amanda got a threatening call tonight. No caller ID. Voice scrambler. Warning her to stop looking for Paul Everett, and for us to stop looking, too. He knew too much about what she was doing at that minute not to have been right there in the hospital."

"You want me to see if I can hack into her phone records?" Ryan jumped right on that. "Maybe I can get something."

"Yes. Try."

"Done." Ryan was already walking over to his laptop, which was sitting on the coffee table. "Is Amanda really freaked out?" he asked as he logged into his secure network.

"Big-time," Casey replied. "She wanted me to send Marc over for protection. I sent Patrick over instead."

"Better qualifications. Better availability," Ryan agreed.

"Not as pacifying, at least to Amanda. But, in this case, I got her to come around. Patrick's the right choice. He took off for Sloane Kettering the minute I called him. He's staying outside the PICU all night. He's also made arrangements with two of his security buddies. They're each taking an eight-hour shift a day. Between the three of them, Amanda will be covered 24/7 until this crisis is over."

"Smart move."

"I'm going over there myself first thing in the morning to check on her."

"You mean in three hours?" Ryan asked, noting that his watch said 3:30 a.m.

Casey sighed. "Yes, in three hours. And, while I'm there, I'm going to ask her if I can bring Hutch on board. He can check the FBI's internal systems and see if there are any warning flags on Paul Everett."

"Good move. I doubt she'll refuse. Hutch's credentials are pretty impressive. Not to mention he's at Quantico. That word alone infuses everyone with awe." Ryan was clicking away on the keyboard as he spoke. "Get a few hours' rest, boss. I'll call you if I find anything. I'm not holding my breath. It was probably a throwaway phone. But, if I'm wrong, you'll hear from me."

Lisa Mercer knew that her father was back in D.C. She also knew that he jogged every morning at 5:30 a.m. So when she got back to her dorm at Northwestern at 4:00 a.m. CST—after cramming all night for finals—and listened to her voice mail, she called him right away.

"Hi, Lisa." The congressman didn't sound a bit surprised to hear from his daughter. It was still 2:30 a.m. in Pasadena, or Tom would be on the phone from Cal Tech, as well.

"What's going on, Dad?" she asked without preamble. "I got your cryptic message. I also read about you and Mom getting tested as donors for that poor little baby, and I think that's superamazing. But why were you calling me about it?"

Cliff Mercer pressed his lips together and sank down onto the bottom step leading into his front hall. He wished he could keep his lips just that way, so he didn't have to open his mouth and dive into this can of worms. But it wasn't an option. His career was on the line. All he could do was to try to keep this as simple and innocent as possible, in the hopes that his secret didn't leak out—not even to his children. They weren't all that close to his father—or rather, the man who'd raised him. But he was the only grandfather they knew. The only person he'd trusted with his secret was Mary Jane. And his wife was as determined as he was to protect it.

As for the rest of the world, if the truth came out, given how deep into Lyle Fenton's pocket he was, his political aspirations would be over before they began.

"Dad?" Lisa repeated.

"Sorry, honey. I was just tying my sneakers. I didn't mean to sound cryptic. It's just that Amanda Gleason, the baby's mother, is a photojournalist who's done media coverage on both my campaign and ongoing events during my current term. She's a real sweetheart. And the idea of her possibly losing her child… It's unthinkable. That's why Mom and I got tested. As a gesture of good faith, I'd like you and Tom to get tested, too. I'm not optimistic that any of us will be a match, but if it inspires others in the district to get tested, it's worth it."

"Knowing you, I'm going to assume this is a gesture of good faith, not a political ploy."

"That's exactly right. I'm not going to use a critically ill infant for political gain."

Lisa sighed. "I'm sorry. This just came at me out of left field. What happens if I'm a match? Do I have to donate an organ or something?"

"Of course not. I'd never ask that of you. It's simply a type of blood transfusion. Nothing more. But we'll cross that bridge if and when we come to it. I can't force you to do this. But I know how bighearted you are. So I wanted to ask."

"It's no problem. I can run over to Evanston Hospital after my last class today. But, Dad, please, no media. No announcements. Just let me do this quietly. If you want to put out a press release about your kids getting tested, just wait until finals are over. Tom's bound to feel the same way. We've got enough on our plates without local reporters banging on our dorm room doors, wanting to interview us about what altruistic kids we are."

"That goes without saying." Cliff rubbed his temples. He felt like the world's shittiest father. "We don't even have to announce this, if you'd prefer. The same goes for Tom. I'm sure I'll be hearing from him in a couple of hours. And I'll tell him exactly what I'm telling you. What you're doing is a wonderful, selfless thing. I'm sure Amanda will be incredibly grateful. How you want it handled—publicly, privately—that's your call."

"Okay." That put Lisa's mind at rest. "I'll take care of it later today. And I'll call you afterward."

"Thank you, sweetheart. You're a great kid."

"Yeah, I think so, too," she quipped. "Talk to you later."

Cliff disconnected the call. By the time he'd finished his run, taken a shower and gotten ready for his day, Tom would be on the phone. He'd go through the whole charade again. It didn't make him feel any better that he wasn't lying about wanting to help Amanda Gleason's critically ill baby. His reasons were still steeped in self-protection. He'd sworn never to be one of those dirty politicians. Yet here he was, being just that.

The whole situation sucked.

Warren Mercer might be a cold SOB.

But Lyle Fenton was a scumbag.

* * *

Patrick walked over as soon as he saw Casey in the PICU waiting room.

"How is she?" Casey asked.

"Not great. Shaky," Patrick replied. "I think the phone call was the straw that broke the camel's back. She was holding on by a thread to begin with. I don't think there's been any improvement in Justin's condition. He's still on the ventilator. And when she got that phone call… Well, you can imagine."

"She knows you're here, though, right?"

"Definitely. She's come out three times in the past few hours to check. She's terrified that someone's going to get by me and hurt her son. We've talked. I think I finally established a rapport with her. I'm not Marc, but I'm kind of a father figure to her, which seems to soothe her. That's why I'm not letting Carl relieve me for the next shift. She's just gotten used to me. I don't want to throw any more changes her way."

Casey patted his arm. "You're a good guy."

"That's true. Maybe you should be paying me more," Patrick replied good-naturedly. "Do you want to see her now?"

Nodding, Casey explained what she was hoping to have Amanda agree to regarding Hutch.

"Excellent idea." Patrick glanced over his shoulder as Amanda appeared outside Justin's room. "Here she comes. You can discuss it with her. I doubt she'll turn you down. The poor woman is desperate."

As he spoke, Amanda caught sight of Casey. She stripped off her sterile attire and walked over. "Hi." It was a tentative greeting, accompanied by a pleading look. "Do you have any news?"

"Not from the phone calls, no. But half the Hamptons population is getting tested, thanks to Congressman Mercer."

A flicker of hope lit Amanda's eyes. "What he did was very kind. I know it was a favor to my uncle, but he did it nonetheless. And his gesture inspired so many others to offer their help. I'm so grateful. I called the congressman's office late yesterday afternoon and asked them to give him my thanks. It would be a miracle if another donor came through. The chances of finding Paul…"

"Are still very strong," Casey finished for her. "We're following up on an unexpected occurrence, one that's too coincidental to ignore. John Morano—the man who took over Paul's hotel project—also took over Paul's office. I don't know if you ever saw it, but it's a shack at the marina on Shinnecock Bay."

"I was there once. Did Paul leave something behind that just now turned up?"

"It's not that. The place burned to the ground last night. And the police don't think it was an accident."

"Someone tried to kill this John Morano?" Amanda gasped.

Casey shook her head. "He wasn't there. It was a warning of some kind. Which leads us to believe that whatever trouble Paul was in somehow related to that project. If we figure out what the connection is, we'll be one step closer to finding Paul."

The hope faded from Amanda's eyes, tears once again dampening her lashes. "An investigation like that could take weeks, maybe more. Justin doesn't have enough time."

"Which is why I'm here." Casey used the opportunity to address what she came here for. "The FI team has a close contact at the FBI. Would you object if I were to share the entirety of your story with him and ask for his help? If Paul is in the federal system—for whatever reason—our contact could try to find that out."

"You really think Paul was involved in a crime," Amanda said sadly. "And now you're thinking even bigger—a federal crime. Who was this man I thought I knew?"

"Don't go there, Amanda," Casey replied. "Yes, we're pretty sure Paul found himself in the middle of some sort of crime. That's no surprise, given the violence of his disappearance. But, as I told you before, it's possible he was a victim, not an offender. We just don't know. And we won't have answers unless we dig deep. I'm asking for your permission to do just that—with the help of a federal agent."

Amanda nodded. "Of course. Get whatever help you need. My life is an open book at this point." She glanced past Casey, her anxious gaze seeking out Patrick, ensuring he was there. "Do you have any leads on the person who called me?"

"Ryan's checking out phone records, but I doubt we'll find anything." Casey didn't try to sugarcoat the facts. "On the other hand, we know that whoever's following us, and now calling you, is hell-bent on keeping us away from Paul. If we understand the 'why,' we'll find the path that leads us to Paul." A compassionate pause. "And stop worrying. Patrick's not going anywhere. He's here for you and for Justin. So concentrate on your son and on staying strong so you can be there for him."

Before Amanda could answer, a monitor from inside the PICU began sounding loudly. The staff all mobilized at once, rushing inside to attend to the emergency.

Dr. Braeburn appeared from another section of the hospital, hurrying into the PICU.

"Justin," Amanda whispered. Sheer terror filled her eyes, and she began running back down the corridor.

The curtains outside Justin's section of the unit had been drawn shut. A nurse was exiting the glass doors to get some medical equipment. She saw Amanda and stopped her in her tracks. "You can't go in there right now."

"Is it Justin?" she demanded. "What's happening?"

"Dr. Braeburn will be out to talk to you as soon as he can. I've got to go back in now to assist him."

"Just tell me what that alarm means."

The nurse was already in motion, heading back toward the room. "It's the ventilator alarm," she supplied. "I'm not sure why it went off. Please, Ms. Gleason, let us do our job."

She disappeared back inside.

"Oh, God." Amanda was trembling from head to toe. "He can't breathe. Justin can't breathe."

Casey and Patrick both hurried to her side.

"Don't anticipate the worst," Casey cautioned, taking Amanda's hands in hers. "These things go off for all kinds of reasons. Not all of those are serious. Let's just wait to hear what the doctor says."

"Casey's right," Patrick concurred. "I've even seen monitors malfunction. So don't let your mind go crazy." He gently patted her shoulder. "I'm sure the doctor will come out as soon as he can."

"It's not a malfunction," Amanda said. "They've been in there too long. Why? What's happening to my baby?"

The door swung open and Dr. Braeburn strode out.

"I can only stay a minute," he told Amanda. "Justin's being prepped for a procedure."

"A procedure." Amanda was as white as a sheet. "What kind of procedure?"

"Justin developed a pneumothorax—a collapsed lung," he explained in simpler terms. "The ventilator can't compensate for that. We have to insert a chest tube to suck the air leakage out of the chest cavity. Once the lung heals, we can remove the tube."

"What if it doesn't..." Amanda began.

"Don't speculate. A pneumothorax isn't uncommon in newborns on ventilators. We caught it right away. And we're doing the procedure immediately." Dr. Braeburn turned to go back inside. "Wait here with your friends. I'll give you an update as soon as the procedure is over. It should take about fifteen minutes."

"Can't I be with him?" Amanda pleaded.

The doctor paused. "Unfortunately, no. This is a sterile medical procedure."

A hard swallow. "Will he be in pain?"

"No. We'll be administering pain medication. Now I really have to get back in there." This time, Dr. Braeburn didn't look back. He walked straight into the PICU.

The door shut behind him.

"Oh, God," Amanda whispered again. She turned away, her hands pressed to her cheeks, her head bowed in unspeakable pain. "My poor baby." She was talking more to herself than to Casey and Patrick. "He's so tiny. So tiny. How can he live through this? More tubes. More procedures. More apparatuses. He's doesn't even weigh ten pounds. How is it possible for him to win this fight?"

Casey didn't care that the questions weren't aimed at her. She answered them anyway.

"He will win this fight, Amanda," she said, walking around so she could face her client. "The tube will work with the ventilator. Between the two, he'll be breathing normally. The lung will heal. The tube will come out. And once the antibiotics do their job, he won't need the ventilator anymore."

Casey's own lashes were damp, but she refused to show anything but calmness and certainty. Because that was what Amanda needed at that moment.

"Amanda, you're so strong," she continued. "So is Justin. He's his mother's son. He wants to live. The doctors are going to make sure that he does."

"As are we," Patrick inserted with a fervor that startled Casey. "We'll find Paul Everett. We won't give up until we do. All you have to do is hold on. I'm a newer member of Forensic Instincts. But I've seen what this team can do. I've helped them do it. Don't lose faith."

Amanda lowered her arms and pivoted slowly to gaze at Patrick. "You have children," she stated with certainty.

"Three. Two daughters and a son. And I'd give my life for any one of them. I understand what you're feeling. Helplessness is one of the hardest emotions to deal with as a parent. But you *will* deal with it. Because all that matters is Justin and the fact that he needs you."

"You're right. I know you're right." Amanda was trying to bolster herself with Patrick's words. "Thank you. I'll pull myself together. I have to."

"I can stay here and wait with you," Casey offered.

"No." Amanda shook her head. "You go talk to your FBI

friend. Find Paul. That's the best thing you can do for me, and for Justin."

"Go ahead, Casey," Patrick said. "I'm here. And I think Amanda mentioned that her friend Melissa was coming by."

"Yes, she is," Amanda confirmed. "She's stopping by right after she puts her kids on the bus. So she should be here soon. Between her and Patrick, I'll have all the support I need."

"Okay." Casey squeezed her hands again. "I'm just a phone call away. And Patrick's right. We're going to find Paul."

Behind the closed doors of his office, Lyle Fenton grabbed his cell phone as soon as he got word about the fire at Morano's place. He didn't have to wait for an investigation to know it was arson.

"Are you fucking crazy?" he demanded the instant his call was answered. "Don't we have enough of a spotlight shining on us with the reopening of Paul Everett's disappearance? Now you're torching his successor's office? Do you think the cops are idiots? They're bound to tie the two together. Why the hell did you do this?"

"The son of a bitch wasn't going to pay us anymore," Franco Paccara snapped. Paccara was a union business manager—and a key member of the Vizzini family. "You're worried about your ass. I'm worried about mine."

"Well, you can stop worrying," Fenton told him. "I pushed the permit applications through. You'll be starting work on that massive construction job two months sooner than expected. So you and your crew will be making a hell of a lot more than the pocket change you've been extracting—and you'll be doing it from outside a jail cell. Enough. Leave Morano alone."

"He spit in our faces."

"And you burned down his shack, his files, his computer, and everything else he had in there. He better have all his building files backed up on a flash drive or you screwed yourselves. Look, you probably scared the shit out of him. Fine. Threaten him throughout the entire project, for all I care. Just don't *do* anything. I don't want another Paul Everett on our hands."

Silence.

Fenton went for the brass ring. "There's a bonus in this if you agree to go along with me."

That woke Paccara up. "How much?"

"How does a hundred thousand sound to you? Half now, half when construction is finished. Share some with your guys. Keep the rest for yourself."

"Yeah, okay, fine. We'll leave Morano alone—as long as he cooperates and doesn't try to screw us over."

"I'll make sure that doesn't happen. Count on it."

CHAPTER TWENTY

Hutch was sitting at the counter in Casey's kitchen, wearing only a pair of jeans, nursing a cup of coffee and working on his laptop, when Casey walked in.

"Hey." He took one look at her, then got up and poured her a cup of coffee. "Here," he said gently, pressing the cup into her hands. "You look like you need this."

"More than you know." She took a deep swallow, then placed the mug on the counter. "Thank you… I…"

In an uncharacteristic emotional meltdown, Casey walked straight into Hutch's arms, pressing her face against his bare chest and winding her arms around his waist. "Watching this…seeing it firsthand…I don't think I could go through what Amanda is," Casey admitted in a watery voice. "Between this—and our last case—I doubt I'll be having kids, ever."

Hutch put down his own cup and wrapped his arms around her. "These cases are the toughest." He pressed his lips into her hair. "I know. That's why I transferred."

She nodded against his skin. "I know you do. And I know you managed to compartmentalize it. I usually do, too."

"I didn't compartmentalize…I internalized," Hutch corrected. "And it never got easier."

Casey drew a deep, shaky breath. "I'm sorry I'm acting so weak and infantile. It's completely unlike me. I'm just…"

"Human?" Hutch finished for her. "Sweetheart, you don't always have to be the formidable president of Forensic Instincts. Sometimes you can just be Casey—at least with me." His palms slid up and down her spine in a soothing gesture. "I think we've come at least that far, don't you?"

"Yes," Casey conceded.

Their relationship was complicated—intense, passionate, meaningful, but long-distance. Two strong-willed, independent people with equally consuming careers. They never talked about a future, never even put a label on what they had. It was better that way.

Still, there was no denying how close they'd grown.

"Tell me what happened at the hospital," Hutch urged. "Is the baby worse?"

"Yes. Maybe. I'm not sure."

Casey stepped out of Hutch's embrace, blinked away her tears and picked up her cup of coffee. "The monitors in the PICU went off while I was there. It seems that Justin has a collapsed lung. The medical team was performing an emergency procedure to fix it when I left. Amanda will call me. She's on the verge of a complete emotional breakdown. And who blames her? Every time she feels a shred of hope, something else happens to beat her down. We've got to find Paul Everett, Hutch. It doesn't matter how."

Hutch evaded that last sentence. He and Casey had different restrictions when it came to operating within the boundaries of the law. So they avoided that topic like the plague.

"Did you ask Amanda if you could unofficially consult with me?"

"Yes. She was thrilled. So here's where we are."

Casey proceeded to bring Hutch up to speed, filling him in on everything—including some things that even Amanda didn't know. But, in order to do his job, Hutch had to be apprised of the FI team's suspicions about Lyle Fenton and his involvement in whatever prompted Paul Everett's disappearance. Casey hesitated when it came to the part about Fenton's relationship to Congressman Mercer. Was it imperative that Hutch know that? Yes. Not only was it a major facet of the bigger picture, but it elevated the entire situation to a bigger, more federal level.

By the time Casey was finished, Hutch was one hundred percent up to speed.

He sipped at his coffee, brows knit, as he digested everything Casey had just told him.

"This is a lot bigger and more complex than I realized," he finally said.

"Exactly," Casey replied. "It might involve a crime family as well as a national politician. We don't know. We will know, because we wouldn't have it any other way. But an infant's life is on the line. We don't have the luxury of time. And you have the ability and the resources to accelerate the process. So anything you could find out would be crucial to our search for Paul Everett." A pause. "After that, the case is all yours. Turn it over to the Bureau. Bring down everyone involved. All signs point to Fenton being a scumbag, so I'd be thrilled. But, for our purposes, all we need is Justin's father."

"Fair enough." Hutch's mind was already racing, considering the best sources for him to approach. "Let me make a few phone calls and send out some emails. I'll see what I can dig up."

Casey's cell phone rang ten minutes later. She'd been sitting on the floor, scratching Hero's belly in the hopes of unwinding. Now, she saw the caller ID and snatched up the phone. It was Patrick.

"What's happening?" she demanded.

"The procedure was successful," Patrick informed her. "Justin's out of crisis mode—for now. Amanda's in the PICU with him. She asked me to call you."

"Thank God." Casey felt a wave of relief. "Whatever time this bought us, I'm using. I filled Hutch in on everything. He's closeted in one of the downstairs offices, reaching out for his contacts, as we speak."

"Good. Meanwhile, there have been no more phone calls at this end. That doesn't mean a thing. Someone's keeping a sharp eye on Amanda and on us. My guess is he's in restraint mode while he gets a read on me. But he'll be back. He's not going anywhere as long as we're continuing this manhunt."

"Which we are—full force," Casey stressed.

"Any word back from Ryan on the phone records? Not that I think he'll find anything."

"No, and I agree. The guy probably used a burner phone. He's not an amateur. He's not going to get caught through phone records."

"And what's going on with Morano's office? Have the cops officially declared it as arson yet?"

"Nope. They're playing it very close to the vest. But I plan on calling our friend Detective Jones in a few hours. He's been busy checking us out. It's time I did a little information pumping of my own."

The captain of *Big Money* eyed the sonar display as he carefully scanned the sea floor for the specially modified container.

Several hours behind schedule and fifteen nautical miles from New York Harbor, he was anxious to recover the last "catch" of the night. The container had been jettisoned two weeks ago in great haste, narrowly avoiding interception by the U.S. Coast Guard, which had stepped up drug interdiction efforts. Fashioned from an old shipping container with large cutouts on all sides, the steel box would have rapidly filled with water and sunk like a massive boat anchor. Steel mesh, welded over the manhole-size holes, would be keeping larger fish out of the container, where they might try to feed off the hermetically sealed bricks of cocaine.

The container and its contents were safe on the ocean floor, but their location, close to the center of the Hudson Shelf Valley, could be problematic.

Extending southeast from the Verrazano-Narrows at a forty-five-degree angle, the Hudson Shelf Valley bisected the New York Bight region of the continental shelf. Depths could reach over two hundred feet, which would make it impossible for the ship and its team of divers to retrieve the valuable cache of cocaine.

But luck was with them today.

The outline of the shipping container appeared on the LCD display—at a depth of 120 feet. Swiftly, the captain motioned to his first mate to dispatch the two divers. In a matter of minutes, the expert underwater team had deployed into the icy waters, attached a grappling hook to the loops of heavy steel cable welded onto the container and begun to haul it to the surface.

Two hours later, *Big Money* and its precious and highly illegal cargo pulled into the Fenton Marine dock in Bayonne, New Jersey.

The fire in Hampton Bays was ruled as arson.

The announcement was made, not by the police, but by the media. As was often the case, they beat the police to the punch—perhaps not with the conclusive findings, but with the revelation.

Within three hours, they'd made enough intrusional headway at the crime scene to put together the pieces and shout them out to the tristate area.

The facts were clear. A shack thoroughly doused with gasoline. The office of a real-estate developer about to embark on a multimillion-dollar project. The successor of a developer who was the victim of a bloody, no-body homicide eight months ago.

It was the kind of story ambitious reporters lived for.

Casey heard the breaking news on her headphones while jogging with Hero back home from the park. It explained why Detective Jones hadn't returned her call. She'd thought he'd just been hiding from her—which no doubt he had been. But he'd also been directing all his resources to shutting down the media.

Unfortunately, not only would that be an impossible task, it would also be like closing the barn door after the horse was out.

Hurrying inside, Casey unleashed Hero, who bounded up the stairs behind her as she made her way to FI's main conference room with its gigantic, multiscreened video wall.

"Hello, Casey. Hello, Hero," Yoda greeted them.

"Yoda, I need to see all local TV news," Casey instructed him.

"Are you looking for breaking news?" Yoda inquired. "Otherwise, you'll find it problematic. It's eleven forty-five—none of the local stations carry news programs at this time."

Casey contemplated that truth.

"Would you prefer local news radio?" Yoda asked. "That would be on the air now."

"I've already heard the radio announcement. I'd like visuals to go along with it."

"I see. Then how shall I proceed?"

"What about midday news?" Casey asked. "A few of the local stations broadcast that."

"Correct. Both CBS and ABC have news at noon. Shall I pull up both stations and we'll await the midday hour?"

"Yes, Yoda, please."

"Certainly." The screens came to life. "I'm showing CBS on your left and ABC on your right. News will begin in precisely thirteen minutes, twelve seconds. Please advise me if you'd like one of the two stations expanded to full screen."

"Thanks, Yoda. I will. One more thing. While we're waiting, can you please search the internet for any stories about the fire at John Morano's office?"

"Beginning search," Yoda replied. Seconds later, he announced, "Nothing found."

"Okay then, please check out the live internet feed from the local TV station in the Hamptons. The rest of Long Island, as well. Then, add those to the video display."

"Very well." A pause. "Local news will now begin in twelve minutes thirty-four seconds. Internet video feeds displaying now."

"Good."

As Casey had expected, the Long Island news stations were the first to scroll the breaking news of the fire across the bottom of the screen. A few minutes after noon, CBS showed a live report on the fire itself. Obviously, they'd had a TV crew in the area filming something else and had diverted them to the scene of the fire for more sensational coverage. The CBS reporter stated that they were awaiting confirmation from the local authorities that the fire was suspicious. Minutes later, ABC echoed the same information.

Casey's phone rang. A quick glance at the caller ID.

"Hey, Ryan. Did you find anything in the phone records?" Casey asked. "Or are you just calling to tell me that the local news stations are jumping the gun on the arson story."

"Actually, both," Ryan replied. "Nothing on the phone records. The burner phone is probably lying at the bottom of the East River. And I'm glad you heard the local news reports."

"I not only heard them, I'm watching them right now. As Yoda pointed out, CBS and ABC have midday news coverage. And the reporters are all over the arson story."

"Did you reach Jones?"

"What do you think?"

Ryan chuckled. "I think he's in deep shit and trying to shovel his way out with a teaspoon."

"For sure. But I'll get through to him. He can't dodge me forever. I'll just drive there and get in his face." Casey paused, a fine tension lacing her tone. "Justin had another setback this morning," she said. "It was pretty rough at the hospital." She went on to explain the pneumothorax to Ryan.

"What happened?" she heard Marc call out from the background.

"Hang on," Ryan said to Casey. She heard him telling Marc the specifics.

"Give me the phone," Marc responded.

No surprise there. Not when there was a baby involved.

"Is he okay?" Marc asked Casey without prelude.

"Right now, yes. He's holding his own," she replied. "For how long? I don't know. I'm no doctor, but it seems to me that Justin's compromised immune system can only fight off so many setbacks." She swallowed, then spoke to Marc with her customary honesty. "If you're asking me if I'm worried—more worried than before—yes, I am. I feel like the clock is ticking away—louder and louder. I feel like we're chipping away at our investigation, making small gains here and there, but nothing substantial enough to write home about. Hutch is on it now. Maybe we'll get lucky and Paul Everett will show up in the Bureau system. But we can't count on it."

"I might still beat the crap out of Lyle Fenton," Marc muttered with none of his usual composure. "You and I both know he's up to his neck in this whole dirty dealing."

"I agree. But the bottom line is, he doesn't know where Paul is. He wouldn't let Justin die. And finding Paul is all we're focused on. Law enforcement can handle the rest."

"Yeah. Right. Fine." Marc blew out a frustrated breath. "We're done here. Ryan slapped a GPS on Morano's car before the guy took off for the arson site. Since then, Ryan's been digging into phone records. Now he's back to cross-checking Everett's and Morano's pasts. He can do that best in the office. We'll pack up and head to the city."

"Fine." Casey knew exactly what was on Marc's mind. "And, yes, Amanda did ask for you. But Patrick is there in his security capacity. And Amanda has started to trust him in a kind of father figure way. So she's in good hands. You can't be in all places at all times, Marc. I know you want to save Justin. We all do. But that's not always accomplished by being Amanda's babysitter. She's a strong woman. And, as for the investigation, she needs to count on all of us, not just you."

"I'm not trying to play knight in shining armor," Marc assured her. "And I know very well what a shrink would say—that I'm compensating for what I've witnessed in the past by trying to save this one infant's life. I'm sure that's true. I'm also sure that nothing is going to erase memories that are burned inside my brain. But I'm the one who took on this case. I feel responsible—not only to Amanda, but to the team."

"I know you do. That's who you are." Casey thought for a moment. "You're right. There's nothing else you can accomplish in Long Island, not at the moment. So come home. You drive. That way, Ryan can keep doing his computer search on the road."

The two men sat across from each other in the private room, their conversation low and intense.

"They're trying to tap into the FBI's resources now," one of them said.

"I know. And we can't let that happen." The second man slammed his fist on the table. "What the hell does it take to scare these pain-in-the-ass investigators off?"

"We haven't found it yet," the first man replied. "But we will."

Fallujah, Iraq

The trip had been arduous—and it still wasn't over.

He'd caught the first flight to Ali Al Salem Airbase in Kuwait City, where he'd taken a military transport to Baghdad. If he was being stationed at the New Embassy Compound, it would be fairly simple, assuming the daily threat condition was in his favor. But he was heading out of Baghdad, traveling to Fallujah and one of the forward operating bases. Ground transportation was an impossibility. He would have to rely on military transport by helicopter. And who the hell knew when that could be arranged? Between the sandstorms that shut them down, the limited seating and the erratic schedule, it could be days before he traveled the ten fucking miles to his destination.

The urgency for this had been off-the-charts, and unnecessary.

Something was going on.

He just wasn't sure what.

CHAPTER TWENTY-ONE

Claire had the oddest feeling.

And it wasn't a happy one.

It was one of deception. And the deception was happening within the tight circle of Forensic Instincts.

She paced around her apartment as long as she could. She had to share this with someone. But who?

Ryan.

She had no idea why his name popped into her head. She could just as easily have talked to Casey or Marc or Patrick. But, for some reason, she knew the one to talk to was Ryan. The aura of deceit didn't come from him. It was elsewhere, cloudy, but real. But Ryan's aura was clear.

They'd probably argue. But she had to take a chance.

She pressed his number on speed dial.

"Hey, Claire-voyant, what's up?" He sounded preoccupied.

"Are you back in the office?" she asked.

"Nope. In the car. Why?"

Instead of an answer, Claire asked another question. "In the car—where?"

"On the way back to the city with Marc." He sounded more attentive now. "Is there a problem?"

"I'm not sure. I'm also not sure why I called you about it. But would it be possible for Marc to drop you off at my place?"

"Now *that* sounds intriguing." The familiar teasing note was back in his voice.

"It is. But not for the reasons you mean." Claire didn't banter back the way she normally would. She was too preoccupied.

A slight pause. "Sure. We're almost home anyway. And I've been working since we left Westhampton Beach. I can take a milk-and-cookies break."

"I have soy milk and organic wafer cookies. I also have full leaf tea and three different kinds of all-natural juice."

"How will I choose?" Ryan asked wryly. "How about a Blue Moon?"

"What?" Claire was genuinely puzzled. "I can't conjure up a blue moon. They only occur on the rare seasons when there have already been three full moons and..."

"The beer, Claire, not the lunar phenomenon."

"Oh." Claire was quiet for a moment, digesting that piece of information. "I'll have a Sam Adams. My father drinks those."

"Thank God for your father. Sam Adams it is. I'll be there in about a half hour."

★ ★ ★

Claire was still pacing around her studio apartment when Ryan arrived.

"Hi," Claire said as she let him in. "Thanks for coming."

"No problem." Ryan was surveying the place, which was so the antithesis of his computer and gadget-crammed apartment, it was almost funny.

Shutting the door behind Ryan, Claire turned to say she would get him his beer when she noticed what he was doing and realization struck.

"You've never been here before," she announced. She'd been so consumed with her sense of unease that she'd forgotten all about that fact. She'd also forgotten to give Ryan her address.

"Yeah, I know." Ryan strolled into the living-room area, still taking in the uncluttered, softly decorated apartment. "Nice place. Very you. Am I allowed to sit on the sofa? Or is that only for show? Do I have to go for lotus position on the floor?"

Claire ignored his taunts. "I never gave you my address. How did you know where I lived?"

Ryan's smile reached his eyes. "Didn't Casey tell you? I hack into everyone's personnel files when they first come on board. It makes me feel more connected to my teammates."

"That's reassuring. Isn't it also illegal?"

"Isn't lots of what we do?"

Claire rolled her eyes. "Good thing I have nothing to hide. Have a seat—on the sofa, since it's allowed. I'll get your beer."

She headed into the galley kitchen, returning a minute later with a bottle of Sam Adams and a plate of cookies. "Isn't it a little early in the day for a drink?" she asked, handing him the bottle and setting the plate on the coffee table.

"Normally? Yes. After the night I've had? No."

"Understood." Claire sat down across from Ryan, her brows knit in concern. "Watching that office burn to the ground must have been pretty unnerving."

"Not nearly as unnerving as wondering if Marc and I were going to be able to escape the scene without being killed by whatever nutcase torched that shack." Ryan tipped back the bottle of beer and took a healthy swallow. "And now Amanda got a threatening phone call. I'm sure Casey told you."

"She did. I called into the office this morning. The threatening phone call doesn't surprise me. I'm constantly bugged by the sense of being watched—not just Amanda, but all of us. We must be getting closer to some truth or we wouldn't be scaring people. I was more upset about Justin's setback."

"Yeah, that poor little kid. I hope he can hold on." Ryan's lips thinned into a grim line. "I never thought I'd be the team member who had to keep it together for the group, at least not outside my area of expertise. But Casey is a wreck, and Marc is practically apoplectic. Even Patrick's getting emotionally involved, I guess because he's a father. And you're always a walking testament to empathy and compassion. So that leaves Hero and me. Oh, and Hutch, who's doing some unofficial poking around for us."

Claire didn't argue the point. The fact that everyone was acting out of character didn't please her. Not in light of what she was sensing.

"So why the urgency for us to talk?" Ryan asked. "You sounded pretty freaked out on the phone."

"I am."

"And you came to me. Should I be shocked or flattered?"

"Neither. I came to you because your energy is positive—at least where it comes to this."

"You lost me." Ryan made a gesture of noncomprehension. "What is 'this'?"

Claire took a deep, cleansing breath. "Here's a ridiculous request for me to make to the guy who hacked into my personnel file, but I'm making it anyway. Please keep this between us. It matters."

"Then it's done."

"Thank you," Claire said simply. She met Ryan's curious gaze. "I'm getting some unusual negative energy. It's persistent or I'd chalk it up to stress. But it's real. And it worries me—a lot."

Ryan did a double take. "You called *me* over here to discuss your psychic vibes? You sure *you're* not the one who's been drinking?"

"Yes, I'm sure. I called you over here because, as I said, the negativity isn't coming from you. But it's coming from inside the team. And that worries the hell out of me."

After giving Claire a long, hard look, Ryan set down his beer. "Are you saying that someone at FI isn't acting in the best interests of the team? Because then I know you're crazy."

Claire dragged a hand through her hair. "It's not as black-and-white as that. It's not necessarily that someone on the team is deceiving us. He or she could just have an additional, separate agenda—one that's not being shared with the rest of the team. Our synchrony is out of whack. I'm sure of it. I'm just not sure of the details. Or of who's throwing our rhythm off." She gave Ryan a pleading look. "Don't dismiss what I'm saying, not without checking it out."

"Checking *what* out?" Ryan was beyond frustrated. "I'm not looking for a traitor at Forensic Instincts."

"Ryan, you're not listening to me. I'm not suggesting any one of us is a traitor. I'm saying that every one of us is reacting strongly to this investigation, in most cases uncharacteristically so. We're all good at pushing boundaries. We need to find out who's pushing in a separate direction. It could be for altruistic reasons. Maybe to protect the rest of the team. I don't know. But something's going on. And I can't figure it out without help."

Softening somewhat, Ryan picked up his beer again, rolling the bottle between his palms. "If it's altruistic, why is it negative energy you're feeling?"

"Because it's hurting, not helping, what we're trying to accomplish. The person doing it might not realize that, or, if they do, they're keeping it from the team for a reason. I'm just speculating. But I need you to check into what everyone at FI has been up to these past few days—when they're not with the group. Or even when they're with the group, but can be doing their own thing simultaneously."

"You're one of the most ethical people I've ever met," Ryan replied. "I can't believe you're asking me to do this."

"I can't believe it, either. But I have nowhere else to turn. And it's necessary. I'm absolutely certain of it."

"Shit." Ryan gulped down the rest of his beer and stood up. "Do you know what's even crazier than what you're asking me to do? The fact that I'm going to do it for you."

"I really appreciate it," Claire said, coming to her feet. "I feel as horrible about this as you do. If I thought there was another way...but there isn't."

"Fine." Ryan shook his head. "I don't even believe in this

crap. Auras. Energy. Flashes of who-knows-what. I must be as nuts as you are."

"Maybe you have a modicum of faith in me."

"Maybe I don't know what the hell I have when I'm around you." A pause. "And maybe I don't care."

Without warning, Ryan reached over and hauled Claire into his arms. He was kissing her before she could breathe, much less protest, and by the time it registered, protesting was the furthest thing from her mind.

"You drive me crazy," Ryan muttered against her mouth. His hands tangled in her hair, anchoring her head so he could deepen the kiss.

Claire wasn't sure who started undressing who first, nor was she sure who started backing them toward the bed. All she remembered was feeling the mattress under her back and Ryan's weight pressing her into it as he dragged off the rest of her clothes.

They both knew that if they thought about what they were doing they would stop. And stopping was the last thing they wanted. So they didn't think. They just shut down their minds and let their bodies take over.

Frantic urgency clawed at them both. Yet they refused to give in, instead savoring each caress, each hungry exploration of the other's body. Ryan was an amazing and experienced lover, but Claire matched him touch for touch, taste for taste. By the time Ryan moved between her thighs, pushing all the way inside her, they were both shaking, desperate for completion.

Their jagged breaths, their harsh moans and the rhythmic squeaking of the bedsprings were the only sounds in the room. And then Claire gave a wild, thin cry, arching up as

her entire body shattered into spasms. Ryan was right there with her, thrusting deep into her climax and shouting as he gave in to his own.

They both collapsed, Claire sinking into the bed, Ryan's full weight pinning her in place. It didn't matter. She wasn't going anywhere. Her limbs felt like water, and her entire body was quivering with aftershocks. Her breathing was as ragged as Ryan's, who was still shuddering from the impact of his orgasm. Clearly, he was in no condition to move.

Claire hadn't the faintest idea how much time passed. The two of them might have dozed, or they might just have floated in a semiconscious state. Claire had no idea. But at some point, she felt Ryan push himself up on his elbows and gaze down at her. Her own eyes were shut, and she wasn't sure she wanted to open them. Right now, she didn't have to think, didn't have to talk, didn't have to address what had just happened. But once she opened her eyes, all that was going to change.

"Claire." Ryan wasn't giving her a choice.

Her lashes fluttered, and with a great effort and even greater reluctance, she cracked open her lids.

"Are you okay?" he asked, sounding as bewildered as she felt. The expression on his face was one of sheer incredulousness.

"I don't know," she managed. "Are you?"

"Beats the hell out of me."

Clare swallowed, turned her head away as the reality she'd held at bay came crashing down like a boulder. This was Ryan. *Ryan.* What in the name of hell had she been thinking? Why had she made herself vulnerable to him? Talk

about exposing one's soft underbelly. She'd all but put the pitchfork in his hand.

"We should get up," she said woodenly.

"Yeah, we should." Ryan rolled away, rising to collect his hastily discarded clothes and to pull them on. He turned, studying Claire from beneath hooded lids.

Damn the guy. Even sweaty and disheveled, he was sexy as hell, with enough charm to melt an iceberg. Meanwhile, she was lying there naked, with nothing but a sheet to cover her. Between that and his looming over her, she felt even more raw and exposed, at a total disadvantage.

"This was a mistake," she pronounced. Wow, she'd managed to sound somewhat normal, and to speak in a relatively strong tone.

"I agree. Probably a big one." Ryan was visibly and totally out of sorts—Claire's only consolation at the moment. He leaned his head back, and blew out a long, uneven breath. "I don't know what to say."

"Let's not say anything. The less we talk about it, the less significance we'll be assigning it." Claire sat up, holding the sheet against her, trying to display the same nonchalance that Ryan's God-knew-how-many-other bed partners displayed. "We acted on impulse. It was dumb. Now it's over. Let's just move on, okay?"

Ryan nodded. "Okay." He finished getting dressed, ran his hands through his rumpled black hair. "I'll head back to my place, shower and change. Then I'll go to the brownstone, where I'll start checking out the activities of our coworkers, and hope you're wrong."

"I hope so, too. But I'm not."

Ryan nodded again. He crossed over to the door, then paused, glancing back at her. "Listen, Claire..."

"See you at the office," she interrupted. Whatever he'd been about to say, she didn't want to hear it.

He took the hint. "Yup. See you."

He walked out, closing the door behind him.

The handwriting was on the wall, and what it said was beginning to be unmistakable.

Still, Hutch wasn't ready to give up.

He'd taken steps in a dozen different directions, tapped into more avenues than he could count. There was a pattern forming, one that was making him distinctly uneasy. Curiosity and determination warred with reason.

He pounded the proverbial pavement a few hours longer, being as thorough and creative as he knew how. Ultimately, he went to the highest ranking contact he had in the Criminal Enterprise division.

The answer was the same. Scripted. Terse. Immovable.

Creating an impenetrable wall.

He'd never expected this outcome. But he had to live with it.

And so would Casey.

CHAPTER TWENTY-TWO

Ryan set aside his sleuthing into Paul Everett's and John Morano's pasts long enough to do what he'd promised Claire. He felt like a shit doing it. There was no "nice" way to justify prying into the lives of his team. He trusted them all with his life.

Still, Claire hadn't accused them of deception, not of the malicious kind. She was concerned that one of them was employing an iffy tactic while trying to protect the others. Was that possible? Sure.

He did a little poking around in the FI phone records, found nothing, and then gave it up for a while. He was too preoccupied to bury himself in work. No matter how hard he tried, he couldn't just forget about what had happened between him and Claire.

Talk about an inferno. They'd practically set the sheets

on fire. How the hell was he supposed to forget about that, much less make sense of it?

"Well, I came down here for nothing," Marc commented, poised in the doorway of Ryan's lair, studying him intently. "I was going to ask you what Claire wanted to see you about. But judging from the expression on your face, you didn't do much talking."

Ryan shot Marc a look. "Casey's the expert with tells. You're out of your league."

"Maybe. But I'm right."

"Drop it."

"That off-the-charts, huh? I'm not surprised. Now what? Where are you going from here?"

"Back to work." Ryan leaned over his computer, deliberately shielding the screen from Marc's view.

"Where's Claire?"

"No idea."

"You're even pissier than you were before. She really got to you that bad, huh?"

Ryan shrank the window he'd been working in on his computer, spun his chair around and faced Marc with a hard expression. "You're not going to leave this alone, are you? You, who are so private no one knows your shoe size?"

"Fair enough." Marc shrugged, unfazed by the verbal attack. "You just look pretty strung out. I thought you might want to talk about it."

"I don't even know what *it* is. And I definitely don't want to talk about it."

"No problem. But, for the record—and because I have ten years on you—don't overanalyze it. Just let it be whatever it is. You're a smart guy, Ryan. You knew damn well it wasn't going to be a quick lay. You two are way too combustible for that."

Ryan's jaw was working. "I hear you. Can we let it go now?"

"It's gone."

"And not a word to anyone."

"That's not my style, and you know it. But I wouldn't expect it to get by Casey."

"If she figures it out on her own and says something, I'll shut her down, too."

Marc nodded. "Since Claire's not the type to ask for a booty call, my original question remains. Why did she need to see you so urgently?"

This, Ryan had been prepared for. "She had some weird vibes about the investigation." *Stick to the truth. There's less to remember.* "All she was sure of was that it had to do with what I'm currently checking into."

"Everett's and Morano's backgrounds?"

"That's what I'm working on. So that's what it must be."

"Did she give you any specifics?"

"Nope." Ryan shook his head, swiveling back around to face his computer. "She hated like hell having to call me at all. She knows how little value I place on psychic insights. But I'm the genius who's going to dig up everything there is to know about Everett and Morano. So she had no choice but to turn to me."

"Got it." Whether or not Marc believed him was anyone's guess. Nothing ever showed on Marc's face—he was a pro at that. "Then I'll leave you to your digging. By the way, how do you want to follow up on our plan to bug Morano's office?"

"Give it a day," Ryan replied. "Morano's already in the process of renting a trailer to operate out of. I'm sure he salvaged a good chunk of his work. He'd be an asshole not to have backed it up on a flash drive and taken it home with him—just in case. He'll be up and running in no time. Gecko will just have a different hiding place to do his reconnaissance."

Marc chuckled. "Right. And I have no doubt that Gecko will adapt beautifully." He headed toward the door. "Just let me know when we're heading back out to the Hamptons. I have some follow-up to do here."

"On what?"

Again, Marc's face showed nothing. But the way he stopped in his tracks and gazed back at Ryan, that searching look in his eyes, spoke volumes. Ryan wanted to kick himself for being so transparent and so abrupt. He'd make a lousy addition to the BAU.

"On Amanda," Marc replied. "I haven't talked to her since Justin took a turn for the worse. Plus, I want to talk to Hutch while he's here. I haven't even seen him yet. I know he's calling his FBI contacts to see what he can find out about Paul Everett—if anything. I still have a few contacts at the Bureau myself. I want to see if I can help him." A pointed pause. "Why? Do you need me for something?"

"No." This time, Ryan kept his interest in check. "I was just curious. I know how invested you are in this case."

"If you're worried that I'll let my baggage cloud my judgment, don't. It never does." Another pause, this one speculative. "Just let me know when Morano has his trailer set up. We'll reverse our tracks and head right back to the Hamptons to install Gecko in the trailer. A baby could break into one of those. We'll have Gecko in place in twenty minutes."

Casey spent a good hour in her private office upstairs, watching Mercer's press conference online. Or, to be more specific, watching Mercer at his press conference.

He was a charismatic speaker, yet he also came across as very warm and sincere—a real family man with solid family values. Some of it was genuine, some was exaggerated. Just like every other politician.

He was definitely uneasy about the whole blood donor situation. Every time the press said something about his altruistic gesture, his lips thinned into a tight smile, and Casey could almost see his internal wince. He wanted the baby to survive. But he didn't want the details of his genetic relationship to Justin to come out. Mercer was also intimidated by his "father." Lyle Fenton was standing on his left. And Mercer was angled away from him, his face slanted to the right, his body positioned as if to shield himself from Fenton.

The whole situation would be fascinating if it weren't so maddening. There was nothing in this clip that could help Amanda. For her purposes, it didn't matter why the congressman had taken the steps he'd taken, only that he had taken them. Now it was back to the waiting game. The complete testing results didn't come back for almost two weeks. While FI knew that Amanda and Mercer were loosely related, Amanda didn't. And the biological connection was weak, at best. So the odds weren't good.

Finding Paul Everett was still the best, maybe the only option. Flying under the radar wasn't working, especially since FI's involvement was public knowledge at this point. Not to mention the fact that they'd put some dangerous people on high alert.

Forget subtlety. It was time to be more aggressive.

"Maybe you should let it go."

Casey started. She hadn't heard Hutch come in.

"Let what go?" she asked. "Mercer? I don't think so. If anything, I'm starting to think we should confront him."

"About what—being Fenton's son?"

"About the fact that we know he's Fenton's son. Also, about the fact that we know he's in Fenton's pocket. It might make him more amenable to telling us anything else he knows about—like Fenton's involvement with Paul Everett's supposed death."

"I doubt he knows anything." Hutch shrugged. "I realize you're getting desperate. But I'd leave that avenue alone."

Casey blinked. "Leave alone a dirty politician? I can't believe this is you. Are you, Supervisory Special Agent Kyle Hutchinson, the most honorable person on earth, actually suggesting I turn my back on corruption?"

Hutch's smile didn't quite reach his eyes. "No, although I thank you for the slightly exaggerated compliment. I'm suggesting you find a donor match for little Justin and stop being sidetracked. That's not just my professional opinion, it's my personal one. Getting Amanda's son healthy is what you were hired for."

Something wasn't sitting right with Casey.

"Did you reach your contacts?" she asked.

"Most of them, yes."

"Good. Because you've been in there for hours. What did they tell you? Is Paul Everett in the federal system?"

"They didn't tell me anything. No one could give me information about Paul Everett or about any investigation involving him in any capacity."

Casey rose slowly, her eyes narrowing on Hutch's face. His choice of wording didn't escape her. "That's pretty vague."

"Actually, it's very definitive." Hutch's expression was totally nondescript. "I tried my best to help you out. But there's nothing I can say. It sucks, Casey. But it's a dead end."

"A dead end," Casey repeated. "Nothing you can say. Nothing anyone could tell you. Nothing you could get. That's an awful lot of nothings."

"I realize that. I'm sorry. I was hoping to help your investigation."

"But you didn't. Then again, you already know that. You told me *nothing*." Her emphasis was pointed.

"That's true." Hutch didn't avert his gaze. "So maybe it's time to widen your search for a donor."

"Or maybe it's time for you to tell me the truth."

"I just did."

"You made sure to word things perfectly. But the truth? That's crap." Casey walked right up to him. "What's going on?"

His jaw tightened. "Leave it alone, Casey."

She was quiet for a long moment, just scrutinizing his face.

"Wow," she said at last. "This is even bigger than I thought. They shut you down, didn't they? Whatever's going on, they don't want Forensic Instincts involved. This must be some major career-building case. No wonder we've got the bad guys so nervous. There's a lot more at stake for them than our search for Paul Everett. He's part of a much bigger picture."

Hutch didn't answer. Then again, he didn't have to.

"You're coming through loud and clear," Casey told him.

"I guess that means that figuring out what the bigger picture is will be FI's job."

"No." Hutch's tone was hard. "FI's job will be to find some other way to save Justin Gleason. Paul Everett isn't an option."

"That's the FBI's opinion. Not mine."

"You're playing with fire, Casey. That's as much as I can say. I don't have too many details—but I have enough to know you're in danger. So drop it."

"There's no chance in hell. Do you have any idea how good the odds are that Paul Everett will turn out to be the best match for Justin? Do you know how fervently Amanda's been counting on that national donor list and coming up empty? Do you know that her son-of-a-bitch uncle, who's her closest living relative, isn't a match? Do you realize that Mercer and his kids are long, long shots?" Anger sparked in Casey's eyes. "Do you understand that you're practically telling me to let a baby die to protect your precious Bureau?"

"That's not what I'm telling you." Now Hutch was getting angry. "But if more powerful forces than you haven't found Paul Everett, FI isn't going to, either. Assuming you're right—and I'm not saying you are—and he is part of some massive investigation, you're wasting your time hunting him down. That's time you could be spending finding a viable donor for Justin."

"Do you know where he is?" Casey demanded.

"I haven't a clue." Hutch's jaw was working. "And, if I did, I couldn't tell you."

"Couldn't? Or wouldn't?"

"Both."

"Dammit, Hutch." Casey was furious. "I'm trying to save

a baby's life. And you're clinging to some stupid bureaucratic rules?"

"Those bureaucratic rules are what define our criminal justice system. Without them—" Hutch broke off with a frustrated sound. "Let's not go down this path for the hundredth time. We don't agree. That's why you started Forensic Instincts and why I'm with the Bureau."

Casey struggled for control—and for objectivity. She knew Hutch was being Hutch, doing what he believed in. But she just couldn't wrap her mind around it, not in this case.

"We're talking about a newborn baby," she said, keeping her tone intentionally calm. "He won't survive much longer without a donor transplant. He might not survive anyway. Hutch, I won't ask you to compromise your principles. Just tell me what you can, what you feel comfortable saying. I'll try to fill in the blanks. Please. I'm begging you. I won't tell anyone, not even the team, where I got the information."

"You know that's not the issue, Casey." Hutch's tone was equally restrained. "Anything I wouldn't feel comfortable with your sharing with the team, I wouldn't feel comfortable sharing with you. This isn't personal. It's professional." A pause, as Hutch grappled with his choice of words. "I wasn't lying. I have no idea where Paul Everett is. Nor do I have the faintest idea how to find him. I'm not sure who, if anyone, does. Classified information is shared on a need-to-know basis."

"I hear you." Casey digested what Hutch was and wasn't saying. Paul Everett was in the federal system and he was a part of some investigation. A significant investigation, if it was classified. And that meant that even Hutch had limited information.

"Is Paul alive?" Casey asked.

"I don't know. I can only speculate."

"Okay, then what would you speculate?"

"I'd speculate that he's probably alive."

"Agreed. Or the Bureau wouldn't be so eager to keep a lid on his part in their investigation."

"Maybe. Maybe not." Hutch shrugged. "It could be that any update on his status is classified. I'm just guessing, based on instinct. I have no facts to support them."

Casey nodded. "When you first walked in here, you had a strong, negative reaction to my watching Mercer's press conference. That tells me that this investigation involves him, too."

"I can't comment on that."

"And Lyle Fenton?"

Hutch sliced the air with his hand. "That's it, Case. Twenty questions is over. I helped you as much as I can—and then some. Any more and I'll be violating my beliefs and my professional ethics."

Casey listened to Hutch's every word, watched his every tell. He was trained and he was good. Downright unreadable, under most circumstances. But in this case, he was trying to convey information without conveying it. So he was definitely more open to interpretation.

Whatever broad investigation the FBI was conducting, Congressman Mercer and Lyle Fenton were key players in it.

"Casey," Hutch added in a grim tone, "I don't think I did you any favors by pushing this with the Bureau. Now that they've been clued in to the fact that you're on a major manhunt for Paul Everett, they're going to do everything they can to block you."

"Did they come right out and tell you that?"

"No, or I couldn't be repeating it. But you and I are both smart enough to figure it out. It's one thing for them to see an amateur YouTube video that was shot by your client. It's another thing to have one of their own reaching out to a handful of insiders, pressing for answers. My relationship with you is hardly a secret among the agents I know. This whole situation isn't good."

"It was a risk we had to take," Casey replied. "And don't tell me to back down, because I won't. The FBI can join the crowd who's watching us. At least we know they won't shoot to kill."

"Very funny." Hutch scowled. "I'm not even going to try to talk you out of it, because I'd be wasting my breath. But I can't be a part of it, either—except to worry about you."

"Fair enough." Casey was as blunt as he was. "By the same token, I can't pass along another shred of information to you. I've already done enough damage to my client by telling you as much as I did. But from here on in, you're out of the loop."

"Fine." Hutch was still scowling. "But I'm not going anywhere."

"Aren't you due back in Quantico in a day or two?"

"Trying to get rid of me?"

Casey attempted a smile, but didn't manage to pull it off. "Nope. You're too good in bed."

"I'm not laughing, Casey." Hutch's jaw tightened another notch. "I don't know who all the key players are here. But you could be walking into a minefield."

"Then let's hope I tread carefully. Because I'm finding Paul Everett."

CHAPTER TWENTY-THREE

John Morano was in the process of setting up his replacement computer system, trying to make it fit within the confines of the narrow trailer he'd hastily bought as a substitute office, when Lyle Fenton walked in.

"Good. You're not missing a beat," Fenton pronounced, marching inside. "I like that in the people I do business with." As he spoke, Fenton glanced out the side window of the trailer, nodding in approval as he scanned the close proximity of the bay. "Smart idea to stay put. From experience, I know it's important to be on-site. It keeps the construction crew on their toes."

"I didn't stay put," Morano said, angling his computer monitor. "I moved to the other side of the marina. The stench of burned wood and gasoline were more than I could take. Plus, that area is a crime scene."

"I didn't mean that literally." Fenton had that hard edge to his voice—and it was unsettling enough for Morano to stop what he was doing and straighten up to regard Fenton.

"Sorry if I'm grouchy," he apologized. "It wasn't exactly the best night of my life."

"I assumed not."

"So what brings you by?" Morano attempted a weak smile. "Did you bring me a housewarming present?"

Fenton didn't smile back. "The news reports said that the police are ruling this arson."

"It was pretty much a no-brainer," Morano replied. "So is trying to figure out who did it."

No change in expression. "The mob."

A shaky nod. "I shut them down, told them I wasn't paying up anymore. So they gave me an unmistakable warning. Hey, at least they didn't kill me—yet."

"You're being very flippant, under the circumstances."

"Flippant?" Morano's voice was hollow. "I'm a nervous wreck. Yeah, I anticipated they'd do something. Their flunky made sure to tell me that during our last visit. I just didn't know what they had in mind. Now I do. The only good thing is that the cops, who wouldn't do a fucking thing until now, are sending out extra patrol cars to police the area and to keep an eye on my apartment. Those are the only two places I plan on being. No detours for me—not for a long time."

"It took balls to provoke them the way you did," Fenton stated. "You're either very brave or very stupid. Which is it?"

"Neither. I was being squeezed to the point where I couldn't breathe." Morano looked like a trapped bird. "Believe me, I'm not suicidal. But I'm not a multimillionaire, either. I don't have the kind of money they're demanding. Do I keep wondering if this is what happened to Paul Everett, and that, when he put on the brakes, he wound up dead? Damned straight I do."

"I would, too." Fenton was never one to sugarcoat things. "That's why I hired round-the-clock security for you."

"What?"

"You asked why I came by. I came by to protect my investment. I don't know what the hell happened to Paul Everett, but whatever it was, it wasn't good. You and I just signed a contract—a very lucrative one for me. I don't plan on seeing you get killed. The cops can't watch you 24/7—there aren't enough tax dollars for that. So I'm taking care of it. You'll have eyes on you at all times until this hotel is finished and up and running."

"That's going to be two years."

"Less," Fenton corrected. "Seventeen months. I want it open at the start of the season after next. You can have a grand opening Memorial Day weekend. As for how long you'll need a bodyguard, don't worry. I can afford it." He glanced around the trailer. "Is everything important safe?"

A nod. "I keep all my electronic documents backed up. And, given how rickety that old shack was, I took home my important files every night. With the bunch of teenagers who hang around the bay smoking up until the wee hours of the morning, I couldn't risk losing anything during a break-in. So we won't have any delays."

"Good." Fenton nodded. "Then I suggest you kick your ass into high gear. The guard that my security company sent over is in his car across the street. The permits are taken care of. The mob will be happier once the union members are working. So it's time to break ground."

"I agree. And thanks." Morano looked more than a little relieved at the knowledge that he was being safeguarded, even if it was just because Fenton was safeguarding an important business asset. "I'll set things in motion within the week."

"Do that." There was no give in Fenton's tone.

Casey called a team meeting just as soon as Patrick could make the necessary arrangements for a relief shift at Sloane Kettering. Amanda was okay with him going, once she met Roger and saw how professional he was. Besides, she was in with Justin every minute, and not as focused on the bodyguard situation.

The entire team gathered around the conference room table. The atmosphere was tense, which announced to everyone that Casey had something important on her mind.

"Good afternoon, everyone," Yoda greeted them. "Will you be needing any assistance?"

"Yes, Yoda," Casey said, shutting the conference room door and walking over to her place at the head of the sweeping oval table. "But first we need some discussion time. Then we'll be calling on you."

"Very well, Casey. I'll be on standby." Yoda fell silent.

Casey sat down, aware that all eyes were on her. Even Hero, who was stretched out at her feet, was gazing expectantly up at her, keenly aware that something was going on.

"You all know that I asked Hutch for his help in finding Paul Everett," Casey began, interlacing her fingers in front of her. "He spent a good portion of the day making phone calls and sending out emails. He came back with nothing."

"So Everett's not in the FBI's internal system," Marc mused aloud. "That surprises me. I tried to connect with Hutch, but he was locked in the office doing his thing. Given how long it was taking, I assumed he was getting some significant information. Guess I was wrong."

"You weren't wrong." Casey had that no-bullshit look about her. "I'm sure he got an earful."

Claire looked puzzled. "But you just said he came back with nothing."

"They shut him down." Marc was watching Casey as he spoke. "Whatever Paul Everett is connected to, the Bureau doesn't want us poking around in it. So whatever they did tell Hutch, he can't pass it along to us."

"That's the gist of it." Casey nodded. "I'm sure there's plenty they didn't even reveal to Hutch. But, whatever he found out, he can't share it. My bringing him into the loop was a mistake. If anything, I hurt us—and Amanda—by sharing details with him. Now he knows how far we've gotten in our investigation, and what our trump cards are. If he feels compelled to, he can pass that on to the Bureau. You know how principled he is. I screwed up. I'm sorry."

Ryan and Claire exchanged glances—the first time they'd looked at each other since he'd left her apartment. But this glance was one of understanding. Now they knew what was causing the negative energy Claire couldn't shake, and what the unintended deception was that she'd sensed.

Claire gave Ryan a quick nod of affirmation, before turning her attention back to the team. He got her message loud and clear. No need to poke around further. The team was, once again, in sync.

"You didn't screw up, Casey," Patrick was saying. "We all knew you were bringing Hutch on board—and that includes Amanda. We took a risk. Marc and I are both former FBI—we know how it works. If this is a classified case, then Hutch's hands are tied."

"Yes and no," Marc amended. He gave Casey a long, hard look. "What exactly did Hutch say—or not say?"

A hint of a smile touched Casey's lips. As always, Marc was right on her wavelength.

"What I inferred from his responses is that Paul Everett is a key player in a broader—and classified—federal investigation. What's more, Fenton and Mercer are both touchy subjects, too, which tells me that they're subjects of interest in this case, too. In what capacity or how deeply they're involved, I don't know. What I do know is that Paul Everett is definitely alive. Whatever Hutch's contacts told him, I can tell he believes that. And, if he believes that, it's true."

"Did you get the feeling that either Fenton or Mercer knew about Everett?" Ryan asked.

"No." Casey shook her head. "I'm not saying they didn't play a role in his disappearance, but I don't think they know where he is now. If they did, the Bureau would be hauling their asses in."

"They're not the same," Claire pronounced.

"Who?"

"Mercer and Fenton. They have different levels of involvement. Fenton's aura is dark. Mercer's is much grayer. It's also more muddied, as if he's torn between dark and light."

"He sounds like a friggin' Jedi knight," Ryan muttered.

Claire shot him an irritated look. "No. He's torn, part victim and part offender. I feel sorry for him."

"You would."

"Ryan, cut it out." Casey was in no mood for this. And, frankly, she was surprised. Ryan didn't sound teasing, he sounded downright obnoxious—a line he rarely crossed, especially during intense team discussions.

He seemed to come to the same conclusion at the same moment, because he looked sheepish and unusually off balance. "Sorry, boss. I'm just on overdrive since the fire last night."

Casey's gaze flickered from Ryan to Claire and back, but she accepted his explanation with a nod.

"I agree with Claire," she said. "Mercer's like a fly in a web. I'm sure he's playing dirty politics. But I don't think he's in this thing anywhere near as deep as Fenton."

"True. Even so, I don't think Fenton knows where Everett is," Marc noted. "If he did, he'd get him here to save Justin."

"Well, someone knows where Everett is," Patrick replied. A long, thoughtful pause. "Unless, of course, Everett faked his own death and disappeared on his own. Anybody considered that?"

"Yes." Casey answered that one right away. "I considered many things. That's the other reason I called this team meeting. I want to explore various scenarios, and either eliminate or confirm them, one by one."

"Getting our answers by whatever methods necessary?" Marc asked quietly.

"Getting our answers by whatever methods necessary," Casey replied. She knew exactly what Marc was implying. She also felt Patrick's scowl. Still, she didn't hesitate or back down. "We're moving forward with one goal in mind—saving Justin's life by finding his father. I don't care how we do it. But it has to be fast."

"Casey..." Patrick interjected.

"I know where you stand on this, Patrick." Casey waved it away. "But the circumstances have changed. We're operating at a federal level now. The FBI now knows we're all over this, and that we're not going to stop. They'll thwart us every chance they can. We've got to anticipate their attempts to do so and sidestep them before they can gain traction."

"You have a targeted plan?" Marc asked.

"Yes. And you're all going to help me fast-track it to completion."

With that, she swiveled her chair around to face the wall. "Yoda, please create a virtual workspace."

Yoda responded instantly.

"Creating a virtual workspace, Casey," he said. A minute passed, and the video wall came alive, bathing the room in an electric-blue glow. "Virtual workspace created and ready."

"Please create topics as follows: Criminal Offender, Fugitive, Confidential Informant, Dead, Witness Protection."

She pivoted again to glance around the table. "Anything else?"

"He's not an illegal. He's not a military deserter. I think you've covered it all," Marc replied.

"That should do it, Yoda," Casey informed him.

"Topics created," Yoda announced.

Immediately, the master video wall was divided into five equal sections, each section headed up by one of the topics Casey had requested.

"Good." Casey spread her notes out across the table.

"Okay, team, let's brainstorm each topic. Yoda, please transcribe all our comments. Summarize the points of consensus and disagreement. Display our progress in real time on a whiteboard for each."

"All right, Casey. I am ready."

"Team, let's begin by addressing the option of Paul Everett being a criminal offender."

"Wait," Claire interrupted. "The moment you spelled out the topics, and then again when I saw them in writing, I got that powerful sense of binary energy again. The pull is way too strong for us to ignore. Casey, whatever he is, Paul Everett is *not* dead. I understand you have to explore every option, but that should be our last. Not only because I know I'm right, but because it's futile to pursue an avenue that's of no use to Amanda. Finding out that Justin's father isn't alive defeats our purpose, and hers. Frankly, it's a waste of time."

The rest of the team nodded. Even Ryan didn't dispute Claire's argument.

"We all seem to be in agreement," Casey replied. "Adding Hutch's reaction to the equation, let's shelve 'dead' for the very end and concentrate on the other scenarios."

"You can save time on the Witness Protection debate," Patrick said with great reluctance. "Ditto with the fugitive discussion. Either possibility is strong, given the possible mob connection and the fact that whoever made Everett disappear went to great lengths to make it convincing."

"And?" Casey prompted.

Patrick cleared his throat, fiddling with his pen and keeping his gaze lowered. Whatever he was about to say, he clearly did *not* want to say.

"I have an old buddy with the U.S. Marshals," he replied

at last. "He owes me a bunch of favors. I'll call one in. He can do the necessary digging to find out whether or not Paul Everett is in the Witness Protection Program or a known and wanted fugitive. He's not going to like it. *I* don't like it. But he'll do it." A defensive pause. "I'm not asking him for any details," Patrick clarified. "So don't press me for them. I'm just looking for a yes or no on both counts. That's the best I can do."

"It's great." Casey knew how much Patrick loathed going this route. It went against every straight-and-narrow grain in him. "We don't need to know your friend's name or any specifics about Paul's situation." A brief pause as Casey tested the waters. "Do you think your friend would be willing to get a message to Paul? Would you be comfortable asking?"

Another scowl. "I doubt that Everett's in the Witness Protection Program. If he were, he'd still have internet access. Which means he'd have seen the YouTube video and reacted. If he's a fugitive, however…" A thoughtful pause. "Then we're probably screwed. But, rather than speculate, I'll make the phone call and ask the question. I'll do it right after our meeting breaks up."

"Thank you." Casey turned back to the screen. "That leaves us with two options to discuss and pursue. Criminal Offender and Confidential Informant. Let's throw out the pros and cons. We'll take our assignments from there."

They discussed and debated those two possibilities until they'd slimmed down the options Everett could have taken within each, and decided on the best ways to proceed.

Marc and Ryan were going back to the Hamptons that night and installing Gecko in Morano's trailer. Ryan was simultaneously going to fine-tune, intensify and finish his in-depth study of Morano's and Everett's histories, going as far back as necessary to find a connection between the men or an inconsistency in Everett's background.

Casey was going straight to Detective Jones. In person. No more cat-and-mouse telephone games. She would get into the troop barracks to see the guy, and to eyeball him face-to-face as she fired questions at him. In addition to that, she'd call in every favor and pull out every stop with the NYPD, since she'd consulted for them before forming Forensic Instincts. They'd hopefully have a handle on the CI angle, especially given mob involvement. Maybe she could even get them to tap into one of their own who was working on an FBI task force and could—and would—get her answers on whether or not Everett was a federal informant.

Claire was driving out to the Hamptons with Marc and Ryan, then going her own way. She was determined to revisit Paul's cottage and Amanda's apartment—alone—and immerse herself in their energies until she finished what she'd started when she went out there the first time. Being alone, without distractions, she felt she'd have a stronger chance of keying into something. Plus, she'd been involved in this case longer now, giving her a better shot at connecting with the people and their circumstances than she'd had a few days ago.

Hero was going, too. But not for Claire.

This was the hard part, the part that Patrick winced at when the discussion turned to Marc.

After breaking into Morano's trailer, Ryan and Marc had another stop to make. This one was Marc's to do solo. Actually, not solo. With Hero.

Ryan was driving them out to the Shinnecock Bay marina where Lyle Fenton docked his private yacht. Ryan had dug up not only that piece of information, but the fact that, during the winter months, Fenton's yacht was housed in a vacant building he'd purchased adjacent to the marina, where it was safe from the elements and readied for the next boating season.

Marc was going to break in. After that, he had three goals in mind. One, to thoroughly search the yacht for anything even remotely incriminating. Two, to take a few of Fenton's personal items—things he'd never miss—from which to make scent pads for Hero for future use. And three, to bring along previously made scent pads of Paul Everett, so that Hero could tell Marc if Everett had ever been on Fenton's yacht.

Breaking into that building and boarding that yacht required a stealthy approach or a search warrant.

Marc was an expert on the former. The latter was not something he gave a damn about. Yes, the risks were higher than they would be when he and Ryan broke into Morano's trailer. Fenton might even have a security guard there. And Marc wasn't going alone, which would have made invisibility a snap for a former Navy SEAL. He had Hero with him. A bloodhound couldn't be concealed. So he and Marc would have to be casually but openly visible. That task didn't faze Marc in the least. He was a creative guy. He'd get himself and Hero in that building and on board that yacht.

The whole team was aware that, if Marc managed to get anything on Fenton, he'd be paying him another visit at his East Hampton home. And this time, the meeting wasn't going to be quite as civil as the last time.

This was the part where Patrick gritted his teeth. He understood what was coming, and it went against everything he stood for. But he'd known what he was signing up for when he'd joined Forensic Instincts. He wouldn't stop the team from breaking the laws he'd spent his entire career enforcing—not because his gut reaction wasn't to do exactly that, but because he'd learned to keep his eye on the prize. FI didn't jump into sketchy operations hastily. But they did what had to be done. And what had to be done now was to find Paul Everett so he could save his son's life.

Patrick forced himself to think about Amanda, and about little Justin who was struggling for his life. Then he steeled himself and kept his mouth shut.

Picking up on Patrick's tension, Casey turned to give him a questioning look. "Are you okay with all this?"

"I can live with it," he replied tersely.

"Good. Because I have one more assignment for you."

Patrick arched a brow. "Does it involve killing anyone?"

A hint of a smile. "Nothing like that. But it is a delicate task, one I don't envy you for having to do. Still, it's time for it to be done. And you're the right person for the job."

There was no need to ask what job Casey was referring to.

"You want me to tell Amanda about her uncle."

A nod. "She's our client. She's got to be brought up to speed—somewhat."

"How much do you want me to tell her?"

"I'm not sure." Casey raked her fingers through her hair. "Suggestions, team?"

"Stick to the basics," Marc responded. "Tell her that Fenton is a person of interest. Say that his business dealings are in question, and that he might have associates who aren't on the up-and-up. Say that any one of those associates might have knowledge of what happened to Paul. Explain to her that we need to obtain the facts, and that we're in the process of doing just that. And emphasize to her that she can't, under any circumstances, alert Fenton to our suspicions—not yet."

"I agree, but make it more personal," Claire amended. "Patrick, tie everything you say to Justin. Tell Amanda that she's holding her tongue to protect Justin. That her uncle might be shady, but that he has no idea where Paul is. That, if he did, he'd produce him because, no matter what, Justin's well-being is what's most important to him. Trust me, Patrick. Take that approach when you break the news to her. It's the only way Amanda will be able to rationally accept what you're saying. Otherwise, emotion will take over and she'll run off to confront her uncle and to demand answers—which is the last thing we want."

"I agree," Casey said. "Marc's procedure, Claire's technique. Combine the two and you've got your strategy." A sigh. "I'm sorry to dump this on you, Patrick. But you're with Amanda the most, and she's come to respect and rely upon you for her safety."

"I'll do it," Patrick agreed. "But don't you think it would be easier coming from Marc? He's kind of her knight in shining armor."

"No." Casey gave an adamant shake of her head. "Marc is definitely Amanda's rock. But you're her father figure. You've got a gentler touch and children of your own. Those are the qualifications that Amanda needs right now."

"Casey's right." Marc spoke with total objectivity. "My connection is with that poor baby. And, yeah, I know Amanda counts on me. But soothing and comforting aren't my strengths, nor is walking the emotional line Claire just described. You'll handle that a lot better than I would." A corner of Marc's mouth lifted. "And I'll handle the illegal missions a lot better than you would."

"No arguments there," Patrick said drily. "I'll take care of it. I'll head back to Sloane Kettering and relieve Roger right after I contact my buddy at the U.S. Marshals office."

"Excellent." Casey glanced around the table. "Questions?"

Silence, accompanied by four shakes of the head.

"Good. Then let's move."

CHAPTER TWENTY-FOUR

It was late when the FI van arrived in the Hamptons.

Ryan was driving. He dropped Claire off at Amanda's apartment. Then, he and Marc continued on. Hero was stretched out on the backseat of the van.

It was going to be a busy night on Shinnecock Bay.

First, they hit the Hampton Bays side of the bay, where Morano's trailer was stationed. Both Marc and Ryan were dressed in black to blend in with the night. They left the van a short distance away. Hero stayed inside, his acute bloodhound instincts telling him this was a time to be quiet and still. Ryan took Gecko. Marc took his waist pack of tools. They headed for the trailer.

"Wait." Like last time, Marc extended his arm to block Ryan's progress. "Get down." He took his own advice, squatting low to the ground.

"What now?" Ryan demanded, following suit. "Is someone torching the trailer?"

"Nope. Watching it."

Ryan's eyes widened. "Where?"

"There." Marc jerked his thumb toward a spot across the way.

It took Ryan a few minutes to make out the black SUV tucked away in the sandy alcove. The damned thing was nearly invisible.

"How the hell did you see that?" he asked Marc. "Never mind."

It was a stupid question. Marc had the instincts of a predatory cat.

"Is it the same arsonists about to do a repeat performance?" he asked instead.

"Uh-uh." Marc shook his head. "I'd say it's either the cops or private security. My guess? Private security. The cops would be patrolling, not sitting in the bushes, doing surveillance. And they can't afford SUVs. Morano's probably scared shitless. He must have hired someone to watch his new makeshift office." A frown. "We need a distraction."

He whipped out his cell phone and pressed Casey's number on speed dial.

"It's me," he said without preamble. "We have company out here. A black SUV, parked diagonally across from Morano's trailer on the Hampton Bays side of the marina." He gave Casey the exact location. "I need you to call 9-1-1 and report it as a suspicious vehicle. When the cops show up to check it out, and while they're busy interrogating the driver, Ryan and I will get inside the trailer. We'll be out and gone by the time they leave."

"We will?" Ryan asked incredulously as Marc punched off his phone.

"Yeah. We will." Marc stayed crouched down, indicating to Ryan that he should do the same. "Follow my lead. When the cops show up, we go. Fast. I'll get us in. You get Gecko installed. We'll be gone in three minutes tops."

"Shit. You're tougher than my MIT professors."

Marc gave a hard grin. "Get used to it. Real life is tougher than any Ivy League school. Now stay put."

It didn't take five minutes before a patrol car came speeding down the street and stopped behind the SUV.

Marc waited until the cop had gotten out of his vehicle and approached the SUV, his back turned toward them.

"That's our cue," he told Ryan. "Let's go."

They sprinted over to the trailer. Marc had the lock picked in thirty seconds. Then they were inside.

"I'll keep watch," Marc said. "You do what you have to." He went to the trailer window and stared out.

Ryan quickly scanned the space, focusing on the area of the ceiling where Gecko would have the widest visibility. Perfect. A gap in the ceiling tile that would allow Gecko's tiny video camera to see the whole room. He climbed onto Morano's desk, used his palm to push the tile up and to a side, and placed Gecko in position. Then he lowered the tile back into place.

"Done," he announced.

Marc was standing like a statue at the window, not moving or making a sound, just continuing his lookout. The cop and his partner were still talking to the driver of the SUV, probably checking out his credentials.

"Good." He spoke to Ryan without turning. "Let's get out of here."

They crept to the door and slipped out, making sure to lock the trailer door behind them.

There was one more tricky feat to accomplish before they took off.

Ryan stopped at the van long enough to extract the all-important small black box and to pull on his boots with the ankle gaffs and his leather gloves. Next came the body belt and safety strap. Once all his gear was in place, he climbed noiselessly up an adjacent telephone pole—away from the view of the cops—where he mounted the black box. That baby would receive Gecko's audio and video signal, encrypt them and transmit them over the internet via a secure tunnel opened between the black box and their firewall.

And Forensic Instincts would be able to watch and hear everything Morano did or said.

They drove away quietly, headlights off until they reached the main road. Then, Ryan flipped on the headlights, accelerated to a normal speed and steered the van around to the Southampton side of Shinnecock Bay where the marina and Fenton's yacht were located.

While Ryan was finding a hidden spot to park the van, Marc shrugged into a down parka. The hunter-green jacket was bland enough to be less than memorable, but contrasting enough so he didn't look like a cat burglar. For this second of his two break-ins, he wanted to seem like a regular guy taking a stroll with his dog.

Ryan parked the van in a desolate area a few hundred yards

from the marina. He unbuckled his seat belt and snapped off a salute to Marc.

"Have fun, you two," he said, indicating Hero. "I'll be in the back of the van with my computer doing the *real* work."

"Good to know I'm getting off easy," Marc retorted, zipping up his parka. "I'll try not to worry about you."

Ryan grinned. Marc didn't waste his time worrying. He just planned, executed and succeeded.

"I'm going back another decade on Everett and Morano," Ryan told him. "Hell, I'll go back to nursery school if I have to. There's got to be some kind of connection. I don't believe in coincidences."

"Neither do I." Marc had jumped out of the van, and was now leashing up Hero and collecting the backpack of items he needed for his excursion.

"I mapped out the location of the security cameras for you," Ryan reminded him.

"Got it." Marc pulled out the printed diagram Ryan had given him. "I'll make sure that Hero and I avoid them."

"The place is fenced in and gated, and there's a friggin' guard sitting in that booth in front." Ryan cast a troubled look at the marina. "The commercial building that Fenton's made into his personal boat garage is way in the back. You can't scale the fence, not with Hero in tow. And who knows what kind of private security Fenton has in place? This isn't going to be as easy as breaking into Morano's trailer."

"Never thought it would be." Marc shrugged, urging Hero to stand beside him. "I'll handle whatever's thrown at me. You just figure out what link there is between Morano and

Everett." He slung the backpack over his shoulder. "See you in a while."

"Yup. See you."

First things first.

Marc ambled along the pavement as if taking Hero for an evening stroll, but using that opportunity to pass by and assess the guard in his booth. The guy looked half-asleep, his feet up on the desk, his chin on his chest. No obstacle there.

Turning around, Marc strolled back to the gate. He assessed the lock and pulled out his tools. No challenge here, either.

Once he'd taken care of the lock, he opened the gate a crack—just enough so that he and Hero could slide through. He shut it behind them, leaving the lock hanging in place so the guard wouldn't notice anything. It was too dark for him to see that the lock was open—not that he was looking anyway.

Marc and Hero were inside.

Referring to Ryan's diagram, Marc walked Hero through the docks in a zigzag pattern that avoided the security cameras. Hero was intently sniffing, taking in every new and interesting scent around.

They reached the commercial building without incident.

Sure enough, there was a burly-looking security guard sitting outside the building. He jerked into a standing position the instant he saw Marc and Hero approach, then come to a halt beside him.

"Who the hell are you and what do you want?"

"I'm a mechanic," Marc replied, using his peripheral vision

to ensure that no one else was around. "Mr. Fenton asked me to check out something on his yacht."

"He didn't say a word to me." The guard fumbled for his cell. "You'll have to wait." He glanced down at his phone. "I've got to verify..."

The guard never finished his sentence.

Marc's arm was around his throat, his thumb pressing down on the carotid artery. With his other hand he pressed the guard's neck sideways in the same direction, and waited the few seconds it took for him to lose consciousness. Marc released his grip as the guard sank to the ground, and caught him as he did. He dragged the guy to the side of the building, where he'd be out of sight. He then tied his wrists and ankles with the thick cord he'd brought with him and stuffed a handkerchief in his mouth—just in case he regained consciousness before Marc's exit.

Hopefully, this wouldn't take long.

The lock on the building was almost as easy to pick as the one on the front gate had been.

He and Hero were inside in three minutes, the door shut behind them.

The building was dark, illuminated only by the faint moonlight that filtered in through the large skylight in the ceiling. It was enough to reveal the outline of a ship. Marc reached into his backpack and pulled out a flashlight. He clicked it on, shining it directly on the yacht. It was an exquisite vessel—streamlined, white, ninety feet long, and with the name *Lady Luck* printed in bold letters on the bow. An apt name for Fenton's private treasure.

Marc didn't waste a second. He gathered Hero up, balancing his ninety pounds of weight against his chest, and climbed up the ladder and over the side, placing the bloodhound onto the main deck of the yacht.

They explored the berth deck, concentrating on the stateroom and the bath. It didn't take long to find a few of Fenton's personal items—an old razor and a pair of swim trunks. Marc let Hero sniff them, then he shoved them into his backpack.

He pulled out the scent pads he'd made with Paul's smell on them, and gave one to Hero to sniff. Hero sniffed at it long and hard. Then, he picked up his head and bounded across to the galley kitchen. There, he sat down and pawed the ground. He refused to move, no matter what.

Bingo. Marc had his answer. Paul Everett had been on this yacht. And Fenton had never mentioned it. Casual business associates? Yeah, right.

With that important knowledge stored away, Marc gave Hero a coveted treat and then led him along the main deck and up the ladder to the bridge. All the controls—including the electronic radio controls—were located there.

Marc went straight for the control panel and quickly zeroed in on what he was looking for.

He pressed the power button on the rack-mounted Sailor Broadband unit and waited for the system to acquire a satellite. Once that was accomplished, he extended the retractable ethernet cable, plugging one end into his netbook, the other into the wall jack adjacent to the mahogany tabletop that served as Fenton's maritime office. When the Power, Terminal, and Antenna status lights on the Sailor 250 were solid green, Marc powered up his netbook. Opening up Firefox, he entered http://192.168.0.1 to gain access to the main menu.

Done.

Marc clicked on the Messages navigation button to look at all of Fenton's recent calls and text messages. He downloaded the call log to his netbook, saving the details for Ryan to decipher later.

Abruptly, while examining the phone book, something caught Marc's eye. It was an entry for *Big Money.*

Interesting.

He went into the software's edit mode, then copied the mobile number—870 area code. Didn't recognize it.

Clicking the Messages navigation button, and selecting the Write Message option, he pasted *Big Money's* phone number into the Recipient field and then composed a cryptic, one-word text message:

Status?

He changed Delivery Confirmation to Yes, clicked the send button and waited.

A brief interval passed. Then Marc got a confirmation. Shortly thereafter, his response arrived:

Why are you on your boat? Thought it was in storage for winter.

Marc considered what Fenton's reaction would be to having his whereabouts questioned. Then he responded:

My business, not yours. WHAT IS YOUR STATUS?

Sure enough, came the reply:

Sorry. All containers retrieved. Heading 4 Bayonne.

Marc did a double take. Then he typed his final message:

Good. Signing off.

Containers retrieved? In Marc's experience that meant one of a couple of things—either of which would put Fenton behind bars for a long, long time.

Ryan was sitting in the back of the van, thoroughly studying his computer screen, when Marc yanked open the back door and instructed Hero to jump in.

"Hey." Ryan's head snapped up. "How did it go?"

"It went." Marc gestured for him to return to the driver's seat. "I've got a call log for you to decipher. And we've got three other stops to make. Let's start with Westhampton Beach. We're picking up Claire."

"And the second stop—you're going to see Fenton."

"Yup. And third stop, Mercer. It's time to blow the lid off this case."

Thirty minutes after Marc left the marina, the captain of *Big Money* was crossing under the Verrazano-Narrows Bridge when the incoming-message indicator on his communications display terminal flashed again. Pressing the icon on the touch screen, he read:

Fenton (mobile).

The captain was puzzled about why Fenton would text him again, this time from his cell phone. While aboard *Lady*

Luck, he'd made it clear he was signing off, the implication being *Don't bother me.*

Quickly, the captain opened the text message. He panicked when he saw Fenton's request:

Status?

He didn't wait. "Goddfrey," he shouted to his first mate. "Call Fenton on his cell phone. It's an emergency."

CHAPTER TWENTY-FIVE

Fenton was waiting for Marc when the van arrived at the iron gates of his estate.

He eased aside his living-room drapes to watch the approaching headlights illuminate his lawn. This time he was worried. Very worried. He had no idea how much damaging information Marc Devereaux had come away with, but what Fenton had been briefed on was bad enough. This wasn't going to be a harmless fishing expedition like last time. It was going to be an ugly confrontation.

He would have called his lawyer and asked him to be present. But that would make him look as guilty as he really was.

He sucked in his breath and readied himself for what was to come.

Outside, the guard posted at the property entrance complied with Fenton's earlier instructions. He opened the iron gates and let the FI van pass through.

"Do you want me to come in with you two?" Ryan asked Marc, as he maneuvered down the labyrinth driveway.

"Nope." Marc shook his head. "I want you to continue your research and share some trail mix with Hero. He must be starved after his long night. As for Fenton, this visit will be most effective if I just walk in and surprise him with the team psychic. That'll freak him out."

"It freaks everyone out, right, Claire-voyant?" Ryan teased.

Claire's brows rose. It was the first normal comment Ryan had made to her since…well, since then. "Not everyone," she replied. "Mostly you."

Ryan met her gaze in the rearview mirror. "*Freaked out* is not the term I'd use. More like *intrigued* and *frustrated*."

Claire swallowed. "That's an improvement over *dismissive*."

"Yeah, well, people change. Although I still don't buy the communing with inanimate objects."

"Then how do you explain Gecko?"

"He's very animate. He just speaks a different language than we do."

"So do victims' personal items."

"Save it, you two," Marc interrupted. "Let's get the truth out of Fenton. And Mercer. Then you can go back to your game of one-upmanship."

"Good idea," Claire said. She averted her gaze and readied herself as the van approached the manor. "This should be interesting."

"Don't flip out if I go after the guy—I mean *really* go after him," Marc cautioned her.

"You mean beat him up?" She shrugged. "If it will help us save Justin, feel free. I'm a lot tougher than the bunch of you think."

Ryan coughed, but he said nothing. He just pulled the van around to the front of the house. "Good luck," he told them. "Shoot some video if you kick the guy's ass."

"Sure," Marc replied good-naturedly. "Claire, you have your cell, right?"

The butler ushered Claire and Marc directly to the study where Fenton sat at his desk. He did a double take when he saw Claire.

"We met at the hospital," he remembered aloud, scrutinizing her.

"We certainly did. Claire Hedgleigh," Claire reminded him.

"Right." Try though he did to keep up appearances, Fenton was definitely thrown. He knew who and what Claire was.

Shuffling some papers around on his desk, he snapped off commands to his butler. "Go. And shut the door behind you. I don't want to be disturbed—not for any reason."

"Yes, sir." The thin, uneasy-looking man disappeared.

"Why did you bring Ms. Hedgleigh with you?" Fenton demanded right away. "She wasn't there when you broke in and trespassed on my boat with your trained bloodhound."

"I have no idea what you're talking about." Marc's expression was nondescript. He glanced around the room. "I hope you're not stupid enough to have this room bugged. Your admissions, or lack thereof, are a lot more incriminating than mine."

"The room's not bugged. I'm an average man, Devereaux, not a spy."

"An average man?" This time, Marc raised a brow. "I wouldn't use that term to describe you. As for Claire, she's my colleague, and a trusted judge of character. I asked her to be here."

"She's a psychic."

"Yes, I am," Claire confirmed. "I pick up on all kinds of energy, good and bad."

"Bad energy isn't admissible in court," Fenton mocked her.

"I wasn't planning on testifying. Why? Should I be?"

Marc bit back a smile. He'd never seen this side of Claire. She was damned good.

"Stop dancing around the issue." Fenton planted his palms flat on his desk. "I know what happened tonight. My guard at the marina regained consciousness. Nice of you to pull the gag out of his mouth so he didn't choke, and loosen the ropes so he could free himself. The minute he did, he took off after you. Of course, you were already gone. But he called me on the spot. And he described you and your dog to a tee."

"Yet you didn't call the police." Marc looked thoughtful. "Interesting. If my property had been broken into, I'd be on the phone with the cops. Then again, I'm not a criminal scumbag like you."

Without so much as a pause, Marc tapped Claire's shoulder and pointed to the marble-framed photograph on the wall. "That's the ship I was telling you about," he said conversationally. "*Big Money.* Impressive, isn't it? It travels to Fenton's dock in Bayonne on a regular basis, retrieving containers as it goes. And it lives up to its name. It rakes in huge money—doesn't it, Fenton?"

Fenton wet his lips with the tip of his tongue. "My entire company is successful."

"I'm sure it is. Transporting illegal cargo really rakes in the cash."

"You don't know what you're talking about."

"Ah, but I do. It's a sweet deal. Your fleet is out there dredging anyway. Why not help out the mob and reap some extra profits at the same time?" Marc took a few menacing steps forward, his sarcastic tone turning cold as steel. "Did you plan on doing the same thing with your ferry service to the new hotel? Is that the deal you made with the mob? To take along their stash of guns or drugs while you transported tourists to the luxury resort? Is that why it took you so long to sign those contracts with Morano—because you were working out the specifics with the mob while they blackmailed him in the meantime?"

Fenton had gone sheet-white.

"It backfired, didn't it? When Morano couldn't afford his blackmailers anymore, they burned down his office. People could have been killed. I bet you didn't plan on adding murder to your list of crimes, now, did you?"

"I'm not listening to another word," Fenton barked. "You don't have a shred of proof to back up any of these outrageous charges."

"Fortunately, I don't need any." Marc's tone was now low, threatening. "My job is not to bring you to justice, much as I'd love to. I work for Forensic Instincts, not law enforcement. My job is to find Paul Everett. As it turns out, he was on your private yacht, *Lady Luck,* right before he disappeared. And that I do have proof of. Solid, admissible proof." Marc stretched the truth—and it worked.

"So you *were* on my yacht," Fenton burst out. "You admit it."

"Why? Because I know her name? Public record, Fenton." Marc leaned over the desk, his eyes ablaze, his stance ominous. "Are you denying that Everett was there?"

Fenton shrank back. Marc was more than a little scary when he looked like this. "No, I'm not denying it. We had a business meeting there."

"One you never mentioned?"

"Why would I mention it? You asked if Everett and I were business colleagues. We were. We had several meetings. One of them was on my yacht. Last I checked, that wasn't a crime."

"Did Everett figure out what you were up to? Is that why he conveniently disappeared? Was it your call or was it the mob's?"

Fenton's pupils dilated, and his jaw literally dropped. "You think I killed Paul Everett?"

"Maybe. Maybe not. Maybe you just made sure he was somewhere else, out of the way."

Fenton was starting to sweat profusely. "My niece's child—my great-nephew—is dying. His father is the only real hope he has. Do you honestly think I'd take away his best chance to live?"

"Justin wasn't born when Paul Everett vanished," Claire reminded him. "So it might have been too late when you realized how vitally important Paul Everett was to his son's life." She pursed her lips. "Very dark energy, Mr. Fenton. Very dark, and very ugly. You're a despicable man."

Fenton raked both hands through his hair. "This is insane. I didn't kill anyone. And I didn't stash Paul Everett away.

I don't know what happened to him or who's responsible. But it wasn't me."

That spurred Marc into action.

He grabbed Fenton by the lapels, dragged him forward. "What did Everett find when he was on your boat? Did he overhear a conversation? Did he put together the pieces? Or did he find something concrete—like the containers themselves? Tell me, you son of a bitch, or I'll make you wish you were never born."

Fenton struggled to free himself. But Marc's grip was unbreakable.

"Let go of me," Fenton commanded.

"I'm just getting started. Now it's only your designer suit that's in danger of being torn apart. In a few minutes, it'll be a whole lot more. Now talk." Marc shook him hard. "What happened when Everett was on your boat?"

"Nothing." Fenton was starting to get scared. The expression on Marc's face was lethal. "We talked about the hotel. We talked about Amanda."

"How touching. I'm sure he confided his innermost feelings to you." Marc's grip tightened again, and he yanked Fenton forward until he was halfway across the desk. "That's a bunch of bullshit. You didn't discuss Everett's social life. He spent the time trying to convince you to sign onto his hotel project. And you kept him at arm's length—for the same reason you were doing it with Morano. How much in kickbacks did you get from the twenty grand they each paid the mob every six weeks?"

"Nothing. I didn't know…"

Marc was around the desk in a microsecond. He pinned Fenton to the wall, digging his elbow into his throat, keeping the threat real. "Yes, you did. You knew everything. Just like you profited from everything. Now, am I going to do some serious damage to your body, or are you going to answer me?"

Fenton gazed past Marc, giving Claire a frightened look. "Are you going to just stand there and let this barbarian physically assault me?"

"Hmm." Claire pursed her lips thoughtfully. "Yes," she replied. "I am."

"I'm not admitting to anything," Fenton gasped as the pressure of Marc's elbow intensified. "Nothing except the business meeting on my yacht. But I swear I didn't have anything to do with Paul Everett's disappearance."

"Who did?"

"I don't know. You don't ask certain people those kinds of questions."

"I'll bet you don't." Marc lifted Fenton by the throat and threw him down to the floor, discarding him like a piece of trash. "I'd love to kick the crap out of you. But it doesn't suit my purposes—not right now. Right now, all I care about is finding Paul Everett. And you don't know shit about his whereabouts. But you're going to find out. You're going to dig as deep as you have to, ask the scariest people you know. And, if you're lucky, they'll have my answers."

Fenton stared up at Marc, his forehead drenched in sweat. He made no move to stand up. "Do you know what they'll do to me if I accuse them, or even press them for answers?"

"Do you know what *I'll* do to you if you don't?" Marc loomed over Fenton, eyes blazing like fire. "Uncle Sam trained me well. I can kill you anytime I want to—no matter where you are or who's protecting you. Do you know what a SEAL is capable of? Bin Laden never stood a chance. Which means you sure as hell don't. Get me information. Tonight. Then I might show you some mercy by only breaking body parts you never knew you had. And afterward, just for laughs, I'll make an anonymous call to the cops and get you thrown into jail for smuggling—plus a whole list of other crimes you don't even know I'm aware of. I may not be law enforcement now, but I was once FBI. One phone call from me, and they'll take care of the rest."

With that, Marc turned and headed for the door, gesturing for Claire to join him. "I'll be in touch in the morning, Fenton. Make sure you have answers."

"Okay, you're officially terrifying," Claire commented as they headed toward the van.

"And you *are* a whole lot tougher than I realized." Marc snapped off a salute. "I'm impressed."

"That man is scum," Claire replied. "Every time you accused him of something, I got a flash of violence and dirty money. The only thing I got nothing on was each time you asked about Paul Everett's whereabouts. I kept coming up blank—well, almost blank. I'm pretty certain that Paul disappeared because of Fenton, but not by his hand."

"I agree." Marc nodded, opening the van door so Claire could climb in. "I'm not even sure he knows who to go to for answers. But he'll torture himself trying. He's going to have one miserable, sleepless night—and put himself in a shitload of danger. Plus, we'll get leads from the calls he makes, since Ryan's monitoring his phone records. That's good enough for me right now."

"He didn't know where Everett is?" Ryan surmised from the tail end of the conversation.

"Nope. But he'll be busting his ass to find out."

"You played your trump card."

"I sure did. Laid it all out for him. Along with some proper incentive, if you get my drift."

"How much blood was there to clean up?" Ryan inquired.

"None." Claire grinned. "Marc's a very neat worker."

"But you accomplished what you set out to do."

Marc nodded. "And once we find Paul Everett and save our client's baby, I'll make sure the details of Fenton's crimes fall into the right hands."

Ryan got it. "Do you still want to go to Mercer's?"

"Definitely. He's back home during the Congressional winter break. It's time we had a little chat and tied up some loose ends. You're welcome to join Claire and me for this one—unless you're in midresearch. No need to spring Claire on Mercer as the omniscient psychic. I've got a different agenda in mind for him."

"I can join you, no problem. I made my own headway while you were roughing up Fenton," Ryan replied as he drove away from Fenton's mansion.

"The call log?" Marc asked.

"Nope. That's next on my list. But I finally found a link between Paul Everett and John Morano. Weird that I missed it until now. It seems the two guys have the same real-estate attorney."

"Interesting." Marc processed that piece of data. "So this attorney is the one who worked with each of them on the hotel project."

"Yup. I saw the real-estate documents themselves, pulled

them up on the computer. The lawyer's name is Frederick Wilkenson. He's got a stellar reputation, a spotless record and an office right in Southampton. I think we should spend the night at Amanda's place so I can pay him a visit tomorrow morning—just to size him up. He's not going to say anything. He'll cite attorney-client privilege."

"I agree. But it's worth you feeling him out. It's interesting—and somewhat unusual—that he represents both Morano and Everett. And it's suspicious that you didn't uncover this until now, not given the in-depth search you've been doing. It makes this whole situation smell even worse. And while you're visiting Wilkenson, I'll make my repeat performance at Fenton's and see what I scared up."

"Works for me."

"Let's just make sure we're not needed at home," Marc said. "We'll check in with Casey after our chat with Mercer. If she agrees, we'll make our morning social calls."

Casey was frustrated as hell.

She was batting zero, having gotten nothing out of the cops and nothing out of Detective Jones. Oh, he knew something. Casey picked that up from his body language. But he'd obviously been told to keep quiet, whether by his supervisor or by someone higher up, she wasn't sure. But, short of getting herself tossed in jail, Casey had tried everything, to no avail.

Then there was Patrick's phone call to his buddy with the U.S. Marshals. Another stone wall. His friend hadn't come out and denied that Paul Everett was in the Witness Protection Program, but he hadn't admitted it, either. Again, whatever was going on with Paul Everett, the U.S. Marshals had also been told to keep a lid on it.

After that unproductive attempt, Patrick had had the unpleasant task of talking to Amanda, telling her about her uncle.

She didn't take it well. In fact, it had taken all of Patrick's abilities of persuasion to keep her from calling Fenton up and demanding answers. Thanks to Claire's advice, which Patrick had employed, Amanda had settled down enough to concentrate on Justin and let FI handle her uncle.

Justin hadn't gotten worse. Then again, he hadn't gotten better, either. He was still on the ventilator, his breathing labored as he continued battling the pneumonia.

Things on Casey's end just plain sucked.

Things weren't going too well with Hutch, either. The tension between them was so thick, it was stifling.

When Casey went upstairs to grab a quick nap before Marc called in, she found Hutch sitting at the edge of the bed, his fingers steepled beneath his chin. His half-packed bag was sitting on the floor beside him.

Casey paused in the bedroom doorway. "You're leaving?"

He turned, his jaw tight. "I'm due back the day after tomorrow. I was just trying to decide whether or not it paid to stay till then. I'm trying to help you, but I'm afraid we'll kill each other if I hang around."

Sighing, Casey shut the door behind her. "I know you're angry at me and worried about me. I also know you understand where I'm coming from. You're torn. I get it. But we've had this discussion a dozen times. I'm not trying to impede an FBI investigation. I'm just trying to save my client's child. And if those two things conflict, then I have no choice but to piss off the Bureau." She paused. "If you'd tell me more, perhaps I could avoid messing up their investigation."

"You know I can't do that. Not that I'm a fountain of knowledge. You already figured out that I was shut down. I just know that the Bureau is not open to discussion on this one. Which tells me you're dealing with dangerous people. So, yeah, I'm worried. And I'm pissed. You're so fucking stubborn. There's got to be another way to help your client."

"Come up with it, and I'll listen."

Hutch frowned. "Maybe we can come up with it together."

"We can do a lot of things together, Hutch. This isn't one of them. I already screwed up by telling you too much. You took it all back to the Bureau. I want to punch you for that. And I want to punch myself for letting it happen."

"I understand." Hutch blew out a long, frustrated breath. "And I'm not sure there's a way around your impasse. Any step you take is going to be the wrong one. It's driving me crazy to watch. It'll be worse if I see something I shouldn't—and I have to report it. Which is why I think I should head back to Quantico."

Casey gave a resigned nod. "I hear you. I don't like it. But I hear you."

Hutch rose and walked over to her, gently caressing her shoulders. "We really have one hell of a complicated relationship, don't we?"

"That's the understatement of the year." Casey sighed. "Hope I'm worth it."

"Oh, yeah, you're worth it. I always did like complicated."

Casey smiled, raising her gaze to meet his. "I've got some downtime right now. I was going to take a nap. But I could be persuaded to change my plans—if you're willing to leave a little later for Virginia."

A sexy grin curved his lips. "Virginia? Where's that?"

CHAPTER TWENTY-SIX

Unlike Fenton, Mercer was definitely *not* expecting the FI team. He looked puzzled and upset when they rang his doorbell.

"Is there some emergency?" he asked. He was dressed comfortably in a pair of sweatpants and a fleece top—the expected attire of a man lounging at home at midnight. "I was just about to turn in."

"We're sorry to bother you, Congressman." It was Claire who spoke up, softening the late-night intrusion. "But, yes, it is urgent that we speak to you right away. Otherwise, we never would have come by this late."

"Okay." Mercer opened the door and gestured for them to enter.

"Cliff? Is everything all right?" Mary Jane Mercer hurried down the stairs, wearing a lounging robe and the frightened look of a mother whose mind had immediately gone to the well-being of her children. She stopped halfway when she saw who was there. "What's happened?" she demanded.

Marc kept his gaze fixed on the congressman. "An urgent matter. We need to talk to your husband immediately."

"Your children are fine," Claire clarified at once. "This has nothing to do with them."

Mrs. Mercer visibly relaxed. "It can't wait till morning?"

"Afraid not," Marc said.

"It's okay, honey." Mercer indicated that his wife should go back upstairs. "This won't take long. And if it concerns Amanda Gleason's sick baby, I want to help."

"Of course." She turned around and retraced her steps.

"Why don't we go into my office?" Mercer suggested. "It's comfortable and private."

Nodding, the three of them followed the congressman and assembled in his spacious home office.

"I don't believe we've met," Cliff Mercer said to Ryan.

"We haven't." Ryan extended his hand. "Ryan McKay. I work for Forensic Instincts, as well."

A nod. "Well, have a seat and tell me what this is all about. Is the baby all right?"

"He's holding his own," Ryan said carefully. "But it's touch-and-go. Which means that every second counts. And that his best chance of survival is still his father."

"Have you had any luck locating Paul Everett?"

"We're hoping for a breakthrough—soon," Marc said, taking over. As planned, he was going to run the conversation.

"How can I help?"

"By telling us about Lyle Fenton."

Cliff stiffened, visibly taken aback by the topic. "Lyle? What is it you want to know?"

"A great deal. We just came from his house."

By now, Mercer was clearly on guard. "And?"

"And it wasn't pleasant. Nor did we get very far. All we found out is that Paul Everett was aboard Fenton's private yacht a short time before he disappeared."

Mercer's eyes widened. "You suspect Lyle of having something to do with Everett's disappearance?"

"Do you?"

"No, of course not. Lyle Fenton is a friend of mine."

"Yes, we know." Marc just pushed right on. "He subsidized your campaign. And now he counts on you to help him out."

This time, Mercer's eyes narrowed. "What are you implying?"

"Nothing that isn't true. You're in Fenton's pocket. We know it. And frankly, we really don't care. But you do." Marc waved away Mercer's oncoming protest. "Don't bother denying it. We don't want your head. We want leverage. We intend to use it to save a child."

"What kind of leverage?" Mercer was starting to get angry.

"Anything you know about Fenton that might help us find Paul Everett. As I said, we don't give a damn about nailing anyone to the wall. All we want is information."

"So you're blackmailing me." Mercer stared from one of them to the other. "With what? The fact that I share the same goals for my district as Lyle Fenton, and that I use my influence in Congress to promote those goals? I think I just described every politician I know."

"Except for the fact that, in your case, the reason you promote Fenton's goals is because he's your father."

Mercer started as if he'd been struck, all the color draining from his face. He said absolutely nothing.

"We're talking about a whole different level of scandal," Marc continued. "So, before you answer, decide what's most important to you."

"Who else knows?" Mercer asked bluntly.

"We haven't gone public. We don't intend to—not unless you force our hand. Just tell us everything you can about Fenton, the people he associates with, any illegal activities he's involved in—anything that might lead us to Paul Everett."

Mercer blew out a weary breath. "I purposely separate myself from Lyle's outside life. Frankly, I don't want to know the answers you're looking for, so I'm careful not to ask questions. Which means I have nothing to tell you. Does that mean you're going to announce my paternity to the world?"

"No." It was Claire who spoke up. "You don't deserve that."

Both Marc and Ryan turned to look at her.

"He's telling the truth," she said simply. "He's weak and Fenton uses that to his advantage. He has a good idea what his biological father is capable of, but he divorces himself from it. So, as I said, he's a weak man, but he's not a bad man. Most important, he's completely in the dark about what happened to Paul Everett or where he might be. We'd have nothing to gain by ruining his career. He can't help us." She rose. "Let's go."

Marc hesitated, then gave a tight nod. "You're very lucky I have so much faith in my colleague, Congressman," he said. "I wouldn't be walking away so readily if she weren't as certain as she is."

"She's right." Mercer was visibly grateful and relieved. "I'll turn a blind eye to a lot of things, but not to violence or murder. Plus, I'm a parent myself. I love my children. I'd never stand in the way of Amanda Gleason's search for her baby's father. Especially not under these circumstances." He paused. "Do you really believe Lyle had something to do with Everett's disappearance?"

"More and more, it's looking that way, yes," Marc replied.

"Then I'll keep my ears open. If Lyle says or does anything that I think you should know, I'll call you."

Again, Marc glanced at Claire, and again, Claire nodded.

"Then we won't keep you any longer," Marc said, coming to his feet. "Thank you for seeing us, Congressman. Good night."

Casey sat up in bed to take Marc's call.

She listened carefully to everything he had to say. "So let's cross Mercer off our suspect list. Back to Fenton. You think that Paul figured out he was involved?" she asked cryptically, and quietly, so as not to awaken—and alert—Hutch. "And that, as a result, he had to be disposed of?"

"Or he disposed of himself," Marc replied. "It's possible that Everett disappeared off the grid out of fear for his own life."

"So thoroughly that even the FBI can't find him?"

"It's happened in the past. You know that. Even fugitives on the FBI's Most Wanted list have gotten away and vanished for years. Everett could be anywhere, in hiding with anyone. Remember, Amanda only knew him for five months. He could have old friends, distant family members, even a wife that she doesn't even know exists."

"And the FBI is searching for him in order to get a solid case against Fenton."

"Makes sense, doesn't it?"

"Actually, yes, it does." A pause as she glanced over at

Hutch, whose slow, even breathing told her he was still in deep slumber. But she wasn't taking any chances. "Uh…I think we should continue this discussion in person."

"Hutch is with you," Marc deduced. "How much did he overhear?"

"Nothing. He's asleep. But I don't want to press my luck. Are you headed home now?"

"We weren't planning on it. We were planning on staying out here till morning." Marc went on to explain Ryan's findings about Everett and Morano's mutual real-estate attorney.

"Ryan should pay him a visit," Casey agreed. "Plus you'll want to follow up on Fenton. See if putting the fear of God in him had any results. If nothing else, you showing up on his doorstep again will probably make him wet his pants." Casey couldn't help but smile. "It wouldn't be the first time you've gotten that response from a suspect."

"True." Marc sounded more matter-of-fact than amused. "So what's on tap for you?"

"Hutch is leaving in the morning." Casey stated it as a fact. She knew that Marc wouldn't ask for, nor require, any further explanation. "As soon as he takes off, I'm heading over to the hospital to check on Amanda. She didn't take Patrick's news too well. And, after what you just told me, it's even more important that she not confront her uncle. She could screw up everything."

"She can't," Marc agreed. "We're right on the brink."

Fallujah, Iraq

It was pouring—a bone-chilling, miserable day.

Rain was a common occurrence in this portion of Iraq in

December. As a rule, if you got off lucky, the precipitation was light and spotty. Not so today. It was coming down in sheets, the heavy winds blowing the palm trees around. Unlike back home, the ground here didn't absorb the water, so it turned the sand into deep, thick mud, making the ground you walked on feel like a vat of peanut butter. In an attempt to deal with the water, the military spread stones over acres of land. It did a decent job, but, between the stones and the mud, walking became next to impossible. And he could forget about his daily five-mile run. That sure as hell wasn't happening.

He was trudging toward his barracks, drenched and ankle-deep in muck, when the military transport drove by. It stopped, deposited its sole passenger and his bag, and then continued on its way.

The two men saw and recognized each other right away. They'd both served in the same U.S. Army infantry squad fifteen years ago.

"Hey, Paul." Gus Ludlock yelled out and waved his arm.

Paul stopped, dragging the hood of his rain slicker higher on his head to block out the rain. "Gus, hey," he called back. "I didn't know you were out here."

"Me, either." His Army Reserves friend grinned. "Do we ever?" He shielded his face against the elements. "We'll talk later. Oh, apparently, you're famous."

"What?" Paul gave a puzzled shrug.

"Famous," Gus repeated. "I saw you on a YouTube video at the NEC. Couldn't catch the audio because I was headed out. But some hot brunette was holding up your picture. You must've done something heroic you don't know about—the video has over a million hits."

The wind chose that moment to pick up, nearly blowing down both men.

"Let me check in," Gus shouted. "We'll catch up later."

Paul stood there for a long moment after his friend had headed off. Oblivious to the pelting rain and the sludge that was oozing up his legs like quicksand, he stared off into space, plagued by a growing sense of unease. This whole trip had felt wrong from the start. Now it was beginning to feel like one ugly, well-planned manipulation. Being sent out to this godforsaken place with a line of bullshit justifying the training he was instructed to provide. Being at a Forward Operating Base in a high-threat situation. Being allowed no internet access, given the three soldiers who'd recently been killed nearby, and whose families had to be notified. Being in an area that just happened to have little to no cell phone reception—effectively cutting off all communication with the outside world.

There were way too many coincidences.

And now this odd piece of news.

Whatever charade he was being forced to live was over.

As a military veteran who knew how the system worked, Paul had no trouble calling in a few favors. When the bad weather temporarily subsided, a military buddy of his picked him and his bags up in a crummy Humvee and drove him to the helipad located on the FOB. The sergeant responsible for the flights was stationed in a tent right on-site. He was expecting Paul and arranged to put him on the first flight out. Someone would be pissed off at being bumped.

Paul didn't give a damn.

It was a fifty-mile trip. A little over an hour later, Paul was back in Baghdad.

He waited awhile, the sergeant having made arrangements for a trusted buddy stationed at the New Embassy Compound to pick him up. A beat-up SUV eventually arrived, driven by Private Kenny Robinson. Fifteen minutes after that, Paul was back at the Embassy.

He didn't waste time. He went into Kenny's office cubicle and used his computer to log on to YouTube. He searched for the name Paul Everett, and the video popped up.

He watched it three times before the impact of what he was viewing fully sank in. He went from shocked to numb to livid in rapid succession.

Culminating in an urgency he'd never before possessed.

Everything that happened next was a frenzied blur.

He grabbed his BlackBerry and tried to call out. The storms in the area refused to make that possible. Well, they weren't going to stop him from getting home.

He used Private Robinson's computer one more time—to send an internal email. He knew that the message would furiously keep trying to leave the local email server, waiting until the storms let up. But eventually it would find its mark.

His boss would cringe. Not at his profanity. Nor at his threats. But rather at the thought of who had been CC'd: the head of the Review Committee.

The email was clear and straight to the point:

I'm done being jerked around. I now know everything. I've seen the video and I'm flying back to the U.S. When I land, I'm going straight to Sloane Kettering to see Amanda and try to save my son. If anything happens to him, I hold you and every other fucking bureaucrat responsible. STAY OUT OF MY WAY!

Paul knew he was racing the clock, not only to get to his son, but to thwart any efforts to prevent him from getting home. He turned to Kenny, asked for his help in getting to Baghdad International Airport. From there, he'd talk himself onto the next military flight to Kuwait. He'd get from the airbase to the airport. There'd be waiting time—a lot of it. But he'd wait for days if he had to. He was heading home.

To Justin.

The emergency meeting took place in a small, nondescript conference room.

The group—and the subject matter—were classified: the head of the entire office, the team leader and the Assistant U.S. Attorney were all there.

"He left the Forward Operating Base," the team leader reported. "No one at the New Embassy Compound has seen him."

The Assistant U.S. Attorney scowled. "Which means you have no idea where he is."

"We've got key personnel searching the whole embassy. We'll find him."

As they spoke, the phone in the conference room rang. The team leader picked it up. "Yes?"

A long moment of silence, and then the team leader hung up.

"He left the embassy. He's already on a flight to Kuwait."

CHAPTER TWENTY-SEVEN

Patricia Carey couldn't shut an eye all night long.

She was in her office, pacing restlessly about at 5:00 a.m. The current situation forced a flood of raw emotion to surface. How darkly ironic life was. As the Executive Assistant Director, she was the highest-ranking woman in the entire agency. All her life, she'd exceeded everyone's expectations. In school. In training. In her rapid rise to a position of power. At forty-six years old, she was still successful at everything she did.

Except for the one thing that would truly have been her legacy.

Despite consultations with the most noted experts in the world, and the hundreds of thousands of dollars she'd paid them, she'd failed.

She blamed herself entirely. She'd waited too long. The

"Shit." The AUSA slammed his fist on the table. "We can't let this happen. We've *got to* stop him."

The phone rang again.

"Yes?" was the impatient response. Then a pause. "Thank you." A few quick clicks on the team leader's laptop. "He emailed us."

Everyone listened as the email was read aloud.

"He's not coming to D.C.," the AUSA realized aloud. "He's going straight to JFK."

"Then we'll have him detained there." The office head paused. "In the meantime, we've got to wrap up this investigation. One day. That's all we've got."

"If we have that," the AUSA replied. "What happens when he tries to contact Amanda Gleason by phone? You know he will. And there'll be no weather to screw up his cell service."

"We'll take care of that."

At that heightened moment, the office head's BlackBerry rang. He glanced at the caller ID and blanched. "It's *her.*" He gestured urgently toward the door, ordering everyone to leave.

Minutes later, urgent instructions arrived at the desk of the head network security analyst on duty. He thrust aside his current assignment and turned quickly to the task at hand. With a few mouse clicks, he disabled the targeted cell phone, transforming it into nothing more than an expensive paperweight.

rise of her career had pushed this onto the back burner. She'd climbed the proverbial ladder, all the while thinking that later would be fine. But when later came, Mother Nature had other plans. And her body refused to cooperate.

Tears. Trials. Injections. In vitro. Nothing had worked.

By the time she'd accepted the inevitable, even adoption was not in the cards. Her age, her now-greater set of professional responsibilities, and, most of all, her depleted emotional reserves—all those factors combined to rule out the prospect of adoption.

A baby was precious. But, for her, it was never to be.

So, yes, her circumstances had colored her thinking. But still she'd debated the current dilemma long and hard, forcing herself to be objective, to view things from all angles. She had the final say. And her primary responsibility was to the agency.

But at what cost?

The hours ticked by, slowly and painfully. Patricia drank her coffee and searched her soul. The decision would be hers. So would the ramifications.

Patricia's bleary-eyed assistant, Sharon, knocked and then poked her head into the office. "It's eight o'clock, ma'am. The contingent from New York has arrived. They've been driving all night to make this meeting. Everyone is assembled in the conference room as you ordered. Will there be anything else?"

"Yes," Patricia replied. "I need to see Richard before I go to this meeting. Have him come to my office now."

"Of course."

A few minutes later, Richard Fieldstone, the Deputy Assistant Director of the Criminal Investigative Unit, and the

Chairman of CUORC—the Criminal Undercover Operation Review Committee—stepped into his boss's office. "You wanted to see me, Pat?"

"Yes." She waved him in. "Close the door behind you and have a seat."

Once he'd complied, she folded her hands in front of her on the desk. "I'm about to attend a very important meeting, one whose outcome will ultimately end up in CUORC's lap. Let me bring you up to speed on the difficult situation we're facing. Then I'm going to lay out the way I want this handled and the outcome I want you and CUORC to achieve."

Richard's brows rose. CUORC was a joint entity that consisted of their own representatives and representatives from the Department of Justice. The Committee met bimonthly at headquarters, and made its own independent recommendations. It was unprecedented—although well within Patricia's power to do so—for her to insert herself in the decision-making process.

"Go on," he said.

Patricia told him the entire story, omitting no details. She didn't want him to be blindsided by a single thing that might and would be said when CUORC held its emergency meeting.

Richard listened without saying a word. When she was finished, he asked, "I just want to be clear about this—are you saying that if CUORC votes in favor of the Bureau and against the individual, you'll override our decision?"

"That's exactly what I'm saying." Patricia spoke calmly and with authoritative finality. "I'm instructing you to hold the emergency meeting today, and I'm giving you the responsibility of shaping the outcome so as to avoid any confrontation. This way, the decision will be CUORC's and no one will be the wiser. That said, if you come to me with any other recommendation, rest assured, I will overrule it. I'd prefer it not come to that, which is why I'm giving you a heads-up."

Richard studied her unyielding expression. "Why this time?"

"Simple," Patricia replied. "I will *not* be the one responsible for letting an innocent baby die. And I will *not* allow the FBI to be held responsible in the court of public opinion for letting an innocent baby die."

Hutch was still asleep when Casey left the brownstone the next morning. But he'd clearly gotten up sometime during the wee hours of the morning, when she'd been out for the count, because his overnight bag was unpacked and his toothbrush was back in the bathroom.

Casey smiled. Tough as the situation was, she was glad he'd decided to stay. He had to be back at Quantico tomorrow anyway. And if they could grab one more night together, it would be worth the professional tension that permeated the air whenever their careers collided.

Nothing good was waiting for her at Sloane Kettering.

The minute she arrived at the PICU, Patrick warned her that Amanda was in a highly depressed state. Justin had had a fitful night, and Dr. Braeburn was concerned that there had been no improvement in his breathing or in his overall condition. The antibiotics should be doing their job by now.

Casey nodded, and then went down the hall.

She stood on the other side of the window, watching Amanda try to hold Justin. It was next to impossible with the ventilator and the chest tube in place. And she was clearly terrified about inadvertently jostling any of the apparatus, for fear that it would cause them to stop working—even for an instant.

It broke Casey's heart to see Amanda bow her head and brokenly sob over this tiny little person who had endured so much in his few short weeks of life. Her shoulders quaked with emotion as she stroked his face, his downy head. Tears slid down her cheeks and fell onto the railing of Justin's crib.

Dammit, Casey thought, squeezing her own eyes shut. Why couldn't the FBI understand this? Why couldn't she drag the whole miserable lot of them into this PICU to see the consequences of their actions, to see the result of their impeding FI's search for Paul Everett? What if it had been their child whose life was on the line? What in the name of heaven could matter more? Some stupid case?

Tears brimming in her own eyes, Casey turned away. She'd lost all objectivity where it came to the FBI's handling of this investigation. Obviously, whatever they were pursuing was major. But that wasn't this poor baby's fault. He deserved the right to live, to thrive. And—if he was lucky enough to do both—he deserved the right to know his father.

Amanda glanced up and spotted Casey outside, her back turned toward her. She resettled Justin in his crib and rose, walking slowly out to where Casey stood.

"Hi, Casey," she said quietly, a tremor still in her voice. "How long have you been here."

"I just arrived." Casey dashed away her tears and turned around. She wasn't fooling anyone with her show of bravado, but it was her job to appear strong. So strong she would be. "No change?" she asked, fully aware of the answer.

"None." Amanda eyelids were puffy, and there were deep, dark circles beneath her eyes. She looked as if she'd aged ten years this week. "Have you gotten any information from my uncle?"

"Nothing concrete. Marc met with him last night. He's going back again this morning. We honestly don't believe he knows where Paul is. But it's possible some of his colleagues do. We won't let it go until we find out."

"His colleagues," Amanda repeated. "Yes, those were the words Patrick used. But I'm not a fool. What you're saying is that my uncle has mob connections."

Casey blew out her breath. "All we have is speculation to go on."

"I don't believe that. You're too thorough of a woman to fly by the seat of your pants. You know something."

"And when that something translates into hard facts, you'll be the first to know it." Casey raked a hand through her hair. "I realize how much we're asking of you. But please trust us. We're pushing this to the limit. If any of your uncle's associates knows something, we'll get at it. In the meantime, just promise me you won't contact him. And don't take his calls. It would only complicate what's already a delicate situation."

"I won't." Amanda's lips thinned. "But if I find out he had any part in Paul's disappearance—or even if he knew a thing about it—I won't be responsible for what I'll do."

"I don't blame you. Just do it after we find Paul."

Marc called Casey as she was driving home.

"What's up?" she asked, emotionally drained and bone weary.

"You sound like hell." As usual, Marc cut right to the chase.

"That's because I just came from seeing Amanda. She's *in* hell. Tell me that Fenton gave you something."

"Only a restraining order." Marc chuckled. "Evidently I'm a danger to him. So I never got through his gates today. On the plus side, he's been making phone calls like a demon. Probably warning off his 'contacts' and telling them they won't be using his fleet to transport illegal cargo anytime soon."

"And Ryan's tracing the calls?"

"Oh, yeah. Your plan was genius—scare Fenton, watch him run. Ryan's hard at work—we'll probably have the names of half the mob by the time he's done."

Casey sighed. "All we need are the ones who took part in Paul's disappearance—if any of them did." A pause. "What happened with Ryan and that attorney?"

"It was a bust, just as we expected," Marc replied. "The guy is a Boy Scout without a blemish on his record. He loves kids and puppies and gives to all the local charities. So you think he'd be the epitome of compassion in a situation like this one. But, nope. He shut down like a clam the minute he heard what Ryan wanted. Didn't give him so much as a clue. He stuck to attorney-client privilege, and said he'd talk to us only if we got written permission from John Morano."

"Right, like Morano's going to give us that."

"Exactly. But, judging from Ryan's description, this lawyer is just too good to be true. It only makes this situation stink even more."

"Agreed."

Marc paused. "Is Hutch gone?" he asked diplomatically.

"No, I think he's staying till tomorrow."

Marc heard her loud and clear. "Good. Then he and I can grab a beer before he takes off."

"I'll let him know." Casey pulled up to the curb and parked the car, grateful that she'd found a spot only half a block from the office. Meanwhile, she could hear Ryan's muffled voice talking to Marc at the other end of the phone.

"Hey, Case?" Marc responded. "Ryan asked if you'd stop in the conference room when you get back to the office and see if we're getting Gecko's transmission from Morano's trailer. It seemed to be functioning well the last time Ryan checked his laptop—which, by the way, was fifteen minutes ago—but he wants to double-check that it's coming through clearly at your end so we have a backup copy on the server."

"No problem. I'm here. I'll do that first thing."

"You won't be seeing anything too impressive," Marc reminded her. "Just the crappy interior of a trailer-turned-office. And a polished, harried-looking guy."

"Morano."

"Yup. Morano."

"Got it." Casey unbuckled her seat belt. "I'm hanging up now. I'll give you a call later."

She went straight upstairs to the conference room and sat down at the large oval table.

"Good morning, Casey," Yoda greeted her. "Will you be requiring my services?"

"Yes, Yoda. Please display the live feed from Gecko."

"Certainly. Would you like me to fill the entire wall?"

"No. Please size the video for optimal resolution."

"Engaging Faroudja video enhancement," Yoda announced. A brief pause. "Video is coming up now. How is the quality, Casey?"

"Perfect, Yoda." Casey focused on the screen and the clear image that had appeared. "Thank you."

"My pleasure. Let me know if you need anything else." Yoda fell silent.

Yup. Gecko was doing a fine job, Casey thought, leaning forward to scrutinize the picture. She could clearly make out the dumpy trailer that Morano was using as an office. Morano was in and at his desk. Casey recognized him from the online photos Ryan had showed her when he traced Morano's background. The guy wasn't doing anything too exciting; just typing at his keyboard and flipping through a few files.

Just as Casey was about to call her findings in to Ryan, Morano's cell phone rang. Not the one on his desk, but another one, which he yanked out of his pants pocket.

"Yeah," he answered. He went rigid. "What do you mean, he's on his way home? How the hell did he get out of there so fast? And how did he put the pieces together?" A pause. "Shit. He'll be flying straight to JFK. That's just thirteen hours in the air. Which gives me one fucking day. How do you suggest I pull this off?" He stood up and began pacing, so agitated that he looked as if he might kill someone. "Okay, good. Just have him stopped. I need a little more time. I know, I know. Just buy me a couple of days."

He punched off the phone. "Shit!" he shouted at the empty room. "Shit, shit, shit!" He picked up a mug and hurled it against the wall. It shattered into fragments. Then, he sank down at his desk, dragging an arm across his sweating forehead. Whatever he had to accomplish, it was big. And it was in the process of being compromised.

A myriad of thoughts flooded Casey's mind.

The person Morano was referring to had to be Paul Everett. And Morano himself was in this as deep as Fenton. Maybe more so, if he were part of the mob.

Without further speculation, Casey punched Ryan's number on speed dial. "Are you behind the wheel?" she demanded.

"Nope, a passenger," he replied. "I just switched off with Claire, since I've been driving since last night. I needed to take a break."

"Well, don't. Tell Claire to pull over to the side of the road. All three of you get in the back of the van. Rewind the transmission from Gecko about three minutes. Then, watch."

"Done." Ryan didn't ask any questions. He just acted.

While Casey stayed on the phone, she could heard a mingle of voices and a rush of activity. Then some slamming car doors and shuffling around.

"We're all back here," Ryan said. "I'm putting you on speaker, and putting down the phone so I can rewind the video feed."

Casey waited impatiently while Ryan reversed the feed and backed it up about three minutes. Then, he shifted back into play mode.

"Yup, that's Morano," Marc identified. "Sitting at his desk."

"Keep watching," Casey instructed. She listened as her other team members watched and heard what she had.

"Holy shit." Ryan reacted first. "I thought Morano was a victim. That must have been a setup. He's one of them."

"One of whoever's keeping Paul Everett away," Marc clarified. "It could be the mob. It could be law enforcement. We just don't know."

"We *do* know that it's Paul Everett on a flight," Claire inserted. "His energy has been in transition since I got to Amanda's. I kept walking around her apartment, going from room to room, trying to understand what I was sensing. But this is it. He's on his way home."

"Which means he's flying into JFK from somewhere," Casey said. "We don't know where and we don't know when. All we know is that it's a thirteen-hour flight, that it's landing at JFK sometime today, and that whoever *they* are, they intend to stop him from getting to Amanda and Justin."

"We might not know any of the details," Marc said in a hard tone. "But Morano does. We could confront him. But that would only backfire. He'd shut down and refuse to tell us a damned thing. We're better off sticking close by and monitoring him. Eventually, he'll be having a follow-up chat."

"I agree," Casey said. "You three stay out there and keep a close eye on Morano. Call me ASAP if you see or hear anything before I do. I'm contacting Patrick and getting him to call in security relief. I want him at JFK's International Terminal. Thirteen hours means the flight is originating overseas. Marc, you've done the most international traveling. Come up with a list of potential origins. In the meantime, Ryan, you search for flights about thirteen hours in length that are landing at JFK. The two of you compare notes to find the most likely time and terminal."

"Done," Marc said.

"In the meantime, Patrick can pick me up and we'll go to JFK together. Two sets of eyes are better than one. Until we get your text, we'll check out the arrival schedule and figure out some possibilities on our own. And, if either one of us spots Paul Everett, or anyone tries to detain him, we can act."

CHAPTER TWENTY-EIGHT

The large fifth-floor conference room at FBI Headquarters was filled to capacity.

Patricia had met with the team from the New York Field Office, together with the Assistant U.S. Attorney, before Richard called the CUORC meeting to order.

CUORC consisted of Richard, the Committee Chairman, plus a dozen FBI Section Chiefs and an equal number of Unit Chiefs spanning every division of the FBI, in addition to a Department Of Justice Director and a dozen DOJ division chiefs. It was up to CUORC to assess the benefits and the risks of the Undercover operation and the sensitive circumstances that existed.

Waiting in the wings to answer any questions their respective Section and Unit Chiefs might have during the meeting were SSA Robinson of the Public Corruption squad and

SSA Camden of the Vizzini family Organized Crime Squad, along with the Assistant U.S. Attorney who was working with the New York Field Office.

Frank Rodriguez, Section Chief of Integrity in Government, spoke first.

"This investigation was initially ours. It began over a year ago. The Long Island Resident Agency got a tip from the original owner of beachfront real estate on Shinnecock Bay. He wanted to build a hotel to capitalize on the business opportunity created by the construction of the nearby Shinnecock Indian Casino. He sought all the appropriate permits from the Town of Southampton. Evidently, Lyle Fenton, using his position on the Town Board, was extorting him by withholding permits, zoning variances, road improvements, environmental approvals—you name it—unless he was guaranteed a portion of the hotel profits. Fenton was already on our radar, and we had reason to believe the corruption extended beyond Southampton to Washington, D.C."

"Are you speaking of Congressman Mercer?" Richard inquired.

"Yes," Rodriguez replied. "The problem was, there was no hard evidence against Fenton or Mercer. So when the case was referred to the New York Field Office, I approved the Public Corruption Squad's request to aggressively pursue the case. We made arrangements for the landowner to sell his property to an FBI shell company with the understanding that, once our sting was over, we'd sell the property back to him at the same price."

"And the new owner of the property became Paul Everett," Richard stated, repeating the facts for the benefit of the

CUORC members. "Or rather, Special Agent Paul Evans of the Philadelphia Field Office. Everett was his UC name."

"Exactly. Paul was the ideal candidate for the job."

"Not so ideal," Richard said drily. "Getting romantically involved with Amanda Gleason was a colossal mistake—one we're all paying for now."

"Agreed." Douglas Sawyer, Unit Chief of Undercover and Sensitive Operations, nodded, taking full responsibility for the case-altering snag. "But none of us, Paul included, anticipated that complication. Paul was the right choice for the assignment. He'd done UC work before, and he had a background in real-estate development, so creating his legend was easy. What happened afterward, his involvement with Ms. Gleason—that was a lapse in judgment we tried to correct. Paul refused."

"Let's stay on point," Richard said. "What was your plan?"

"Our plan was for Paul to make himself very visible and to play ball with Fenton. Only Fenton got smart. He wanted to size Everett up before he showed his full hand. So he softened his tactics by simply delaying the permits and waffling about Fenton Dredging taking part in the construction project. No extortion, not for the time being."

Sawyer paused to drink some water.

Rodriguez continued. "Where Fenton left off, the Vizzini family took over. Their leverage was the unions. So now we had two targets—Fenton and the Vizzini crime family." He gestured toward James Kirkpatrick, Section Chief of Criminal Enterprises for the Americas. "We brought in CE. Together, we arranged for Everett to make his payments to the mob and to strike up a working relationship with Fenton.

We hoped to bring them all down, including those in Washington, D.C., who were involved."

Rodriguez went on to explain that their investigation had revealed that Congressman Mercer was Lyle Fenton's son, that he was in his pocket, and that they intended to find out how deeply.

"The problem was budget constraints," Kirkpatrick said, taking over from Rodriguez with the Criminal Enterprise point of view. "We had limited funding. And the PC unit had already overextended itself with the land purchase. Paul was frustrated, and right on the brink of nailing Fenton. He took a weekend off and went to Boston, where he ran in a law enforcement charity 10K marathon. Evidently, he did this every year. Should have been no problem. Except that he ran into a buddy of his, Ron Pembrooke, his former roommate as a New Agent Trainee in Quantico. Pembrooke's now a backup media specialist at the Boston Field Office. Even that would have been okay, if Pembrooke hadn't placed in the damned race, if Paul hadn't gone over to slap him on the back, and if a local photographer hadn't snapped a shot of them together right in front of the Law Enforcement Officer's charity banner—a photo that later appeared in American Police Beat magazine."

Everyone in the room nodded, as the sequence of events became clear. Paul had compromised the investigation—not only by getting involved with Amanda Gleason, but by failing to maintain anonymity.

"We had to pull Paul out," Sawyer said. "We were planning on scrubbing the entire UC op. If Kirkpatrick's people hadn't come up with their proposal, and if the ADIC and CE hadn't approved the funding to support it, we'd have been dead in the water."

"Which is how you made it look like Paul Everett was," Richard commented.

"Yes," Kirkpatrick confirmed. "We faked Everett's death and made it look like a mob hit. We got the cooperation of the local State Troopers, who closed the murder investigation ASAP. CE bought the shell company from the Political Corruption unit. CE took over the entire operation and supplied one of our own UC agents—John Macari, now John Morano. We're about to bring this case to fruition. We just need a few key pieces of evidence. And with so much invested by the Bureau, we can't afford to back off or to compromise the investigation—certainly not for the personal needs of one agent."

"We're not discussing an agent," Richard corrected. "We're discussing a dying infant. And you wouldn't be compromising the investigation. We could have Paul Evans escorted to Sloane Kettering and kept in hiding until you complete your operation." A heartbeat of a pause, after which he played Patricia's trump card—the one she had briefed him on just before the CUORC meeting. "Plus, as you yourself just said, you don't have certain pieces of key evidence. We could change that."

Kirkpatrick frowned. "What does that mean?"

"It means we can obtain the evidence we need while simultaneously ensuring that Paul Evans will not be seen or identified at the hospital."

"With all due respect, Rich, can you truly make assurances like that? Amanda Gleason is Lyle Fenton's niece. What's to stop him from visiting the hospital at the exact time that

Evans is being donor tested? What's to stop anyone in the New York area who knew Evans as Everett from recognizing him? And what's to stop these Forensic Instincts people from inserting themselves yet again and screwing things up? Can you guarantee that none of that will happen?"

"Yes." Richard didn't miss a beat. "I can." He carefully described Patricia's entire plan, just as she'd instructed him to.

The room was filled with a deadly silence, as all the attendees contemplated the proposal, glancing at one another to gauge how others might vote.

Minutes later, Richard walked into his boss's office to deliver the verdict.

Hutch was showered and dressed when Casey came upstairs to her apartment and walked into the bedroom.

"Good morning." She smiled, went over to him and kissed him hello.

"Sort of." Hutch wrapped his arms around her. "I would have preferred a proper good morning to a cold bed and a belated kiss."

"Sorry. Duty called." Casey kissed him again, then stepped away. "It's been a crazy morning. It's about to get crazier. Patrick's picking me up. I have to race off again. I wish I could share the details with you." A sigh. "Maybe when it's over and we've saved little Justin."

"You'll save him, Casey. I have faith in you." That was something Hutch could say with complete candor.

"Thank you. I hope you're right. And, for the record, I hope we can do it without jeopardizing an FBI investigation."

Before Hutch could reply, his cell phone rang.

He picked it up off the nightstand and answered it. "Hutchinson."

"Hello, Hutch," was the reply. "It's Patricia Carey. I know you're in New York, taking a few days off. Are you free to talk?"

Hutch couldn't mask his surprise. He'd known Executive Assistant Director Carey for a dozen years, and they'd even worked together on several violent crimes investigations earlier in her career. They'd always shared a mutual respect, and even an occasional beer. But now that she was an Executive Assistant Director, they didn't exactly travel in the same circles. And they definitely didn't exchange social calls.

"Uh, yes." He glanced up at Casey, about to request some privacy. "Just give me a minute."

"If that minute involves asking Casey Woods to leave the room, don't. I want her there. Or am I being too presumptuous?"

Hutch sat down on the edge of the bed with a stunned expression on his face. "You're not being presumptuous. I just don't understand why you'd…"

"Why I'd know you were involved with Ms. Woods? Or why I'd want her participation in this telephone conversation?" A hint of humor. "The former is common knowledge. As for the latter—please ask her to stay."

"All right." Hutch held up a detaining palm.

Casey halted in her tracks, a puzzled expression on her face.

"One last thing before we have Ms. Woods join in," Patricia said. "You and I have worked together in the past. I've since followed your career. Your reputation is stellar. Plus, I trust you. So here's my question—I'm aware of the fact that

Forensic Instincts is trying to locate Paul Everett—and uncovering a wealth of information in the process. Please put your personal feelings about Ms. Woods aside. Are she and her team trustworthy?"

Trustworthy meant different things to different people.

"In what regard?" Hutch asked, trying to discern whether Patricia meant honorable or lawful.

Patricia read his mind and chuckled. "I don't mean, do they follow the rules. I'm more than cognizant of the fact that they both bend and break those. What I mean is, if I were to strike a deal with them—one that would benefit their client—would they honor it?"

"Absolutely." That one was a no-brainer. "I can vouch for their integrity, beyond the shadow of a doubt."

"I assumed you'd say that. And I'm relieved. Now, would you please put us on speaker?"

Still totally at sea, Hutch did as she asked, beckoning Casey over as he did. "You're on speaker, ma'am," he said. "Casey, you're talking to Executive Assistant Director Patricia Carey."

Casey's brows arched. Patricia Carey was the FBI's highest ranking female, reporting to the Director himself.

"It's a pleasure, Ms. Carey," she said.

"The feeling is mutual," Patricia replied. "Forensic Instincts has earned itself quite a reputation in a few short years—along with a few bent noses here at the FBI. Congratulations."

"Thank you." Casey paused, dying of curiosity as to the reason for the call.

"I'll cut to the chase," Patricia said. "You want to find Paul Everett. I want to successfully complete an investigation that might require a little creative energy—all within legal bounds, of course. Please understand that the FBI is unyielding about the interpretation of legal. Am I making myself clear?"

"Perfectly."

"Good. Bearing that in mind, I believe that you and I are in a position to help each other. Are you interested?"

Casey inhaled sharply. "Are you telling me you know where Paul Everett is and you're willing to turn him over to us?"

"I might be. *If* you comply with certain stipulations in order to protect him and our investigation. And *if,* in return, you supply me with what we need to bring this case to a successful close."

Her wheels turning, Casey considered the confidentiality agreement that FI had with Amanda, and weighed it against the results being promised to her. She knew very well what Amanda would want her to do.

"I'll give you everything I have," Casey assured Patricia.

"Excellent. Then we have a deal."

Casey glanced at Hutch. He knew that look. She was about to test the waters. "Is Paul Everett on a plane en route to JFK?" she asked.

Another brief chuckle. "I'm impressed. I had no idea you'd come so far. The answer is, yes, Paul is due back in New York at 4:00 p.m. on Flight 117 from Kuwait City. Now, let me lay out my stipulations. The first one is that I want SSA Hutchinson to be part of the operation I'm about to initiate. You and I both trust him, so it's a win-win situation. Agreed?"

Casey shot Hutch a quick smile. "Agreed."

"Good. Now here's the rest—after which, I'll need every shred of information you have on Lyle Fenton."

"And John Morano?" Casey asked.

"No. John is one of ours."

A long pause.

Abruptly, awareness exploded in Casey's brain. "As is Paul Everett," she realized aloud.

"Precisely," came Patricia's confirmation. "Paul is most definitely one of ours. Oh, and by the way, so is attorney Frederick Wilkenson. We added him to the equation to divert you. So you can tell Mr. McKay he isn't losing his touch."

Casey nodded, even though Patricia Carey couldn't see her. "Tell me what you need of us. And then I'll tell you everything you don't already know. It's more than enough for a conviction—and not just for Lyle Fenton. For key members of the Vizzini family."

"That's what I'm counting on, Ms. Woods."

CHAPTER TWENTY-NINE

The plane landed smoothly at JFK's International Terminal.

Paul leaned under the seat and grabbed his carry-on bag, which was his only form of luggage. He was frustrated enough that he had to endure the time necessary to pass through customs. He'd be damned if he'd stand in a baggage claim area, watching a stupid carousel go round forever before it spit out his bags.

The plane was still taxiing to the gate when Paul's cell phone rang.

He stared at the "unknown" caller ID, weighing his options. It had to be the Bureau. There was no doubt they intended to stop him. And they'd had hours to fine-tune their plans.

Answering the phone was his best bet. Any clue he could get about how they were going to go about this might help him circumvent the obstacles. But, the truth was, he didn't care if he had to report a bomb scare and evacuate the whole airport. He was getting to Sloane Kettering.

He punched on his phone. "Yes?"

"This is Casey Woods, Mr. Evans." Casey rushed on, getting in the crucial words before Paul could decide to hang up on her. "Amanda Gleason hired me to find you."

A pause. "How do I know that?"

"Because you saw the YouTube video. That toll-free number was set up by my company, Forensic Instincts. You can dial it yourself and ask if you don't believe me."

"Actually, I can't. My phone seems to have been deactivated."

"It was. But it's been reactivated. Again, if you don't believe me, you can check for yourself after we hang up. But we're in a time crunch. So right now, I need to give you instructions so we can get you to Amanda and your son as soon as possible."

Paul did a double take. "Let me get this straight." He spoke quietly, so as not to be overheard. "Obviously, if you know about my travel plans and my cell phone, you've been in touch with the Bureau. You're telling me that they're just allowing you to usher me out of the airport and straight to Sloane Kettering?"

"They're working with me to make it happen and to protect your anonymity. But we have a certain protocol we need to follow. So please listen to me now and ask questions later. You're almost at your gate. I need to talk fast so you'll be ready to proceed as soon as that door opens."

The ambulance pulled directly up to the plane the instant it came to a complete halt and was safe to do so. The captain had already advised the passengers to stay in their seats until further advised. The information given was that a fellow passenger was suffering what appeared to be a heart attack, and would be escorted directly to a waiting ambulance before everyone else could deplane.

Everyone, including Paul, stayed in their seats, although all eyes were on him and the doctor who was examining him.

"We should start oxygen therapy," the doctor said, forehead creased in concern as Paul clutched his chest and left arm, his breathing short and uneven.

"We'll do that, Doctor." Two paramedics burst onto the plane, rushing directly over to Paul. He was quickly examined.

A minute later, he was on a stretcher, an oxygen mask over his face, and he was being carried out to the waiting ambulance.

Once the patient and his EMTs were inside, the ambulance driver took off, sirens blaring.

"I hope you brought my bag," Paul said drily, as he sat up and removed the mask. "I carry my own aspirin."

"We got it." Hutch patted the travel bag, then leaned back on his haunches. "I wouldn't get too comfortable. That mask has to be on your face when we go screeching up to the emergency room entrance. You're being carried in there the same way you were carried out of the plane." He extended his hand. "SSA Kyle Hutchinson," he said. "It's nice to finally meet you."

"SA Paul Evans, although I doubt I have to introduce myself." Paul shook Hutch's hand. "Are you from the New York Field Office?"

"Nope. Quantico. I'm BAU-2."

Paul's brows rose. "They sent the BAU to get me?"

Hutch grinned. "Not in the way you mean, no. It's a long story. You'll hear all the details later. For now, let's just get you to the hospital and your son."

"Where is that woman who called me—Casey Woods?"

"She's with Amanda, telling her what's happening. You're a lucky man, Evans. You've got a great woman, a fighter of a son and the best private investigative team there is all in your corner. Without Casey, this could never have happened."

Paul's eyes narrowed as he tried to absorb what was happening. "How did she get the FBI to cooperate?"

Another grin. "She's not only one hell of an investigator, she's one hell of a horse trader."

"She dug up information on Fenton," Paul realized aloud. "She knows what's going on. She's helping the Bureau complete their operation."

"You got it."

"Damn." Paul shook his head in amazement. "So this is for real. Casey Woods was being straight with me."

"As an arrow," Hutch assured him. He indicated the man next to him. "This is SA Mike Shore of New York's violent crimes squad."

"I'm at the Long Island RA," Mike said, shaking Paul's hand. "I was part of the initial investigation into Lyle Fenton, before the whole UC operation began."

"Good to meet you." Paul still looked a bit dazed. "Can either of you fill me in on my son's condition?" His voice quivered on the word *son*.

Hutch was frank. "All I know is that he's holding on. I don't know the details of his illness, but I'm sure the doctor will fill you in. He's been advised you're on your way.

You'll be donor tested immediately—right after you have a chance to see Amanda and to meet Justin."

"Justin." Paul tasted the name on his lips. "I still can't believe this." He dragged his hand through his hair, then lay back down on the stretcher. "Give me that oxygen mask," he instructed. "And tell the driver to ignore rush hour traffic. Turn on that siren and drive up the shoulder of the Van Wyck and over the goddamned Queensboro Bridge. As far as I'm concerned, there's no one else on the road."

Casey sat Amanda down in a quiet corner of the waiting area, so that she could finally tell her client the news she'd been aching to hear. Amanda looked like a fine thread that had been frayed and was about to snap, as if she'd hung on just about as long as any human being could. This poor woman, this poor mother, had endured—and was still enduring—a living hell. She'd visibly aged this past week, internalizing each emotional blow that threatened to take Justin away. God, it would feel so good to share this wonderful, positive news with her.

"What is it?" Amanda searched Casey's face. "The way you dragged me out of the PICU, I know it's urgent. What's happened?"

Casey took Amanda's hands in hers, not even trying to conceal the tears of joy that were glittering on her lashes. "We found Paul," she said simply. "He's on his way to Sloane Kettering right now."

Amanda lurched with shock, all the color draining from her face. For an instant, she looked as if she might faint. "You... He's..." She couldn't seem to form a coherent sentence. "How? When?"

"I've known since earlier today. I just didn't want to tell you until we'd successfully pulled it off. Now we have. His plane landed just after 4:00 p.m.—about forty-five minutes ago. We helped him stage a heart attack. He's arriving by ambulance. He'll be here before six."

"A heart attack?" Clearly, Amanda was only absorbing pieces of what Casey was saying.

"He's fine," Casey assured her. "It was all an act. We needed to get him here as fast as possible." Casey waved away the rest of Amanda's questions. "Let Paul fill you in on the rest. Just know this—the instant he found out about Justin, he moved heaven and earth to get here. So don't doubt his commitment."

As Casey spoke, Patrick walked over, followed by the rest of the team, who'd just arrived. Everyone wanted to be here to see the culmination of their relentless search.

"They'll be here soon," Claire told Amanda with a smile. "Paul's energy is overwhelming. I almost can't breathe past it. The only thing rivaling it is *your* energy."

Amanda laughed, something she hadn't done in an aeon. "I don't believe this. You're miracle workers."

"We can discuss how awesome we are after Paul's been tested and confirmed as a strong donor match," Marc said in true Marc style.

"Any psychic hints?" Amanda asked Claire.

Claire gave an apologetic shrug. "Right now, all I'm picking up on are relief and joy. Both are emanating from you and Paul. I can't tell if that positive energy relates to anything more than your current feelings. We'll have to wait and see. But my prayers—all our prayers—are right here with you."

"Thank you," Amanda whispered. "I..." She wanted to say more, but couldn't find the words. "Thank you."

"You'll thank us afterward," Casey said.

"And tell us how awesome we are," Ryan reminded her with a wink.

"With pleasure," Amanda assured him. She turned back to Casey. "Does Dr. Braeburn know? How is this going to work?"

"Dr. Braeburn has been advised, as has the hospital lab. Paul will come up here first to see you and Justin and to meet with Dr. Braeburn. Then he'll go directly down to get tested. The lab results will be prioritized and rushed. We'll have our answer in three days."

"Oh, God." Amanda pressed her palms to her cheeks. "I don't believe this is happening."

"Believe it," Patrick said, patting her shoulder. "Because it is."

Hutch and Mike, still dressed as EMTs, carried the stretcher out of the ambulance and rushed it inside. Paul lay still, his face partially concealed by the oxygen mask, a blanket pulled up to his chin to help do the job.

It was only in the closed elevator that Hutch said, "Okay, time to get up and get into this."

Paul rose, yanked off the mask and shrugged into the hooded parka Hutch handed him.

"You obviously can't put up the hood. You'd stick out like a sore thumb," Hutch said, shrugging out of his uniform. "But keep the jacket zipped. The hood will bunch up around your neck and hide a chunk of your face. Mike and I will walk ahead of you, so we'll block you from view. And remember what I said. We've arranged to have the waiting room cleared, supposedly for cleaning. We'll guide you straight to the PICU and to Amanda. The rest is up to you."

Amanda was in the waiting room with the Forensic Instincts team when the approaching bustle of movement made her snap around. Two men in suits were striding down the hall toward her. They stopped inside the waiting room, and the taller man gave her a wink. Then, they veered off, going over to join the FI team on the sidelines.

Left standing alone, Paul stared at Amanda, unzipping his parka and pulling the sides apart so that she could make out his whole face.

The action wasn't necessary. She already knew who he was.

He just stood there for a moment. Then he made his way toward Amanda at the same time as Amanda ran forward to meet him.

They hugged each other fiercely, holding on to each other for strength and comfort as much as for a reunion.

"I'm so sorry," Paul murmured, when he finally stepped back, gripping Amanda's shoulders in his hands and searching her face. "If I'd had any idea… If I'd even guessed." He gave a self-deprecating shake of his head. "And you had to go through this all by yourself. There's no way I can ever make that up to you."

"Oh, yes, there is," Amanda told him fervently. "Be a healthy donor match for our son. Please. Help me save his life."

Paul sucked in his breath, squaring his shoulders to take

on the responsibility that should have been his from the start. "If I am a viable match, will that be enough?"

Amanda shook her head. She'd gone through every detail with Dr. Braeburn, every possible best- and worst-case scenario. As much as any layperson could understand, she did. Her son—their son—had a huge uphill battle, even if all Paul's infectious disease testing checked out, and he was the donor. Paul's peripheral blood stem cells would have to be purified. The purity would have to be high enough and the quantity of stem cells sufficient enough for transplantation. Then, once the peripheral stem cell transplant took place, there was always the chance of graft versus host disease, if Justin's body rejected Paul's cells. She couldn't allow herself to consider that, not after all they'd gone through to find Paul. He was here. God wouldn't have brought them all this way just to fail now. Paul had to be the answer.

Still, he was entitled to know everything—including exactly what he was getting into.

"This won't be just a simple blood test," Amanda explained, "not after you've been officially ruled a donor. You'll have to get four days of injections to stimulate your blood marrow so it will release more stem cells into your blood. The fifth day will be the transplant itself. They put you on a special machine that collects and separates your blood. Then, there's a stem cell purification process that takes place in a sterile lab. Dr. Braeburn can explain the whole process to you."

Paul waved away the entire matter. "I'm not the issue. I'll do whatever has to be done. But, once that's over, once my cells are in Justin's body, what are his chances? How long will it take till we see results?"

"A few weeks." Amanda clenched her fists at her sides as she spoke. "We need engraftment to occur. That means your donor cells have to successfully take, so to speak, at which point Justin will begin to develop an immune system. Then he can start to fight off all his infections." A watery smile. "We have to pray. But now that you're here, I believe in miracles again."

Paul's expression softened. "As do I." He glanced past Amanda, and down the hall. A hint of awe flashed in his eyes. "Is he... Is Justin...in there?"

Amanda felt her heart swell, and she nodded. "He looks so much like you," she said. "He has your eyes, not just the color, but your shape and your eyelids. Oh, and your eyelashes. Remember how I used to tell you how every woman would kill for those thick lashes of yours? Well, now they're Justin's, too. And his nose, Paul. It's a tiny version of yours. He even has your dimple." She touched Paul's cheek with her fingertip. "He's got so much of you in him. He's curious about everything. He's easygoing—until he really wants something. And he's always moving. He kicked me nonstop my entire last trimester. I'm sure he's going to be a marathon runner like his father. I'm sure..." Amanda fell apart, her body racked with sobs as her stoic veneer shattered.

Only this time, she had someone to hold her.

Paul wrapped his arms around her and gave her a fierce hug. "We're going to make this right, Amanda. *I'm* going to make this right. You'll see. Our son is going to be just fine." Emotion clogging his voice, Paul asked, "May I see him? Even through the window?"

"Of course." Amanda stepped back, dashing away her tears. "I'm sorry. I just still can't believe that you're here.

That you're alive. That you're real. That you didn't intentionally stay away."

"I didn't," Paul stated fervently. "If you believe nothing else, believe that. I have so much to fill you in on. But later. After I've done everything I can for Justin."

Amanda took Paul by the hand. "Come on. Come meet your son."

As they disappeared down the hall, Casey turned to Marc. "Everything's in place," she murmured. "The FBI delivered, as promised. Now it's our turn. Go ahead and take care of what we discussed."

Marc nodded. "With pleasure." He sauntered off, leaving the PICU and taking the elevator to the hospital lobby.

He'd already selected the deserted spot in the alleyway where he was going to make his phone call. And, in his pocket, he already had what he needed: the spare burner phone he used for just these types of occasions, along with a voice scrambler.

Calling the FBI tip line was going to be Marc's pleasure. The information he provided would take care of Lyle Fenton and his mob buddies.

With a grin, Marc set the scrambler in place.

Damn, he loved his job.

CHAPTER THIRTY

Hutch and Mike took off to report in. But the FI team stayed on, hanging out in the waiting room to hear the results of Paul and Amanda's conversation with Dr. Braeburn.

"I really am good," Claire announced.

Ryan did a double take and stared at her. "Did I just hear my voice come out of your mouth?"

"Nope. That voice you heard, along with the words, were mine. Everything I sensed was accurate. The binary energy? Paul's double life. The running? Not just Paul's disappearance, but the marathon that made it necessary. The covert phone calls I kept picking up on the other side of Paul's bedroom? His undercover work. And the sense of being followed? Mostly, the FBI. The times when I sensed danger? Fenton, keeping tabs on our search for Paul." Claire eyed

Ryan victoriously, like the cat who swallowed the canary. "You can't argue with success."

Patrick gave an exaggerated groan. "God, I think he's rubbing off on her."

An interesting choice of words, Casey thought.

Quickly, she glanced at Claire, then Ryan. She watched Claire avert her gaze, her cheeks tinged with pink. And she saw Ryan, who would customarily be delivering one barb after the next, remaining uncharacteristically silent, an odd expression crossing his face.

These two had *so* slept together, it wasn't funny.

"You know, Patrick, I think you're right," Casey said. "They're definitely rubbing off on each other. So tell us, guys, when did this start?"

Claire blanched. "What?"

"This sudden self-confidence that smacks of Ryan—only a tad less arrogant." Casey was the picture of innocence. "When did it start?"

"I'm just acknowledging how right-on my awareness was this time," Claire said, recovering herself. "I'm pleased that I was connecting. That doesn't mean I'm professing to be a world-class genius, as do others we know."

"Like you, I only speak the truth." Ryan had clearly regained his composure, as well. It was business as usual.

"I speak it. You flaunt it—*and* exaggerate it," Claire corrected him.

"Nah. Gecko and I were definitely the heroes of the day." Ryan grinned. "Although you didn't do too badly. I don't begrudge you a few self-congratulations."

Claire rolled her eyes. "Acknowledgment, Ryan. Not self-congratulations. I didn't win the lottery. I helped locate a man who's desperate to save his child. I did my job."

"Yes, you did," Casey said quietly, bringing the conversation around to the grave situation at hand. "We all did. But it's not enough." She lowered her gaze for a moment, then looked up to regard her team soberly. "Technically, our jobs are over. But they're really not, are they?"

The rest of the team grew equally sober.

"No, they're not." Patrick answered for all of them. "And they won't be until this crisis comes to a successful conclusion. We're professionals—damned good ones. But we're also human. We care. We're emotionally invested in this case. That's one of the things I most admire about working with this team."

"Ditto," Ryan said.

"We're not even close to being out of the woods." Claire made the statement with a faraway look in her eyes. "I don't understand all the medical jargon. But it's complicated. And it will be a long road till it's over."

"And when it is?" Casey asked. "What will the outcome be?"

A frustrated shrug. "I wish I knew. The energy I'm picking up on is overwhelmingly emotional—on so many levels—and it's coming at me from all sides."

Marc rejoined the group at that moment. Briefly, he met Casey's gaze and gave her a quick nod. The call had been made, the wheels set in motion. As they spoke, FBI agents would be descending on Fenton's home, his New York offices and his maritime operations in Bayonne. And that was just the start. The dominos would begin to fall, one by one.

And, by the time they'd all crashed down, the Bureau's interviewing rooms would be as full as the AUSA's docket.

Casey nodded back.

"I ran into Hutch in the lobby," Marc informed the team. "Evidently, he and Mike put the necessary items in Paul's bag to help disguise his identity. Since he'll be at the hospital for at least three days—more, if he's a donor match, he needs to be unrecognizable. That was part of the deal. This way, he can move freely to the lab for blood and diagnostic tests, and stay in the PICU with Amanda and Justin without worrying about anyone spotting him."

"He won't be leaving Sloane Kettering," Claire responded. "Not for a long time. Whether or not he's a match, he won't leave Amanda's and Justin's sides. Not after all they've been through to become a family. He'll be here to see Justin through this crisis. Damn the Bureau."

Standing with Amanda outside Justin's window, Paul was thinking exactly that. Right now, everything he cared about was right in front of him. He saw all the apparatus, all the tubes helping Justin with his struggle to survive. But he also saw his son. *His* son. Amanda was right. He could see himself in the tiny person whose eyes would occasionally open as if he was somehow aware that someone new had been added to his life.

Paul could actually feel his chest constrict. The emotion, the fierce sense of protectiveness, the entire feeling that seized him was indescribable. And, in that moment, he knew he'd move heaven and earth to make sure his son lived a healthy, normal life.

While they waited for Dr. Braeburn, Paul filled Amanda

in on his real name, his job with the FBI and the fact that he was involved in a deep undercover operation throughout their time together. He couldn't share the details. Nor did they matter. All that mattered now was Justin.

Dr. Braeburn came out of his office and approached Paul and Amanda. He'd already explained all the specifics to Paul, starting with the preparation Paul would undergo for the four days prior to the transplant. Then came the day itself. The apheresis—the actual technology during which Paul's blood would pass through an apparatus, collecting and separating out the cells necessary for the transplant and returning the remaining blood to his circulatory system—was a four-hour procedure, followed by a ten-hour purification process to enrich the stem cells as much as possible before the blood was ready to transfer to Justin. The transplant itself would be done right in the PICU and was an IV infusion of Paul's purified stem cells into Justin's body.

At Paul's insistence, Dr. Braeburn had reviewed what to hope for afterward, although he warned Paul not to accept the timetable as ironclad.

"Each case is different," he'd explained. "Engraftment can take place anytime between ten and twenty-eight days. So I don't want you losing faith if it takes longer than the two-week period I've suggested. Also, I know Amanda's mentioned graft-versus-host disease to you. We're hoping that won't happen, but we'll have our experts in several pediatric subspecialties—hematology, gastroenterology and dermatology—monitoring Justin for fever, rashes, diarrhea and anything else that could indicate GVHD. We'll also have our infectious diseases specialists monitoring him for infections of any kind."

Paul couldn't help himself. He had to ask the question that Amanda had sidestepped with him earlier, only because she so desperately wanted to put it out of her mind. She knew the answer. But to hear it said aloud—again—she just couldn't bear it.

Still, she understood. Paul had to know.

"If I'm a healthy donor match," he asked Dr. Braeburn, "and if the transplant takes place, what are Justin's immediate chances for survival?"

Dr. Braeburn regarded him soberly. "If Justin weren't as sick as he is right now, I'd say close to ninety percent. But I won't lie to you. Given his physical condition, his chances are a little better than fifty-fifty."

Amanda's insides twisted, and she turned away, tears clogging her throat.

"But we're not going to focus on odds," the doctor continued. "We're going to focus on a positive outcome. If the engraftment takes place and clears the pneumonia—which I'm hoping it will—Justin's long-term survival rate will increase to ninety percent, after which there's every reason to believe that he will live a full and healthy life."

For the umpteenth time, Amanda found herself silently praying. But she also knew that, between now and then, there were so many hurdles to conquer, so many "what-ifs" to face.

"It will be all right," Paul murmured, as if reading her mind. His fingers closed around hers. "We're going to beat this, Amanda. Justin's going to beat this."

She nodded, determined to stay as strong as she'd been before Paul's return. She'd coped with this all alone. Now she'd cope with it together with Justin's father.

One step at a time.

Paul was anxious to take step one.

"Everything's been arranged," Dr. Braeburn informed Paul. "Once your blood's been drawn, you'll go through a battery of tests, just to make sure you're healthy and there's nothing to rule you out as a donor. Then, you'll come back up here. Amanda will show you the visitation protocol, and the sterile attire you'll have to wear before going inside. After that, you're welcome to spend time with your son. I know you want to hold him, but that will have to wait. The fewer people who handle him right now, the better."

"I understand." Paul nodded. He looked ashen.

"Let's get you tested," Dr. Braeburn said gently. "We'll take it from there."

The FI team was waiting when Amanda and Paul—now with blond hair, glasses and two-inch lifts in his shoes—emerged from the PICU and into the waiting area. Paul paused, gave Amanda a quick kiss and squeezed her hands hard. Then, he waved at the FI team and headed purposefully off toward the elevator.

Amanda walked over to join the team.

"I was instructed by Agent Hutchinson to stay here with you," she told them quietly. "My being by Paul's side would make him more recognizable. This way is safer." She gazed anxiously after Paul. "I wish I could be there. I wish they could tell him the results on the spot. I wish..." She broke off and gave a hard shake of her head. "I'm not letting myself think that way. I'm just going to be grateful that you found Paul, and believe in my heart that it's a good sign. I have to think positively, for Justin's sake."

"That strategy has worked up until now," Marc reminded her.

"You're right." Amanda's expression changed. "Your team and I haven't had a chance to talk. We do now. How guilty was my uncle? Where do things stand on that front?"

"Listen to me, Amanda." It was Casey who spoke. "You're a very intelligent woman. You realize this situation goes a lot deeper than any of us realized. Let's just be grateful that Paul was one of the good guys."

"That doesn't answer my question." Amanda's gaze was steady. "And I need to know. Obviously, Paul is an undercover FBI agent assigned to a high-level case. So who was following us? Was it other agents sent to prevent you from finding Paul?"

"Most of the time, yes. They were keeping a close eye on our progress. They were also the ones who made that unnerving phone call to you in an attempt to scare you off."

"Most of the time," Amanda repeated. "Well, since the FBI wouldn't go so far as to kill us, that means the danger you were sensing about us being watched came from a different source, like from organized crime."

No response.

"Whatever you're not saying, it involved my uncle," Amanda pressed. "What has he done?"

"A lot," Marc answered her bluntly. "None of which we can discuss with you. And none of which you can take to your uncle. We located Paul and got him home. We didn't do it without some assistance. So it's time to respect the FBI's wishes not to have their investigation compromised. Once things are out in the open and arrests have been made, then we can talk and you'll have plenty of time to hurl accusations at Fenton. Until that time, all you can know is that he's committed more than one crime. But he didn't know that Paul was alive, and he didn't keep him away from you and Justin. Leave it at that."

Blowing out a breath, Amanda studied Marc's face, which, as always, was carefully blank. "All right. I won't ask you any more questions. But it makes me ill to think that my own uncle did something that made it necessary to erase Paul's existence. Paul *Everett's* existence," she amended. "That man is gone forever. But Paul Evans is here. And he won't be disappearing or going undercover again. No matter what, Justin will have his father. And when the FBI gives you the okay, I plan to find out every single thing my uncle is guilty of. Then, I'll tell him exactly what I think of him."

"Just don't do it now." Marc's words were more than a request. They were a command.

Amanda's chin came up in surprise. Marc had never before used that sharp tone with her.

Now she saw what had triggered it.

Marc's penetrating stare was fixed on a point over her shoulder. She turned to see her uncle Lyle striding into the PICU waiting room, clearly on his way to see Justin.

"Don't, Amanda," Marc instructed her. "Be cold. Be aloof. But don't tip your hand—not if you want to keep Paul safe and to see justice done."

Amanda nodded. She took a few deep breaths, then walked away from the FI team and toward her uncle.

Patrick took an instinctive step in their direction.

Marc seized his arm. "Leave it alone. We can't tip our hand any more than Amanda can tip hers. We're all here en masse. He won't try anything stupid."

"What the hell is he doing here to begin with?" Ryan muttered.

"Probably stopping by on his way to sewers unknown." Marc's tone hardened. "He can save himself the trouble of fueling up his jet. After my phone call, Fenton's not going anywhere but to jail."

"But he doesn't know that yet," Casey reminded him.

"True. But I'll find Hutch. He can't have gone far. That means that the longer Fenton's here, the better the chance that he won't walk out a free man. So let's let things play out."

"In the meantime, I hope Amanda can pull this off."

"She'll pull it off," Claire said quietly. "She'll do it for Justin, and for Paul."

"Uncle Lyle." As if proving Claire's point, Amanda greeted him in nothing more than a guarded tone. "I didn't realize you were coming by today."

"Amanda, hello." Fenton halted. At the same time, he glanced to his left and saw the entire FI team standing in the waiting room corner.

Clearly, he was *not* happy with that scenario. He couldn't be in control of the conversation, not when he was uncertain about what the team had told his niece. Plus, Marc intimidated the hell out of him.

As if in disgust, Marc turned and stalked out of the room.

That gave Fenton some hope.

It also gave Marc the time he needed.

He went into the men's room and turned on his phone. He didn't give a damn if it was allowed or not.

He pressed Hutch's number on speed dial.

"Hey," he said the instant Hutch answered. "Where are you?"

"I just joined Mike outside the lab. Why?"

"Fenton's here. He's with Amanda. We've got our eyes on him. But call whoever you need to. Put a rush on those warrants. My gut tells me this is a stopover to the airport. You stay with Evans. Keep him away from the PICU until you hear from me."

"Done."

CHAPTER THIRTY-ONE

Back in the waiting room, Fenton was testing the waters.

"I wanted to check in on Justin—and to talk to you," he said, gauging his niece's reaction.

"About what?" With or without realizing it, Amanda was blocking her uncle's path with her body, erecting an invisible but protective wall between her uncle and her son.

Fenton played his cards with great care. "About the future—Justin's future."

"The only aspect of Justin's future I'm interested in discussing is the one where Dr. Braeburn tells me that my son is out of the woods and is going to live a full and healthy life."

"I understand that." Fenton went for a softer approach. "And I have no doubt that's going to happen. Since Cliff Mercer's plea, half of his political district has come forward to be tested. So have the student bodies of both his kids' colleges. Between that and your online video, word of Justin's condition is on the front burner, coast-to-coast. You *will* find a match."

"I pray you're right. But, in my heart, I know the best match would be Paul. That's the person I really want to find."

Fenton wet his lips. "Any progress?"

Amanda's nails dug into her palms, but she remained composed. "I get the sense that Forensic Instincts is getting somewhere. But they're reticent about discussing it with me because they don't want to get my hopes up."

"So they haven't told you anything?"

"Only that they're interviewing a number of people, including some slimy ones. And that some of those slimy individuals might be colleagues of yours." She gazed pointedly at her uncle, awaiting his response.

He looked relieved. It didn't take a psychic to figure out why. If that was all Forensic Instincts had revealed to his niece, then Fenton was in a good place.

"You know the kind of business I'm in, Amanda." He went for a factual approach—but one that was devoid of self-implication. "It's a tough one to run, and I run it. I can only speak for my own actions. No one else's."

Amanda had a hard time hiding her disgust. "I understand that," she forced herself to say. "And, I know that if you had any information at all that might help find Paul, you would have shared it."

"Of course I would." Fenton's stance was relaxed now. He was back on sure footing. "Are you holding up all right?"

"Touch-and-go." Amanda didn't have to fake the pain in her voice. "Justin is in a very precarious state. He's sick. He's gotten sicker. And all the antibiotics in the world can't cure him—not without an immune system to fight things off."

"I know." Fenton looked genuinely concerned, which he was, even if it was for all the wrong reasons. He cleared his throat. "But, as I said, I know you'll find a donor. Which is why I want to discuss Justin's future—especially now when I'll be away for a while."

"Away?" Amanda gave him a quizzical look. "Where are you going?"

"On a business trip. I have to check in with some of the Fenton Dredging operations on both coasts. I have several large maritime contracts in the works."

Fenton paused. "In any case, tending to my empire has made me think about the future of my company. Because of that, I've made some changes in my will."

"Don't do anything for me, Uncle Lyle," Amanda couldn't stop herself from saying. "In your world, money might be a panacea. Not in mine."

"It's not a panacea. But it does help. It's also not about you, although you've been well-provided for." Fenton didn't avert his gaze. "I've set up two separate trust funds for Justin, both of which you'll manage until he comes of age. The first will pay for any health-related issues that might arise because of his condition. You'd be surprised how many items slip between the medical insurance cracks. The second will provide for his future—college, grad school, anything else he might need. It's a substantial sum."

Amanda hadn't been prepared for that. She wasn't quite sure what to say. On the one hand, she hated taking anything from her uncle. On the other hand, the money was for Justin. Altruism was one thing. Real life was another. If anyone had learned that in the past month, it was she.

However, if any of that trust fund money was dirty…

"Thank you," she said simply. "That's a very generous gesture on your part. But I'll have to think about it."

"There's nothing to think about. It's done. And it's not about generosity." Fenton wasn't finished yet. "It's about blood ties. Justin is your son, and my great-nephew. He's also the future of Fenton Dredging."

Amanda blinked. "Pardon me?"

"I'm leaving my entire empire to him," was the blunt response. "I have no grandchildren. But I do have a great-nephew. And I have a business empire that I built from the ground up. It's my legacy, the only one I have. I want it in the family. So I'm leaving it to Justin."

This time Amanda had an immediate reaction. "That's way over-the-top," she said. "It's also unrealistic. We have no idea what Justin's goals or interests will be. He might not have any desire to be a business mogul. And, if he does, he may have no affinity for dredging or for building jetties or docks. I don't want to saddle him with that responsibility."

Fenton sucked in his breath. "It's not a responsibility. It's a gift. If I don't leave it to Justin, it will just become part of my estate, which will go to the two of you anyway. I prefer to believe your son will keep my business empire going—no, thriving—even if he opts not to take an active part in running it. It's not just a gift, it's a favor. In a sense, Fenton Dredging is my only child. I want it to flourish. So please don't refuse my wishes. Should the time come and should Justin refuse to have any part of my legacy, he can sell it or dissolve it as he sees fit. At least I won't be alive to know about it."

Amanda had never heard her uncle speak so fervently or so emotionally. It took her aback.

"All right," she agreed, studying his face and wondering how many facets of Lyle Fenton existed. "I won't make that decision for Justin. He can make it himself when he's old enough to do so. That's all I can promise you."

"That's all I'm asking—and one thing more."

"Which is?"

"I'd like to see Justin before I leave."

Amanda stiffened. "He's in a reverse isolation unit, Uncle Lyle. You know that. No one but a restricted few are permitted in there. Plus, he's on a ventilator and he has a chest tube. He's very sick. There are no visitors allowed. Period."

"I didn't plan to go inside," her uncle replied. "I just want to see him through the window."

"You just saw him the other day."

"Humor me." Fenton shifted, casting a quick, uncomfortable glance at the FI team. Their lack of reaction to his presence was starting to unnerve him. Especially Devereaux, who'd rejoined the group a little while ago. Why was he just standing there? The last time they'd been in a room together, the SOB had practically crushed his windpipe. Was it the restraining order? Was it the fact that there were other people around and he couldn't risk physical violence?

Whatever it was, Fenton wanted to put as much distance between them as possible.

"I'm going to be away for a while," he told his niece. "I'd like to see my great-nephew before I leave."

A tight knot formed in Amanda's stomach. "Is this your

way of saying goodbye, just in case…" She didn't finish her sentence. "Because I don't want any of that negative energy around my son. We're all thinking positive thoughts."

"As am I." Fenton shook his head. "Would I have gone to so much trouble to provide for Justin's future if I believed we were going to lose him? No. I just need to do this. Call it a solidification of my plans."

A long pause, during which her gaze darted quickly to Marc, then at the clock on the wall.

Marc got it. Amanda was asking him what to do. Paul was due back. And she didn't know that precautions had already been taken.

He let her know.

Mouthing the words, "no problem," he gave her a thumbs-up, indicating that things were fine, that they had the situation covered.

That was the only reassurance Amanda needed.

"Okay," she agreed. "I'll walk you down there." She turned and, staying two steps ahead, led her uncle down the corridor.

"I think I'm going to puke," Ryan muttered, averting his head. "What next?"

"Hutch is on it," Marc said simply. "He's also with Evans, so we have that base covered. As for Fenton, let's buy Hutch some time." He glanced at Patrick. "Go to your usual security position. Watching Amanda and Fenton will be your job. Keeping Fenton here will be ours."

"Are you going to finish what you started at his estate?" Claire inquired. "Because I don't advise it. There are people around. Assault is a crime, and Fenton already has a restraining order against you."

A corner of Marc's mouth lifted. "Thanks for the concern. But, no, I won't be beating the shit out of him this time. He's scared enough of me so I can manipulate him just by getting in his face. As for the restraining order, I doubt it'll hold much water next to warrants for federal crimes."

"Scaring him off is not our goal here," Casey reminded Marc. "Keeping him here is. You can leave that part to me. Once he walks out of that PICU, I'll keep him occupied and off balance until the Feds show up."

Fenton stood at the window for a good five minutes, just staring at Justin.

"You're his mother," Fenton finally said to Amanda. "So you see your struggling baby. I'm his great-uncle and a successful businessman. I see the kind of fight that makes a real leader. He's going to beat this enemy. Winners always do. Percentages and odds mean nothing. Take it from one who knows."

Amanda didn't answer. The words of encouragement were nice. The analogy was sickening. Justin was going to be fine. But he'd never be like his great-uncle.

She shifted uneasily, wondering where Paul was and who was ensuring that he and her uncle didn't run into each other. She couldn't count on a disguise to protect Paul's anonymity, not where her uncle was concerned.

Fenton stepped away from the window and glanced down at his watch. "My pilot will be waiting. I'm not sure when I'll be back. But I'll be checking in to get updates on Justin's condition and to see if you've found a donor."

"That's fine." Amanda wanted to push him down the corridor and out the door.

When they finally did emerge into the waiting room, Patrick was standing at his post, stony-faced. Marc, Ryan and Claire were nowhere to be found, and Casey was sitting and reading a magazine.

She rose as soon as she saw Amanda and Fenton walk out, and headed over to them.

"Hello, Mr. Fenton," she greeted him coldly. "Did you come to visit Justin? Or to see if Amanda was still in your corner?"

Once again, Casey's assertive demeanor threw Fenton off balance. He worked in construction, which was still a man's world. Strong women were not something he often encountered.

And Casey was well aware of that.

Fenton cleared this throat. "It's none of your business, but I came to see Justin and to talk to Amanda. Is that a problem?"

"Not at all." Casey loved seeing the rapid pulse beating at his neck. He might be afraid of Marc physically, but she intimidated the hell out of him mentally. "Did you have information to pass along to her, or were you just on a fishing expedition?"

His eyes glittered. "I've made provisions for Justin. Amanda needed to know."

"My uncle is leaving on a business trip," Amanda provided, gazing quizzically at Casey. Now was hardly the time for an interrogation. They had to get her uncle out of here before Paul returned.

"Is he really?" Casey's brows arched. "Where will you be headed, Mr. Fenton?"

"To my various subsidiaries."

"Hmm. I assume your itinerary is available, should it be needed."

Red splotches were forming on Fenton's cheeks. He was livid. And he was starting to feel trapped.

"I don't really see—"

"Amanda," Casey interrupted, inclining her head in Amanda's direction, "make sure you know how to reach your uncle. You're bound to have good news to share with him. In which case, he'll want to know immediately, especially given his attachment to Justin. Who knows? Maybe Congressman Mercer will be a donor match." Her curious gaze flitted back to Fenton. "Or will he be going on this business trip with you?"

"Of course not," Fenton snapped. "Why would he?"

"Oh, I don't know. Maybe he just needs a little getaway."

"Hardly. His kids are coming home from school. He'll be with his family."

"Right. His family." Casey's stare bore right through Fenton. "The congressman strikes me as a loyal and devoted husband and father. I'm sure the same applies to him as a son—if his father is deserving." A purposeful pause. "From what I hear, his father is a tough and demanding man. I'm sure the congressman's loyalties can only be pushed so far. Don't you agree?"

Fenton started. Clearly, Mercer hadn't mentioned to him that Forensic Instincts knew about their blood ties. That was to the congressman's credit. It meant he'd been sincere when he told FI he'd be keeping his eye on—and his distance from—Fenton's suspicious activities.

But Casey had just taken care of that omission in grand style. It had to throw Fenton big-time to know that Mercer wasn't quite the lap dog he'd assumed, and, more important, that Forensic Instincts had uncovered yet another secret of Fenton's—this one explaining the leverage he used to "encourage" congressional support for Fenton Dredging.

His hostile expression said it all.

"You're acquainted with Warren Mercer, right?" Casey asked, the vision of innocence. "Although, if I recall correctly, the two of you haven't spoken in many years."

"Warren and I lost touch, yes. But Cliff is a fine man, so I'm sure he's a fine son." Fenton was trying. But, hostile or not, he was panicking. Casey could see it in every gesture, hear it in every syllable.

Amanda, meanwhile, was staring at Casey as if she'd lost her mind. And Casey could certainly read hers: why the hell was Casey making small talk, however useful, when Paul was about to return to the PICU and run smack into Fenton?

Casey wished she could explain.

As it turned out, she didn't have to.

The waiting room door opened, and a man and a woman walked in. They didn't warrant a second look—just average professionals, with a brisk Manhattan stride and everyday business attire.

Except that Casey's trained eye spotted the pistols clutched subtly at their sides. Even without that giveaway, she'd know they were plainclothes FBI. She'd interacted with the Bureau long enough to recognize the demeanor. All the tells were there—the sense of purpose, the sharp look in their eyes as they sought out and found their target, and their casual yet intense way of closing in.

Fenton had his back to them, so he didn't react. And Amanda noticed nothing unusual about the pair, so she didn't react, either—not until she saw Marc, Claire and Ryan clustered in the corridor, standing to the side as a set of three armed plainclothesmen stepped just inside the doorway.

Spotting the M4 rifles, Amanda's eyes widened, and her whole body tensed.

Casey remained intentionally relaxed, and she didn't meet Amanda's gaze. She simply watched the SWAT team position themselves along the periphery of the doorway, their M4 rifles raised.

Fenton saw his niece's expression and started to turn around.

He didn't have the chance.

The two agents had raised their pistols into ready gun position, the female agent announcing in a clear, firm voice, "Lyle Fenton. FBI. You're under arrest for racketeering and corruption." A moment later, his arms were pulled behind him and handcuffs were snapped onto his wrists.

The male agent then searched him for weapons and contraband.

"This is outrageous," Fenton snapped, too stunned to struggle. "I want my attorney." He shot a scathing look at Casey. "You bitch," he muttered between clenched teeth.

"I've been called worse." Casey gave him a saccharine-sweet smile. "And I'm happy to oblige. Thank you both," she added, speaking to the FBI agents.

"Our pleasure," the female agent replied. "We have a car waiting out back with Mr. Fenton's name on it. Let's go," she addressed Fenton, urging him toward the door.

"Amanda..." Fenton opened his mouth, then shut it again.

"Don't talk to me," Amanda replied in a hard, livid voice

that Casey had never before heard her use. "Just go. Justin and I don't need you or your money. Get out of my sight."

His jaw working violently, Fenton said nothing more, forcing himself to go quietly with the agents.

"Who are those other armed men?" Amanda asked Casey, pointing to the doorway.

"A plainclothes SWAT team," Casey supplied. "My guess is there are probably two other teams at choke points, probably at the top of the stairwell and the elevator banks."

"My God." Amanda was visibly dazed. "You were purposely stalling my uncle. That's why you were making small talk. You knew the FBI agents were coming."

Casey nodded. "I also knew that Agent Hutchinson and Agent Shore were keeping Paul in the lab, so there was no chance of him running into Fenton. As soon as I get a phone call saying the FBI team has left the premises, I'll have Paul brought upstairs, and the two of you can visit with each other and with Justin."

Amanda was still trying to absorb what had just happened. "Racketeering? Corruption? Do I even want to know?"

"It's just as well if you don't, because you can't." Casey was blunt. "The U.S. Attorney's Office is building a case. Until the facts become public record, the details can't be discussed. Just accept the fact that your uncle has a lot to answer for. Oh, and I wouldn't count on that inheritance. I doubt it was obtained legally."

A disgusted shudder. "I don't want his dirty money—not for me and not for my son. We'll do fine without it."

"I know you will." Casey paused. "One suggestion. Don't press Paul too hard. He's not going to be at liberty to tell you too much. Concentrate on the fact that he loves you, that he loves and wants Justin, and that he's here to do all he can—and to stay. The details of his assignment are unimportant in comparison."

Amanda nodded. "I understand. And I agree. I'll listen to whatever Paul can and chooses to share. And I won't interrogate him. I'm just so grateful to you for finding him and bringing him home." Tears clogged Amanda's voice.

"A few days ago, I told you not to thank us until we found Paul. Now I'm telling you not to thank us until he's saved Justin." Casey meant every word she was saying. "Knowing Justin will be well is all the thanks my team and I need."

EPILOGUE

Winter was clinging on with a vise grip, as March did indeed come in like a lion, showing no signs of relenting. Two weeks into the month, the wind was blowing fiercely, menacing gray clouds hung overhead, and snow was in the forecast.

Bundled up and shivering, the entire Forensic Instincts team hurried into Sloan Kettering and down the hall to the first-floor hospital chapel. They wanted to get there early, to help make the necessary preparations.

They shrugged out of their winter coats, scarves and gloves, and hung them all away, surveying the solemn interfaith chapel and thinking about how many times Amanda had visited this sanctuary over the past three months, praying for her son's recovery. And about how many times the team itself had been in this hospital.

From the time Amanda had hired them last December, there had been more hours spent here than any of the FI team cared to count—painful hours, emotional hours, tension-filled hours, prayerful hours.

This time it was none of the above.

This time the hours would be joyous.

The whole team, together with others who were near and dear, were gathering together to celebrate two extraordinary events, both of which were long overdue and which no overcast skies could eclipse.

The first would be taking place at nine o'clock this morning.

The exact timing of the second was still under discussion.

But it would be soon.

"The candles add a nice touch," Claire announced, having arranged a line of them on at the head of the room. She stood back, assessed her handiwork, then nodded. "Just the right balance of elegance and warmth. A roomful of positive energy."

"No occasion is complete without positive energy," Ryan replied drily.

"Don't play Scrooge with me." Claire didn't so much as blink at the subtle taunt. "Not when you called me at some ungodly hour and asked me to rush over to the lair and check out three ties so you'd know which one worked best."

"Now that's a moment I would have paid to see." Marc chuckled. "The debonair Ryan McKay, seeking fashion advice."

Ryan shot him a look. "I usually avoid these kinds of parties. My wardrobe lends itself to less reverent occasions."

"So, Claire, you were in the office—and down in the lair—at dawn." That one hadn't gotten by Casey. "Just to choose a tie? Because you two seem to spend a lot of alone time downstairs these days."

"Not cute, Casey," Ryan warned. "Also not work related."

"Not work related? Funny, I always thought that's what offices were for. I assumed you two were having meaningful strategy sessions, the union of spiritual and scientific input."

Ryan looked like he might hit her.

Casey arched a brow. "Did I put my foot in my mouth? Sorry. But I do own Forensic Instincts. I have to ensure that all the team members' hours are spent effectively."

"Not to worry. They are." Ryan turned his back and walked over to the table they'd set up on the side, making sure the champagne they'd been given permission to serve was chilling.

Claire's cheeks were pink, but she ignored the conversation entirely. Her relationship—or whatever it was—with Ryan was not something she wanted to talk about. It was all wrong, except when it was all right. It had no definition and it made no sense. It was sporadic and it was extreme, and its ambiguity was driving her crazy.

"I like the floral arrangements, don't you?" she asked Casey, changing the subject even as she arranged the vases. "I think the pastel colors suit the couple."

"I agree." Casey nodded. "I think you did a beautiful job. I think Amanda and Paul will be very touched."

"After all they've been through, they more than deserve it."

Casey nodded again. It was hard to believe that three months had passed since they'd found out Paul was not only an adequate donor match for Justin, he was a strong one. Starting with that reality, and adding the scientific advancement of the purification process, it gave them solid reason for hope.

The next five days had been intense as Paul's injections and preparations commenced, and he and Amanda hovered over Justin, continually praying that their tiny son would be strong enough to hang on.

He did. Somehow that precious little one-month-old baby continued to fight, as if he knew that help was on its way.

The big day arrived.

First, the four-hour procedure where Paul's stem cells were collected. Next, the grueling ten hours of waiting while the stem cells were processed and enriched.

And finally, the crucial procedure they'd been waiting for—the IV infusion of Paul's stem cells into Justin's body.

It had been the longest fifteen minutes that Amanda and Paul had ever lived through.

They'd known it would be at least two weeks before they saw any evidence that engraftment had taken place. And even though Justin was closely monitored by the entire transplant team for any sign of complications, the ticking clock had been unbearable. Fortunately, there'd been no signs of graft versus host disease.

And then came the fateful day, four weeks later, when the heavens smiled down on them. Justin's tests came back, revealing some good cells with early function—enough so that his oxygen requirements were decreased, and the chest tube could be removed.

A month after that, he'd been off the ventilator. And now, three months after the transplant, the infections were gone and Amanda and Paul were sitting down with Dr. Braeburn to discuss discharging Justin from the hospital.

There would be frequent follow-ups, but Justin was out of the woods and ready to begin his life—with his mother and father.

Who were ready to begin their lives as a married couple, and as a family. A *fully* healthy family, since Amanda had already undergone three months of her six-month treatment to cure her hepatitis C.

Even the cynical Ryan McKay couldn't deny that this was the ultimate happily-ever-after.

The chapel was theirs to use for the brief but meaningful ceremony. Patrick was giving away the bride, and Marc was acting as Paul's best man. Amanda's dear friend Melissa was the matron of honor, and two of Paul's close friends at the Bureau were driving in to attend the wedding.

But the most important guest of honor would be the four-month-old baby boy who'd be brought in by a nurse and allowed to remain in attendance as his parents were joined in matrimony.

It was the most precious wedding gift Amanda and Paul could be granted.

Immediately following the service, Justin and his newlywed parents would return to the pediatric unit. Very little in their routine would change between then and release day. Amanda and Paul would sit by Justin's side, holding him, playing with him and marveling at the wonder they'd created—and the strength he'd exerted to survive.

But homecoming was imminent. Dr. Braeburn had given Amanda the green light, so long as she brought Justin in for his regular follow-up checkups. They were just waiting for some final blood results, and for a slightly less blustery day. Then, Justin would be securely buckled into his car seat and driven to Hampton Bays, and his new nursery in Paul's cottage.

The small bedroom adjacent to the master had gone through a major renovation during these past months, and was now a bright and cheery room for a baby to thrive in. Amanda's apartment would go back to serving as her workplace—a photojournalist's studio, keeping the nursery for Justin to use on those occasions when he was with her while she worked.

The wheels of justice were turning, as the AUSA prepared his case against Lyle Fenton and key members of the Vizzini family. Congressman Mercer had resigned from office, citing family issues as the cause, and had privately agreed to testify against Lyle Fenton in exchange for not being prosecuted. The truth was that any favors Mercer had done for his "father" had been done under duress. He'd used his influence to sway political decisions, but he hadn't bribed anyone or committed any egregious crimes. His guilt fell in the area of gray, and it was far easier to accept his resignation and his agreement to help the U.S. Attorney's Office nail Fenton than it was to go after him and lose the sway his witness testimony would provide.

Paul was still working for the Bureau, only now he was in the Counterintelligence division at the Long Island Resident Agency. His undercover days were over, which suited both him and Amanda just fine. From here on in, he could be Special Agent Paul Evans, and Amanda could openly become Mrs. Amanda Evans. And Justin's name was being legally changed on his birth certificate to read Justin Gleason Evans.

For the first time, Forensic Instincts was truly ready to consider this case closed.

Which was a good thing, considering how busy they were.

"This one hit hard," Patrick commented, coming up behind Casey and reading her expression. "It took a lot out of all of us."

"Not nearly what it took out of Amanda," Casey replied.

"You know what I mean. An innocent baby whose life was in our hands. Quite a responsibility—one that we each personalized in our own way. Today is a celebration for Forensic Instincts, too."

Casey turned to give Patrick a knowing look. "You're full of it, Mr. Former FBI. You were so invested in our last case—your first big one with us—that you ate, drank and slept it."

"Different circumstances," Patrick responded. "That kidnapping was a long-term thorn in my side. It haunted me for years. This case was another thing entirely." He paused. "But you're right. I do internalize our cases. We all do. That's part of what makes us the team we are."

"Even *I* was on shaky ground this time," Marc freely admitted as he walked over to join them.

"You had your reasons." Casey didn't elaborate. She didn't need to. Marc's background and his Achilles' heel were common knowledge among the FI team. "Plus, you brought this case to us—as a fait accompli." She couldn't help but add the slight dig.

"Yup. My overstepping of the boundaries. My rule-breaking. My responsibility." That's how it was with Marc. Short and to the point. "Just another reason I wasn't going to fail."

"Among others."

Marc nodded, that sober, faraway look in his eyes. "Among others."

"This time we made a difference," Casey reminded him quietly. "It can't erase past atrocities. But it can make one family very happy and give one baby the life he deserves."

"You're right." Marc snapped back to the present, acknowledging the feat they'd accomplished.

"We done good," Ryan announced, strolling over. "We should make one toast to ourselves. Too bad dogs aren't allowed in hospital chapels. Hero should be here to share in the celebration."

"Not to worry," Claire assured him, still arranging flowers as she spoke. "I left Hero an interactive toy filled with treats. He'll be wrestling with it all morning to extract his prizes." She shot Ryan a look. "And, no, they're not loaded with fat. He won't gain an ounce. Besides, he was part of this victory. He sniffed out Paul. He helped us bring down Fenton. He deserves a reward."

"No arguments, Claire-voyant." Ryan gave her that lazy grin. "Each of us gets some of the credit for this one—even you and your energy-sensing."

"Wow. A compliment." Claire rolled her eyes. "Can I get that in writing?"

"Nope. I reserve the right to deny everything—especially if you piss me off during our next case."

"Which I'm sure I will."

Casey shook her head, laughing as she did. "We make quite a team. No wonder the FBI wants to choke us half the time."

"Ah, but that other half of the time..." Ryan was as

smug as always. "Look at our track record. Look at our rep. Enough said."

"For now." Casey the boss kicked in. "Let's celebrate this hard-fought victory. Then it's back to reality—and to work."

★ ★ ★ ★ ★

AUTHOR NOTE

The Shinnecock Indian Reservation is located on the east side of Shinnecock Bay in the town of Southampton. While the Shinneock Indian Nation's gaming authority is planning for a long-awaited casino, that casino does not yet exist. When it does, it will not be built on their reservation, which is their ancestral home, but elsewhere on Long Island. Therefore, the casino in *The Line Between Here and Gone* is a fictitious place, the product of this writer's fertile imagination.

ACKNOWLEDGMENTS

A host of people contributed to my writing this book, and I want to express my appreciation to each and every one of them for their time, their expertise, and their tolerance of a novelist who's a relentless perfectionist.

My thanks go out to:

Angela Bell, Public Affairs Specialist, FBI Office of Public Affairs—and the real-life equivalent of a fairy godmother!

Former SSA John Mandrafina, FBI Undercover Coordinator/Sensitive Operations Program

SSA James McNamara, FBI Behavioral Analysis Unit 2

Dr. Morton Cowan, Chief, Allergy Immunology and Blood and Marrow Transplant Division, UCSF Children's Hospital

SA Laura Robinson, Senior Team Leader, Evidence Response Team, FBI Newark Field Office

SSA Rex Stockham, Program Manager for FBI Laboratory's Forensic Canine Program

SA James Margolin, FBI Office of Public Affairs, New York Field Office

SSA Gavin Shea, FBI White Collar Squad, Long Island Resident Agency

Sharon L. Dunn, Department of Pediatrics, Hematology/Oncology, University of Chicago

Detective Mike Oliver, retired NYPD

Simon Jorna, owner of Simon's Beach Bakery Café, Westhampton Beach, Long Island, New York

Michael Greene, Simon's Beach Bakery Café and tour guide of "Amanda's" apartment

And to a very special core of people:

Adam Wilson, the best (and most deeply missed) editorial partner any author could ask for

Valerie Gray, who stepped in at the crisis hour and finished the process with grace, enthusiasm and commitment

Andrea Cirillo and Christina Hogrebe, my incredible agents and diehard advocates

Peggy Gordijn, the quiet force of nature who stays in the background and moves mountains

And most of all my family, who, every day and in every way, give me the love, the incentive and the creative input to make each book the very best it can be.

Thank you all. You're the very best of the best.